Say You Love Me

Marion Husband

Published by Accent Press Ltd - 2007
ISBN 1905170866/9781905170869
Copyright © Marion Husband 2007

Printed and bound in the UK

Cover Design by Joëlle Brindley

The publisher acknowledges the financial support of the Welsh
Books Council

For Hazel, with thanks

Also by Marion Husband,
Published by Accent Press

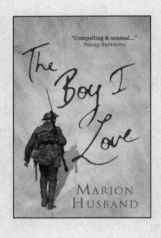

The Boy I Love
1905170009 / 9781905170005
£6.99

Paper Moon
1905170149 / 9781905170142
£6.99

Chapter 1

Mark said, 'I've decided to go home.'

In the flat above their florist shop, Luke and Tony looked sympathetic. Carefully, Tony said, 'When you say home, you mean...?'

'Thorp.'

'Because ...?'

Mark bowed his head, embarrassed by their concern and the careful way they avoided the relevant words. There was a vase of lilies on the mantelpiece and their intense perfume filled the room and deepened the silence he seemed unable to break. He almost blurted out that he was too strange to be sitting here in their tidy living room, that didn't they think he was polluting the very air they breathed? He was filthy after all – couldn't they tell? His flesh crawled. He mumbled, 'I just thought I'd go home – see Dad. A bit of a holiday, really.' He thought how northern his voice sounded when he couldn't be bothered. It was a sign of his depression: these slack, Teesside vowels. Luke and Tony exchanged looks and Mark tried to read their expressions, knowing he looked too hopeful. He wanted them to tell him not to go, and that it would all be all right to stay and do nothing. But their pity had become exasperation; he looked down at the glass of wine cradled in his hand. 'Sorry,' he said, 'I'm afraid I haven't been much company tonight.'

The two men were quick to deny it. Luke glanced towards the dining table, still littered with coffee cups and wine glasses, the plate of ravaged cheeses sweating and weeping amongst grape stalks and biscuit crumbs. All the

1

other guests had left; only Mark outstayed his welcome. Mark thought of the woman who had sat across the table from him, a dentist with dark, clever eyes, good-looking enough. Luke and Tony had high hopes that he and the dentist would hit if off, hopes that were unspoken, but demonstrated in the way the two men became more flirtatious around them, as though some of their playfulness would rub off on their awkward guests. The dentist was called Helen. She was the kind of woman he ought to like but didn't; adding to his sense of hopelessness.

Tony said, 'Mark, why don't you come and stay with us for a while?'

Mark thought about staying in Luke and Tony's spare room, of waiting in bed, listening to the two of them preparing to go downstairs to work. Luke would sing; he sang often, the latest song by Madonna or Kylie, and Tony would nag him to be quick: they had deliveries to attend to, wreaths to assemble. The smell of their coffee would drift into his room like a gentle hint that he should get up and stop moping, although neither of them would use such a word as mope. Luke and Tony believed what he was going through was far too serious for the kind of stiff upper lip, grin-and-bear-it words his father would use. Suddenly he longed to be home, in his bedroom where the bright colours of the Persian rug broke the shadow of the plane tree that grew outside his window, only to remember that it had been days since he'd slept a full night in his bed. Lately he fell into fitful dozes on the couch, afraid of sleeping, of his violent, chaotic dreams.

Tony said, 'Listen, love, the offer stands. If you go home and find you can't cope with all that family stuff, come back here and stay with us. Or one of us could stay with you. You're not alone in this.'

Luke said, 'Of course you're not.'

I am alone, Mark wanted to say. Utterly, totally. He looked at the two men sitting opposite him on the china blue silk sofa. Tony's arm stretched along the sofa's back, his fingers dangling millimetres away from Luke's shoulder. Such casual intimacy used to reassure him: here was love and respect and tenderness. Now it just seemed smug and condescending. He got up, surprising himself with the suddenness of his move so that he felt too big and awkward amongst the knick-knacks and artful arrangements of flowers. He downed the last of his wine in one swallow and knew that he must look rude, in too much of a hurry to leave.

'Sorry,' he said. 'I should go.'

They followed him down the narrow flight of stairs that rose from the doorway leading out on to the street. On the pavement they embraced him in turn. Holding him at arms' length, Tony searched his face. 'You'll be all right,' he said. It was a statement, as though he'd seen something in his expression that reassured him. Tony had told him once that he was strong, that he could sense his northern grit beneath the soft veneer living in the south had lent him. Mark was tempted to ask him if he truly believed he was a hard man. How ridiculous he would sound.

In his car, he sat for a moment before turning on the engine. He pictured his flat, how he had left a lamp on in each room, how the feeble, forty-watt bulbs would leave too much shadow and darkness. He needed one hundred-watt bulbs, the kind of harsh, no-nonsense light that illuminated his father's house. Simon didn't go in for the soft ambience of lamps. Simon had to have blinding, white, overhead light as though he was about to examine a patient.

A week ago Mark had been to see his GP. Years since he had visited the practice, he found that the doctor he remembered as being a little like Simon had retired, replaced by a girl a good ten years younger than himself. On her desk she had pictures of a fat toddler clutching a baby, on her wall a poster informing that *Breast is Best*. He had felt like a trespasser. She had ended up taking his blood pressure, listening to his blood pounding with a professional little frown. He couldn't bring himself to say what he'd intended to say if the doctor had been the older, old-fashioned man he'd expected. *'I am so tired,'* he'd wanted to say. And, if he'd felt brave, *'I think I should be put away.'* And the kindly, twinkle-eyed doctor who wore a tweed suit and smelt faintly of cigars would not be shocked or disgusted as he coaxed out his confession but rather brisk and even dismissive. 'My dear boy,' the doctor would cry, 'I daresay we all think of ourselves as monsters from time to time!'

Mark put on his seatbelt and started the car. He thought of Susan, who had told him that if he was a monster he was one of a rare and exotic breed, a line that must be nearing extinction. 'You're the last of your kind,' she said. Straddling his body she'd leaned forward and brushed her mouth against his. She'd whispered, 'I'm not scared,' and the smile in her voice had made him laugh in despair.

'I am,' he'd said.

She had sat up and frowned at him thoughtfully, her head cocked to one side. At last she'd said, 'I wish you were a monster, Mark, a larger than life shit – I wouldn't feel guilty about fucking you then.'

They never mentioned guilt and she had glanced away as she said it, only to look at him again, not quite meeting his eye as she smiled crookedly. A few minutes earlier she had been wrapping her legs around his waist and groaning his name in a climax he only half-believed she faked. Now the guilt she'd conjured made her look sheepish. 'It's just *sex* that's all,' she said. 'I do what I do because you're the most beautiful man I've ever seen.' She laughed a little and rested her forehead against his. 'Think of it as a basic urge I have to satisfy, like thirst. I would shrivel up without you.'

He remembered holding her head between his hands and lifting her face away from his. The fresh wounds on his back and buttocks stung and he knew the sheets would be

4

spotted with blood and he would feel ashamed as he stripped the bed and bundled the linen into the washing machine. But for that moment he wanted her to tear at his broken skin with her finger nails, to open him up and make him bleed more. He had almost asked her to stay the night in his bed so that later, later... Instead he had closed his eyes, sickened by his own basic urges. She had kissed him. 'I should go,' she'd said. 'Or he might begin to wonder where I am.'

Mark turned the car into his street. He parked in a space only a few doors from his flat and locked it with the remote, only to try the door to check it was secure. The street was quiet but he was afraid that the car would be stolen and that its theft would topple him over the edge. He was afraid too that the flat would be burgled, that one day he would return home and find it plundered and vandalised, graffiti sprayed on the walls, fresh faeces on the carpet – the shit-scared leaving their calling card. Climbing the steps that led from the street to his front door he saw it in his mind's eye – drawers pulled out and spilling their contents, his books and papers fanning across the floor, pages fluttering in the draft from the jemmied window. He hesitated before turning the key in the lock and going inside.

The hallway at least was as he left it, the lamp on the table spreading its yellow glow on the polished floor and the muted colours of the rug. Next to the lamp the lilies he bought each Saturday from Tony's shop had changed in his absence from heavy buds to half-unfurled blooms, their scent already filling the hall. He caught a glimpse of himself in the mirror above the table, saw that he looked haggard, as though he'd been drinking all night in some filthy dive rather than struggling to make small talk with a pretty dentist. Resisting the compulsion to peer at himself, he turned away and walked though to the kitchen where his answering machine beeped its quiet, persistent alarm. Two messages.

He pressed play and poured himself a scotch as Simon's recorded voice said, 'Hello? Mark? It's Dad – just wanted to say I'll expect you about two o'clock tomorrow. I'll rustle up some lunch. Anyway...are you all right, my boy? Sorry I missed you....' He trailed off, an old man uncomfortable with machines that didn't allow for mistakes, that he knew made him sound older and more unsure of himself and the world than he had ever been in his long life. Sipping his drink, Mark deleted his father's message. At once the confident tone of his brother had him setting down his glass and listening carefully to the nuances in his voice.

Ben said, 'Hi Mark. Dad's just told me you're coming home tomorrow. Spur of the moment decision? Well, good, we need to talk, don't we? I'll look forward to seeing you – safe journey.'

Mark played his brother's message again. Ben's voice was light, friendly, the voice he no doubt used to reassure his patients. He pictured his older brother standing at the French windows of his study, looking out over his large, manicured garden as he spoke into the phone. Behind him his desk would be bare except for his laptop and an orderly pile of strictly relevant reference books. His diary would be open on the day. Mark imagined his own name written in red and underlined on its page. He wondered if Ben had hesitated before punching his number into the phone, if he'd felt that sudden, nervous quickening of the heart. Ben would have taken a breath, been firm with himself: it was just a phone call to his brother. Mark played the message again. He fancied he could hear Ben's baby son crying in the background. He picked up his drink and pressed delete, erasing his brother's voice mid-flow.

He went into his own sitting room. His flat was the ground floor of a Victorian terrace house. The builders had taken care with its conversion and all the original features that estate agents liked so much were still in place. The flat's rooms were airy, with high ceilings and deep skirting

6

boards. He had an open fireplace that was much admired but never lit. In the alcoves on either side of the marble mantelpiece were floor-to-ceiling bookcases so crammed with books that some had to be stacked on the floor. Most of the books he hadn't opened for years; often he imagined getting rid of some of them, but knew that the process of selection would take hours, that he would be caught up in reading dust jackets and opening lines and that the words would drag him into the past and hold him prisoner there. These books were best ignored, but certain books, the first editions and flea market finds Susan had inscribed with clever dedications, he had hidden away in a suitcase in the spare bedroom. One day, with a decisive bravery he could barely imagine now, he would dispose of those.

He sat down in a leather armchair beside the fire, a pile of books on Renaissance art at his fingertips, the next tentative idea for a novel to research. He rested his head against the chair's high back and closed his eyes, too tired to go to bed to wrestle with sleep. He took the remote control and switched on the television. On BBC twenty-four hour news American soldiers had been killed in Iraq; a child had gone missing from the Rosehill housing estate on the outskirts of Durham.

He turned up the volume. The estate was close to Simon's house and he remembered its rows of 1950s semi-detached council houses, flat-fronted and pebble-dashed, that he and Ben used to pass on their shortcuts to the park. The news camera panned along the missing child's street and he noticed that the houses looked less raw than they had in his 1960s childhood. Trees had grown in front gardens, cars were parked bumper to bumper along the kerb, suggesting a kind of prosperity that was missing in those days. Despite the fact that they had moved away to the leafy suburbs of Thorp, Ben would still play football with the boys from Rosehill on the green spaces between the squares of houses and tower blocks.

He had always been excluded from these games, considered too weedy, too much of a girl, a *puff*. He was an embarrassment; Ben disowned him whenever he thought he could get away with it. As a child Ben led a double life and a large part of the subterfuge was making sure his association with such a useless boy didn't taint him. Ben could easily act the part of the posh boy from the big house but he was also one of the lads, a rough kid who swore and fought and smoked *Embassy* cigarettes openly in the street.

The news turned to sport and Mark switched off. He went over Ben's message again and thought how the lightness of his voice was faked to disguise his urgency. Ben needed to talk to him and for the moment this need was the most important thing in his brother's life. For the first time Ben craved his approval. Mark felt his stomach turn over at the very idea of his brother's new obsession.

Last month, late one evening as he worked at his desk, he had answered the telephone absently, only to sit up straighter as Ben said, 'Mark. Hello. Hello?' His brother had laughed self-consciously. 'Mark? Are you there? Can you hear me?'

'Yes. Yes, I can hear you. Sorry –'

'You sound distracted. Do you have someone with you?' Ben laughed again, an edge to his voice as he said, 'Is this a bad time?'

'No. How are you?' Mark had looked down at the last line he had typed, deleting an adjective despite himself. He said, 'How are Kitty and the baby?'

'They're great. Well, Nathan is teething again, so perhaps not so great…a few sleepless nights, nothing Kit can't cope with.'

Mark thought of the girl Ben had married a year earlier. Ben's child-bride, Simon called her, his voice gruff with affection. Kitty was beautiful, an elfin girl Simon adored. Whenever they met Mark felt huge and clumsy beside her; he also felt old, of course, every day of his forty-three years an unbridgeable chasm between himself and his sister-in-law.

Ben said, 'How are you, Mark?'

'Fine.'

'Good. That's good.' He paused. On a rush of breath he said, 'So, you're OK?'

'Is there something wrong, Ben?'

'No! No, not wrong. Not really…' He'd sighed. 'I don't want you to be upset, that's all.'

Mark's hand had tightened around the phone. 'Go on.'

'It's just that I've been thinking, since Nath was born…Mark, I want you to understand…'

And his brother had gone on, cajoling him to understand. When he had finally put the phone down Mark had rushed to the bathroom and thrown up. For some minutes he sat on the bathroom floor, his head against the cold tiled wall. He tried to think clearly, to be calm and rational as Ben had insisted he should be. Ben had said, 'I'm not asking for your permission, Mark – I just wanted you to know…I wanted you to hear it from me…'

Mark remembered the pauses Ben had left for him to fill. He hadn't been able to speak. Already the bile had risen in his throat and Ben had been exasperated with his silence. 'Mark, for God's sake! I can't believe this has come as a surprise!' Then, more gently, he had said, 'I know this might be difficult for you. But Danny is my father – *our* father, our flesh and blood. I have to find him.'

Mark got up and turned the television off. He finished his drink and went into the kitchen to place the glass in the dishwasher. He would wake to a tidy home, everything in its place. His flat was beautiful – everyone said so. He was told he had exquisite taste. His guests admired the oil paintings of seascapes on his pale walls, his elegant, antique furniture, the way his few rooms seemed so full of light, of a kind of *grace*, Tony had once said, and had looked at him

9

curiously as though he couldn't quite accept that they weren't lovers.

Mark undressed for bed. He brushed his teeth and avoided his eyes in the bathroom mirror. He hated the sight of himself, more so since Ben had told him he was set on finding their natural father, Danny. Since then his face was even more a reminder of trouble. He looked so starkly like Danny, so unlike the blond, blue-eyed Simon that it was obvious that he was only an adopted son. Ben could pass for Simon's blood but not him. He was Danny's, through and through. And yet it was Ben who wanted to find Danny, Ben who wanted to reach back as though their blood held some knowledge he couldn't get along without.

Mark gripped the edge of the sink, sickened again by the idea of Ben excavating their shared past. For the first time it occurred to him that his brother might have dug up more than he'd admitted to, and he pictured Ben meeting him outside Simon's house tomorrow with Danny at his side. He wondered if he would faint with fear or run like a madman. He forced himself to look at his reflection full on. Danny gazed back at him. He turned away quickly and went to bed.

Chapter 2

Annette Carter watched as the man who had insisted on being addressed as Simon poured her a sherry from a sticky-looking bottle. He was tall, about six foot two, his shoulders were broad, his waist slim and his hair was thick and blond, often falling over his eyes so that he pushed it back impatiently. He wore a tweed suit with flecks of green in its weave, a suit that may have been expensive once but looked old-fashioned now. His dark blue tie was stained and his shoes needed polishing. He smiled often. Earlier he'd told her that he was a surgeon. She'd noticed his hands then, and thought how strong and capable they looked.

If she'd had to guess she would have said Doctor Simon Walker was only thirty or so. He was forty-five – she'd calculated his age quite early in her interview as he explained why he limped. Aged twenty-one he had lost a leg during the liberation of France in 1944. Smiling he'd said, 'It didn't used to slow me down quite as much as it does nowadays.' His smile was lovely; it had made her feel shy and she'd looked down at her hands clasped in her lap. Nervous from the start, his gentle manners and good looks made her feel anxious. Danny would hate this man.

Doctor Simon Walker handed her a schooner of sherry and sat down in the armchair opposite her. He said, 'Annette – may I call you Annette? Annette, as I said, my wife is in hospital and will be for the next couple of weeks. I would like this house to be spic and span for her return –

11

comfortable, welcoming...' He glanced around the large, untidy room. There was a stain on the brown wallpaper above the mantelpiece, the same paper curling away from the corners of the room. Cobwebs collected dust around the light fitting, a single, unshaded bulb that dangled from the chipped ceiling rose. The doctor's furniture was as old and grand as the stuff she dusted in the homes of the solicitor and bank manager she cleaned for, but neglected, its fineness almost obscured by accumulated junk.

Doctor Walker frowned. As though he was seeing his home for the first time, he said thoughtfully, 'It's not a very homely house, is it? I'd forgotten how cold and damp it is. But I would like my wife – Joy – not to be too dismayed when she finally gets to see it.'

'I'll do my best, sir.'

'Simon.' He smiled. '*Sir* makes me feel terribly old.'

'Sorry.' To avoid his gaze she glanced away towards the damp patch above the French doors. The doors led out to the garden, a huge lawn enclosed by a high wall. Daffodils bloomed beneath a row of trees, the branches shading the veranda of a summerhouse. The summerhouse had a hole in its tarred roof; its door hung open on its hinges. Small birds flew in and out of the snow-white blossom of a hawthorn hedge. She had never seen such a beautiful garden; she would like to lie down on the grass and soak up its peacefulness, to drift into sleep knowing she would be safe. She thought of Sleeping Beauty's garden, its wildness shielding her from the outside world until the Prince hacked his way through.

She realised the doctor was speaking. Startled, she looked at him as he said, 'I'm afraid the place has gone to rack and ruin since my mother's illness. I hope you don't feel too put off by its shabbiness. Look – why don't I show you around? You can decide for yourself whether it's something you would want to take on or not.'

12

Annette had seen the postcard advertising for a cleaner in Brown's window. She had been on her way home from taking Mark and Ben to school and straight away she had gone to the telephone box at the end of her street and dialled the number on the card. She hadn't given herself time to think about it. When Doctor Walker answered on the fifth ring he had asked if she could be interviewed immediately. Standing in the smelly phone box she had looked down at herself. She was wearing her tartan miniskirt and a skinny-rib jumper, American Tan tights and the black coat Danny had rescued from a bin on the posh end of his round. She had brushed the coat down and sewn on new brass buttons and it looked all right if she didn't show its torn lining. As Doctor Walker gave her directions to his house she decided that she was presentable enough to be offered a cleaning job. She had told him she would be there in half an hour.

The doctor led her through the house, from the sitting room and dining room that looked out over the garden, through the hallway and upstairs to the grand bedrooms with their thick, faded curtains and Persian rugs and views of the graveyard across the road. There were graves as far as the eye could see. Her own parents were buried there, their grave unmarked in a shady spot way beyond the obelisks and urns and weeping angels that marked the resting places of the prosperous. For a moment she and the doctor stood side by side looking out at the sobering view. Then, wordlessly, he turned away and led her up more stairs to the attics, full of suitcases and tea chests, then down again to the kitchen and scullery.

It seemed that the kitchen hadn't been touched since Victorian times. There was still a black-leaded range and a stone sink with a single tap, and a Welsh dresser loaded with china cups and plates and servers and soup tureens – the kind of delicate stuff no one used any more. The Spode and the Wedgwood gathered dust that dulled the pretty patterns of Chinese bridges and willow trees, roses and windmills. It would take a day just to strip the dresser to its bare shelves and wash each piece in soapy water.

In the pantry she noticed a mousetrap and guessed that the house would be over-run with mice and cockroaches, silverfish and moths, all the little creatures that had such noses for the dirt and grime old women left in their wake. Simon Walker had told her that his mother had lived to a grand old age in this house and would not be moved from it until the very last. Annette imagined her living solely in this kitchen, close to the heat from the range, surviving on bread and milk and sweet tea, just as her own grandmother had – a squalid, deranged existence.

Standing in the middle of the kitchen Doctor Walker said, 'You're very quiet, Annette. I'm afraid you're going to run away in horror.'

'No – really, I'm not afraid of hard work.'

'Do you think you might be able to start straight away? Tomorrow, say?'

'I've got the job?'

'Of course – why not?'

'I could come in the morning, about half past nine?'

'Half past nine it is.' He smiled. 'Now, may I give you a lift home?'

She thought of Danny and the interrogation he would subject her to if he saw her getting out of a stranger's car. She had an idea that she could keep this job a secret, the money she would make would be hers alone, hers and Mark's and Ben's. Thinking of her boys, she said, 'I don't need a lift, thank you. I only live a short walk away.'

He showed her to the door. On the black and white tiled path that led to the gate he held out his hand. 'Goodbye, Annette. I'll see you in the morning.'

His hand was warm and dry in hers. As she walked away she felt his eyes on her and looked back. It must have been her imagination because already the door was closed and the house looked as empty and undisturbed as it had when she first arrived.

Simon finished the last of the sherry and went outside to throw the bottle in the bin. He walked along the side of the house and into the garden and thought about picking some of the daffodils to take to Joy in hospital. Joy loved flowers, the wilder the better. Not for her the roses and lilies and chrysanthemums his mother had preferred. His mother had dismissed as vulgar the fat headed daffodils that grew like weeds in this garden. Joy, no doubt, would think them pretty. He sighed, profoundly miserable.

He walked across the lawn to the summerhouse and sat on its steps. Four months ago, newly married to Joy, he had given up cigarettes on her insistence but now he longed for a smoke. He had smelt tobacco on that girl's clothes and had almost asked her for a cigarette. Perhaps he should have, it might have helped her to relax a little. He frowned, remembering how tense she was, jumpy as a feral cat. He remembered how she couldn't bring herself to meet his eye and how she had blushed when he'd explained his bloody leg. Perhaps he'd said too much, he often did when he thought it might put others at ease. Gushing, his mother had called it. Well, his gushing had backfired with this girl. She must have thought him a fool, an old soldier for the love of God.

As well as cigarettes, the girl had smelt of Lily of the Valley perfume, a sweet-sharp, oddly old-fashioned scent for such a young woman. And she was young, only about twenty-two or three. He'd expected someone older, a matron in a flower-sprigged overall, pink spiky curlers showing beneath a dull headscarf. When he'd opened the door to Annette Carter he'd thought that she was a gypsy like those that occasionally called at his London home selling white heather or offering to read his palm. Annette

15

had the same dark looks, the same wary suspicion in her eyes. Such arresting eyes she had, a curious, lovely green. He'd noticed how full her breasts were beneath that tight, cheap sweater. He had watched her as she walked ahead of him up the stairs to the bedrooms, her skirt skimming her mid-thighs and showing off her shapely legs and swaying hips. She was one of the sexiest women he had seen for years, since the war, probably, when all girls seemed to be as gorgeous as Annette Carter. He thought of Joy lying in her hospital bed, pale and plain and spinsterish as the day he met her, and felt ashamed of himself.

His mother had called him a fool and asked him why he had wanted to marry such an old maid as Joy Featherstone. 'You could have any woman you liked – any! If only your father was alive to talk some sense into you!'

'Dad would have liked Joy.'

'He *loved* Grace.'

'Grace is dead, Mum. Please, let's not talk about Grace.'

Grace, his first wife, had been killed during one of the last air raids on London. They had been married for two years. In his memory she had become incandescently lovely and for more than twenty years he'd believed no woman could replace her as his wife. He had taken lovers instead, discreetly, one after the other; these women were other men's wives mainly – women he imagined would be less trouble to him. Then he met Joy, who wasn't married, who he suspected had barely been kissed, and had been so horribly easy to seduce, so grateful to him for being kind and gentle as he took her virginity. So kind and gentle he had forgotten his usual precautions and a few weeks later Joy told him she was pregnant.

From the summerhouse steps he gazed unseeing at his new home. It was Joy's pregnancy that had brought him here, that and his mother's sudden death, a beginning and an ending conspiring to wreck his comfortable, careless life. When Joy had told him she was expecting his child he'd felt as though he'd been punched in the head. In the photographs of their wedding he looked dazed. He looked old, too. After so many years of thinking of himself as young he saw the wedding pictures and felt a kind of dismayed embarrassment, realising that if he hadn't made Joy pregnant he would have blithely gone on with his old life. In no time at all he would have become a laughing-stock, a middle-aged Lothario.

He got up from the steps and walked restlessly around the garden. His parents had bought this house a year after the war, his father pleased with the idea that another doctor had lived here, a man who had run his practice from its large, stately rooms, just as he was about to do. His father believed that he would join him, becoming one of the new National Health Service GPs like him, but he had wanted to stay in London where he had trained. Londoners seemed to need doctors more than the people of Thorp, a town that had come through the war relatively unscathed. Besides, he had no connection to Thorp; he imagined he would despise its small town narrow-mindedness. He'd been a soldier. He'd seen and done and wanted to do more. His father, a veteran of the first war, had told him he understood. His mother raged. Remembering her impotent fury, Simon smiled despite himself. She seemed to have been angry all his life. Even when her stroke silenced her, her eyes blazed.

From the kitchen garden Simon looked back at the house. It was certainly big – five bedrooms, three attics, three receptions rooms, one of which had been used as his father's surgery. He remembered the first time he had visited his parents here, how his father's patients waited on chairs lining either side of the wide hallway: men who had worked too hard for too long and too little and were prematurely old; young, skinny women with too many children. Many of the women were pregnant; their pregnancies had struck him quite forcefully. Inevitably he had thought of Grace, who had wanted children, who hadn't

17

thought that his new disability would make a jot of difference to his capabilities as a father. In 1945 in his father's surgery, as the poor and desperate and ill coughed outside the door, he had wept for this lovely, dead wife as his father waited patiently for him to collect himself.

Joy too had thought he would make a good father, even after he had suggested that she have an abortion. They had sat in her flat, a tray of tea on the table between them, and he had been surprised at the way she squared up to him. He remembered how she sat on the edge of her horsehair couch, her back sergeant-major straight and her knees tight together below the hem of her thick woollen skirt. Her eyes were defiant – he remembered being in awe of her as she said, 'I want this child. *Our* child. I'm prepared to bring him or her up alone. I won't be made to feel ashamed and I won't have a termination as you call it – a horrible word for a horrible act. I don't want anything from you. I just thought you should know.'

She'd smoothed her skirt over her still-flat belly, looking up to catch him staring at her. There must have been some scepticism in his expression because she said, 'I *am* pregnant, Simon. I've had the tests. July – I've been given the date of 10th July.'

In the garden Simon stooped to pick a daffodil. He picked another and then another until he had an armful, some barely out of bud, others in full bloom and almost ragged. He thought of a nurse placing them in an ugly, hospital vase beside his wife's bed. Joy was in a side room off the maternity ward, within earshot of mewling newborn babies. It seemed a particularly cruel place for her to be. But that's what his profession often was, cruel and thoughtless and dismissive of feelings.

Joy had begun to lose the baby on the train from Kings Cross to Darlington. Sitting beside him in the packed carriage she had suddenly let out a surprised yelp, like a puppy whose tail had been stood on. She had grasped his hand tightly, turning to him with such a look of horror he had realised at once what was wrong. The train sped on between stations so that they lost their child in a kind of nowhere land where he could do nothing except hold her and make his feeble reassurances that the blood soaking into the train seat didn't necessarily mean she was miscarrying. At the next station the other passengers helped him support his wife from the train, others passing out their luggage. He wondered if they could smell the blood, or whether its warm iron, ironically fecund, smell was just in his imagination. The blood was a large, dark patch on the seat; he remembered wondering if British Rail would send him a bill for cleaning it up. This was shock he realised now, shock and horror and grief – all emotions that since the war he had tried to protect himself from experiencing again.

He walked back inside the house and stood the flowers in the sink. A bumblebee crawled from one of the yellow trumpets and bumped against the window. He let it out, watching as it flew low over the grass. He noticed how quiet his new home and garden were. The air was sweet with the smell of his neighbours' gardens, gardens which ran down to Thorp Park with its swings and slides and flowerbeds full of Corporation daffodils. This would have been a safe place for a child to grow up, a far cry from the busy, polluted streets surrounding his flat in Hampstead. Joy had been pleased to come here, pleased, too, that he was willing to change his life so drastically.

He had taken a new job as chief of general surgery at Thorp hospital, he was to start in a week's time, a breathing space intended to allow him to show his wife around Thorp and settle them both into their new home. As it was, Joy had never even seen this house. Last night, when he'd visited her in her cell-like room she had turned her face away from him. When he tried to comfort her with a plan for their new future together she had refused to speak. She was right to ignore him because it wasn't much of a plan, only that she could choose new paint and wallpaper and furniture for the house and plants for the garden. Joy had green fingers; she could also sew and knew how to decorate a room so that it looked homely and welcoming. But she wasn't interested in such things any more. All she wanted was her child growing inside her again.

In the panic and pain of those first few hours after she'd lost the baby he had told her they would have other children. Last night he had lain in bed and wondered if he really did want another child with Joy. He found himself gingerly probing at his own feelings as though they were rotten teeth; he didn't reach any conclusion, couldn't come up with any concrete plan of action. All he could think was that his life had somehow come off the rails; he was stranded in a small town he barely knew with a wife he wasn't sure he loved enough. At least he would have his work – a new department to make his mark on. He wondered if it would be enough.

Staring out of the window he thought of the girl who was to be his housekeeper. She hadn't been very talkative, rather silent in fact. She had answered his questions bluntly, telling him that yes, she was married, and yes she had children, two boys. She had lived in Thorp all her life, her husband too. He thought that for a moment she'd looked at him with curiosity, as though wondering why he had so many questions about her life, although she had smiled fleetingly when he'd asked her children's names. She'd said, 'Mark and Ben, they're five and six.' There was such pride in her voice that he had almost expected her to forget her reticence and take out a picture of these boys. He was relieved when she didn't. Since Joy's miscarriage he'd found he couldn't look at other people's children without a painful, surprising surge of jealousy.

He closed the kitchen window and looked at his watch. It was almost visiting time. He pictured driving to the hospital in the car he'd hired that morning. The hospital was only a couple of years old, a plain, forbidding block of concrete surrounded by car park. There, he would wait for the lift to the fifth-floor maternity ward, surrounded by young men, each a new father carrying flowers or holding the hand of a small child, a brother or sister to the latest arrival. For a moment he imagined disguising himself in a white coat, his stethoscope dangling casually around his neck. Those young fathers wouldn't pay him any attention then. No longer one of their number, he could be totally anonymous. He sighed. Taking a sheet of newspaper, he wrapped the daffodils up and went in search of the car keys.

Chapter 3

Turning the corner into Tanner Street, Annette saw Ben and Mark sitting on their front door step. Ben had his arm around Mark's shoulders, his other hand pressing a bloodstained handkerchief to his little brother's nose. Annette ran the last few yards towards them. Seeing her, Ben shoved the handkerchief into Mark's hand and scrambled to his feet, jerking Mark's arm so that he stood up too. As she crouched in front of them Ben said, 'He's locked us out.'

'What are you doing home from school so early?'

'He came to fetch us.'

This was something new. Danny had never set foot in Skinner Street Infants before. Wondering what he was up to made her heart race faster. To hide her panic she forced herself to smile as she gently lifted away the handkerchief he was holding to his face. His nose was caked in drying blood. He looked dazed, like a boxer who had lost too many rounds. She lifted him into her arms and he buried his face in her neck. He was silent as always; she barely noticed his silence any more. She patted his back absently, rhythmically.

Sullenly Ben repeated, 'He's locked us out.'

Carrying Mark, Annette began to walk along the street. She turned into the alley that led to their back gate. Ben slipped his hand into hers. She looked down at him. 'Were you being naughty?'

'No. He just told us to get out. He hit Mark because he wasn't quick enough.'

Annette squeezed Ben's hand reassuringly although fear made her guts feel loose, a shaming, cowardly feeling. Cautiously she asked Ben, 'Was he shouting?'

'No.'

'Did he smell of the pub?'

Ben shook his head. They had reached their gate. The large, European-style number seven that Danny had painted across its panels like the insignia of a dictator made it stand out starkly from their neighbours' gates. They stopped and Mark held on to her more tightly; he whimpered, the first sound he'd made since she arrived home. As if to show that he was more grown up, Ben let go of her hand. He squared his shoulders and glared up at her, a defiant look in his eye that was pure Danny. Stubbornly he said, 'He's locked us out.'

She tried to laugh. 'No! He'll let us in now. Besides I bet the gate's only stuck.' She pushed it gingerly as though it was a delicately sprung trap. The gate creaked open. Across the yard she could see the closed back door. *Yellow Submarine* blared through the open kitchen window; she could hear Danny singing along. She let go of the breath she'd been holding.

'There,' she said. 'He probably only wanted to listen to his music in peace.'

Gently she disentangled Mark's arms from around her neck and set him down, holding on to him for a moment to make sure he was steady. As she released him he clasped her hand, turning to press his face against her thigh. Wanting to hold him again instead she said, 'Stand up straight now Mark. Like a soldier, eh? Soldiers don't cry, do they?'

Annette felt him shiver. After a moment he stepped away from her and let go of her hand. He kept his eyes fixed on the yard's cracked flags as Annette whispered, 'Good boy. If we're good Daddy won't be cross.'

The music stopped abruptly and she felt her heart leap as Danny swung the door open. He stepped back, bowing deeply and theatrically. 'Queen Annette – welcome to my humble abode.'

Danny said, 'Don't take your clothes off, I just want a quick fuck.'

Annette paused, her jumper half off and covering her face. She pulled it down again and lay on the bed. Danny knelt beside her, grinning. He reached out and hooked a strand of her hair away from her face. Through long practice she stopped herself from flinching.

He asked, 'Where have you been today?' He was still grinning, watching her closely.

'I went to the shops.'

'But you didn't buy anything.'

'No.'

He snorted and lay down on his back beside her. Looking at the ceiling he said, 'You can take your tights and knickers off. I can't fuck you if you keep them on, can I?'

Downstairs, when he had straightened up from his bow, he'd grabbed her arm and jerked her inside. To Ben he'd said, 'Didn't I tell you to stay out in the street until I told you to come back in?'

Trying not to sound frightened she'd laughed a little. 'Danny – they're cold and tired. Let them in, eh? They'll be really quiet and good–'

He'd frowned at her. 'You're wheedling. Don't wheedle.' Turning back to the boys he said, 'Fuck off until I call you.' He closed the door. To her he'd said, 'Get upstairs now.'

On their bed Annette squirmed out of her underwear. Rolling on to his side, Danny pushed her skirt up to her waist and placed his palm heavily on her thigh. 'You should be here when I get home. You shouldn't be out gallivanting.'

'Sorry. I didn't expect you back.'

'*Didn't expect you back.*' He mimicked her, his fingers digging into her flesh. In the morning there would be a ring of fingertip bruises to fade to yellow beneath her skirt. With his head propped on his elbow he looked down into her face. 'Where were you really this afternoon?'

Fearfully she said, 'I told you, I looked round the shops.'

'Honestly?'

She attempted to laugh. 'Yes, honestly.'

'You've got blood on your shoulder.'

She couldn't think what to say, knowing that if she told him it was Mark's blood it might re-ignite his anger. Both of his sons provoked him but it was Mark who seemed to irritate him the most. It was Mark's silence, Annette thought, his total lack of defiance. Danny hated to see such blatant fear.

Danny circled the spot of blood with his thumb. 'I gave Mark a bloody nose. Little bastard. Mummy's boy!'

Cautiously she said, 'He's just a baby, Danny.'

'He's growing into a right bloody pansy! I'll have to take my belt off to him again.' He rolled on to his back and groped for her hand. They stared at the ceiling; she felt her exposed flesh grow cold.

At last Danny said, 'Mark's not mine, is he?'

He had said this before; sometimes she could believe he was joking, other times when he was roaring and spitting and jumping with rage she knew he thought it to be true. Now though his voice was calm, there was even a hint of a smile on his face as he turned to see her reaction.

As calmly as she could she said, 'He's yours, Danny. He's the spit of you.'

At once she realised she'd said the wrong thing. His eyes closed. He sighed heavily. Wearily he said, 'If I find out you're lying to me…'

'I'm not, honestly. Really I'm not.'

He unzipped his fly. 'Lie on your front.'

She began to tremble. 'Danny – please…Not that…'

'Get on your front! Unless you want your little bastards to stay out all night?'

The other girls in the sugar factory were jealous of her when Danny Carter asked her to dance one Friday night at the Corporation Hall. All the girls were after him; he was gorgeous, like Elvis: a slim, slight Elvis, neat-looking, clean. Most Thorp men looked like they'd been hastily modelled from clay; they had big hands and heavy, muddy-looking features; their fingernails were dirty and they smelt of sweat and the steel they worked with. Given the slightest encouragement they pushed their big hands up inside your bra, all the time gobbling up your face as though you were made of pastry. Annette had dated enough of them to know she could never bring herself to go all the way with one of them. They were too awkward, too charmless; she wanted to lose her virginity to someone who knew the right words.

She began to gain a reputation for being a cock tease, then for being frigid, then, with more malice, for being stuck-up. As her reputation morphed Danny Carter watched and waited. She sensed him watching her, was pleased by it; it was her secret. She knew he would step in one day and claim her.

That Friday night at the Corporation Hall she had been standing with Mary and Carol. The two of them nudged her as Danny, on the other side of the hall, stubbed out his cigarette and walked across the emptying dance floor towards her. He was wearing his uniform; he was a corporal in the Marines, home on leave. As he approached her she felt such a want for him she pressed her thighs together against her body's softening; it was indecent to want a man so badly. He fixed his gaze on her, ignoring her friends completely.

'Dance with me?'

She nodded, transfixed. She had hardly heard him speak before and his voice was lovely, like serious, clever music. He held out his hand and she took it, thrilled at its coolness, its hardness. The floor was filling with couples for the first of the slow, smooching dances. His arms went around her waist and he pulled her to him carefully as though she was fine porcelain. He moved sensuously. She wanted him to speak but he was silent; he seemed to concentrate on the steps he took, on the way he held her. Resting her head on his shoulder she swayed with him in time to the music, mesmerised.

Towards the end of the last dance he began to whisper, his mouth close to her ear. He said, 'You're lovely,' and 'You're not like other girls.' He held her tighter. A moment before the music ended and the lights came up he said intently, 'I'm in love with you.'

She'd drawn away from him. Around them other couples snogged or laughed and broke apart, staggering from the floor drunk or weak-kneed. Danny stood his ground, holding her with his dark, sober eyes. A man bumped past her and his eyes moved towards him, a flicker of anger that passed so quickly she believed she'd imagined it. He met her gaze again, his face expressionless. Around them the bustle of the emptying dance hall seemed to recede, she felt as though there was just the two of them in the whole world, each watching the other. She realised he hadn't smiled. Soft with desire, she stepped towards him. He looked away, towards the crowd streaming out on to the street.

'I'll walk you home,' he said.

Annette watched as Danny slept. She had to make sure he was sleeping, not just pretending so that when she tried to get up he would catch hold of her and force her to stay in bed with him. He snored and broke into garbled speech. He

27

rolled on to his side, dragging the covers away from her. She was naked from the waist down, her jumper pushed up over her breasts, her bra cutting beneath her arms; she looked filthy, like a dirty picture. She stank of him, his stink leaking from her. Afraid to move, to breathe, she lay on her front and tried to listen for the boys.

She could hear other children playing in the street. Ben might join in with them but Mark wouldn't; Mark was too shy, too frightened of anyone who was even a little bit bigger than he was. More likely, Ben would stay with him, mindful of his duty, and the two of them would watch whatever game was going on like grave little linesmen.

She hoped the other women in the street wouldn't notice the rusty stains of blood on Mark's grey school shirt, or the fact that Ben's socks didn't match or that both boys' clothes were too small for them. But of course they would notice. She imagined Joan from next door grasping Mark's face and examining his bloody nose. She would tut-tut-tut. She would take his hand and lead him into her house and sit him on her draining board to clean him up. She would feed him bread and jam. If she got the chance she would give Danny a mouthful of abuse. The other women on the street weren't afraid of Danny as she was. The other women thought she was weak and useless. They had begun to shun her. Even Joan sometimes told her off; she would tell her to stand up to him, to 'Show the bastard you're not his bloody punch bag.' How easy it seemed to Joan, whose own husband was mild and patient and took his boys fishing; laughably easy, as though Danny was a fly to be swatted away when he got too annoying.

Lying very still, Annette listened to Danny's snores. They seemed real enough. His body looked relaxed, it had a sleeper's looseness, but it was hard to tell, he was a good mimic. She held her breath and gradually tugged her bra and jumper down. He rolled on to his back and her heart almost stopped. Still as stone she watched him, relieved when he began to snore again. Very carefully she swung her legs over the side of the bed. She sat up. She waited, listening, her body stiff and aching from his assault on her. The next stage would be to stand up and she knew that the bed would dip and that the floorboards would creak treacherously. She could only pray that he would sleep on long enough for her to escape, although once she had got half way down the stairs before he charged after her. She had been made to pay for that.

She stood up, her legs trembling. Her skirt lay in a crumpled heap on the floor and she put it on quickly. She pulled on her knickers not bothering with her tights, which would involve sitting back down on the bed. Watching him, she edged past the bed and dived towards the door. Breathlessly she ran down stairs, unlocked the front door and, barefoot, went out on to the street.

Ben and Mark were sitting on the kerb. They both turned to look up at her, a heart-breaking mixture of hope and anxiety on their grubby faces. She smiled at them reassuringly.

'Come on in.'

Warily they glanced past her through the open door.

'It's all right – he's asleep. Fast asleep. We'll be quiet, eh? Like little mice. We won't wake Daddy, will we?'

They didn't need to be told. In the house neither of them spoke much above a whisper. Ben stood up. Sullenly he said, 'Mark's wet himself.'

'It's all right. Don't worry. Come on in now, quickly. We'll have some tea.'

Chapter 4

Half way up the A1, Mark stopped for petrol. He leaned against the car, watching the dial on the pump roll up the pounds and pence. At the pump on the other side of his an Indian woman in a sari distributed tubes of sweets to the three children squabbling on the back seat of her Volvo. Her plait swung against her back. She turned and caught him watching her. She smiled. 'Kids, eh? Who'd have them?' Petrol overflowed from Mark's tank, spilling onto the forecourt. He cursed, a mild, soft curse, the only kind he ever used and the woman frowned and got back into her car. From the Volvo's back window three faces poked out their Smartie-coated tongues at him.

In the petrol station he paid by credit card, massing more of the points he never used, the accumulation of which would be enough to buy an ipod or a Dyson vacuum cleaner – it wasn't as if he didn't flick through the points catalogue imagining sending away for such stuff. He walked back to the car, shoving the receipt and card into his wallet and wondering if Ben and Kitty might have a use for his points. When Nathan was born he had sent them a cheque for a thousand pounds. It was too grand a gesture – he realised that now. Kitty had written him a thank you card purporting to be from the baby himself, all baby language and *thank-you-thank-you-thank-you Uncle Mark*. The card had a picture of a cartoon pram with a baby throwing its bottle over the side. He tried to imagine what was going through Kitty's head when she bought such a card. He suspected she thought him humourless and that this was a way of making him laugh.

Mark rejoined the motorway. Radio Two was running a debate about noisy neighbours that became an argument over the usefulness of ASBOs. He pressed the button tuned to local radio. Otis Reading sang *Sitting on the Dock of the Bay*.

Mark gripped the steering wheel more tightly. He felt himself easing his foot from the accelerator as he listened. This was Annette's song; it always conjured her: Annette washing dishes in the house on Tanner Street, her slim waist clinched by her apron strings, the little transistor radio at her elbow, her voice sweet and yearning as the song's lyrics. Mark watched her from the kitchen doorway, not wanting her to turn around and see him but to go on singing. He knew he made her sad and he wanted to be invisible so he could watch her being happy.

Mark sang along softly, '*I left my home in Georgia, heading for the 'frisco bay...*' Tears ran down his face, unnoticed.

Annette sang, '*I had nothing to live for...*' She turned from the sink, soap suds dissolving on her arms. She smiled at him and for once she didn't look sad. 'I love you,' she said, 'you're my sweetheart.'

He went to her and she lifted him into her arms. She kissed him. She smelt of sharp flowers and smoke. Shyly he pressed his hand against her cheek. 'Mummy,' he whispered.

He thought he might say something so she would help him. He couldn't think of the words he might use.

A car horn blasted behind him, a long, angry burst of noise. Mark jerked himself back in to the present, correcting the car's veer to the right. Blood pounded in his head. The metallic taste of fear numbed his mouth. The other driver over-took him and Mark lip-read *arsehole – stupid fucking arsehole!* Aloud Mark said, 'Sorry. Sorry.' Advertisements chimed on the radio. He hadn't noticed that *Dock of the Bay* had finished. Opening the car window he breathed in the rush of cold air and his cheeks felt tight where his tears had dried.

Two hours later he pulled in to Simon's drive and parked beneath the last of the chestnut trees. Years ago Simon had had a tarmac drive laid and he remembered the smell of its hot blackness on the warm summer air, the labourers stripped to their waists, the sweat gleaming on their bodies as the nutty substance they shovelled shone like jet. He had watched them from the doorstep, afraid because the men reminded him of Danny who was still vividly stalking his dreams. Ben was bolder: he had talked to the men, carried them cups of tea and plates of biscuits on a tray, had his hair ruffled, was teased. The men had tattoos. Mark had wanted to touch the dragons and mermaids and anchors that coloured their flesh. But he was timid, a frightened little boy, and Ben would look at him as though he was something disgusting and pitiable, disgust winning out. His brother hated him for his feebleness, always had. To Ben he was nothing but embarrassment and shame.

The tarmac was breaking up now, strong and determined dandelions pushing through its cracks. Mark took his case from the boot of the car and walked up the path to the front door expecting Simon to charge out at any moment. For a man with a false leg, Simon moved fast; he had always been surprised by how quickly he got about. But the front door remained closed. Although he had arrived at the expected time, his father wasn't watching at the window as he usually did.

His disappointment was ridiculous. As he walked into the house with its familiar smells and clutter he made himself smile to cover such a childish feeling, calling out cheerfully, 'Hello? Dad? It's me.'

Simon came out from the kitchen in to the hall. He grinned at Mark, at once putting his finger to his lips. In a stage whisper he said, 'Mark – dear boy. Welcome home! We have to be quiet – Kitty's just got Nathan to sleep.'

Mark felt his heart sink. 'Kitty's here?'

'Yes, and Nathan – come through. Say hello to the little chap – just don't wake him, for heaven's sake.'

Kitty stood up as he followed Simon into the kitchen. She smiled at him, stepping forward and standing on her tiptoes to kiss his cheek. 'Hello, Mark.' She coloured slightly and he was surprised again by how shy she was when she looked so bold.

Simon said, 'Would you like a cup of tea? Or a drink? Kitty and I were just about to go out into the garden and enjoy this sunshine.' He went to the fridge and brought out three small bottles of French lager. 'I expect you could do with some fresh air after that long drive, Mark. And a drink, eh? Come on – I've set the deckchairs up on the lawn.'

There were only two deckchairs. Kitty sat on the grass, her legs crossed like a squaw's, her back straight; she held her bottle of lager on the ground between her knees, her fingers loose around its neck. She was slight and slim; she had good cheekbones, beautiful, sharp, high bones and a full, soft mouth. Last time he'd seen her she had been eight months pregnant, the bump neat and hard looking. She hadn't bothered trying to disguise it but had worn jog pants and tee shirts that barely skimmed her belly button. Her belly button was pierced and on her left shoulder blade was a pretty tattoo of a humming bird. Kitty's tattoo amused Simon, who had once asked him if he thought it common. When he'd told him no, Simon had laughed. 'Then don't look at her as though you think it is! My God, Mark – my grandfather was more with it than you are!'

'Saying with it means you're not, Dad.'

Simon had clapped him on the shoulder. 'Kitty's wonderful! A breath of fresh air!'

Mark remembered how awkward Ben had been when he introduced this girl to him. Later, taking him to one side Ben had said, 'Don't say she's too young for me, I've heard it all. Just don't say what you're thinking.'

'What am I thinking?'

'Don't be gnomic.' Ben had looked at Kitty who was talking to Simon on the other side of the room. 'She's lovely – fun. God knows what she sees in me.'

Mark could have given him a list of things a girl like Kitty would see in a man like Ben.

Sitting in the old-fashioned, candy-striped deckchair, Mark sipped his lager, aware that his too-big feet were too close to Kitty's knees. He shifted uncomfortably, never fully trusting of folding chairs; he wished he'd sat on the grass too, he might feel less staid.

Simon lowered himself cautiously into the other deckchair, his artificial leg stretched out awkwardly in front of him. He smiled at Mark. 'Getting old,' he said. 'Old as the hills.'

Kitty asked, 'How old are you, Simon?'

'Don't you know?' He pretended astonishment. Winking at Mark he said, 'I'm seventy.'

'That's not too old.'

Simon laughed. 'No. *Seventy* isn't too old.' Looking at Kitty he said, 'Where's Ben today?'

'Amsterdam. He's back this evening.' She glanced towards the house and the open back door. 'Maybe I should have brought the buggy outside.'

'He'll be fine. You shouldn't fret so. When he starts to cry Uncle Mark here will fetch him.'

Kitty bowed her head; she began plucking at the grass around her and making a miniature haystack. Mark noticed the dark rings beneath her eyes and remembered what Ben had said about the sleepless nights she endured. 'Kitty manages,' he'd said. 'She's a little trooper.'

Little soldier, little trooper. These were the words Annette had used; it was strange to hear such phrases from Ben. It was as though he had regressed.

Simon rested his head back and closed his eyes. 'I'm going to go to sleep. You'll excuse me, won't you?' Within moments he was snoring softly.

Mark glanced at Kitty, wondering if she felt as awkward as he did without Simon's conscious presence acting as chaperone between them. They were almost strangers to each other, after all, and there was her surprising shyness. When he'd first seen her, her vest top showing off her tattoo, a fake diamond glinting in her abdomen, he'd thought such a girl couldn't possibly be shy of anyone. She'd worn large hoop earrings and he remembered that her hair had been dyed blonde, her dark roots showing like a tiger's stripe. Despite what he'd said to Simon, he had thought she was common, and had immediately felt ashamed of his snobbishness. It was at moments like that when Mark remembered most forcibly that it wasn't Simon's genteel blood that ran through his veins.

Kitty's hair was dark now, thick and shiny as freshly shelled conkers. The change in her was Ben's doing, he guessed, Ben's taste and Ben's money shaping her as though she was Eliza Doolittle. Her voice remained the same, though; she kept the Teesside accent he and Ben had lost years ago. Perhaps, given time, her voice would be moderated, too.

He glanced at Kitty who had begun plucking at the grass again. He wondered if Ben had told her about his search for Danny or if he kept secrets from his young wife. He had an urge to quiz her and he imagined her squirming under his interrogation, afraid of saying the wrong thing, of somehow betraying her husband. Suddenly he thought of Susan, who wouldn't have been able to resist being cruel to a girl like

Kitty, and the pain of remembering her made him draw breath.

Kitty looked up at him sharply. 'Are you all right?'

'Yes. Cramp, I think, from the drive.'

'Can I get you anything?'

'No, thank you.' He smiled at her but she looked away, spreading the little mound of grass out with the flat of her hand. She looked as if she was about to cry. Carefully he said, 'Ben told me you've had some sleepless nights with the baby?'

She nodded miserably.

'Why don't you take a nap now, while he's sleeping? Dad's old couch is terribly comfortable...'

'No. I'm all right. We'll go soon.'

'You don't have to rush off.'

She laughed shortly. 'No, I know.'

She was wearing jeans, low slung so that the white lace of her panties showed. Only a few months since the birth of her son, her belly was flat, its diamond stud winking in the sunlight below her cropped vest. Her breasts were small, as though they had been depleted by months of breast-feeding. The soles of her bare feet were blackened, her toenails painted pale pink, delicate like her. Sometimes Simon called her waif, his voice tender with love, unable quite to believe that he had been blessed with this girl and her baby so late in his life. He had all but given up hope of a grandchild, had begun to talk of regrets. Now Kitty was the love of his life and Nathan a small, spoilt god.

Kitty seemed to force herself to look at him. 'I saw your book in Tesco.'

'Did you turn it so its cover faced out?'

'No, I didn't think...'

He laughed. 'It's OK. It's just what Dad does.'

'Ben wants you to sign his copy. It's at home – I should have brought it...' She took a drink from the bottle of lager.

Quickly she said, 'I've read it. I liked it. Although I hated the girl. Was I meant to?'

The girl was Susan, only thinly disguised so that Ben would still recognise her. Not that Ben read his novels. He kept them on his living room shelves, their pristine condition marred only by the author's signature on the title page. Susan had called Ben a Philistine, a joke because she didn't think his books worthy enough for it to matter if they went unread. Susan read Henry James and Virginia Woolf. She had once asked him why he bothered to write at all.

Kitty was watching him as though his silence disturbed her. Lightly he said, 'What's Ben doing in Amsterdam?'

'A conference. He's speaking.' There was a note of pride in her voice that made her sound even younger. As if she thought she had been boastful she coloured a little and glanced away towards the house.

Her mobile phone began to ring. She took it from her handbag and flicked it open, immediately getting to her feet as she said, 'Hiya!' Turning her back on him, she walked away towards the summerhouse as she said, 'No, I'm fine. I'm at your Dad's.'

Mark took a drink and set the bottle down on the grass beside him. The lawn needed mowing, the flowerbeds weeding. A couple of weeks ago the daffodils that mobbed the borders would have made quite a display but now their trumpets were forlorn. He remembered how he used to help his stepmother Joy tie the flowers' leaves into neat packages so that the garden looked tidy again. He'd heard years later that this was bad for daffodils and remembered being surprised. Joy always seemed to know so much about gardening. When he helped her weed or prune or plant out seedlings from the greenhouse she called him her apprentice and talked to him about how planting should be kept in time with the moon's cycle. He'd suspected that this was just another story adults told to make children believe there was magic in the world; he'd hoped that it was not. He'd needed Joy to be as she seemed – sensible and honest.

Kitty had walked further away. She kicked idly at the frame of the greenhouse, her body hunched, her head bowed over the phone as if her conversation was top secret. He felt irritated by her; not for the first time he wondered how Ben could have brought himself to marry such a child.

He remembered his brother's wedding day; Kitty's family filling the small Norman church of St Hilda's, the men standing around the graveyard in their cheap suits, smoking their Lambert & Butlers. At least some of them wore suits; some could hardly be bothered to dress properly at all. Kitty's father and grandfather, her stepfather and brother wore hired morning dress, just as Ben and he did, cream rose buds in their lapels, cream silk cravats at their throats. Kitty's brother still managed to look like a yob, her father like someone who had spent his life on social security, smoking himself halfway to death in dim pubs. The women put on a better show – some even wore hats. The fat cousins who were Kitty's bridesmaids wore identical off-the-shoulder dresses made of some purple, satiny material. They bulged obscenely.

Only Kitty had surprised him. Standing behind Ben at the front of the church, he had turned as the bridal march began to see her walking up the aisle on her father's arm. Her face was veiled, her white dress modest and simple and lovely. She looked like Audrey Hepburn.

From the deckchair beside him Simon said, 'Little Kitty – so adorable. She reminds me of a sweetheart nurse who looked after me when they cut my leg off.'

Mark laughed despite himself and looked from Kitty to Simon. 'You never talk about the war.'

Simon snorted. 'Bloody awful time, that's why. Anyway – you never talk about your war.'

'So we're even, then.' Watching Kitty pace back and forth along the edge of the lawn Mark said, 'Do you think she's happy?'

'Yes. Of course.' Sharply Simon said, 'They're very happy. I've never seen Ben so contented.' He was looking at him steadily, the same stern expression he'd use when he'd angered him as a child. 'Do you think you can be happy for them?'

He gazed back at him. 'I'll do my very best.'

Simon sighed. 'Mark, Ben has told me what he's doing – poking about in the past –'

Mark looked away. His father's concern made him feel pitiable; he had a horrible feeling that he might cry. Simon reached out and squeezed his hand briefly.

'Mark? Believe me I tried to talk him out of it. All he kept saying was that he had a right –'

Kitty walked towards them. Smiling at Simon she said, 'You're awake.'

'Oh, I was only dozing. Was that Ben on the phone?'

'Yes. He'll be home in an hour.'

Simon got to his feet painfully. 'Then you should go. Come along, let's get that little chap ready to welcome his Daddy.'

Chapter 5

Mark washed the supper dishes and put them away. He went through Simon's fridge, discarding long out of date yoghurts and shrivelled, bendy carrots that had begun to grow fur in the bottom of the vegetable drawer. Jars of jam cultivated mould in the back of the cupboards and the shelves were littered with crumbs. He didn't go into the pantry. Sorting out Simon's pantry usually took a half-day, all the time Simon pretending bemusement that he was going to so much trouble.

His father read *The Guardian* in his armchair. Sensing that Mark had finished what he called *fiddling about*, Simon folded the paper and tossed it on the floor. 'Is that wine finished?'

'No. Would you like a glass?'

'Will you have one, too?'

Handing him a glass Mark said, 'You didn't eat much.'

'I haven't any appetite these days. It's natural at my age – besides, who wants to see an old man gorging himself?'

Mark sat down in the chair opposite him and Simon studied him critically. 'You've lost weight. You look gaunt.' After a moment he said, 'I know you're worrying about Danny.'

Mark had never heard his father mention Danny by name before. He was shocked by the familiarity of it, as though Danny and Simon had once been friends. Unable to trust his voice he kept silent. Simon sat forward. 'This will blow over, Mark. Ben will lose interest...but if he *does* find him –'

Mark got up and poured himself another drink. Simon watched him anxiously.

'Mark? Don't you think you should talk about the possibility –'

'No.' He turned to face him. 'There's nothing to say. Ben can do as he likes – I don't have to be a part of it.'

'But you're here – you could have stayed in Hampstead.'

'I'm here to see you.'

Simon laughed shortly.

'I've never neglected you, Dad.'

'No. You're a dutiful son.' After a moment he said, 'I think you should go home, Mark.'

'Run away?'

He sighed. 'Mark, if you won't go home then you should talk to Ben, a real heart to heart –'

Hating the bitterness in his voice Mark said, 'Man to man?'

'Yes – if you like. For pity's sake, boy! If you and Ben could sit down together, talk it through instead of always sniping at each other...just tell him how you feel.'

'He knows how I *feel*.' Mark paced the room, too agitated to keep still. So often lately he had tried to imagine talking to Ben about his search for Danny, knowing how contemptuous his brother would be of his fear. Ben didn't know enough to be merciful. *Merciful!* As though he was a hapless criminal to be judged leniently. He remembered how Ben would silently pass him a hanky after Danny had given him yet another bloody nose. Ben would be angry with him, as though he believed he had deliberately caused their father to punch him in the face. In Ben's opinion theirs would have been a happy home if only he had stopped provoking Danny.

Mark finished the wine. He went to the sink and washed and dried his glass, all the time feeling Simon's eyes on his back, the old man's anxiety too pressing to be ignored. Wanting to explain himself he turned to him.

41

'Ben told me once…' Mark laughed, feeling that he might cry, that he was being sentimental and foolish, but he realised that Simon had all at once become still, sitting a little further forward, the better to catch every word. This breathless interest in what he was about to say sobered him; it seemed indecent that Simon should be so curious. Coldly he said, 'It doesn't matter.'

'What did he tell you, Mark?'

Mark gazed at him, wondering if his silence would hurt Simon more or less than what he was about to say. But keeping silent would only make his father think he was playing some kind of game, he would think even less of him and so he said quickly, 'Ben used to tell me that Danny was going to buy him a bicycle.'

Simon laughed harshly. 'Yes. When you both first came to us Ben used to tell me that. For months the only time he could bring himself to speak to me was to boast about how wonderful Danny was.' Shaking his head he said, 'That bicycle! I never heard the last of it!'

'But he really believed that Danny would buy him it —'

'Perhaps he only wanted to believe.'

'But it's still the difference between us — what we expected from him.' Flatly he said, 'He loved him. He loved Danny and he hated me.'

'Mark, he was just a little boy trying to make sense of what had happened to him. He was bound to be angry—'

'*Bound* to be.'

'Don't be childish, Mark. Don't pretend you don't understand that Ben suffered too. And he didn't hate you. Of course not.' Stiffly, Simon got to his feet. 'I'm off to bed. I think you should get off, too. Get a good night's sleep — it's a long drive back tomorrow.'

'You really want me to go?'

'I think it would be best, if you won't talk to your brother I can't see the point of you staying.'

'But I came to see you, not to talk to him.'

42

'Well, all right. But in the circumstances perhaps now is not the best time.' About to leave the room, he turned on him. 'I'm still angry with you, Mark! So angry that sometimes it's hard for me to be in the same room with you! There – I've said it! You will just have to bear with me.' He sat down. 'Dear God, I feel old! I've lived too long.'

Mark stepped towards him. Cautiously he said, 'Please forgive me, Dad.'

Simon raised his head. 'Why, Mark? How will my forgiveness help us?' After a moment he said, 'May I ask you something? Did you love Susan?'

'Yes.'

'It wasn't revenge?'

To his shame, Mark began to cry. Simon watched him impassively. At last he handed him a handkerchief. 'Here,' he said, 'dry your eyes. Go to bed. It seems to me you need your sleep.'

Susan said, 'Hi, I'm Susan Day. You're Mark, yes? Ben's brother?'

In the single bed he'd slept in as a child, Mark remembered how Susan had thrust out her hand to him, a surprisingly masculine gesture. Her handshake was firm, she smiled that amused smile of hers that always seemed on the edge of mockery. Her long, blonde hair was loose around her bare shoulders and she wore some kind of corset, tightly laced so that her breasts were pushed together and her tiny waist was emphasised. The short skirt she wore showed off her long tanned legs and in her three-inch heels she was as tall as he was. She looked him in the eye and seemed to weigh him up in a moment. Her smile became knowing. Touching his arm lightly, she said, 'You write, Ben tells me?'

She had made him sound like a dilettante. He'd laughed. Looking towards his brother on the other side of the room he said, 'What else did Ben tell you?'

'Nothing.'

Ben began to weave his way through the press of their parents' friends until he stood at Susan's side. He slipped his arm around her waist and hugged her to him, kissing the side of her head before holding out his hand to Mark.

'Mark. How are you? Sue's introduced herself?'

It was Joy and Simon's wedding anniversary. Helium-filled balloons were tied to the dining room chairs and bobbed together as though imitating the party guests. Cards crowded the mantelpiece and sideboard and the remains of the buffet littered the table, although the cake was still to be cut. Bottles of champagne waited in the fridge. Ben jerked his head at the cake.

'Do you think Dad will make a speech?'

'Yes.'

Ben groaned. Laughing he said, 'Sue, Dad adores making speeches! He used to make speeches at our *birthday* parties, for pity's sake!'

He couldn't remember seeing Ben look so animated, so less like his usual cool self. It was as though Susan Day gave off an electrical charge that had his proud, ironic brother twitching like a gauche boy. Ben shifted from one foot to the other; he drew Susan closer and kissed her shoulder. He laughed. Mark almost put a hand on his arm to steady him. Instead he took out his cigarettes and offered him one.

At once Ben said, 'I've given up.'

Mark lit his own cigarette. Exhaling smoke he said, 'Good for you.'

'Susan persuaded me.'

He looked at the woman who had entwined her arm around Ben's. She looked back at him steadily. It seemed to

44

him that she was willing him to be quiet and accept that his brother was now under her control.

In the room he'd slept in as a child, Mark lay on his back, half undressed, unable to be bothered to finish the job and resign himself to bed. He'd folded his trousers over the back of the Lloyd Loom chair that had always stood in this bedroom. He'd washed and brushed his teeth at the sink in the corner; he'd wondered about taking one of the sleeping pills he'd bought. The pills hardly seemed to work, only left him feeling groggy the following day. He believed they stopped his dreams, though, or at least lessened their vividness and made them less disturbing. Running the cold tap until the water was freezing, he'd filled a glass and washed two tablets down his throat.He'd left the lamp on and the room was full of shadows. Opposite the bed was the wardrobe, something else that had lived in this room long before he had. When he was a child the wardrobe had been cavernous enough for him to hide in. He remembered its close smell of mothballs and varnished wood; he'd realised that it would be the first place Danny would look when he came to drag him home, but all the same he liked its quiet and darkness. Besides, wherever he hid, his discovery would be inevitable. Danny didn't give up.

Mark finished undressing and climbed between the cold sheets. He closed his hand around his limp cock as if to comfort it. He thought of Susan at Joy and Simon's anniversary party, how she had circulated with a plate of the cut cake, charming his parents' guests as Ben watched her with a rapt, admiring expression. Tearing his eyes away from her for a moment Ben had said, 'Isn't she fantastic?' He laughed joyously. 'She's everything I ever wanted! I can't believe I've found her!'

Watching her too, Mark had said, 'How did you find her?'

'She came to work in the hospital last month – she's a gynaecologist.' He grinned at him. 'What do you think?'

Ben never asked for his opinion. He remembered feeling flattered and that he'd smiled. 'I think she's very attractive.'

Quickly Ben said, 'I haven't told her about Mum and Dad – that they're not our real parents. I will, tonight, probably, after the party.' He sighed, and for the first time that evening he seemed his old, controlled self. 'She'll understand, I think – Christ – most women are fascinated. Besides, I don't have to tell her the whole bloody story.'

Susan came back, insisting they eat some cake. He had wondered if Ben *would* tell her the whole bloody story, or at least all that Ben knew of it. He'd imagined her listening intently as his brother confessed that the kind, gracious, happy couple whom he'd introduced as his parents really had nothing to do with him. He imagined that she would guess that Ben was ashamed he wasn't the bona fide middle-class boy he acted so well; Susan would recognise his shame as his gift to her. Susan would recognise the gift's worth; she would know that it was utterly priceless.

Mark covered his face with his hands. He groaned softly, for once allowing himself the theatrics of pain. At times like this he felt Susan's presence so strongly it seemed all he had to do was speak her name and she would step from the shadows and kneel beside him. She would take his hand and press it to her mouth; she would beg his forgiveness. She would climb into his bed and he would hold her tightly and it would be as if his heart had never broken and his life was as it should be.

Susan had said, 'Sign it. Sign *To my dear sister-in-law, who knows the truth about me.*'

He'd looked up in surprise from signing a pile of his latest novel in a bookshop. She grinned at him, hooking a strand of her hair behind her ear as she held out the book. 'Where are the adoring fans?'

He took the book from her, signed it. Handing it back he said, '*To Susan, with best wishes.* Will that do?'

Looking down at the inscription she said, 'I have to buy it now, don't I?' She took out her purse.

'You pay at the till.'

'So no money will change hands between us?'

For an hour or so he had sat at his table behind his stacked books. The shop's customers had ignored him, its staff had been indifferent. He imagined the signed books being remaindered and a familiar sense of pointlessness over took him. He had looked up at this smirking woman and it was one of the few times in his life he remembered losing his temper. 'What are you doing here, Susan? What do you want?'

Her eyes widened in mock surprise. 'To see you, of course, to support you. Families should be supportive, shouldn't they?' All at once her expression softened, she glanced away, seemingly embarrassed, as though her teasing had gone a little too far. Her fingers drummed on the cover of his book and he noticed that her nails were short and blunt, as they should be for probing inside other women's bodies. She stood by as a man approached and asked him to sign a copy for his wife. Scrawling his name, Mark watched from the corner of his eye as Susan opened his novel and closed it again, turning it over and over as though books were as alien to her as a surgeon's instruments would be to him.

When the man had gone she stepped towards him. 'You're angry with me,' she said.

Disconcerted, he said too sharply, 'No, surprised to see you, that's all. I'm sorry. I didn't mean to be rude.'

'Was that you being rude?' She'd smiled, still soft, still unlike the woman he'd thought she was – the woman who teased and mocked him with such sharp perceptiveness. It was as though he had never truly seen her before. Here she was, smiling at him as though he had the power to break her heart, as though he might guess that she was in love with him. It was an epiphany, an extraordinary moment to be re-

47

visited and re-lived over and over: Susan was a sweet girl, vulnerable; *she wanted him.* He forgot about Ben and thought only of himself, his sudden, mindless desire. He found himself getting to his feet, saying, 'Why don't I buy you lunch?'

They went to a wine bar, a dimly lit, crowded place where she led him to a corner table, where she sat close to him, her thigh against his. She drank most of the bottle of wine she had ordered, for courage, she said. She said, 'I think you think I'm a bitch.'

'No – no, of course not –'

'I *am*, sometimes. To you, especially.'

He attempted smiling, but it was a foolish, besotted smile. 'Why? Why to me especially?'

She'd gazed at him. 'I don't really know the truth about you.'

'No?' He'd smiled his idiotic smile, unable to take his eyes off her, not understanding a word. There had been no other time in his life when his guard had been so completely down. Impulsively he said, 'The truth about me is I think you're the loveliest woman I've ever met.'

Such ordinary words – such a predictable line so that it felt as though she was a stranger he was trying to pick up. Immediately he thought that he should try to say something that was profound, that would have her falling at his feet in awe, but words were useless, failing him as they often did. There was only his desire for her, his prick governing his head and his heart, and his conscience of course. Ah – his conscience! His conscience was nothing, as useless as an appendix, so easily over-ruled! He was weak and he was disgusting and he told her so, there and then as she sipped her wine, as she placed her glass down and turned to him, giving him a look that made him feel she'd reached a hand inside his guts.

'Disgusting?' She'd frowned. 'No. I shall cure you.'

Lying in bed, Mark tossed the covers aside and got up. He went to the wardrobe and opened its mirrored doors, desperately pushing aside coats and jackets, remembering how Susan had once told him that as a child she too would hide. She liked the power she had over the adults as they searched for her, their worry palpable even in her hiding place. The coats and jackets swung on their hangers and he stared into the wardrobe's dark interior, at a loss. He thought of Joy, cautiously extending her hand to him, patiently coaxing him to come out; how she sounded like a frightened girl forcing herself to be brave.

The first night he'd spent at Simon's house, Joy had left a light on by his bed – a lamp in the shape of a gingerbread house, the bulb's yellow glow shining through the little windows with their sugar cane sills. She stood with him at the threshold of his new room, the gingerbread house casting its dim glow, and suddenly she seemed shy of him. Too brightly, she said, 'We're not sure what little boys like – you can change whatever you care to.' He had looked up at her, saw that her sharp features were softened by anxiety, and all at once she was crouching in front of him, her hands grasping his arms firmly. 'Mark, this is your home now and you're safe as can be. You understand, don't you? No one will hurt you ever again.' Glancing over her shoulder to the bed she turned back to him and said, 'That's Tubs on your pillow. He used to be mine, when I was just your age. I thought how nice it would be if you were to take care of each other.' Carefully she asked, 'Would you like me to help you undress for bed?'

He remembered shaking his head. When she'd gone he'd turned the teddy bear face down; no one would see him naked again, not even a baby's toy. When the woman came back she pretended not to notice that her bear was sitting on the chest of drawers, its gaze pointed away from the bed. He'd dressed in the pyjamas that had been left folded on the pillow, he could smell their newness, the stiff feel of them

49

next to his skin; he had buttoned the striped jacket up to his chin, pulled the white cord tightly around his waist. He was afraid he would wet the bed and its soft, pastel sheets and blue blankets that also smelt new. He had an idea that he might sleep on the floor but the woman said, 'Well now! Look at you – what a good boy to get dressed for bed so quickly! Hop into bed now, let's tuck you up snug as a bug, eh? Then we can read a story.'

She sat beside him on the bed, she smiled and said, 'Comfy?' She still looked shy and sad and he was afraid he'd hurt her feelings over the bear, Tubs. Screwing up his courage he whispered, 'Sorry.'

'Sorry? Whatever for? You have done absolutely nothing wrong! Nothing at all.'

He knew better, though. It was just that she didn't know him, just as Susan didn't know him, even when he had told her the story of how Joy would seek him out, and the story of Tubs, and the story of how the gingerbread house cast its shadows so peculiarly on the ceiling. He told Susan everything and she asked for more so that perhaps she felt that he was making up stories to please her, as if he believed that when the stories ran out he would be killed, like the princess telling her tall tales over her thousand and one nights. But he only ever told her the truth. He told her the truth about Danny and it seemed that she held her breath and the power shifted between them for a moment. But in the end the power was all hers and he knew he had made a mistake in that bookshop when the dead scent of books was all around. He had a conscience, but he had discovered it too late so that all he could do was go on and try to square it with himself. Didn't she love him, after all? Didn't she *have to*, after all he had revealed?

Mark closed the wardrobe doors and went back to bed. Leaving the lamp on he waited for the sleeping pills to work.

Chapter 6

Annette said, 'Do you have a Hoover?'

Doctor Walker frowned as if the answer might come to him if he thought hard enough. 'A Hoover? Now, I don't know. Perhaps. Perhaps there's something like that under the stairs.'

They were in the kitchen and she followed him into the hall where he opened a door. A smell of damp and old, muddy shoes wafted out and he smiled at her apologetically before rummaging about amongst the accumulated rubbish. He came out again, a cobweb caught in his hair. 'No Hoover, I'm afraid.'

'A Ewbank?'

'I'm sorry – I don't know what a *Ewbank* is.'

'A sweeper kind of thing.'

He laughed. 'No. I'm afraid my mother wasn't much into sweeping things. Only under the carpet, eh?'

He probably expected her to laugh but she didn't feel like it. That morning Mark's teacher had waylaid her and asked her if she knew what might be troubling him. 'He's very withdrawn, Mrs Carter. Is everything all right at home?'

She'd felt herself blush. 'Everything's fine.'

'I noticed during PE that Mark has a nasty bruise on his back.'

'He slipped in the bath.'

The woman held her gaze as though giving her time to think of more lies to trip herself up. Annette had felt her blush darken, a trickle of sweat ran down her back.

51

Picturing the welfare officer on the doorstep she felt her guts turn to water.

Doctor Walker said, 'Annette?'

She jerked her head up and tried to look as if she'd been listening.

'I said would you like a cup of tea before you start?'

'Oh – no. No thank you. Best get on.'

'As you like. Right – well. If you start on the bathroom and then the main bedroom, I think that should be more than enough for today.'

The toilet had a mahogany seat and roses painted inside its bowl. From the cistern high on the wall a piece of string dangled, tied to what was left of the chain. In the bath a brown stain spread beneath the cold tap that dripped even when she tightened it. She shook Vim on the stain, a thick, caking layer, and its smell caught at the back of her throat. She wished she had a pair of rubber gloves but there wasn't enough money for such niceties. Perhaps the doctor had some in that black hole of a kitchen. Not that she would go down and ask – she couldn't be bothered with his friendliness, his talk. She would just have to put up with chapped hands. If Danny noticed he would call them scrubber's hands and laugh or not, depending on his mood.

Last night she'd managed to feed and bathe the boys and tuck them in to bed before Danny woke up. He'd come down to the kitchen in his trousers and string vest, the dark hair on his chest showing through the diamond patterned mesh. He lit a cigarette and narrowed his eyes against the smoke.

'What's for tea?'

Warily she said, 'I've made you a cheese sandwich.'

'Pickle?' He sat down at the table.

'Yes. Cheese and pickle.'

As she set the sandwich in front of him he caught her round the waist and pulled her close, his face nuzzling into her body. 'I'm sorry, angel.' His voice was muffled, his breath warm through her jumper. She touched his hair cautiously and he broke away to look up at her.

'Don't leave me,' he said.

'I won't!'

'I'd kill myself if you left me.'

'I won't leave you, Danny.'

'I promise not to hurt you again.'

Not judging his mood well enough she said hurriedly, 'Or the kids? Little Mark – he's so good –'

He stared at her. 'Shut up about that little bastard.'

'I'm sorry, it's just –'

He slammed his fist down on the table, causing her heart to leap. 'If you're going to go on pretending he's mine I'm going to bring him up as I see fit, do you hear me? I won't have him growing up into some fucking little fairy!'

Scrubbing at the stained bath Annette tried to remember when Danny had started to accuse her of going with other men. It was probably during their first date together after he'd been discharged from the Marines. He'd called for her, dressed to the nines in a new suit and tie, his shoes polished as glass. He had a bunch of white chrysanthemums and a box of Milk Tray for her gran. Her gran had eyed him suspiciously and left the chocolates on the kitchen table as though they were tainted.

Outside on the street Danny had laughed. 'Is she like that with all your other fellas?'

'I haven't got any *other fellas*!' She'd smiled at him. 'I told you that in my letters – I was staying in until you got back.'

'And you think I believed you?'

She'd laughed, unsure of herself. 'It's true.'

'It'd better be.' He squeezed her hand tightly. 'Are your mam and dad dead then?'

'Yes.'

'I'd heard they were. Just you and the old bag, eh?'

'Don't call her that!'

He'd looked at her. 'Orphan Annie, aren't you? Little Orphan Annie.'

He liked the fact that she was almost alone in the world. Stupidly, she'd imagined that this was because he wanted to take care of her.

She rinsed the last of the Vim away. The stain remained, only a little lighter. She started on the sink, moving aside Doctor Walker's shaving things, his toothbrush and toothpaste. It was what she hated most about cleaning, being forced into intimacy with other people's most personal things. And it was always worse with a new employer; in the other houses she cleaned she'd become so familiar with the stuff they left about that she almost didn't see it any more. Here, though, everything was strange. And he was a man on his own – at least for the time being. She felt shy of making his bed: an intimacy too far.

Reluctantly she went into the bedroom. His bed was already made. She heard the sound of a lawn mower and looked out of the window. She watched as he pushed the mower back and forth, creating neat stripes. His limp seemed less pronounced and she wondered if he suspected she may spy on him like this and so make an effort not to appear too crippled. His blonde hair caught the sun. As if he sensed he was being watched he stopped and looked up. He smiled at her, wiping sweat from his brow with his forearm before miming that she should open the window.

The sash stuck but eventually it gave and the smell of cut grass filled the room. He called, 'There's some lemonade cooling in the kitchen sink. Why don't you bring it out here with a couple of glasses?'

'I haven't finished in here yet!' She laughed, embarrassed by how her voice had rung out so loudly over the quiet gardens. Glancing towards the blank, listening windows of his neighbour's house, she imagined the gossip had already begun about the new doctor and his absent wife.

He followed her gaze. Turning back to her he grinned and cupped his hands around his mouth. He shouted louder, 'I might die of thirst, you know! You don't want to be responsible for my death, do you?'

'All right – I'm coming!' Leaving the window open to fill the room with the spring-scented air, she went downstairs.

They sat on the summerhouse steps, the bottle of pop between them. She'd noticed that a little of the cobweb still clung to his hair and itched to brush it away. She itched too for a cigarette, but didn't think it seemly that she should smoke in front of an employer. The sun was warm and she lifted her face to it, closing her eyes. If she concentrated on its warmth and the way it seemed to intensify the garden's scent, she might forget her craving. A bird called out; she tried to think only of the song it made and to keep her mind in the present. Inevitably she thought of Mark's teacher, the stern, closed look on her face that had softened only when the woman told her how lovely Mark was. It was obvious the woman thought she didn't deserve such a child.

Doctor Walker said, 'It's a blackbird. They nest every year in that tree over there.'

She opened her eyes and the bird swooped down to land a few feet away from them. It pulled a worm from the ground and despite the warmth Annette shuddered.

Gently he said, 'Are you all right, Annette?'

'Yes.' Realising how abrupt she sounded she added, 'I'm fine, thank you.'

He frowned at her. 'I'm sorry, but I think you don't look well.'

'No – I am. Just tired.'

'Then forgive me.' He sipped his drink, watching the bird hop across the grass. After a while he said, 'My father used to teach me to recognise species of birds from their songs. He was a bird watcher. I thought it was the most boring, pointless thing a grown man could do. Now I'm not so sure.' The bird took off and he turned to her and smiled sadly. 'Must be getting old, eh?'

'I like watching them – though we only get sparrows where we live.'

'And where do you live?'

'Tanner Street. Behind the sugar factory.'

He nodded. 'I think I know where you mean.'

'They're going to knock it down soon. For the new road.'

'Are they? How do you feel about that?'

She shrugged. 'We'll get a new flat in the tower blocks they're building on Rosehill. Ben can't wait.'

'Ben's your husband?'

'My son.'

'Of course – you told me yesterday. Ben and Mark? Five and six years old.'

She looked down at her drink. At lunchtime, as she did everyday, she would go to the school and look through the railings to see if she could see her boys. Almost always Ben would be playing football and Mark would be standing alone against the school wall watching him, bumping his head gently, rhythmically, against the red bricks. She felt ashamed for him, for his isolation, his strangeness that made the other children keep their distance. He looked like he wasn't quite right in the head, even though she knew how bright he was, or had been as a baby. When he was a baby Danny had ignored him; it was only when he started to talk that the trouble began. *Trouble*! The word didn't seem big enough to describe what Danny did.

She stood up. 'I should get on, Doctor Walker.'

'Sit down, Annette. Enjoy the sunshine – everything else can wait.'

She did as she was told, even felt grateful. She was sick and tired and her heart felt like a stone, a painful, useless weight. Her hand went to the pocket of her overall, closing furtively around the outline of her cigarette packet.

On impulse she said, 'Do you mind if I smoke?'

'Do you mind if I have one with you?'

They smoked in silence, the garden's quiet seeming to deepen around them. Even the birds had become still. The sun warmed the summerhouse roof and the smell of its tar mingled with the smoke from their cigarettes. She thought of Danny not knowing that she was here with a strange man, smoking in such peaceful silence. If he knew he would kill her.

Doctor Walker said, 'My wife may have to stay in hospital a little longer than I'd first thought. She has to have quite a major operation.'

'I'm sorry.'

Looking straight ahead he said, 'She was pregnant but she miscarried and now she's to have a hysterectomy.'

'I'm sorry.' It seemed inadequate just to keep repeating that she was sorry. Too quickly, she said, 'I lost a baby. I know how sad she must feel.'

'I'm sorry to hear that.'

She laughed painfully. 'Mark was only a few months old when I fell again. I would have had three babies under three. Everyone thought losing that baby was for the best.'

Doctor Walker said, 'I don't suppose you thought it was *for the best*.'

'No.'

'People say stupid things, don't they? Doctors especially, I'm afraid.'

'It was a girl. I thought there might have been something wrong with her, for me to lose her like that.' Shyly she asked, 'Do you think so?'

'Perhaps.'

'I called her Heather. Not that I've told anyone I gave her a name.'

'You've told me.'

'Yes.' Guiltily she hung her head. She hadn't told Danny. She never talked about that time – the memories were too shaming. The doctors had treated her as though she was stupid. One of them had said, 'Do you understand about contraception, Mrs Carter? It's 1963 – no one needs to have a baby a year these days.' She felt herself grow hot at the memory, ashamed all over again.

She looked away to avoid Doctor Walker's gaze, knowing that his sympathy would make her cry. Crushing her cigarette out beneath her foot she said, 'I feel guilty not doing any work –'

'Don't. Talking to you gives me an excuse not to do the weeding.' He looked out over the garden. After a while he said, 'When you move to these new flats do you want to be on the top floor with the view of the hills, or the ground so you don't have to bother with the lifts?'

She smiled. 'The top. Right at the top so you can see for miles.'

'I think you're right – I would prefer the view, too. What about your sons, though? They'll need somewhere to run about.'

She remembered the plan of the new estate she'd seen in the library: the model tower blocks stuck onto a green board with darker green bits of spongy stuff representing trees and shrubs. Each block was on its own little island surrounded by the sponge trees, a parkland where the children would play. She couldn't imagine living in such a place.

She said, 'Maybe we'll get a council house. Not everyone's going to the flats.'

'Perhaps that would be best for the children.' As if to disguise his curiosity he said lightly, 'What does your husband do?'

'He's a bin man.' Even the words for Danny's job sounded rough: a bin man, a *rubbish* man. The words shut up people like Doctor Walker. She glanced at him surreptitiously, wondering if his expression would give anything away. Contempt, perhaps, or boredom – the small discomfit of finding himself with absolutely nothing to say about such a job, no questions to ask.

Catching her eye, he smiled. 'My first wife's father used to say that bin men were life's true heroes, that we would all go to hell in a handcart without them.' He laughed a little as if remembering. 'Edward. He was a nice man. Grace – my first wife – used to call him the absent-minded professor. All the same, she adored him.'

Annette wondered what it would be like to adore your father; she had barely known hers. All at once she felt jealous of this Grace. From the soft expression on the doctor's face she'd obviously been adored just as she adored others. Long ago Annette had decided that the supply of love in the world seemed only to gather around certain people; the more they had the more they got, like iron filings drawn to a magnet.

Doctor Walker said, 'Grace was killed in one of those V2 rockets attacks right at the end of the war. I was still in hospital – *convalescing*.' He laughed bitterly. 'Ironic, don't you think? I survived the Normandy beaches and she was killed buying flowers on a London street.'

'I'm sorry.'

'Well – long time ago now.'

'You miss her though.'

He looked at her curiously. At last he said, 'You said that as though you'd looked into my heart.'

She blushed.

'I'm sorry,' he said. 'I've embarrassed you.'

'No.' She stood up. 'Would you like me to dust the front room? Or I could clean the kitchen floor if you like...'

He sighed. Getting awkwardly to his feet he said, 'All right – we'll get back to the grindstone. If you wouldn't mind dusting the living room?'

Relieved she smiled. 'I don't mind – it's what I'm here for.'

Simon finished mowing the lawn, all the time thinking about his last visit with Joy.

Joy had said, 'I won't be able to give you children.'

He'd taken her hand, so small and white and cold on the hospital counterpane. 'Joy, I only want you to be well – and you will be. I've heard the gynaecologist here is a good man – a fine surgeon.'

She drew her hand away. 'It all seems so pointless now.'

'Don't say that.'

'Why not?' A tear rolled unheeded down her face. Calmly she said, 'I've been thinking about divorce.'

'Oh Joy – no! Don't think about that! Thoughts like that won't help you to get better.'

'*Don't think about that*! *Don't say that*! Why shouldn't I think and say these things? It's what you're thinking – wondering why you're trapped in a pointless marriage like ours!'

'Is it pointless, Joy? I don't think it is.'

'But you don't love me. And you married me out of some sense of duty – although I'd told you I could manage on my own with the baby...' Baby was a taboo word now, of course, and she covered her mouth with her hand, appalled that it had escaped her lips. Fresh tears streamed down her cheeks.

Helplessly he said, 'Joy, I'm so sorry. I wish I could make it better for you – I'd do anything in the world –'

'No one can do anything!' Her voice rose angrily. 'No one! Least of all you! You're useless! I wish I'd never, *never* laid eyes on you! I must have been mad to have anything to do with such a useless, feckless, *faithless* man!'

She wept, terrible, keening cries of pain, all the control she'd managed to hold on to over the last few days finally breaking down. Other patients and their visitors turned to look at her, startled that such a loud, ugly noise should come from the neat, demure little woman who had arrived amongst them that afternoon. Simon pulled the curtains around the bed, focusing his emotions on his anger at the hospital for moving her in to a public ward so soon.

Sitting on the bed he tried to pull her into his arms but she pushed him away. 'Go home! I don't want you near me!'

'Joy, please…'

'Did you want our baby? Did you?'

He must have hesitated a beat too long because she gazed at him with the kind of bitter triumph that comes when a bad opinion is justified. 'You don't care, do you? In fact, I think you're relieved!'

Later, when she had calmed down a little and a pretty nurse had brought them both a cup of tea, he had told her that he loved her and that he had wanted their baby as much as she had. He held her hands, keeping them trapped between his own so she wouldn't pull away. He half expected her to smack his face if he let go. But all her anger had spent itself and she was meekly tearful. She had even apologised to him for her outburst. For the moment it seemed she would accept his lies. When the nurse drew back the curtains he had an idea that all the other men sitting by their wives' beds were wondering how he might get away with it.

Simon put the lawn mower away in the shed packed with the junk his father had always gathered around him. Rooting around earlier for the lawnmower's grass box, he'd found a biscuit tin full of the toy soldiers he'd played with as a child. Alongside, amongst tins of solidified paint, was the fort his father had made.

He smiled, remembering how patiently his father had cut out the plywood with his fret saw and glued the pieces together. The fort had a drawbridge that worked by winding a tiny handle connected to its string and bobbin mechanism. It had a platform running around the interior on which his soldiers stood and pointed their rifles at the enemy. His father, who never once talked about his experiences during the two years he'd spent in the trenches, would sometimes help him to arrange his armies and Simon would ask his advice about formations, but he would pretend not to know about such things. Later he came to think that perhaps he really didn't know. A soldier was the very last thing his gentle, unworldly father had wanted to be. Whatever he'd learnt in France he'd decided to forget.

He lifted the fort down and blew away the years of accumulated dust. He thought of Joy, who would surely want to claim this shed as her own, a place where she could store all her tools for the gardening she loved so much. He should clear the rubbish out, make it the neat and tidy space she would approve of. He set the fort down gently beside the tin of soldiers. He stared at it, thinking of his father who had loved Grace so much and would have been so sad for Joy and the loss of the baby.

He caught his breath and tears welled up in his eyes. Joy was right, he was feckless, a useless man. He'd wasted his life.

Behind him Annette said, 'Doctor Walker?'

He spun round, hurriedly wiping his eyes. She frowned at him. 'Are you all right?'

'Yes! Hay fever. Blasted nuisance!'

Stepping closer she said, 'It makes you look as though you've been crying.'

'Does it?' He laughed brokenly. 'No. Not really.'

'Not really?'

'Self-pity.'

Shyly she said, 'I just came to tell you I'm going now.'

'Yes. Right. Of course. Off you go.'

'I could stay if you like – make you some lunch…?'

'No, I mustn't keep you. But thank you, you're very kind.'

About to go, she said suddenly, 'It's not self-pity to feel sad about your wife and baby.'

Ashamed he said, 'I was crying for myself, really.'

'That's all most of us ever do.'

Surprised by the bleakness in her voice he said, 'Perhaps. All the same, best not to wallow, I think.'

She seemed about to say something, only to stop herself. Glancing towards the house, she said, 'Should I come back same time next week?'

'Would you come sooner than that? Say Friday? I feel the house is so untidy – so much clutter to clear out…Would you mind?'

'No. Friday would be fine.'

He took the envelope containing her wages from his pocket and held it out to her. 'Thank you for all you've done today.'

She took the envelope without looking at it, as though it was something to be embarrassed by.

Chapter 7

Kitty watched as her mother changed Nathan. Julie was much quicker than she was at this – more slap-dash. But she supposed the end result was the same: a clean, sweeter-smelling baby, the dirty nappy folded in on itself to form a tight ball and fastened down with its sticky tapes. Nathan smiled up at his grandmother from the changing mat; he laughed as Julie lifted him onto her knee and rubbed her nose against his.

'Who's my lovely boy? Who's gorgeous? You are! Aren't you? Yes you are!'

Kitty sighed. 'Do you want a coffee, Mam?'

Julie barely glanced at her. 'I have to be back at work soon.'

Julie worked at a mortgage call centre. Recently she'd been made team leader; Kitty believed she would take the place over. Julie had more energy than anyone she knew; it made her feel weary just thinking about her mother's non-stop go. She yawned, wanting to close her eyes and sleep, wanting her mother to stay and keep watch, or take the baby out on a long, long walk. But Julie didn't do walking. Her purple Micra stood on the drive outside the window; she imagined its engine was still hot from her mother's too-fast driving.

Julie frowned at her. 'You look awful.'

'Thanks.'

'You could put a bit of lippy on, comb your hair at least. Have you had a shower this morning?'

'Yes!'

Her mother raised her eyebrows, holding her gaze as she used to when she was little and had sniffed a lie. Kitty looked down at her bitten fingernails.

Julie said, 'You're not depressed, are you?'

'No.'

'You shouldn't be, not with all you've got going for you.' She looked around the large lounge with its polished wooden floor and deep, bright, modern rugs. The cream leather sofa she sat on matched the one opposite, a large glass coffee table between them. Beyond the sofas, French doors led to the garden that was almost as big as Simon's. Bookcases lined the alcoves either side of the fireplace, full of books she hadn't read – Ben's first wife's books, clever-clever books by writers Kitty had never heard of. Books written by Mark. The first question her family asked was where the telly was. In the snug, she told them, or at least she did until she got sick of their teasing. '*The snug?*' Her brother Sean had laughed scornfully. '*What the fuck's a snug?*'

Julie said, 'Kitty, love, I know you're tired –'

'Yes. I am.'

'It's the same for all young mums. And think if you were living in some grotty council flat with kids running riot outside and music blaring day and night. It's lovely here. Look at the blossom on those trees!'

Kitty laughed but tears rolled down her cheeks. 'Blossom doesn't get him to sleep, Mam.'

'Oh, don't cry, pet!' Julie frowned, looking from her to the baby as though torn between them. Coming to a decision she put Nathan down on the changing mat and crossed the room to where Kitty was sitting on the window seat in the bay. She put her arm around her shoulders; never having been a motherly type, her embrace was stiff. She kissed the side of Kitty's head awkwardly.

'Don't be sad, eh? Everything will be all right, I promise. This is just a phase babies go through. I know when Sean was little – I was at my wit's end...'

'But you had Dad helping –'

Julie laughed as though amazed. 'Helping? Your Dad?'

Kitty wiped her eyes. 'At least he was there.'

'Aye – getting in the way, wanting his tea and his ironing doing. I'd have loved it if he'd buggered off abroad for a few days.' She glanced at her watch surreptitiously.

Kitty sat up straight, allowing her mother not to feel so bad about withdrawing her embrace. 'You'd best get going. You'll be late.'

'Oh, I'm all right for a few minutes. Should we have that coffee?'

Julie followed her into the kitchen carrying Nathan and talking her baby talk. She sat down at the table, keeping up her stream of nonsense words as Kitty switched on the coffee machine and fetched milk from the fridge. This was her mother's most favourite room in a house full of favourite rooms. She liked its sunniness, its buttermilk walls that set off the soft, honey glow of the pine cupboards. Beyond the table where her mother sat were doors leading out into the conservatory and beyond that the decking area and another table with its eight matching chairs made of some dark, heavy wood. There were too many big tables in this house, a table for every kind of formal and informal occasion. The first wife used to give dinner parties.

Julie said casually, 'Did Mark get here all right?'

Kitty placed a coffee on the table in front of her. Taking Nathan she said, 'He arrived when I was at Simon's.'

'Oh? Still as gorgeous as ever, is he?'

'Mam! Honestly you're embarrassing.'

'Rubbish!' Unashamed she said, 'How is he, then?'

Kitty sat down. Cuddling Nathan closer she said, 'He doesn't like me.'

Her mother laughed. 'Don't be childish.'

'And he hardly looked at Nath.'

'No! I don't believe that! How could *anyone* not be interested in this little prince, eh?' Julie grinned. 'Maybe he was tired after that long journey. Mark's nice. He was kind to your gran at your wedding. She still asks after *that lovely young man.*'

'He's not young.'

'Everyone's young to your gran, pet. And he is young! Younger than me.'

Kitty reached for the salt cellar, fiddling with it to avoid her mother's eye. Usually, when she wasn't thick with tiredness, she avoided mentioning anyone's age in case the conversation turned to the twenty-two years between her and Ben. Everyone had an opinion on it; everyone was surprised or curious as though she'd done something weird in marrying him. A couple of her friends had made gagging noise when they'd discovered Ben's age, like he was eighty, or something. She shook the salt cellar at Nathan, remembering her own surprise when he'd told her just how old he was. She'd thought he was thirty; she'd thought thirty was getting past it.

Julie sipped her coffee. Smiling at Nathan she said, 'Why don't you ask Mark and Simon to Sean's twenty-first?'

Kitty laughed.

'What? What's so funny?'

'Nothing.'

Julie said, 'You think Mark's stuck up.'

Kitty thought of Mark dancing with her mother at her wedding. He had been attentive, smiling and laughing at her mother's jokes so that she began to worry that her stepfather, Alan, would be jealous. But Mark had also seemed partly absent. She had thought of the prime minister on TV visiting some do or other – smiling for the show of it, looking like he was wondering when he could politely leave the plebs to it.

Julie said, 'Mark's only a couple of years younger than me.'

'So?' Too sharply she said, 'What's that got to do with anything?'

Julie laughed. 'You're too serious, you are. I'm just saying – I wouldn't crawl over Mark to get to Alan.' She stood up, smiling at Kitty's look of disgust. 'I'm going. Will you be all right?'

'Why shouldn't I be?'

Her mother sighed. 'Cheer up, eh? Take Nathan out for a walk – fresh air will do you both good.'

Kitty took her mother's advice and walked Nathan in his pushchair along the lane towards St Hilda's. The church stood in the centre of the village, opposite the one shop, a post office-cum-grocers-cum-newsagent. On her way back from strolling around the graves in the churchyard she would buy *Cosmopolitan* and a bar of fruit and nut. Not that Nathan would allow her to read or eat chocolate; she bought these things in hope rather than the expectation of the peace they represented.

She pushed Nath through the church's lych gate and along the path that led around the church. A bird hopped ahead of her, as if leading her on to some secret place; she thought of the fairy tales she'd read as a child, where animals and birds were knowing and could speak. As a little girl she had wanted to live in a village such as this, the type where such stories seemed to be set – an old place, full of the past and its ghosts. She'd imagined she would be happy away from her family's bickering.

The bird took off and perched on Mary Edward's angel. Mary, who died in 1864, had been the same age as her when the Lord welcomed her into heaven. Kitty stopped and read the inscription carved into the plaque the angel held. Mary had been a mother, too. She crouched beside Nath's pushchair, feeling protective of him suddenly. He slept, a trickle of drool at the corner of his mouth. She wiped it away gently.

To her relief, Ben's first wife wasn't buried here, but had been cremated and her ashes scattered over a meadow close to her parents' home in Kent. Ben had told her once that in spring the meadow was full of cowslips, a half-tame, half-wild place. He had told her in his matter-of-fact voice as though he was teaching her something she might find interesting.

Kitty sat down on a bench. This was her bench, hers and Ben's. Their wedding video featured them kissing here, the full skirt of her dress covering its graffiti-scarred wood. There was confetti in Ben's hair. She remembered how he had kissed her so sensuously she'd been embarrassed when she saw it replayed on the video. After the kiss he had told the photographer to leave them alone. He'd whispered how much he wanted to make love to her, that perhaps they could skip the reception, that *my God!* – he had never wanted anyone so badly! He wanted her right then and there, behind that tomb. He wanted to make her pregnant. He'd pressed her hand against the bulge of his hard-on. She remembered how shocked she'd been at the darkness in his eyes, how the intensity of his lust made him seem angry.

The first time she saw Ben Walker what struck her most was how sophisticated he looked. He wore a dark, pinstripe suit and a flawless pale shirt with complicated cuffs fastened with heavy gold cufflinks. His collar was undone, the fat knot of his blue silk tie loosened. He was laughing, a delighted, head-back, uninhibited laugh. Standing a few feet away from her at the bar of the Cross Keys, he had caught her eye and smiled. Before she could look away he said, 'My friend here has just told me the worst joke I've ever heard.'

Surprising herself with her boldness, she'd said, 'If it was so bad then why did you laugh?'

'Now, there you have me. Max – why do I laugh at your awful jokes?'

'Because you're an idiot,' Max said.

Still smiling at her, Ben said, 'There's your answer – I'm an idiot. My best friend thinks so and so it must be true. An idiot called Ben. What's your name?'

She'd told him and he'd taken her hand and kissed it, bowing deeply from the waist like a prince in a Disney cartoon. He was only a little drunk. Ben never got more than a little drunk. Later, as they'd walked to the next pub behind the combined group of their friends, he'd stopped, catching her hand so that she'd stop too.

He waited until the others were out of earshot. 'May I see you again?'

No one said *may I*. No one she knew, anyway. At first she thought he was making fun of her. She'd noticed how his friends spoke in loud, posh voices, how they had sized up her friends as if they were trying to decide if they were as easy as their clothes suggested they might be. They even looked faintly amused, as though all their expectations of Thorp girls had been met. She'd guessed that Ben and his friends had heard of the Cross Keys reputation and had found herself growing angrier at the knowing, sniggering looks they gave each other.

On the street between the Cross Keys and The Green Tree, she had pulled her hand away from his. 'I've got a boyfriend.'

'Oh.' He smiled, reinforcing the idea he was laughing at her. 'I suppose I couldn't compete, could I? Rather too old to be a *boyfriend*.' Becoming serious he said, 'Listen, I know you think I'm a prick who hangs around with a lot of other pricks –'

'How do you know I think that?'

'You've quite an expressive face.' He'd gazed at her, a direct, appraising look that made her think he was trying to figure her out. Eventually he said, 'Whatever you think, I'd like to take you out to dinner on Saturday.'

She'd glanced after her friends. One of them staggered and Max caught her elbow, the two of them laughing uproariously. Kitty thought of Gary, the boy she was seeing. He'd never said she had an expressive face or asked her out to dinner.

Turning back to Ben she'd said, 'All right. If you like.'

He'd grinned. 'Good. Now, let's get you inside. It's freezing out here.'

Kitty remembered that later, as they waited in the queue for a taxi, he had taken off his jacket and draped it over her shoulders. It was heavy and warm, its silk lining soft against her bare arms. She had wanted to wrap it tightly around her and inhale the subtle, expensive smell of him. How quick and easy it was to fall in love with someone just because they were kind and attentive, because they spoke beautifully and listened when you told them about your boring life. How badly she'd wanted him just because his eyes smiled and smiled and his body was hard and muscular-looking beneath that pristine shirt. He worked out at a gym and played rugby every Saturday in winter. The first time he made love to her she had ached for days afterwards, growing hot every time she thought of the way he'd looked at her as he brought her to orgasm. For all her experience she had never come before. There had only been lads like Gary, banging away on top of her, eyes shut tight as though sex was a trial.

On the graveyard bench Kitty took her mobile from her handbag and re-read the last text Ben had sent her. *Will be late tonight, 10pm. Love you, my darling girl, love to Nath xxxx*. Earlier that morning he had telephoned her during a break between one operation and the next. He'd sounded tired. 'I can't think straight,' he said, and she'd felt a flurry

71

of alarm, a feeling that was subsumed in her ordinary anxiety as Nathan began to cry. Holding the phone between her shoulder and neck she'd lifted Nath from his cot, hush-hushing him. She heard Ben laugh bleakly. 'I'll ring you later,' he said. She'd forgotten to tell him that she loved him.

Two women walked up the path and went inside the church. The church had a cleaning rota and a flower arranging rota and a church hall that held Women's Institute meetings and a mother and toddler group on Wednesday mornings. Church services were held at 10.15am and 6.30pm each Sunday led by the Reverend Graham Winterton. All were welcome, or so the notice board concluded. She was sure she *would* be welcome. People in the village smiled at her and asked about the baby. She felt shy of them, these neighbours who had known Ben's first wife. She knew she was being compared. Afraid one of the two women might come outside and ask her if she'd like to be part of some group, she got up and walked towards the gate that led down to the river path.

On their first date Ben had taken her to a country house hotel, all huge fireplaces and tall windows that looked out over a lawn where peacocks strutted and shrieked. In the dining room, oil paintings of women in ball gowns looked down on tables set with white linen and silver that glinted in the late evening sun. Their table looked out over the garden, away from the swinging door the waiters used and the discreet, green man fire exit sign. The waiters told Ben how nice it was to see him again.

Alone with their menus, Ben had smiled at her. 'You look lovely.'

She had been cutting a bread roll in half and she must have looked up at him too sharply because he said, 'Was that the wrong thing to say?'

'No.' Remembering her manners she said, 'Thanks.'

She'd worn a dress she found in the *H&M* sale, black and short and plain with a scooped neckline. The hanger had stated it was a size ten. It was actually a size eight and it cut a little beneath her arms and pushed her small breasts together so that for the first time in her life it appeared she had a cleavage. She'd borrowed a pair of her mother's evening sandals, the heels higher than she was used to so that Julie had laughed as she'd tottered down the stairs. She'd applied lip-gloss sitting on the edge of the settee as her stepfather watched TV. He'd frowned at her. 'Where you going dressed like a tart?'

Ben said, 'The scallops are very good here.' He'd looked up at her from studying his menu. 'The Parma ham, too.'

'What are you having?' How nervous she'd sounded. She'd never tasted scallops, or Parma ham. On the next table a middle-aged couple toasted themselves with Champagne. A group of Japanese men came in and silently took their seats. Ben caught her eye. He smiled. 'I'm having the soup then the steak.'

'Do you come here a lot?'

He closed his menu and placed it down. 'Sometimes. I like its grandeur.'

'It's nice.' She glanced out of the window, awkwardly aware that she'd hardly strung more than a few words together since they'd arrived. She realised she was shy of him; he looked older than he had in the pub, he seemed more serious. She began to wonder if he thought he had made a mistake by asking her out – not that she cared, she was sure she would never see him again after this evening. He was too old; she had nothing to say to him; he made her feel she wasn't up to his standards.

A waiter came and took their order. Another came and Ben ordered wine. She watched the peacocks spread their tail feathers. A bride walked across the lawn, her little bridesmaids running ahead of her. Music from the wedding disco could just be heard from another part of the hotel.

Ben cleared his throat. 'Have you always lived in Thorp?'

'Yes.'

He nodded. 'Never wanted to leave?'

'Why should I?'

'No reason.' He seemed lost for words. He turned towards the window. Outside the bridesmaids were having their photograph taken. They watched as the girls kissed each other solemnly for prosperity. The bride laughed as her new husband came up behind her and lifted her off her feet. The sun was setting behind a distant line of trees. It was like a film set, Kitty thought; she wanted to walk out onto the lawn and be part of it.

A waiter brought their first course. Ben made small talk. She decided she liked scallops. During the second course he was quieter. After the waiter cleared their plates Ben said, 'Kitty, is there something wrong?'

'No.'

'It's just that you're so quiet –'

'Sorry.'

'Don't be sorry. I wanted you to enjoy this evening.'

'I have.'

A waiter approached them. 'Would you like to see the dessert menu?'

Ben looked at her enquiringly. 'Would you?'

'No. Thanks.'

'Coffee?'

Kitty shook her head.

'Just the bill, please.'

He drove a Mercedes soft-top that smelt of the showroom and was so clean he might have been handed its keys that morning. He opened the passenger door for her, closing it softly only when it seemed he was sure she was safely inside.

About to start the engine he turned to her. 'Should I take you home?'

74

He gazed at her and she thought how handsome he was. But he didn't look like the boys she usually went for – slim, slight lads who barely needed to shave, lads like Gary who wore the soft, indie clothes her mother accused them of sleeping in. Gary wore plaited bracelets and a tongue stud; he had acne. Ben had the beginnings of crow's-feet around his eyes. Although he was only a little taller than she was, he was broad and tough-looking; he was the kind of man you would want on your side, a man who looked as if he knew how to handle himself in a fight. Despite his Hugo Boss suit and beautiful, modulated voice only the intelligence in his eyes, that serious, sad expression of his, stopped him from looking like a thug.

Sitting in his head-turning car she thought how much she wanted to sleep with him, if only for the experience – for *his* experience – she knew she would learn from him. But it was more than that; the difference in their ages wasn't only to his advantage. She wanted him to see her naked, to hear him gasp, to have that power over him.

She said, 'If I asked you a question would you tell me the truth?'

'Yes.'

'Are you married?'

'Is that what you've been thinking all night – that I want an affair?'

'I suppose so.'

'Maybe you should have asked me when we met.'

'Maybe. But I'm asking you now. Are you married?'

'No.' He started the car. 'No, I'm not.'

She thought she had offended him and expected to be driven home. Instead he drove her to his house. Without a word he showed her inside and led her through the big square hall along the black and white tiled passageway into a huge, unnaturally tidy kitchen. He made coffee as she sat at a table big enough to seat ten. Beyond the kitchen was a conservatory, its glossy palms casting huge, jungle shadows on the slate floor. Behind her was a dresser, its open shelves displaying fine, discreet white china. There were no photographs on display, no books or newspapers or piles of raggedly-torn envelopes spilling bills such as those that cluttered her mother's kitchen. She thought of the show houses she had once looked around with her Dad. He had laughed at the just-so arrangements of furniture and ornaments; she had wondered what it would be like to live in such a calm, orderly space. Looking around Ben's kitchen, she imagined coming down to this peaceful room each morning, with no spilt cornflakes underfoot, no piles of last night's washing-up in the sink.

Ben had caught her looking around and smiled. Awkwardly she turned away to the lilies crowded in a vase on the table. She touched one of the buds and remembered the way he had opened the car door for her and closed it so carefully. No one had treated her with such respect before. She found herself wanting him with a fierce longing that felt immoral, as though it owed too much to his obvious wealth.

Pouring coffee he said, 'We should have *After Eight* mints or something, shouldn't we? I'm afraid I don't have any.'

As he set her coffee in front of her she said, 'Mam used to bring us mints if she'd been out for a curry. Alan used to get really embarrassed because she'd ask the waiters for handfuls of them.' Quickly she said, 'Sorry about earlier, in the car...'

'Have we got off on the wrong foot, do you think?'

She avoided his gaze. 'Probably.'

'All right – let's be honest with each other. I'm not married, I'm a widower.'

It seemed that there was a change in the air between them, as though he had just opened a door on to a room he would never allow her to step inside. She shifted uncomfortably. 'I'm sorry.'

After a while he said, 'May I ask you something?'

'Yes.'

'How old are you?'

'Twenty.' She attempted a flirtatious smile. 'How old are you?'

He hesitated, then said quickly, 'I'm forty-two. Ancient, eh?'

Carefully she asked, 'Do you have children?'

'No. Do you?'

'No!'

'Some women your age do.'

'Well I'm not one of them!'

'Do you think having children when you're young is something to be ashamed of?'

'No – I'd like to have children –'

He'd smiled. 'Would you come out with me again? '

Nathan began to wake up. Realising how far she'd walked she turned the pushchair around and hurried home before he began to scream.

Chapter 8

Annette knelt beside Ben and Mark's bed. She kissed Mark's forehead, smoothing his hair back from his face. Quietly she said, 'Try not to wet the bed tonight.'

He gazed at her, his big dark eyes so sad and serious that she laughed a little. 'You're my sweetheart. I know you'll try to be good for Mummy.'

From the door way Danny said, 'Where's Ben?'

As soon as he heard his father's voice Mark squeezed his eyes shut and curled himself up small beneath the sheet. Annette wanted to weep for him and glanced away quickly so that Danny wouldn't accuse her of paying Mark too much attention. She stood up.

'Ben's brushing his teeth.'

He stepped towards her and from the corner of her eye she saw Mark flinch. 'Are you ready?'

'Yes.' She made her voice bright. 'All ready.'

'Come on then, what we waiting for?' Danny sighed. Suddenly he bellowed, 'Ben! Get in here now and get into bed. You've got two seconds!'

At once Ben was edging past his father and climbing into bed beside Mark. Annette kissed him briefly, whispering, 'Goodnight. I'll be back soon.'

'What are you saying to them?'

'Nothing.'

Shaking his head Danny said, 'Then stop wasting time and let's go.'

Danny was in a good mood. His horse had come in at fifteen to one and he had money in his pocket. He'd held a pound note out to her only to snatch it away. 'You have to earn this. I'm not giving it away.' Smiling he'd said, 'We'll go out tonight. I feel like getting pissed.'

As they walked towards the Castle and Anchor pub on the corner of their street, Danny grasped her hand. Squeezing her fingers tightly he said, 'Look twice at anyone and I'll kill you, do you hear me?'

'Yes.'

'And don't go off talking to those bitches from the factory, either.'

'No, Danny.'

He stopped walking and let go of her to smooth back his hair with both hands. 'Link your arm though mine. And stop looking so fucking petrified.' He glanced at her. 'Ready?'

She nodded, talking his arm as they crossed the street. As Danny pushed open the Anchor's door she saw his face assume the forced-smile expression he wore in public. The noise of the crowded pub spilled out onto the pavement as arm-in-arm they walked inside.

Joan said, 'Who's with the kids?'

'Maureen from across the way.'

Joan snorted. 'You mean Maureen who's stood over there at the bar?' She shook her head. 'You've left them bairns on their own, haven't you?'

Annette felt her cheeks burn. 'He won't have strangers in the house.' She looked furtively towards Danny who was buying another round of drinks. Quietly she said, 'I'll slip back in a few minutes to check on them.'

'Sure you will.'

'They'll be all right.'

'Aye, maybe.' Joan looked at Danny malevolently. 'Why was he shouting at the poor bairn last night? I heard him – effing and blinding and going on like a lunatic.'

Mark had knocked over a glass of water. At once Danny had slapped him across the head so hard he knocked him off his chair.

Joan sighed. 'Here, he's coming back. Don't worry, I won't say owt to the lousy sod.'

Danny set a tray of drinks down on their table. He smiled at Joan. 'Half a stout, wasn't it?'

'Aye.' Grudgingly she added, 'Ta.'

Joan's husband Bill came back from playing darts. Danny smiled at him too. 'Got you a pint in, Bill.'

Bill hardly glanced at him. He sat down next to his wife and raised his drink at Danny in a half-hearted salute. Annette sipped the Babycham Danny had bought her, hoping the atmosphere would lighten a little. Catching her eye Bill smiled at her sympathetically. She looked away quickly, afraid to respond in case Danny saw her.

Joan said, 'I've heard old Doctor Walker's son has moved back home.' She smiled as if remembering. 'Oh he was a lovely man old Doctor Walker. Wasn't he, Bill?'

'Aye.' Bill sipped his drink. 'A gent.'

Danny said, 'Bloody snobs, the lot of them.'

'Well, maybe she was, the wife.' Joan looked at Annette. 'Your Gran used to clean for her, did you know?'

Danny laughed nastily. 'That old cow, clean? You must be joking.'

'What would you know about it?' Joan shook her head. 'Nowt.'

Annette could see Danny's mask begin to slip. If Joan carried on like this in a few minutes all his smiles and friendliness would be done with and he'd be dragging her home. She hoped Joan would shut up about Doctor Walker. Danny always picked up on her responses to Joan's gossip;

he would read from her expression that she was keeping something to herself. Bill came to her rescue.

'Fancy a game of darts?'

Danny smiled, resuming his play-act. 'All right.'

The two women sipped their drinks in silence. Someone fed coins into the jukebox and Tom Jones began to sing *It's not Unusual.* Joan glanced at her.

'Bill's only being civil to him for your sake, you know. Bill's heart bleeds for those poor bairns of yours. I wouldn't be surprised if he has a word with him.'

The idea caused her voice to rise in panic. 'He won't say anything, will he?'

'No. Probably not. But if it goes on – all that shouting and bawling...'

'Don't let him say anything to Danny, please Joan. I don't know what he'd do –'

'All right, don't cry.' She took a handkerchief from her bag. 'Here. Don't let him see you're upset, it'll make his night.'

Joan's friends from the sugar factory joined them and Annette found herself on the edge of this group of women, excluded from their work gossip. It seemed Bill could only stand Danny's company for so long because he drifted off to talk to a group of men he worked with and Danny stood at the end of the bar alone, drinking steadily. She watched him light a cigarette from the butt of the last and order another pint. He didn't mind his own company, he'd told her that often enough. He'd told her he'd rather be on his own, that most people were too stupid to be tolerated. Danny was clever. Even when she'd begun to hate him, she acknowledged that he was cleverer than anyone she knew.

On their first date he had taken her back to the room he rented. It was only a small bed-sit, at the top of a flight of stairs that creaked noisily, embarrassing her as she imagined creeping down again, Danny's neighbours speculating behind their closed doors. She remembered being struck by the bed-sit's tidiness, how neatly the bed was made with its white sheet turned down over the grey, coarse-looking blankets, how clean he kept the little corner where the gas ring and sink were. There was an old horsehair two-seater sofa beside the gas fire and on the scarred oak dining table were piles of books. She had picked one up and leafed through it curiously. Its pages were thin, its print small and dense. Unable to make head nor tail of the passage she read she closed the book and put it down. Watching her, he said, 'Das Kapital.'

'Oh.'

'*Oh*.' He mimicked her inflection exactly. Flatly he said, 'Karl Marx. He predicted the violent overthrow of the capitalist class by the proletariat. He thought the workers should own the factories and the mines.'

'Is that what you think?'

'No.' He gazed at her until she blushed and looked away. At last he said, 'You're shy, aren't you? I don't mind. I like it. I can't stand mouthy girls.'

She noticed that there were exercise books on the table, too, the kind she'd used in school. She made to pick one up but he said sharply, 'Don't touch that. Don't you dare.'

There was menace in his voice but when she looked at him he smiled. 'Private stuff. Sit down, over here.' He sat down on the sofa and patted the seat next to him. When she hesitated he said, 'Sorry if I was sharp with you.'

She sat down. The sofa sagged; she could feel its worn-out springs through its prickly upholstery and imagined the metal breaking through to stab her thighs. Danny sat as far away from her as the sofa allowed. She thought how oddly prim he looked, his knees together, his small, delicate hands clasped in his lap. He was thinner than he'd appeared to be in uniform; he looked younger, too, a skinny lad with a soft, grown-man's voice.

Annette smiled nervously, unsure of him. She cleared her throat. 'You don't sound like the lads from round here.'

He snorted. 'Thank Christ. My father knocked it out of me. I had to speak *prop-er-ly* on pain of a good hiding. So I did. So he gave me a good hiding for something else instead.'

She remembered the rumours she'd heard about Danny's father, a slaughterer in the abattoir on Thorp Road, a unionist always agitating for strikes. He'd been a conscientious objector during the war but it didn't make him peaceable.

Danny said, 'My father stank. He stank of blood and bone.' His voice was matter-of-fact and he smiled at her. 'Blood was ingrained in the skin around his fingernails.' He held his hands out and inspected his splayed fingers, frowning. 'He used to take off his belt, like so,' he mimed undoing his belt buckle and pulling off his belt. 'Then he'd tell us to drop our trousers and underwear and bend over the table.' He smiled again as though he'd told some mild joke. 'And then – thwack! And again – thwack! I used to recite the Lord's Prayer in my head. He was usually finished by the second amen.'

'That must have been awful.'

'It was…undignified.' He reached out and took her hand. 'Annette. I'm not sure if I like your name or not. Do you have another?'

She laughed uncertainly. 'No.'

'Oh well. *Annette* – you know I'm only joking, don't you? You don't have to look so scared.'

'I'm not scared.'

He laughed and put on a high, frightened voice that sounded like hers. 'No – I'm not scared!' Smiling he touched her cheek. 'Sexy little thing.'

She bowed her head surprised at the jolt of desire she'd felt at such a brief touch.

Softly he said, 'I'll be so careful of you. Your first time will be like all the stars falling down around your head;

you'll be enraptured.' After a moment he said, 'It *will* be your first time, won't it? Don't disappoint me now.'

Mortified she'd whispered, 'Yes, it will.'

He breathed out sharply. 'I'll wait,' he said. 'Until our wedding night. I have to do this properly.'

In the Castle & Anchor Annette watched Danny down the dregs of his pint and grind his cigarette into the ashtray on the bar. He took change from his pocket and spread the coins out on his palm. As though he'd become aware of her watching him, he looked up and held her gaze across the noisy pub. She thought how handsome he was and that if only he was kind to the boys she would love him no matter what; she wouldn't mind his strangeness, which only showed how vulnerable he was, if only he wasn't so cruel.

Joan said gently, 'Get home to your little lads, pet. Go now, while he's not looking.'

Danny was feeding coins into the jukebox. As he deliberated over his choice she got up and hurried from the pub.

He came home drunk and forced himself on her, biting at her breasts and clawing at her thighs, pushing his hand inside her when he couldn't get hard enough so that she cried out in pain, although she tried to be quiet, for the boys' sake. He gagged her by making her take him in her mouth, his fists full of her hair so she thought he might pull it out by the roots when he tugged her head away. He pushed her down on the bed and knelt astride her. 'Say you love me.'

'I love you.'

'Say it as though you mean it!'

'I do! I love you, Danny.'

He stared at her and it took all her courage not to look away from him. She hoped he wouldn't notice how much she was trembling and tried to smile, to keep her voice steady as she said, 'I love you.'

He went on staring at her although his body lost some of it tautness. His face crumpled. 'I'm sorry. I'm sorry, babe.'

He began to cry. Still kneeling astride her he covered his face with his hands. Annette held out her arms to him. He lay down, burying his face against her breasts, and cried as though his heart was broken.

Chapter 9

Doctor Walker was out when Annette arrived at his
house at the time they'd arranged. After she'd knocked
on the front and back doors and peered into the windows
to make sure he wasn't home, she lit a cigarette. She
watched the little birds feed from the toast crusts on the
bird table, keeping an eye on the cat that crouched half-
hidden beneath a bush. She thought how Danny hated
cats, seemed actually to be afraid of them. He hated dogs,
too. If he heard a dog barking he would say how much he
wished he had a gun so that he could shoot it and shut it
up for good. She had laughed the first time he said this
and he had looked at her as though he wanted to shoot
her as well.

Last night, when he had stopped crying, he had said,
'They hate me don't they?'

She'd thought he meant the boys and so she said gently,
'No – you're their Daddy, they love you –'

'No! Not them! The neighbours. *They* hate me.'

She'd held him tighter, wishing he would sleep. She
wished she hadn't mentioned the boys, she tried to keep
them out of his sight and mind because it seemed to her he
could forget he had children quite easily if only they
weren't around to remind him. She stroked his head, afraid
to speak even to comfort him. He was right anyway – their
neighbours despised him.

He'd pushed himself away from her and held her face
between his hands. She could smell her own scent on his

fingers, her fearful stink. 'We should go away – me and you – away from this bloody hole.'

'Where to?'

'America.' His eyes were bright. 'I'd get a decent job there.'

'All right.'

He lay down again and pulled her to him. 'Never walk out on me again like you did tonight. You hear me?'

'I won't.'

'You showed me up.'

'I'm sorry.'

'That's all right. Now go to sleep.'

The cat began to stalk across Doctor Walker's lawn, keeping its body close to the ground. Annette clapped her hands together and the birds took off. The cat ducked as they flew over its head. 'There,' she said. 'That's you foiled.'

'Annette!'

She turned to see Doctor Walker hurrying towards her. Breathlessly he said, 'My dear, I'm sorry – I went out for some milk and a paper.' He held up his shopping as if to prove he wasn't lying. 'Forgive me for keeping you waiting.'

She hastily crushed her cigarette out beneath her shoe. 'It's all right, Doctor Walker, I've only just arrived.'

'Really? Oh, that's good. I didn't forget about you, not at all.'

He unlocked the back door, putting his shoulder against it when it stuck. He glanced at her, smiling. 'Does *anything* work properly in this house? Perhaps I should sell it – buy a nice little bungalow instead.'

Without thinking she said, 'You're too young for a bungalow.'

He laughed. 'You think so? I'm terribly flattered. But I was thinking more about my leg. It doesn't like stairs, I'm afraid.' Going into the kitchen he placed the bottle of milk in the sink and tossed the paper down on the table. It was the *Guardian*, the paper Danny sometimes read. There was a headline about Vietnam; Danny was following the war's progress avidly.

Doctor Walker said, 'Let's have a cup of tea! We must discuss a plan of action for today and I need your advice, Annette. You know Thorp better than I do – where will I find a plumber and a good decorator?' He looked at her as he lit the gas beneath the kettle. 'Do sit down, my dear. I'd thought we'd got over all this standing about on ceremony.'

She sat gingerly, still tender from Danny's assault on her last night; that morning she'd had a burning sensation when she'd gone for a pee. Trying not to think about what damage he might have done to her, she found herself looking around the room and noticed that it seemed a little cleaner and tidier than the last time she'd been here. A tea chest stood in one corner, spilling shreds of straw. Around it were ornaments, half out of their protective wrappings. A figurine of a shepherd boy smiled up from the floor beside an elegant-looking coffee pot.

Doctor Walker said, 'My wife's things – some of them, at least. They arrived this morning – there're more chests in the hall. All of them need sorting – I'm just not sure if she would rather do it herself.'

'I'd want to unpack myself, if I were her.'

'Would you? It was just that I don't want her to come home to a house that looks like the removal men have just left.' He laughed wearily. 'When she's a little stronger I shall ask her what she wants me to do.'

'How is she?'

'Not too bad. Very sad, of course.'

He made tea briskly and sat down opposite her. 'Now, then. Plumbers. Can you recommend one?'

'No, I'm sorry – I don't know any.'

'Decorators?'

She shook her head.

'Oh. Oh well. I shall resort to Yellow Pages. See if I can spot the cowboys by the cut of their jib, eh?'

She smiled. 'You could try the hardware shop on Palmer Street. They might know some handy men.'

'Thank you – I'll pay them a visit. So, how are you today?'

'Fine, thanks.'

'And those little boys of yours – happily off to school? Or are they like I was – dragging their feet all the way?'

'No, they like school. Ben especially – he's made lots of friends.' She thought of Mark, who seemed not to have made any friends, who stood alone each playtime. She imagined how scared he must be of going home, a place where he should have felt safe. Guilt at her failure to protect him rose inside her. She fought against it, aware of the strained silence that had grown between her and the doctor. After a moment she said, 'Mark's very shy. I worry about him.'

'How old is Mark again?'

She looked down at her tea. 'Five.'

'Very little, then. He's probably just trying to find his feet, holding his fire until he knows what's what and who's who – a very sensible little boy.'

She smiled and was appalled to feel tears sting the back of her eyes. She kept her head bowed to hide them from him.

Gently he said, 'Annette?'

She wiped her eyes quickly. 'I'm being daft.'

'No – if you're worried about him...' He sighed. 'My dear, forgive me if I'm prying but you really don't look well to me. Would you like to go home?'

'No – really. I'm all right.' Forcing herself to look at him she smiled. 'Really. It's just when I think about Mark –'

He looked so sympathetic, so kind and concerned, that she began to cry. At once he got up and walked round the table to sit beside her. He waited patiently, silently, until she stopped. Fishing out the handkerchief Joan had given her she blew her nose. 'Sorry.'

'Tell me about Mark, Annette. Tell me why you're so worried.'

'I'm not! Not really. It's probably like you said – he's just finding his feet...'

'Have you talked to his teacher? Perhaps she sees a different side to him when you're not there.' He was quiet for a while. At last he said, 'I'm afraid I know so little about children. I only know how to treat them when they're poorly. I wish I could be more help.'

She stood up, stuffing the handkerchief into her pocket. 'I should get on, Doctor Walker.'

He didn't protest as she thought he might. Instead he stood up too. 'I've bought a vacuum cleaner. It's in the hall – I think I've set it up properly.'

Simon read the paper, reading the same line over and over and still not making sense of it. The drone of the vacuum kept drawing him back to thinking about Annette. He looked up as the vacuum was switched off and her footsteps sounded across the room above him. There was a bump as something was moved; the vacuum was switched on again. He realised he was sitting on the edge of his chair as if about to spring to his feet.

He couldn't stand that she was cleaning for him; he wanted to sit her down and feed her something nourishing; he wanted her to rest in the fresh air with the sun on her face. Most of all he wanted to understand what was troubling her and offer a solution. But he was afraid of his own motives: she was beautiful; in his old life he would have pursued her, asking her to share her problems a useful way into her bed. He knew he hadn't changed and yet there was a vulnerability about Annette Carter that made him want to act with the best of motives. He had almost told Joy about her. But it was in that *almost* where his true character lurked.

Her vacuuming went on, the noise becoming more distant as she moved to another room. He should ask her to stop, to go home, she'd done enough for one day. She would think that he was strange to pay her for a half day when she'd only worked an hour.

He slumped back in his chair, tossing the paper to the floor. Last night he'd gone to dinner at the house of the senior gynaecologist at his new hospital. The man was called Iain, his wife Sarah and there were two other couples there, junior doctors and their wives. Usually he avoided such get-togethers – there seemed to him few worse prospects than an evening with colleagues – but these were new colleagues and he wanted badly to fit in, or at least assess what he was up against. So he'd bathed and pressed his good suit and tried to memorise his hostess's name as he drove across town to the modern house that Iain had told him he'd had a hand in designing.

Iain and Sarah knew about Joy, of course; such news always travelled swiftly and he'd prepared himself for sympathy, for those *so sorry to hear* openers that cloaked curiosity. He'd left Joy's bedside early in order to be on time and he thought about her guiltily. Only as he'd parked on Iain's gravel drive did he realise that it probably would be Iain himself who would be operating on his wife the next day. The realisation made him feel sick; he'd almost turned around and gone home.

Sarah had greeted him at the door wearing a full-length flowing gown patterned in abstract purple flowers, her hair piled in a beehive, kiss-curls artfully slicked into place. She smelt of Chanel Number Five and when she kissed his cheek she rested a manicured hand on his arm and told him that she had visited Joy to welcome her to Thorp. He had felt so grateful he had almost cried. Sarah had patted his arm briskly. 'Come through,' she said. 'Allow me to introduce you to everyone.'

As they were finishing the Beef Wellington, Sarah had asked, 'Have you found any help, Simon? I have a very good cleaner – would you like me to ask her to pop over – she lives quite close to you, near town.'

'I've found someone, thank you.'

'Oh, that was quick! How on earth did you do it? It took me months to find someone reliable!'

He'd wondered if Annette was reliable and thought how frail she seemed, how distracted; his mother would have dismissed her as a will-o-the-wisp. In Iain's brightly modern home he had sipped his wine and wondered if she would turn up in the morning as arranged, surprised at how worried he was that she might not.

But this morning she had arrived on time and had even waited for him. She'd jumped when he'd called her name, for a moment she'd looked truly frightened. There were dark rings beneath her eyes, standing out starkly against the pallor of her complexion. He noticed how thin her arms were; he'd be able to encircle her forearm with his thumb and forefinger.

Upstairs the noise of the vacuum ended. He found himself on his feet and walking out into the hall and upstairs.

She looked at him from dusting the chest of drawers in the second bedroom. Simon smiled, suddenly at a loss, only to be inspired.

'Annette, I've been sorting out some things and I've come across all my old toys my father kept. They're in rather good condition – would you like them, for Ben and Mark? There are books, too. *Peter Rabbit* – a whole set of Beatrix Potter –'

She looked terrified. She shook her head. 'No, no thank you – really. It's very kind...'

'Not at all.'

'I couldn't.'

He smiled, feeling even more foolish. 'Why not?'

'I'm sorry, Doctor Walker...'

'All right. Don't worry, I'll take them to the hospital, for the children's ward.'

'Yes. That would be best.' She wrung her hands, twisting the duster into a tight, grubby knot.

Afraid that she might cry again, he said carefully, 'Annette, perhaps you should go home.'

'Have I lost my job?'

'No!' He was horrified. 'No, of course not! I just think —'

'I'm all right to finish off here – until the time we said.'

'Annette, I only think...' He sighed, unable to say that he thought she looked too ill to be out of bed, let alone cleaning for him. 'I'll pay you for the whole morning, of course.'

'It doesn't seem right.'

'Oh, I'm sure you'll make up for it.' Feeling he owed her some kind of explanation he said, 'My wife, Joy, is having her operation today. I should go and be with her.'

She stepped forward timidly and he realised he was still standing in the doorway, blocking her exit. He stood aside and she pushed the unplugged vacuum past him.

'Let me take that downstairs,' he said.

She turned to him. Quickly she said, 'Thank you for the offer of the toys. Could I take a couple of the books for Mark? He loves to read.'

The relief he felt was ridiculous. He beamed at her. 'Of course. They're in a box in the sitting room. Come and chose which ones you'll think he'll like best.'

Chapter 10

Ben said, 'I met Kitty in this pub.'

Mark looked around the Cross Keys. The bar was crowded and he'd had to wait for several minutes to be served, time enough to notice the groomed, thirty-something women that waited alongside him or stood around with their glasses of white wine in groups of three or four. The Keys was a big pub but its low ceiling and dark, old-fashioned décor made it seem intimate. It was possible to promenade around the Keys, circuiting out into its garden with its industrial-sized patio heaters and hanging baskets full of trailing ivy and dwarf geraniums, and back inside, edging through the elbow-to-elbow crowds of casually well-dressed drinkers. The promenade would be slow; there would be frequent stops to chat, or simply to wait while a jam of bodies cleared. The noise of so many people had made Mark wish his brother had chosen somewhere quieter.

That morning, as he was preparing to go home, Ben had telephoned. Simon had answered, almost at once holding the phone out to him. 'I think you should talk to your brother,' he said. So Simon had allowed him to stay in order that he might talk to Ben, nodding his stern approval when he'd told him that this meeting was arranged. All day Mark's nerves had jangled. Now it was all he could do to stop his hands from shaking.

They had found a table that faced the bar, quite a vantage point for watching the ebb and flow. Mark sipped his pint, noticing two slim, pretty blondes pass them for the third time only to stop a few feet away. Mark said, 'Is it singles' night?'

'Unofficially.'

'Trying to fix me up?'

Ben looked at him coldly. 'No. I'm sure you don't need any help in that department.'

Regretting his thoughtlessness Mark said, 'How's Kitty?'

'Fine. As is Nathan.' Taking a long swallow of his own pint he wiped his mouth and looked around. 'We should have gone somewhere else. I'd forgotten what this place is like on a Tuesday night.' His lip curled as he watched a trio of men move in on the blondes. 'Bloody cattle market!'

Ben had picked him up from Simon's house in his new BMW. He had driven, as he always did, without speaking. A CD of Mozart's *Magic Flute* played softly. Mark had rested his head back against the leather upholstery and tried to concentrate on the music. He'd felt jumpy with nervousness. Now, in the noisy pub, he wondered when his brother would see fit to begin on the reason why they were pretending it was natural that they should have a drink together and the sick feeling in his guts intensified. He half drained his glass in one long swallow. He wondered if being drunk would help.

Ben said, 'Do you think Dad's managing in that house?' He shook his head. 'I wish he'd sell, buy something smaller. You know he never goes upstairs now, don't you? He sleeps in the dining room.'

'Yes, I know. Does it matter?'

'No, it doesn't matter – not if you don't care whether he's comfortable or not, whether he's even safe in that bloody mausoleum.'

'He's safe enough.'

'Yeah? He puts on a front for you – won't admit to being scared –'

'Scared?' Mark frowned. 'Scared of what, for God's sake? Simon doesn't get scared.'

'*Simon*?'

'Dad.' Mark picked up his drink only to put it down again. As calmly as he could he said, 'Dad's fine. But if you like I'll talk to him about moving somewhere more suitable.'

'Do that. He listens to you.' He laughed bitterly. 'Doctors don't listen to other doctors. Susan was the same.'

Mark avoided his gaze. He watched as the blonde girls flirted with the three men. One of the girls caught his eye and looked away quickly, her smile faltering as though she'd been caught out in a lie.

After a while Ben said, 'God only knows why Dad kept the house on after Mum died.'

'Memories? The house is full of her, it's obvious why he wants to stay there.'

'He should move on.'

'He's an old man.'

'It's a cold house – impractical. I've always hated it.' Vehemently he said, 'From the day I set foot in that house I hated it. Don't you remember how it was? So dark and freezing cold? So bloody disorganised? You would have thought they might have cleaned up a little... Do you remember all the tea chests in the hall when we first arrived, as if they were *going* somewhere? How bloody tactless was that?'

The chests had been made of pale, rough wood stamped with black letters he couldn't bring himself to make sense of. The woman who had gently suggested that he should call her Joy had ignored the chests as she led him to the kitchen where tea and toast was promised. 'Or would you prefer squash?' Her voice had risen a little; she'd sounded anxious. Her anxiety had frightened him; like the ominous tea chests it reminded him that grown-ups weren't to be trusted.

Ben looked down at his drink, turning it round and round on the beer mat. The mat read *It's Your Licence! Don't Drink & Drive!* Ben's lip curled as though the idea of drinking at all disgusted him. He blinked and his fingers went to his eye as if to stop a twitch. Mark watched him and wished he had the courage to leave, but he knew that Ben would follow him and that there would be a scene. He smiled grimly, knowing he would do anything to avoid a scene.

Angrily Ben said, 'You hated the house too.'

'Yes. You told me it was haunted.' Mark remembered the creaks and rattles of the old house settling for the night. He had known the noises weren't caused by ghosts but was convinced that Danny had come for him. He would lie very still; he felt that he could will his heart to stop beating, to be utterly silent if he tried hard enough. Once, Simon had looked in on him and he'd lost control of his bowels.

One of the blonde girls approached them. She smiled at Mark. 'Do you have a light?'

'Yes, of course...' He fumbled in his pocket and took out his cigarettes and a book of matches. As she took the matches from him she laughed nervously. 'I'm sorry, but you are Mark Walker, aren't you? The writer?'

Mark heard Ben snort and saw the girl glance at him as if she was afraid she'd said something foolish. Quickly Mark said, 'Yes, I'm Mark Walker.' He smiled, feeling foolish himself. 'Hello.'

'I recognised you from the photo on your book jacket...I'd heard you came from round here. I've just read *The Burial Party*.' She blushed. 'I loved it. I love all your books...sorry. I'm bothering you, aren't I?'

'Not at all, you're very kind...'

Ben said, 'I can't believe you recognised him from a photo.'

The girl glanced at him, unsure of his tone that was thick with mock surprise. Awkwardly she said, 'It's a very good photo.'

Ben laughed and looked down at his drink, turning and turning the glass.

When the girl had gone back to her friend Ben said, 'I forget you're famous. Sometimes I see your books stacked up in Waterstones and I think *My God! Who'd have thought it!*' Looking at the girl who had moved away to the bar he said, 'You could have had her knickers off, no effort at all. Oh – but she's not your type, is she? A bit young, a bit eager to please.'

Mark ignored him. He thought, I hate you, I want you to die. It was a silent chant he'd used as a child; he used to feel it gave him power. He lit a cigarette and drew smoke deep into his lungs; he felt some of the tension in his chest give a little.

Suddenly Ben said, 'I read *Burial Party.*'

Mark looked at him in surprise. He wondered if he had recognised his portrayal of Susan in the novel because sometimes it seemed so obvious that he had written about her and at other times he knew he wasn't a good enough writer to make Susan live again. He tried to read from his brother's expression whether he had understood the book or not but Ben only smirked.

'Yes, I read it – start to finish. Good ending. Well done.'
'Thanks.'

Ben nodded thoughtfully. 'Susan would have loved it.'
Cautiously Mark said, 'You think so?'

'Yes! Well, it's a woman's book, really, isn't it?' He cast him a sly glance. 'Sue used to say…' He frowned. 'Now, what was it? Ah yes – that you write like a woman who hates men. Did you know that the first time she saw you she asked me if you were gay?'

Mark concentrated on rolling the tip of his cigarette around the edge of the ashtray. He forced himself to say, 'I think you told me that.'

'Did I? I know, I'm a boring bastard.' Ben picked up the cigarettes. 'Can I have one of these?' Without waiting for an answer he took one out and lit it. Exhaling, he said, 'Yes, she asked if you were gay.' He laughed shortly. 'Remember when we were kids? That family that lived across from us on Tanner Street? The Harrisons? Three brothers – always one of them ready to give you a thumping. You were terrified of them, remember?'

'No, I don't.'

'No? I had to keep rescuing you from them – Brian Harrison – he was the biggest – built like a brick shit house? He used to call you fairy cake – remember? I thought that was quite imaginative for a thick bastard like him.'

'I don't remember you ever rescuing me.'

'Well I did. I used to tell you that if you just stood up to them instead of being so petrified –'

'I was *five*, Ben.'

'And I was six, but I still knew you had to stand up for yourself.'

'You never rescued me from those boys.'

'You just don't remember –'

'No, Ben, I do remember. Christ – I remember when we were at Thorp Grammar –' He stopped, thinking he wouldn't stoop to re-living old hurts from their childhood, it would seem as though he hadn't grown up enough to forgive him. He thought of Ben, captain of the fifth year rugby team, keeping his distance from him, denying, even when asked directly, that he was his brother. The other boys thought that it was a great joke that Ben should lie so blatantly – it give them more ammunition with which to wage their campaign of bullying. And the more he was bullied the more ashamed of him Ben became. And so the cycle went on. Try as he might he couldn't break it. Even when he joined the Marines, even when he fought in a war, in Ben's eyes he was always the terrified little boy who rocked Danny's boat so catastrophically.

Mark glanced at his brother, anger and resentment rising inside him despite his best efforts to suppress it. Catching his eye, Ben said, 'Don't look at me like that.'

'Like what?'

Ben laughed wearily. 'Like you hate my guts. I don't know, Mark – maybe you should have a think about how much hate I deserve.'

'Can it be measured?'

Ben snorted. 'Jesus, you're a portentous sod sometimes. Susan used to say your portentousness came out in your writing.'

Mark thought of Susan tossing down one of his novels so that it skittered across his bedroom floor, her voice full of impatience as she said, 'All right, tell me something – *anything* – is going to happen in chapter two. Tell me he murders the silly bitch with a meat axe.'

He had laughed in an effort to disguise the hurt he'd felt. He'd been unsure of how to respond to her in those days, still believing that she would lose interest soon enough and that he could go back to being ordinarily immoral. In those days he still relished his badness; decency was for the dull.

Ben said, 'Look – I'm sorry. Don't go all silent on me like you usually do. I want us to talk –'

'Isn't that what we're doing?'

'We're bickering, aren't we?' He smiled at him and Mark had the feeling that if he were his patient he would be about to receive some very bad news indeed. Drawing deeply on his cigarette, Mark avoided his gaze. He heard Ben sigh.

'Mark, it's important we talk about what's happened.'

'Has something happened?' He looked at Ben, as shocked as if he'd pulled a knife on him.

100

'Not *happened* – that's the wrong word. I know you find this difficult but I need to discuss it with you.' He stubbed out his half-smoked cigarette. At last he said, 'I want to tell you what I've found out about Danny.' For a moment Ben looked as he had as a child, scared of his own defiance, and Mark felt sick; he wondered what Ben would do if he rushed to the gents; whatever his reaction it would be a way of distracting him.

Ben said carefully, 'Danny's still alive. But I suppose you'd guessed that, hadn't you?'

'No.' His voice was flat, like that of a man who had been tortured into giving himself away. He cleared his throat so that he might sound more resilient. 'No – how could I know?'

'Not known, guessed. I guessed that Dad would have told us if he'd died.'

Mark imagined that conversation, how Simon would sit them both down either side of him, how he would take their hands and hesitate a moment as if searching for the right – the very best – word to begin. '*Your father –*' no, that would be wrong. '*Your real father –*' Even more wrong. '*Danny,*' he could almost hear Simon sigh with the relief of realising this was the right way of referring to the man who had sired them.

Becoming aware that Ben was waiting for a response from him, Mark said, 'You think Dad kept in touch with him?'

'I think he found a way of keeping track, as it were.' He laughed shortly. 'He had his *sources*. You're naïve if you think he didn't keep himself informed.'

Mark had a picture of Simon employing a private detective, of furtive telephone conversations made from Simon's study. Simon would have revelled in such dramatic secrecy. Bitterly he asked, 'Has Dad helped you to find him?'

'No. I asked him to. He said he couldn't help, that he didn't know anything. Maybe it's true. Maybe since we grew up he thought the danger was past and gave up keeping track.' Quickly he added, 'The danger has past. Danny's an old man. Incapable.'

'You've found him.'

Ben nodded. For a moment he looked guilty and Mark half expected him to apologise. Then Ben seemed to remember that he'd decided not to be guilty. He sat up straighter; he picked up his glass and took a long drink. Placing the glass down again he glanced at him only to look away. 'You've gone green, Mark. If you're going to be sick the toilets are along there.'

'I'm not going to be sick.'

'Good.' Angrily he said, 'Because that would be a bit of an over-reaction, wouldn't it? Christ, Mark! I've found Danny. That's all. I'm not suggesting we have a grand reunion!'

About to speak, Mark heard his voice break and he cleared his throat. At last he managed, 'Where did you find him?'

Ben frowned. 'What? I didn't hear –'

Louder, Mark said, 'Where is he? In Thorp? Where?'

'Calm down!' Ben glanced around as though afraid they were causing a scene. Turning back to him he said, 'He's in Thorp.'

'Where in Thorp?

Ben sighed. 'Listen Mark, I know this is hard for you. Don't you think it was hard for me? I struggled with this, I didn't want to upset Dad, or you...'

'Tell me where he is!'

'South Durham General.'

'He's sick?'

Ben hesitated. 'He's dying.'

Mark laughed, a harsh burst of noise, and Ben pursed his lips in distaste but seemed prepared to allow him his outburst. Eventually Ben said, 'He has lung cancer.'

'Good. Excellent. There is justice in the world.' He looked at Ben, a bright, strained smile on his face. 'How long has he got?'

'Christ, Mark! Don't you have any pity? Have you any idea what it's like to die like that?'

'Is it painful?'

Ben shook his head. 'I didn't expect this, even from you.'

'What did you expect? Tears?'

'No Mark. I know you only cry for yourself.' He laughed shortly. 'You'll be feeling happier now, eh? Don't have to be scared of the bogeyman any more.'

'Yes, you're right. I'll be even happier when he's safely in the ground.' He stood up. 'Do you want another drink here or should we celebrate somewhere else?'

'Sit down.' Ben looked up at him in disgust. 'Sit down, I haven't finished.'

Mark sat. To his surprise he felt curious now. He wanted to know everything that Ben knew, to wallow in information. He wanted to picture Danny in a hospital bed, see that pain had shrunk him so that he was nothing but grey skin and bones, an oxygen mask clamped around his face. He would be completely alone – even the nurses would sense his wickedness and see to him only when strictly necessary; he would be afraid. Mark wished that he believed in hell.

Ben said, 'We have three brothers.' He glanced at him as if to gauge his reaction. 'Colin, Graham and Steven. They all live in Thorp – on the Rosehill Estate. Steve is the youngest –'

Mark stared at him. He held up his hand. 'Stop. I don't want to hear this.' Shaking his head in astonishment he said, 'I don't want to know.'

'Well I think you should know! For once in your life listen! There's this boy – our brother, Steve –'

'I don't care.' He felt afraid again. The idea that Danny may have had another family had never occurred to him. He tried to imagine his sons, these half-brothers, and it was as if Danny had been resurrected from the grave he'd only just buried him in. He stood up and his legs felt shaky.

Ben stood up too. He grabbed his arm but Mark shook him off and began to push through the crowded pub. Outside, the pub's bouncers eyed him suspiciously as he stood drawing breath like a man who had just ran a marathon.

Beside him Ben said, 'Mark, don't behave like this.' Exasperated, he said, 'I thought you should know! There are three young men walking around who are our family – close, *blood* family! We've never had so much as a distant cousin –'

'We had Simon and Joy! They are my family, Ben! I'm not interested in some scum from the Rosehill Estate!'

'They're not scum, you bloody snob! Steve's a decent lad –'

'Where's the taxi rank?'

'What? You're just going to go?'

'Why not? You've told me all I need to know. There wasn't anything else was there? Listen, let me know when he's dead, I'll crack open the champagne.'

Behind them a voice said cautiously, 'Hello, Ben...'

Ben spun round and at once he smiled, embarrassed and apologetic at once. A boy had stepped from the shadow of the pub doorway into the yellow light of a street lamp and Mark stared in disbelief. Danny stood in front of him, smiling and holding out his hands in a placating gesture as if he was afraid he was about to run away. Mark thought his heart might burst through his chest. Above the pounding of his own blood he heard Ben say, 'Mark, this is Steven, our half-brother.'

*   *   *

It was like I was surrendering to him – holding out my hands, palms up – as if to say *don't shoot*. I was smiling, like one of those monkeys that act up to show the alpha male he isn't worth killing, but I was still angry. I'd heard what he'd called us. Scum. We live on the estate – *the* estate, mind, it's notorious – ergo we are scum.

They have very nice voices my half brothers. They sound intelligent, gentle, a bit wry. Especially Mark. I'd heard him on *Front Row*, being interviewed by that Mark Lawson, and I remember thinking then how nice he sounded. Nice. It's not a word I use much – it's a bit wishy-washy. But it suits the middle-class, middle-aged, white sound my half brothers make. Listen to them and you imagine all they ever talk about is Art and Literature, with Radio 4 presenters hanging on their every round, soft, perfect syllable. You could fall in love just listening to voices like theirs.

Mark is beautiful. There, let's get that out of the way first. If he wasn't my brother (half) I'd want him. Even now I'm thinking, well, it's not as if we were brought up together, it's not as if I *feel* related to him. But that's disgusting, isn't it? We are related; it's even obvious we're related. Ben told me I was Mark's double. He couldn't get over how much I looked like him; the first time he spoke to me he kept shaking his head and frowning in disbelief. I think it disturbed Ben that I was so much his brother's image. A chav like me! I think Ben thought he'd fallen through a hole in time, into a parallel universe. He didn't expect me at all when he started out on his quest. To Ben I'm the fairy that pops up in a puff of pink smoke on the road to the ogre's castle.

Mark isn't queer, I'm pretty sure. Not even half queer like me. He's not right, though – anyone can see that once you get past his lovely manners and heart breaking voice. It's as if he traded in his life supply of happiness for being head-turning beautiful and realised long ago what a poisonous deal he'd got. I couldn't take my eyes off him; I wanted him to look at me so I could somehow convince him that I was a good person and would help him not to be so sad. Ambitious, eh? I suppose I just wanted to comfort him. But he wouldn't look at me, not even when Ben persuaded him to have a drink with us in the Green Tree.

I don't drink. I asked for a mineral water and Ben raised his eyebrows in that mild way of his, 'Sparkling or still?' Mark and I stood a couple of steps behind him as Ben was served at the bar and I've never felt so awkward in my life, as though I'd just said something really thoughtless and hurtful and was desperately trying to think of something to say to make up for it. I hadn't said anything at all, only that chirpy *Hiya!* as I shook Mark's hand.

Ben handed me my glass of water. He said, 'Shall we sit down?' He looked at Mark as though he thought he'd been rude to keep me standing. The Green Tree is a quiet pub, there was even a free table by the open fire, three armchairs arranged around it as though it was set up especially for us to have a cosy family chat. The table was crowded with wine and beer glasses stained with lipstick; an ashtray overflowed with the stubs of menthol cigarettes. I thought, *at least the girls had a good time*. I helped Ben clear the glasses to the bar but Mark sat down. Immediately he lit a cigarette. I noticed that his hands shook a little.

As I set my handful of glasses on the bar I said, 'Ben, I think maybe I should go –'

'No.' His voice was hard. 'I want you to stay.'

'He's upset…'

Ben laughed nastily.

We sat down. Straight away Ben said, 'Steven works as a porter at the hospital, Mark. That's how we met. I saw him and I thought…Well, you can imagine what I thought.'

106

Mark flicked cigarette ash. 'Can I? Actually I'm afraid I can't.'

'Oh, come off it, Mark!' Ben laughed. 'Look at him!'

I squirmed. I looked down at my drink, watching the bubbles rise to the surface. I felt my face colour and I never blush. I head Ben sigh and he sounded just like Dad – the same angry, fake patience that makes that horrible shock of fear dart through you. I glanced at Ben, wondering if he realised he sounded so much like Danny. Catching my eye he smiled apologetically and the likeness to Dad disappeared.

Looking at his cigarette Mark said, 'I'm sorry about this, Steven. I can see it's embarrassing for you.'

'No – really. I know this must be a shock –'

For a second he managed to meet my eye. Coldly he said, 'You're not shocking, Steven. I only wish Ben had saved you from all this awkwardness. He should have told you I want nothing to do with you or your family.' He drained the half-pint of beer Ben had bought him and stood up. 'Now, if you'll excuse me I'm going home.'

'Oh for Christ's sake, Mark!' Ben stood up too and caught his arm. 'Why do you have to be such a bloody child? The boy's here now – he wanted to meet you! He's actually a fan of yours! Read all your books, haven't you Steven?'

I didn't know where to look. The two of them were standing over me, both of them like prize fighters squaring up to each other. I imagined standing up between them, a hand on each of their chests saying, 'We want a nice, clean fight, boys,' calm as any referee. Instead I took a sip of my drink, hoping they wouldn't notice my blushes.

Ben sat down again. After a second Mark did, too. Just for something to break the silence I said, 'That fire's hot, isn't it?'

'Do you want to sit somewhere else?' Ben asked.

'No – it's fine. I like it.'

'We have an open fire at home,' Ben said. 'Only ever light it at Christmas. Messy things. Lovely but messy. You have a fireplace in the flat, don't you, Mark?' Ben turned to me. 'Mark lives in Hampstead, Steven. Quite near the heath.'

I nodded as if I knew where he meant. Then, just to make a bigger fool of myself, I said, 'I've never been to London.'

'No? Honestly?' Ben laughed as though truly amazed. 'Good God!'

Mark leaned forward and for a second I thought he was going to pat my knee like people do when you've been patronised. Of course he didn't, only flicked ash into the ashtray. I noticed his hands, capable, strong-looking. I started to imagine the weight of one of those hands on my thigh; I started getting a hard-on and felt disgusted with myself. I cleared my throat.

'I've heard of Hampstead Heath.'

Ben said, 'Our parents lived there, before they came to Thorp. Mum often used to take us back to visit friends of hers. Do you ever see Moira and Charles, Mark?' Ben frowned. 'No, of course. Charles died, didn't he?'

Mark ignored him. Afraid of the silence I said, 'They're Londoners, then, your Mam and Dad?'

'No, Mum came from Stoke-on-Trent, I think. Dad's family was from York, that's right, isn't it, Mark?' It was obvious he didn't expect a reply. He went on, 'Granddad came to Thorp just after the war, to set up his own practice as a GP.'

Mark snorted. '*Granddad*? You speak as though we knew him!'

'He died before we were born.' Ben turned to me. 'I feel as though I know him from all Dad's told me.'

Mark seemed to force himself to look at me. He said, 'Ben's told me your father is dying?'

I thought of Danny as I'd seen him that morning, sitting in his high-backed chair by the ward window in a square of sunlight. He liked the sun on him; he said he could never get warm enough. He was wearing the worn out tartan dressing gown the hospital had found for him and his wrists stuck out of the sleeves thin as twigs. The backs of his hands were purple and orange and black where they'd stuck needles. No one had bothered shaving him and the grey stubble made him look like an old tramp so that I'd thought I might have a go shaving him myself, only I knew I couldn't bring myself to be so intimate with him. I'd pulled up the visitor's chair and sat at arm's length. The nurse came, that cheerful redhead. She'd smiled at Danny, 'How are we feeling today?' and Danny smiled his don't-concern-yourself-with-me smile, cringing like Uriah Heep.

Mark said, 'He has lung cancer?'

'Yes.'

Ben said, 'Did you visit him today?'

'Yes, he was out of bed, sitting up –'

Mark frowned as though deeply concerned. 'He was sitting up? How long does he have?'

'For pity's sake, Mark!' To me, Ben said, 'They have good and bad days. I've spoken to his consultant Mr Hughes about his pain relief.'

'Thanks.'

Mark stood up. 'I really have to go. I'm sorry, Steven, but I can't listen to this.'

Ben and I watched him walk out. Ben said, 'Sorry. Perhaps you were right, I should have made sure he was used to the idea of you before allowing you to meet.'

Allowing. Ben couldn't help talking like a boss. I sipped my drink, knowing he was watching me. At last he said, 'Mark is a difficult man.'

'He's all right.'

'He's self-conscious around strangers.'

109

He hadn't seemed self-conscious to me, only angry as though we'd conspired to play some nasty trick on him. Suddenly I wanted to follow Mark outside. I wanted him to know that I wouldn't cause him any trouble and that I really admired him and would like to be his friend if I could. But more than that, I wanted to tell him I knew what it was like to *be* him. I knew I would have sounded mad, though, like some sort of psycho stalker.

I was looking towards the door, still thinking of chasing after Mark, when Ben said gently, 'Steven, do you mind if I ask you something – something rather difficult?' He sat forward, his hands clasped together so that his knuckles were white. He opened his mouth to speak, only to close it again and glance towards the door as though wishing he could make the same escape Mark had. At last he said, 'Did Danny ever hurt you and your brothers?'

I had an urge to laugh: that was it, the big question he had to work himself up to ask! I gazed at him, wondering what he wanted to hear, what would disturb him least.

He said, 'You're smirking. You think it's a stupid question.'

'No, not really, not if you need to know.'

'I don't know what I need to know.' He exhaled sharply. 'I'm sorry. This is difficult for me.' Looking down at his drink he said, 'When Mark and I were taken into care...well, Mark was very ill, in hospital. Simon – the man who became our father – would sit me down and tell me how poorly Mark was...he didn't actually say it but I knew he meant that Mark might die.'

'That must have been scary.'

'It wasn't intended to scare me. He meant me to take sides, Mark's against Danny's, my dad's.' He laughed shortly. 'Dad – Simon – was always taking me out for walks, just the two of us, trying to talk to me, to get me to understand the seriousness of it all...that Danny wasn't about to come back.' Sighing, he said, 'All I wanted was to

110

go back home to my dad. I didn't care about Mark. Mark was a cry-baby – I thought he was pretending to be sick just to get Dad into trouble.' He smiled crookedly. 'Mixed-up kid, wasn't I?'

I tried to picture him as a child, a tough little boy ready to kick this Simon in the shins and run off in search of Danny, loyal to him. I finished my drink. Nodding at his empty glass I said, 'Do you want another?'

'No.' He sighed. 'I should go.'

He had a very young wife – a beautiful wife and a baby boy. I knew all this before I met him; you hear a lot hanging round a hospital ward waiting to take a patient to theatre. The nurses would say to some poor sod on the gurney, 'Mr Walker is lovely – the very best, there's absolutely nothing for you to worry about!' Most of the nurses had a crush on Ben Walker, although he wasn't my type – too butch, too hard. He glanced up at me from twisting his empty glass around and I felt this pity for him, this soft, sentimental feeling that made me reach out and touch his hand lightly.

'Don't look so sad.'

He laughed, fishing in his pocket for his car keys as if to have an excuse to draw his hand away from mine. 'I'm not sad – not really. Do you need a lift home or anywhere...?'

'No, thanks.'

We walked to his car. A few metres away he pressed the remote on his keys and its lights flashed as if it was excited to see him. He stopped and shook my hand. 'Steven, thank you for coming to meet Mark tonight.'

I wasn't sure why he felt the need to thank me. I'm sure he knew how much I wanted to see Mark. Perhaps he didn't – I was afraid of giving myself away, after all, of appearing too desperate, too scarily *me*.

He climbed in the car. He said, 'I'll see you at the hospital. Tomorrow afternoon, if I have time.'

Ben knew that I visited Danny each lunchtime. I'd take my sandwiches and sit by his bed instead of sitting in the staff canteen or outside on the scrubby bit of grass that used to be the hospice garden. The hospice had moved years ago to a bigger, brighter plot past the Church of the Holy Trinity and the little garden was forgotten, its rose bushes leggy and diseased, the Leylandii, planted to give the dying a bit of privacy, racing to block out the sky. No one else seemed to know about the garden. It was peaceful there, just me and the starlings that shared my sandwiches. When Danny was first admitted I used to think that one day I'd borrow a wheelchair and take him to the garden. I imagined asking him stuff there. Stuff! There was only one question, really, the big *Why?* The wheelchair was never borrowed, of course. I couldn't have him in my peaceful, private space; taking him there was just a fantasy I had.

I had lots of fantasies when I was a kid. The most enduring was the one where I'd been stolen as a baby, that Mam had liked the look of me and lifted me from my shiny, well-sprung pram and whisked me off to her mad house. Mam was always telling me how bonny I was and that she didn't know where I'd come from. Her family is ugly as sin, her brothers especially. Graham calls them the Potato Men, not realising that he's becoming a Potato Man himself. Our Uncle Mick brought Graham up. When Colin was eleven he ran away and when the uncles found him trying to sneak on a train to London, Uncle Mick took him in as well. That left me and Mam. Mam and me and Danny, when he wasn't inside.

The first time I went to bed with Nichola, after the sex when we were cuddled up and she was all soft and loving, she said, 'You're funny, aren't you?'

'Funny?' My heart skipped because I thought she'd found me out.

She lifted her head from my chest to smile at me, her face all stupefied like a happy drunk's. 'Different. Weird. In a good way.'

'How good?'

She groaned softly and flicked my nipple with her little pink tongue. 'Lovely. *Gentle*.' She seemed pleased with this adjective. She frowned, nodding as if tasting the sound it made. 'Gentle.'

The first time I went to bed with Carl, as I was getting undressed, scared, desperate, he said, 'I'll be careful with you.' I didn't want care; I wanted him to be careless, cruel, so I didn't have to think. I didn't know Carl very well then, didn't realise that cruel was beyond him.

I watched Ben drive away and walked home. I thought about Mark and the best way of reaching inside his heart and head. I was thinking about him as I went to bed, as I drifted off to sleep. I dreamt of him, that I'd somehow saved him.

Chapter 11

With breathless care Kitty lowered Nathan into his cot. She covered him with his quilt then waited, keeping as still and silent as she could in case any noise or movement might wake him. His bottom lip trembled and for a moment she was afraid that he was about to start crying again, but he slept on and she allowed herself to hope that he was too exhausted to wake. Piglet lay at her feet, dropped a couple of hours ago when she'd lifted Nathan from his cot, soaked and screaming. She hugged the pink plush toy to her chest before tucking it gently beside her baby and creeping from the nursery.

She'd been about to run a bath when Nathan had woken, now she couldn't be bothered. Lying down on the bed she looked at the alarm clock. Ben would be home soon. He would smell of cigarettes and beer; he would be angry – tetchy; he wouldn't speak, wouldn't be able to bring himself to discuss his evening with his brother. She wouldn't dare ask how their discussion had gone, afraid of his temper that lately seemed so ready to erupt.

Outside an owl hooted. Ben had told her once that a mouse skeleton could be assembled from an owl dropping, the tiny, indigestible bones and skull all neatly wrapped and disposed of so that boys like him could come along and fit the mouse together again as though it was an *Airfix* toy. There was something about bones, Ben said, that was utterly fascinating; as a child he would dissect the dead creatures he found, rats and sparrows and mice, even a mole once. He said he had wanted to discover how they worked and how they died. He had laughed at the disgust on her face. 'The mole,' he'd said, 'was particularly exciting – such shy creatures, you hardly ever laid eyes on them.' He'd smiled, remembering. 'Poor thing. Its paws were almost like human hands.'

Kitty rolled onto her back. If she undressed quickly she could be under the covers, eyes closed feigning sleep before Ben came home. Not that he'd believe that she was sleeping, or particularly care. He would pull her into his arms, slipping his hand inside her tee shirt to cup her breast. He would murmur into her hair and call her his sweet girl, his *baby*. His erection would nudge her backside, its hard urgency contradicting his soft words.

Eventually she would roll over to face him, pretending still to be sleepy, malleable, just as he liked and expected her to be. She wouldn't have to do anything energetic; he would slip inside her easily as she lay on her back and it would be over quickly. There would be no performance to prove his youth and virility and skill. But she would wrap her legs around his waist still, she would still moan a little and cry out as he came. But she would be thinking of the mice trapped inside the owl pellets waiting for Ben's dextrous fingers, for their resurrection. She would be thinking of the little mole's hands, pink and pathetic, and she would be reminded how powerless she was although she loved him and fancied him still. *Fancied*. It was a word from her school days, those wasted, restless years, when no one had found certain boys as beautiful as she did. She had kept her peculiar fancies to herself. She didn't want her friends to think her weird, after all.

She began to undress, dropping her clothes into the Ali Baba basket in the corner of the en-suite bathroom. She stood in front of the wash basin and stared into the mirror above it. Her mascara was smudged as though she had been crying, but it was only the tears that came from yawning. She noticed that the mirror was splattered with tiny flecks of toothpaste. The glass where their toothbrushes were kept had built-up a white sludge and should be cleaned, as should the basin and the bath and the beautiful, expensive floor Ben's first wife had chosen. The whole house needed a thorough clean, although it looked presentable enough. The dirt, Kitty knew, lurked in places where visitors wouldn't notice it, and this seemed terrible to her and dishonest. The dirt was real slut's dirt; she was slovenly, lazy, she couldn't be bothered. She wished her mother would come, energetic, organised, quick, and take her in hand. She needed to be rescued.

She sat on the edge of the bath and brushed her teeth. In bed, she listened for the owl and for Ben's car, watching for the pattern its lights made on the ceiling as he turned into the drive. She sometimes thought she could sense his impatience in this pattern of light; she wished he were calmer, like her father. Her father was easy going and fatalistic, certain always that life would work out if left well enough alone. 'Don't pick at scabs, pet,' he told her, and 'Don't go looking for trouble, not when it looks for us so determinedly.' She guessed that Ben thought her father was a waster.

The day after their first date in the posh hotel, Ben had taken her to Whitby. They had walked hand in hand up the abbey steps and looked out over the grey North Sea. He had put his arm lightly around her shoulders and pointed out a ship on the horizon and suddenly he said, 'My brother Mark was in the Marines. During the Falklands War. His ship was torpedoed – or bombed or something – and he only just escaped with his life.' He'd turned away from the sea's horizon to frown at her. 'Do you remember the Falklands War? Have you even heard of it?'

She'd bristled. 'Yes, I've heard of it.'

He turned back to the sea. 'Why did I tell you about him?' He smiled at her awkwardly. 'Mark and I aren't close although we pretend to be for our father's sake. And for our

116

mother's sake too, when she was alive.' After a moment he said, 'Mum died last year, of cancer. Dad and Mark are the only family I have.'

She had taken this as her cue to tell him about her family and the ordinary broken home she came from. As she talked he took her hand again and led her through the abbey's graveyard. She sensed he was listening carefully. He asked blunt, incisive questions and she found herself telling him more than she had intended to, about her mother who she suspected was disappointed in her, about her father who she wished had stayed, or at least asked her to go with him. That night, when Ben had kissed her goodbye and she waved to him from her mother's front door-step, she realised that she knew next to nothing about his family, except that he had a brother who had been a Marine and was almost killed in a war she'd barely heard of. She'd imagined Mark as much older than Ben, a doddery man, frail as the veterans that laid their poppy wreaths at the Cenotaph on Remembrance Sunday. She'd been shocked when she finally met him.

Mark had said, 'Hello, Kitty. I'm pleased to meet you at last.'

He had taken both her hands and kissed her on each cheek and smiled his shockingly beautiful smile. He was as expensively dressed and as powerfully built as Ben, but a bit taller, just enough for the difference to be noticeable. When the brothers stood side by side it seemed to her that Ben realised how much Mark out-shone him; Ben became a different, diminished man and even the sentences he spoke became poor, stunted things, as though he could hardly bring himself to speak for bitterness and jealousy. After that meeting, half-drunk and off-guard, she had asked Ben if he hated his brother.

He had turned on her angrily. 'Why do you say that?'

She'd retreated at once. 'Sorry – of course you don't hate him –'

117

'Don't I? No – of course.' He snorted. 'Have you fallen in love with him?'

'No!'

'Don't protest too much. Most women *do* fall for him.' He frowned, studying her for a moment. 'Perhaps you're too young to make that mistake.'

Later that night as they lay in bed together, Ben asked her to marry him. His proposal wasn't unexpected but all the same she had struggled from his embrace to kneel at his side. 'You really want to marry me?'

'Yes, I really do.'

'Why?'

He laughed and reached out to press his palm against her cheek. 'Because I love you. Because I find you sweet and sexy and lovely. Perhaps the better question is why you should want to marry me, if you do want to, of course.'

'I do!' She remembered laughing and thinking that this was how it felt to be truly happy. Unable to contain herself she'd stood up on the bed and looked down on him. 'Can we have a big white wedding? Can we have a horse and carriage and loads of bridesmaids and a marquee and a massive party –'

He'd laughed and held out his hand to steady her as she bounced on the bed. 'You can have anything you want. Choirs of angels, if you want.' He pulled her down, holding her close as he guided her hand to his erection. Softly he said, 'I want a child, a son. I don't want to wait.'

What is happiness, anyway? Kitty thought. An excitement that's quickly over. It's not contentment. She used to imagine contentment was only for the old. Happiness was nothing very much more than sparks from a Catherine Wheel.

The day Nathan was born Ben had bought her three dozen yellow roses. On the card he wrote, *'Well done, my darling girl.'* Her mother, reading the message, had laughed shortly. Her mother and husband successfully made her feel like a child.

Ben's car spread its light across the ceiling. She listened to the car door slam, the beep that meant it was locked and alarmed; she heard his footsteps on the gravel, his key turn in the door. She tensed, wondering if he would go into the kitchen or come straight upstairs to bed, to her, wanting her with the single-mindedness that had recently transformed their love-making so that she felt her only part in the process was as a receptacle for his sperm. Nathan was no longer enough; there was more to prove.

She turned on her side and curled into a ball, her back to his side of the bed. She thought of the hedgehogs that bumbled across the lawn at night and wondered if Ben had ever found one to dissect.

Simon was still up when Mark returned home. He came out from the kitchen as Mark hung up his jacket and said, 'Iain's here,' his voice flat so there could be no doubt he was still upset with him. Mark sighed.

'In that case I'll go straight to bed.'

'No. You won't be rude to my friends. You'll come through and say hello.'

Mark imagined arguing, whining like a child, saying that he was tired and that Ben had been nasty to him and couldn't he take his side, just for once? He imagined telling him about Steven – a good enough excuse to be allowed to be alone. But Simon was gazing at him, expecting him to argue, expecting to be let down and disappointed. Through the open kitchen door Mark could see the chess set on the kitchen table. The two men would stay up late into the night and in the morning he would come down to the half-finished game, the captured pieces lined up against the whisky bottle and two sticky tumblers.

Simon went into the kitchen. Cheerfully he said, 'Iain, fetch another glass, Mark's going to join us for a night-cap.'

Iain Weaver stood up. He went to a cupboard and took out a glass, perfectly at home. Pouring a generous measure of Simon's whisky, he smiled at Mark as he handed him his drink. 'You don't take water with it, do you Mark? I should know, shouldn't I – you're my Godson, after all. I don't see enough of you, Mark – read your last review in the *Observer*, though. Terribly proud of you, my boy. Terribly proud.'

The Observer had said he was back on form after a disappointing run. He remembered tossing the paper down, thinking *wankers*. He smiled at Weaver. 'How are you, Iain?'

'Oh, you know – when you get to my age...' He laughed. 'You've lost weight, my boy. Good for you! Fat at fifty, fat forever, that's what I say.'

Dryly Simon said, 'Mark's nowhere near fifty, Iain, and he's never been fat. Please don't upset him.'

Iain frowned at Mark. 'You're not upset, are you?'

'No, of course not.'

Weaver went on frowning at him. He had a way of sizing him up that had always made him uncomfortable. Iain Weaver knew too much about him, knew everything, in fact. When he was a teenager Weaver's knowledge of him made him blush to the roots of his hair. For years he couldn't stay in the same room as him; even now he longed to get away. He thought of the boy, Steven, and wanted to be alone to begin to understand how he felt. The boy had Danny's voice; his voice more than anything else dragged him back to his childhood.

Simon said, 'How's Ben, Mark?'

'Fine.'

Weaver said, 'Your father's told me what Ben's been up to. I have to say I think he's a bloody fool.' He shook his head. 'I can't think why he would want to do such a fool thing.'

120

'All right, Iain.' Simon glanced at Mark, embarrassed. 'I think enough has been said on that subject.'

'Yes. Of course. I just wanted Mark to know I don't support what Ben's doing.'

The two older men sat down, facing each other across the chessboard. Mark realised he'd been dismissed and set his barely tasted drink down gently. 'I'll say goodnight.'

'Goodnight, Mark!' Iain smiled at him. Simon hardly glanced up as he made his first move of the game.

Later Simon knocked on his bedroom door, waiting only a moment before coming in. He said, 'I saw your light was on. Can't you sleep?'

Mark put down the book he'd been reading. 'I haven't tried to sleep.'

'No?' Simon sat on his bed. He smiled awkwardly. 'Months since I climbed those stairs. Quite an effort...' Sighing he said, 'I didn't think you'd be asleep.'

'Has Iain gone?'

'He's contemplating his next move – could take an age...I wanted to find out how you'd got on with Ben.'

'Not very well.'

'No, I supposed you hadn't. What did he have to say for himself?'

'Nothing very much.'

'No news?'

Mark laughed bleakly.

'Mark, please don't keep things from me – if Ben's discovered anything at all I'd like to know.'

'He hasn't.' He looked at him, feeling blatant, knowing that he could lie well when he chose to.

Simon exhaled as though he'd been holding his breath. 'That man! That disgusting swine! Why should Ben want to look for a swine like that? Why? He should have been hanged! I would have put the rope around his neck myself!'

Such vehement hatred was disturbing, it exposed too much that was better shut away. Quickly Mark said, 'Don't say that.'

'Why not? It's the truth! Iain always said he should have hanged for what he did and I agree!'

Iain had said, 'Now, young man, you're going to have to be very brave and good whilst I examine you. It won't hurt, you just take some good deep breaths...' A nurse had held his hand and stroked his head and said 'It's all right, good boy, good boy, good boy,' as the doctor hurt him. They had laid him on a high narrow bed covered with a roll of white paper as though he was dirty and there was a sharp, bad stink and shiny metal objects arranged on a trolley and glinting in the hospital's bright, white light. The doctor and the nurse seemed to know what Danny had done to him. He thought he would die of shame.

Mark turned away, unable to face Simon after such memories. He said, 'I'll go home in the morning, Dad. I think that would be best.'

'Oh Mark. How did we come to this? You know what Iain said to me just now? He said how proud I must be of you and Ben that you both over-came so much and turned out so well –'

Mark shook his head, smiling in disgust. 'I suppose he considers your experiment a complete success now he can see how well we've *turned out*.'

'My experiment?'

Ashamed of himself he said, 'I'm sorry. Forget it. I'm tired –'

'You say foolish things, Mark.'

'Yes, I do. Sorry.'

'Your mother and I adopted you and Ben because we loved you and wanted to give you a proper home.'

Mark hung his head. 'I know, I'm sorry.'

'All I wanted – all your mother wanted – was for you to feel safe and loved enough to put your past behind you.'

'Yes, Dad. I know. And we did, *I* did, at least. I knew you loved us...'

'Did you?' He laughed a little. 'I wondered. When you first came to us you reminded me...' He pressed his lips together, clamping down on the words he was about to say. 'Anyway – long time ago, now.'

'What did I remind you of?'

Simon gazed at him. At last he said, 'You reminded me of a kitten my father brought home once. A farmer had given it to him. He had thrust the poor creature into a sack, tied the top and handed it to my father as a present for me. As soon as Dad opened the sack in our kitchen the little cat leapt out and ran straight up the wall. Such a look of shock and fright on its face...' He sighed. 'I'm sorry – it's a silly comparison.'

'It's not. I was a timid child.'

'No – not really. You could be a fearless little thing!' He laughed. 'I remember the first time I took you and Ben swimming, how you took to the water so naturally while Ben flayed about... and if you were timid around strangers, well, maybe you had every right to be...' Fervently he said, 'I just wanted to protect you – like I wanted to protect that kitten – make you see that you were safe and wouldn't be harmed again! But I couldn't – you had to learn that for yourself. I just had to wait for you to trust me. I was impatient, though. I remember feeling terribly impatient.'

'Yes, I remember too.'

'Do you? Then I'm sorry.' To Mark's surprise he reached out and took his hand between his own. 'I wanted to be a good father.'

'You were.'

'I could have been better –'

Mark drew his hand away gently. 'All parents make mistakes.'

'Do you think I loved Ben more?'

123

'No!' He frowned at him. 'Please, Dad, there's no need to talk like this –'

'There is! I need you to know I treated you both as fairly as I could.'

'I know you did.'

'Then why...' He closed his eyes. Painfully he said, 'Then *why* did you set out to hurt Ben so badly –'

'I didn't set out to hurt him.'

'You had an affair with his wife.'

'He didn't find out.'

'But you wanted him to.'

'No! It had nothing to do with Ben or you, or the past. Nothing to do with the way you brought us up. My childhood doesn't have to be the reason for everything –'

'I'm just trying to make sense of it!'

'The sense is I loved her.'

'Love! For God's sake be honest with yourself if not with me –'

'It's the truth.'

'How could you?'

'How could I what? Love someone? I don't know, Dad. It's amazing, isn't it? Who'd have thought I'd be capable of love, eh? A dirty, filthy, damaged creature like me!'

'I never thought of you like that and you know I didn't!' He frowned at him as though coming to a realisation. 'You'd do it again, wouldn't you? You have no remorse –'

'I loved her!'

'She was your brother's wife! Whatever you felt for her you should have left her alone! You set out to wreck his marriage, I know you did –'

'All right, you're right. I was so jealous I hated him and wanted revenge and it's your fault for being such a bad father. You should have left me with Danny. Is that what you want to hear?' He picked up the book that lay face down on his lap. Closing it he kept his gaze fixed on its cover. 'Anyway, it's over now. Ben has Kitty and Nathan; he has what he always wanted.'

He thought of what he wanted. Susan. The way she held him, how her body fitted with his so well, how she could be so quiet sometimes he half-believed he calmed her and made her different from the woman his brother knew. At such times he had wanted to tell her how much she had made him different; but already he had told her too much. Better just to hold her and to imagine that because they fitted so well it was normal to love someone so badly, that nothing else could matter so much. They were *made* for each other. All at once he was seized by the desire to make Simon understand that his need for her wasn't wicked.

'Dad – Susan was everything to me…' He trailed off, aware of how empty the words sounded, so drained of meaning through over-use. It was a line from a popular song, from a poem put together by someone who hadn't thought deeply or clearly enough. Everything – *the air that I breathe, my moon and stars and sun.* Desperately frustrated, he said, 'She understood me –'

Simon laughed shortly. He said, 'Mark – do I have to repeat myself? Do I have to tell you again that she was *your brother's wife*? Everything else is romantic nonsense –'

'No. No –'

'She was the only woman in the world for you? The only one from so many – of course! Just an unhappy coincidence that she was Ben's wife and he loved her, because she was the one, the *only* one who understood you!'

'It wasn't like that.' He could hear the sulkiness in his voice, could hardly bear to meet his father's eye, just as he couldn't as a child, because Simon knew him too well, as well as Iain Weaver who sat downstairs. Both of these charming, easy, *worldly* men knew him and from the moment they set eyes on him he had always made their flesh crawl. He had to make another effort to make him understand.

Quickly he said, 'I think about her all the time. Some days the grief is so bad I can't keep still, can't concentrate on anything but the fact that she's gone and I'll never see her again. I panic. It's as if I can't believe that it can't somehow be fixed, that I can't find someone who can make it all right again. All my life someone has always rescued me...but I can't be rescued from this. I wish I had died instead.'

'Don't say that. If I lost you – well, I couldn't cope with that.'

'What can I do?'

'Carry on? When I lost your mother –' He sighed, exasperated. 'Oh, Mark, hush now! Don't start crying! Come on, don't behave like this...pull yourself together. Perhaps you should go and see a doctor, you're obviously depressed –'

'I'm not depressed – pills won't help how I feel!'

'Not pills, then, a counsellor, perhaps.'

Scornfully he said, 'Someone to talk to? Aren't we talking now? Can't I talk to you?'

'I'm sorry, Mark, I can't. I'm not the right person.'

'You're the only one who knows.'

'Ben is my son, just as you are. You must understand...please try to understand.' He took his hand again. 'Mark, listen now. The pain gets better, I promise, you won't always feel it so badly...'

'I want to feel it – what else do I have?' He made an effort to compose himself. 'I'm sorry. I didn't mean to upset you. I'll go home in the morning.'

Simon got up from the bed. 'Iain will be wondering where I've got to. I'll leave you to get some sleep.'

As he reached the door he stopped. He turned to him with such an expression of shocked bewilderment on his face that Mark got up and went to him. 'Dad?'

'Mark, oh God...' His knees buckled and he collapsed into Mark's arms.

Chapter 12

The Tale of Peter Rabbit was inscribed on its facing page with the words, *'To Simon, who understands all too well what soporific means. With Daddy's and Mummy's very best love, Christmas 1927.'*

Annette smiled at the words. On her knee, Mark reached out and touched the copperplate writing. He whispered, 'Read it, Mummy.'

'You. You read it.'

He struggled a little with the strange, ornate letters but she broke down the words into syllables, dragging her finger beneath each one. When they'd made sense of it he looked up at her. 'What does it mean?'

'I don't know. We shall have to look it up in a dictionary. Shall we read the story first?'

He nodded and relaxed a little against her chest. She kissed his head, inhaling his soapy scent. She'd just bathed him; his hair clung damply to his head. Beneath his clean pyjamas bruises bloomed blue and yellow and black, some of them old, others more recent. She had dabbed at them gently as she dried him.

She began to read, pointing out the words as she spoke. She was shocked that Peter's mother told her babies that their father had been eaten in a pie, it seemed too terrible for words in a baby's story. She had stopped reading but Mark had looked at her impassively, turning back to the book to read the story aloud to himself. She listened, watching as he pointed out the words as she had.

Outside in the street Ben played football with his friends. She heard their shouts, heard the ball bounce hard against the cobbles. The sun streamed through the open window and she could smell the fish and chips frying in the chip shop on the corner. She remembered how hungry she was, and at once felt guilty. The boys were hungry too and it didn't matter how she felt. She'd considered going to Joan and begging a couple of shillings to buy chips. Only her pride stopped her. Listening to Mark's timid little voice she began to think that her pride was nothing against her children's hunger. When the story was finished she would carry Mark next door and ask Joan for the money. Joan wouldn't refuse her when she saw Mark. She adored Mark, was always amazed at his ability to read the labels of the tins and packets in her kitchen. As she fed him bread and jam she would sometimes test him with the evening paper and was always astonished. 'Genius,' she'd say as he read the bold black letters of the *Gazette's* headline. 'Real genius, aren't you pet?'

If she asked for money Annette knew Joan would say that she should make Danny hand over his pay packet every Thursday. She'd say, 'You take the thick end of it, he gets the rest. That's what happens in this house. I wouldn't see my lads go without food.'

She'd said it before; Annette wondered if she'd ever tire of saying it. She thought of Bill who had smiled at her so gently in the pub the other night. She remembered that only a thin wall divided his and Joan's bedroom from hers and Danny's. Bill would have heard the filthy things Danny shouted as he forced himself on her. All the terrible names he called her were shouted so loudly she wondered if the whole street heard. She'd noticed that some of the men on the street looked at her as though she was dirt. Some of them sniggered when they thought she wasn't looking. She guessed what they were thinking: surely only a slut could be treated like that.

Danny had gone out an hour ago; she wasn't sure where and she didn't care very much. He had clipped Mark round the ear as he left. 'See the little bastard's in bed when I get back.' As if she would keep him up, waiting to be assaulted. She wished she could whisk her kids away, somewhere safe and quiet where they wouldn't hear the terrifying, disgusting words Danny used. The words shamed her as much as anything he did.

That afternoon as she'd stood in Doctor Walker's sitting room choosing children's books from the many in the box, she'd had a sense of being outside herself. It was as though her mind was cut off from her body and she could watch from a distance the way she stood and picked each book up, hear her own voice as if it belonged to someone else. She'd liked the feeling, even began to allow herself to drift further away so that Doctor Walker's voice began to sound as if it had an echo, but he had touched her arm and her mind had jumped back. Reality clattered around her as he said, 'Annette – my dear! Are you all right? Here, you must sit down!'

He'd made her sit on one of the dusty armchairs, bending over her with such a look of concern she was scared.

'I thought you were about to faint.' He'd frowned at her, picking up her wrist and timing her pulse. His manner changed, becoming like that of every doctor she had ever met. 'Have you eaten today?'

'Yes.'

'The truth?'

'I had a cup of tea.'

'Stay there.'

He came back a few minutes later with a plate of ham sandwiches and a mug of hot milk. He'd watched her as she ate; because she was ravenous she forgot to feel self-conscious and finished the food quickly.

'Thank you.' She became ashamed of herself, realising how she must have looked as she'd gobbled the sandwiches down. She got up and made to carry the plate and mug to the kitchen. Doctor Walker took them from her again. 'Sit down, Annette.' In his serious, doctor's voice he said, 'You should eat a proper breakfast before you go out to work.'

'Yes. I know.'

'You need to keep up your strength for the sake of your children, at least.'

'I know that, too.' She met his gaze, angry with him for saying what was so obvious; she'd thought better of him than that.

He sighed and his voice became softer again. 'Annette, I know you and I have only just met and you may feel this is presumptuous of me, but I think we're becoming friends, wouldn't you agree?'

She nodded, unable to look at him any longer. No man had ever said he was her friend. It was embarrassing and touching and she was afraid she might cry again. She mustn't cry. She'd made enough of a show of herself today.

He said, 'I'm worried about you –'

'There's no need to be!'

'How did you get those bruises on your hand and arm?' When she didn't answer he said, 'Annette?'

'I don't know how I got them.' Forcing herself to look at him she said, 'I don't know. I'd like to go home now.'

'Then let me give you a lift.'

'No, really – it's not far.' She stood hurriedly, desperate to get away. 'Besides, you have to go and see your wife. You shouldn't worry about me.'

He'd pressed the books on her, two of them. She had hidden them under the boys' mattress, terrified Danny would come in and catch her in the act, scared even now that he would find them.

Mark said, 'Mummy?' He touched her face anxiously. 'Mummy...?'

130

She brought herself back into the present. 'It's all right sweetheart. Come on. Let's put your lovely book away. We're going to see Aunty Joan.'

Simon sat at Joy's bedside. She was yet to come round from the anaesthetic and he held her hand, wanting her to somehow sense that he was there. She looked smaller in the intimidating hospital bed; he tried to dismiss the thought that she looked old, too. Older than him, although they were the same age. Joy had an older way about her, an old-fashioned, matronly air.

And yet she made so little fuss; everything was taken calmly in her stride. The first time they'd gone to bed together in her tiny Hampstead flat her modesty had made him feel as though he'd stepped into the past, to a time before the war, perhaps before even his father's war. Standing in her bedroom she'd asked, 'Should I undress? Or is that something I should leave to you?'

She'd looked at him as though it was common sense to seek his direction and he'd smiled as the desire he'd begun to feel for her slipped away. 'Let's lie down first,' he said. 'I'll hold you for a while.'

'I'm rather nervous. I'm sorry.' She'd taken off her shoes and laid down on her back, her hands folded over her stomach so that he was put in mind of a patient about to be examined. He lay down beside her. 'Joy,' he said. 'Are you sure about this?'

'Yes. Absolutely. I'm just rather surprised you're here. And I don't know if I'm surprised despite your reputation or because of it.'

'I'm here because I want to make love to you.'

She laughed slightly.

'I didn't make a joke, Joy.'

'No. I didn't think you did.' She turned on her side to face him. 'I *am* nervous; but also I feel such a...such a *want* for you. Indecent. I suppose I feel indecent with desire. And

131

I laughed just then because to hear you say you want me, too, well…how wonderful.'

He smiled, touched by her honesty. 'I'll make it as wonderful as I can.'

She gazed at him. 'Of course you will. That's why I chose you.'

She was a secretary to one of his senior colleagues. She was fiercely efficient. It was rumoured she made junior secretaries cry. It was rumoured too that she was a lesbian and that had made him laugh. In his heart he didn't actually believe in lesbianism but all the same he'd looked at Joy Featherstone with new eyes. He found himself drawn to her coolness, her trimness and clipped way of talking. He forgot the silly rumours and found excuses to visit the little office she shared with his own secretary. On one such visit Joy was on her own. She'd looked up from her typewriter and smiled wryly. He'd asked her out to dinner. In her clean and orderly flat, both naked beneath her crisp white sheets, her surprising passion spent, it had crossed his mind that she was just the kind of woman he needed. It was only a fleeting thought, and one he quickly got rid of. Joy wasn't his type, not at all.

In her hospital bed Joy stirred. She opened her eyes and looked at him, her eyes confused and full of pain. He stood up and smoothed her hair back from her brow. 'Darling, it's all right, everything went well. How are you feeling?'

'Don't leave me.'

'I'm here to stay, as long as you want me.'

'Simon –' She tried to sit up and her face became even paler. Guessing what was coming he reached for a clean bedpan and held it for her as she vomited.

He left Joy sleeping more peacefully and went to see Iain. He was just leaving and they walked along the pea-green hospital corridors together.

'What a sensible woman your wife is, Simon. Asked all the right questions, didn't cry or go on like some of them do.' He glanced at him. 'She's very brave.'

'Yes. Yes, she is.'

'It's horrible for you both, I know.'

A patient fresh from theatre was pushed past them, the porters either end of the trolley exchanging banter. The patient was an old woman, tiny and frail as bird bones, curled on her side. Her face, even in her drugged state, looked anxious. The world was full of pain and he couldn't escape it, it was the life he'd chosen. He was sick of it, he wanted to say that he was sorry but he couldn't go on with it any more. He wanted to lie down for a long time and not think about anything. His leg hurt. He drew breath and exhaled heavily. This was self-pity; whenever he started taking notice of his leg he knew he was letting himself down.

They walked out into the hospital car park towards the *Doctors Only* spaces. Iain drove a Jaguar, brand new and red as fresh blood. Simon's hired car was parked beside it, a black Morris Minor. Iain laughed at it as he took his car keys from his pocket. 'Fancy one of these instead?'

He almost said that cars were the least of his worries. But he smiled and said, 'Thank you for taking such care of Joy.'

Iain slipped his keys back into his pocket. He stepped towards him and patted his arm. 'Listen, come over for supper tomorrow evening – I'd say tonight but Sarah's got tickets for the theatre. But tomorrow – seven-ish. Nothing as stiff as the other night – just the three of us and a spag bol or something, how about it?'

'Thanks, you're very kind, but do you mind if I don't? I'm rotten company, Iain, really.'

He smiled. 'You're not, but all right, it's an open invitation if you change your mind –' He got into his car.

'Cheerio. And don't worry about that lovely wife of yours. Everything went exactly as expected.'

Iain had two children. One was at Cambridge, the other about to have her first child. Iain was only a couple of years older than he was and in a few weeks he would be a grandfather. Simon waited until Iain had backed the Jag from its reserved space and driven away; he couldn't bear to tootle along after him in his laughable car. Iain was a nice man – more than that, he could imagine him as a friend and he had few enough of those, God knew. But at that moment he hated him, a jealous hatred that wanted him dead so he could take over his life, his sexy, warm wife and bright, successful children, even the grandchild, a baby not yet born.

He closed his eyes and rested his head against the steering wheel. He didn't want them, of course he didn't. He wanted what he'd lost. He wanted Joy to be as happy and excited as she'd been the day they packed up her Hampstead flat. He wanted the baby, *his* baby. No matter how much he tried to think of it as just a cluster of cells, he knew how badly he'd come to want it.

He sat up straight. He put the key in the ignition and started the engine. Ignoring the throbbing pain in his leg he shoved the car into gear and drove away.

Joan said, 'I was just about to send our Ray out to the chippie. How about you and the bairns stay and we'll all have a fish supper here? How about that?'

Annette hadn't needed to ask for money. Joan must have seen right through her and decided to save her the embarrassment. Feeling weak with gratitude she said, 'Are you sure?'

'Well aye. Bill and Frank have gone up to the fishing club so there'll be two less mouths to feed anyway. Sit down. Me and little Mr Clever Clogs here will butter some bread.' She ruffled Mark's hair. 'You going to help Aunty Joan, honey?'

Mark nodded shyly and was lifted up to sit on the table. Joan took out a loaf of *Mother's Pride* and a block of *Stork* margarine. She bellowed, 'Ray! Ray, get yourself down here!'

Annette saw Mark jump and his eyes widen with shock at the sudden loudness of Joan's voice. Joan noticed it too. She frowned at him sympathetically. 'Oh – did I scare you, pet? I'm sorry! Come here, let's give you a love.' She lifted him into her arms and jigged him up and down singing, 'He's got eyes of brown – I've never cared for eyes of brown – but he's got eyes of brown...' She paused, laughing as she kissed his forehead. 'And he's my baby now! There!' She sat him on the table again. 'You're handsome, aren't you? Good looks and brains – the girls'll be beating a path to your door, pet.'

Annette said, 'He's only a baby, Joan.'

Joan handed Mark a piece of bread and margarine. Her youngest son Ray appeared and she glanced at him, rooting in her apron pocket for her purse. 'Here, fish and chips five times. And get a bottle of pop for the bairns.' She smiled at Mark. 'We're having a party, aren't we, honey?'

When Ray had gone Joan said, 'Where's that husband of yours tonight, then?'

'I don't know.'

Joan snorted and her lips set in a thin, grim line.

Needing her to be jolly again Annette said brightly, 'I've got a new job – with that Doctor's son you were talking about in the pub, Doctor Walker. I'm cleaning there twice a week – good money too.'

'Money he's taken off you?'

Annette bowed her head, ashamed of how Danny robbed from her purse. At least she'd managed to pay the rent with the money Doctor Walker had given her, although there was nothing left for anything else.

135

Joan set a slice of bread in front of her. 'What's he like, then, Doctor Walker?'

'Nice.' She thought of the way he'd walked her to the end of his drive that morning, how he'd stood watching her cross the road and how he was still there when she looked back. He was worried about her. She wasn't sure if that made her feel safe or more frightened.

Remembering the books he'd given her she said, 'He let me have a couple of his old books for Mark.'

'*Very* generous.'

'No – it was! It was kind of him…'

Joan sighed. 'Don't let him take advantage of you like all the other buggers you work for.'

'He wouldn't.'

'Oh?' Joan looked at her quizzically. 'Too *kind* is he? Aye well, maybe. His dad was kind. He delivered our Ray that terrible winter of '48 – the snow was piling up in the streets but he still came, I'll never forget – he says to me, "Just call me Eskimo Nell." Mind, I wasn't in any state for laughing. Eat your bread. You look half famished.'

Ray came back with a newspaper parcel under one arm and Ben under the other. The boy, thick set and as powerful looking as his mother, said, 'Look at the monkey I found in the street!'

He set Ben down and immediately began to tickle him. Mark watched, his eyes wide as if he was deciding whether he should be frightened or not. Ray set the parcel beside him on the table and ruffled his hair. 'Hiya! You finished that War and Peace yet?'

'Leave him be. Now, let's not bother with plates. Up you get, Mark. You can sit on your Aunty Joan's knee.'

The parcel was unwrapped and its released heat filled the kitchen with a smell that made Annette's mouth water. Sitting down Ray said, 'I asked for scraps.' He winked at Ben, who grinned happily, showing off the gaps where his baby teeth had fallen out. Sometimes she forgot how little

136

he was, he was always so serious and sensible, so protective of Mark that it seemed sometimes he was the grown up and she was the child. He had become her confidant and true ally, never judging her as Joan did. She smiled at him and his grin melted away as though she reminded him of trouble. She felt as if she'd been slapped in the face and she hung her head, her appetite gone.

Later they all watched Joan's telly, Mark asleep against Joan's breast. She looked at Annette while stroking his hair. 'Stay here with me tonight, the three of you. In the morning we can go down the council and ask if they could re-house you and the kids –'

'I couldn't!'

'Couldn't what – ask for a safe place for your bairns? Look at this!' She lifted Mark's limp arm and pointed at a chain of bruises. 'You said yourself – he's a baby. He's just a baby and he doesn't deserve what that bastard's doing to him!'

'It isn't so bad, not really...'

'No? Sounds like he's killing him some nights!' She lowered her voice as Ben turned to look at her. 'Listen, you could stay here and if he comes anywhere near, my lads will knock him into the middle of next week.'

'No, Joan – we'll be all right. I don't want any trouble.'

'You've got trouble now! What more trouble could there be? He could kill this baby – then you'd know bloody *trouble*!'

'We should go home.' She got up and lifted Mark from Joan's arms. 'Thanks for the fish and chips.'

'Are you going to leave the rotten sod?'

'How could I? He'd only find us...it would be worse then, you don't know him.'

'Oh, I know him, all right.' She sighed and pushed herself up from the sagging settee. 'Come on, Ben, pet. Let's see if I've got some sweeties for you before you go.'

137

*   *   *

Danny didn't come home that night. In the morning Annette found him sitting at the kitchen table, his head in his hands. He looked up at her and his eyes were bleary and red rimmed; he stank of beer and cigarettes and dirty houses. He caught her hand as she brushed past him to put the kettle on.

'You not speaking to me?'

'Course I am!'

'*Course you are*!' He took out a packet of cigarettes. Finding it empty he tossed it down on the table. 'Got any money?'

'No, sorry –'

'No secret stash? You sure?'

'Where would I get money from?'

'You could try opening your legs for it.'

'Danny, don't talk like that.'

'Don't lie to me, then.'

'I'm not lying. Honestly.'

'Should I go and have a look around?' He smiled at her. 'Now, where – if *I* were *you* – would I hide a bit of cash?'

'Nowhere.'

He snorted. 'All right. I can't be bothered with you now. Where's Ben? Where's my lad?'

'He's getting ready for school.'

'What about that little bastard of yours? Where's he hiding?'

'Danny, please, please leave him alone. I don't know why you have to be so hard on him…'

'Oh – are you all worried about him now? All – *Oh please don't hurt him, Danny! He's only little, Danny!* Look at your face – fucking petrified. My mother used to hold us down when my father gave us a hiding, she didn't whinge and moan on like you! In fact – yes, that's what you'll do –

138

next time he needs disciplining you can hold on to him and keep him still!'

'No, I won't. You won't hurt him, I won't let you.'

He laughed. 'Oh, go on. Let me. You always have up to now.'

She felt her face flush with shame and anger. Danny reached up and touched her cheek with one finger. He made a hissing sound like spit on a hot iron.

'Annette. Some bloody mother you are, aren't you? I wonder what Ben thinks of you – should we ask him? I bet he thinks you're worse than fucking useless.'

She closed her eyes and tears spilled down her cheeks. Danny wiped them away with his thumb. 'Do you want to ask me where I've been all night?'

It felt like a trick question. Too scared to say the wrong thing she said nothing and he squeezed her hand hard.

'You can ask. I won't bite your head off.'

'Where –' She cleared her throat to try to rid her voice of tears. 'Where have you been?'

'With another woman. She's pregnant with my kid. Her name's Anne-Marie. *Anne-Marie* and *Annette*.' He grinned. 'I quite like the sound of your two names together.' He stood up suddenly. For once he ignored the way she flinched away from him and he smiled at her. 'It's all right – I'm not going to leave you and Ben. I thought she could move in here.'

Her legs felt weak and she leaned against the table. 'Danny, don't say things like that.'

'No. Action not words, eh?' He laughed. 'Honestly, you should see yourself. You believe every word I say, don't you? Quite gratifying if it wasn't so fucking infuriating. I'm going to work. We'll discuss Mark when I get back. Don't think I've forgotten about him.'

She sank down on a chair. Upstairs Ben and Mark were getting dressed for school but she was shaking too much to go and see to them. After a while Ben came down. He sat beside her, her dogged little ally. She made herself smile at him. 'All ready for school?'

He nodded. After a moment, reluctantly, he said, 'I'm hungry.'

'I know. But you can have your milk at school – that'll be nice, won't it?' She got up, wiping her eyes quickly although he always knew when she'd been crying. Brightly she said, 'Is Mark ready?'

'I hate Mark.'

'No you don't!'

Unnoticed by either of them Mark had come downstairs. He gazed at them both from the doorway. After a moment Ben got down from his chair and went to him. He took Mark's hand. 'Come on,' he said, 'we have to go to school now.' Glancing at her he said, 'You can stay here, if you like, we can go on our own.'

Chapter 13

Simon said, 'I've taken on a girl – to clean the house ready for when you come home.'

Joy nodded. She was sitting up in bed, a blue bed-jacket draped around her shoulders, the pearly buttons of her white nightdress fastened to her throat. A nurse had washed her hair and it fell softly around her shoulders, less severe than when Joy was in sole control of its styling. He smiled at her. 'I like your hair like that.'

Two pink spots appeared on her cheeks, the first colour she'd had since her miscarriage. Taking her hand, he squeezed it gently. 'You're making good progress – Iain's really pleased with you.'

She drew her hand away from his. 'He's a nice man.'

'Yes, he is. And he and his wife Sarah have invited us both over for dinner as soon as you're well enough. Which will be soon. You'll be fit as a flea in no time.'

'A flea.' She snorted dismissively. 'A *flea*!'

She'd barely glanced at him since he'd arrived. The flowers and chocolates he'd bought her, the get-well cards from her friends in London, all were ignored beside her on the bed. Buying the chocolates, he'd realised he didn't know which type she preferred and so he had bought *Quality Street*, a mix, a compromise. Her nostrils had flared in contempt when she saw the box with its soldier and crinolined girl.

He cleared his throat. 'Is there anything you need? Anything else I can get you from the shops, or from home?'

'No. Thank you.'

He sighed, 'Joy –'

'What?' She looked at him with such hatred he was shocked. He looked away but felt the weight of her gaze.

She said, 'I had a letter from Doctor King. He said I could have my old job back any time. Any time at all.'

He frowned at her. 'Why should he offer you your job back?'

'Because yesterday morning I telephoned and asked him. He told me on the phone he'd be delighted to have me back. He very kindly wrote to me, too, reiterating the offer. A very nice letter which I received this morning. He was always very prompt.'

'Is that what you want to do? Go back to London?'

'It's an option.'

Matching her matter-of-fact tone with a coldness he didn't feel he said, 'And what are the other options?'

'One would be to go back to Stoke. My mother's quite frail now. I could go home to Stoke and care for her. Perhaps get a part-time job – I still have some contacts there and friends who would help me.' Her hands clenched and unclenched on the hospital counterpane. He reached out and covered them with his own. Again she drew away. 'Please stop touching me, Simon.'

After a while she said, 'Actually I've thought of emigrating. My sister lives in Toronto. She's always been very keen for me to go out there, too.'

Anger rose inside him. Too loudly he said, 'For goodness' sake, Joy! What else? What else can you think of to say to hurt me?'

She looked at him astonished. 'Me hurt you? Is that possible, do you think?'

'Of course it is! You're my wife! I don't want you to leave me!'

'Keep your voice down.' She glanced along the ward as if checking to see if any of her fellow patients had reacted to his outburst. Turning to him again she said, 'Simon, I over heard two nurses talking about you. They called you the *dishy* new doctor. Of course, they didn't realise that I was the *dishy* new doctor's wife. I'm sure they wouldn't dream that someone like me was married to you.'

'Why wouldn't they? Who the hell am I? *Dishy*!' He spat the word out in contempt. 'What are you talking about?'

'About how others see us – ill-matched. Unsuited. Ridiculous. I'm ridiculous.'

'This is self-pity, Joy. It's really too far beneath you.'

'Nothing is too far beneath me now. You've reduced *me* to nothing. I am alone without a job or friends in a town I'd never heard of before I married you. I've lost everything. And that is not self-pity, that is fact. I have to face facts.'

'You could face the fact that you're married to me. For better or for worse. That's what you promised me and that's what I promised you!'

He couldn't remember feeling so angry. It was such an unexpected emotion he got up, wanting to find some physical out let for this rage, making him forget about his leg so that he put too much weight on it too quickly. The pain was a sharp reminder, and he closed his eyes, clenching his jaw against it. He sat down again, feeling idiotic.

She said, 'You've gone white.'

'Of course I've gone bloody white!' He opened his eyes to look at her. 'I've never sworn in front of a woman before, Joy. So, are you satisfied?'

She turned away. 'Just go, Simon. Please, just go.'

'No. I'm not going. I won't be treated as though none of this affects me! *I* had a life in London, too, Joy! A life I can't go back to as easily as it seems you can go back to yours. And *I'm* miserable and sad. Believe it or not, I am.'

She remained silent, kept her head turned away so that she reminded him of a stubborn infant refusing the last of its dinner. Her lip trembled.

More quietly he said, 'I want you to stay. I want us to mourn our baby together and I want us to help each other come to terms with what's happened. Please don't tear another big hole in my life, Joy. I don't think I could bear it.'

'But can't you see we're not right for each other?'

'Aren't we? Perhaps we are...' He shook his head as if he could clear his muddled thoughts. 'Perhaps in time...'

She cut in, her voice shrill with misery. 'In time? In time what? Will we look at each other and see what a waste of our lives our marriage has been? Is that what *time* holds for us?'

'Oh, this is nonsense! I can't see the future, Joy!'

'I can – it seems so obvious: the two of us stuck in a loveless, childless marriage! What is there that might hold us together? Nothing! There's nothing to build on...'

She began to cry and he watched her helplessly. Desperate to say something that might comfort her he said, 'Joy, we have each other.'

'I'm not the woman you want to be married to! You want someone young and pretty like that little nurse you can't help but look at!'

'That's not true!'

She glared at him. Taking a handkerchief from her sleeve she wiped her eyes impatiently and blew her nose. A little more composed she said, 'I have been a fool. This is a foolish mess I have to clear up, that's all there is to it.'

'You're writing me off as a foolish mess? Our marriage *a foolish mess*? Well I don't think it is!' He felt even angrier and knew it was because she suspected him of being the kind of silly, insubstantial man he knew himself to be. Wanting only to prove her wrong he said heatedly, 'You mean more to me than you think – ever since our first evening together you've been in my thoughts – I don't think anyone has ever preoccupied me so much.'

She avoided his gaze but he saw something in her expression change, a kind of doubt in her convictions he seized on. He took her hand and held it tightly. 'Joy, do you really think I would have asked you to marry me if I didn't feel something for you?'

Without looking at him she said, '*Something*, though. Not love.'

He sighed. Facing defeat he said, 'If I'm honest I don't think I've ever loved anyone.'

'Except Grace.'

He had told her about Grace during their first date. He had talked about her briefly, lightly, as though she was a part of his past as incidental as the first hospital he'd worked in. He hadn't told Joy how much he still thought about Grace, or that his dreams were still full of her so that when he woke he felt newly bereaved. Perhaps all of that had shown in his face, perhaps she'd heard it in the softening of his voice. Even now he felt something inside him contract at the thought of his loss. He hung his ahead, ashamed to meet his new wife's eye.

After a while Joy said, 'It's all right that you loved her, you shouldn't deny it.'

He kept his gaze on the hospital's tiled floor. He said, 'We were so young, the war put its mark on everything –'

'But you *loved* her.' Quickly she said, 'I loved a man during the war. I wasn't as innocent as you think.'

'I never thought you were…'

'Yes. You did. I know what you thought, Simon, what everyone thought. Well maybe everyone was right – I should have stayed unmarried, a spinster, an old maid, keeping my sad little secret, pining for a dead man.' She plucked at the counterpane, folding a fan of creases in the cloth. He noticed how thin her wedding ring was and felt shocked by the meanness of it. He remembered how hastily it had been bought and was overcome by a new sense of shame.

Covering her fidgeting hand with his own he said, 'I only ever thought how lovely you were…'

She laughed harshly and drew her hand out from under his.

There was an uneasy silence between them. Around other beds visitors spoke in low, hospital voices. Outside in the corridor a trolley rattled past and a man laughed and Simon glanced toward the ward's swing doors as though laughter was the most astonishing noise in the world. He turned back to Joy and found her watching him. He smiled crookedly. 'I suppose he must have told you how lovely you are?'

Holding his gaze challengingly she asked, 'Who?'

'The man you loved during the war.'

She looked down at the fan of creases she'd made and smoothed them out. 'I can't remember.'

'Was he in the army? Air force?'

'Army. He was a Captain.' After a while she said, 'His name was Peter and the Japanese murdered him'

Simon remembered the newsreels he'd seen of the liberation of the Japanese camps, the skin-and-bone men in ragged loincloths who staggered towards the camera; they barely looked human, still less like British soldiers. He remembered thinking how foreign they seemed, as though no English man could ever be reduced to such a pitiable state. He thought of this Peter, his wife's one time lover; no doubt he had been kind, ordinary, like any one of the officers he himself had served with. He thought of how much this man must have suffered, and he thought of all the pain and suffering there had been in the world and was yet to come and knew that for the first time in his life such thoughts could unhinge him.

Joy picked up the box of chocolates and turned it over and over, her eyes fixed on it. 'I do *like* you, Simon. When I met you I thought that you were funny, perhaps too frivolous – but that was good, I knew there would be no hard feelings on either side when we'd both had what we wanted from each other. I knew I wouldn't feel embarrassed when I passed you in the hospital corridor because it would have all been just fun to you. And I wanted some fun. I wanted to feel that my life hadn't just been a weekend in 1940.' She laid the *Quality Street* box down on her lap and her hands became still. At last she looked up at him. 'Look where fun has got us, eh?'

'I'd do anything to turn the clock back.'

'To when? Before we went to bed together?'

'No!' He frowned at her. 'To before we got on that train…if I could have saved our baby…' Overcome by grief he covered his face with his hands. Unable to help himself he saw dead foetuses, all the would-be babies whose remains he had dealt with so clinically. Just like those babies, his would have been afforded no more respect than surgical waste.

Gently Joy said, 'Are you crying, Simon?'

He wiped his eyes quickly. 'I'm sorry.'

'Don't be.'

'No – I should be strong for you…'

She held his hand as he cried. At last he drew his hand away and fumbled in his pocket for his handkerchief. He attempted to laugh, heard it as it was, a harsh, hollow noise. Wiping his eyes he said, 'The other week I found myself looking in a toyshop window at a rocking horse. Almost bought the thing! But you know what was really foolish? I didn't buy it because I thought it was tempting fate! As if we have any control over our destinies, as if we can make any difference to anything! You know – looking in that toyshop window was the first time I've felt truly happy for years? And I didn't even realise it!' He met her gaze. 'Joy, please don't think of leaving me. You're the only person since Grace that has made me believe my life is worth anything. I don't want to return to being that idiotic man you met.'

For a while she said nothing, only held his hand, her eyes searching his. At last she said, 'My heart's broken, Simon. I don't know what I can offer you...it's so painful...I never guessed I could feel like this. I can't imagine it getting any better.'

'It will. In time, it will...' He wiped the fresh tears from her eyes. 'Joy...my poor girl...'

A nurse came, the pretty, blonde nurse who smiled at him so readily. She said, 'Oh now Mrs Walker – not more water-works!' She looked at him sympathetically. 'She was being so brave this morning when I was doing her hair.'

Joy sat up straighter. 'I'm fine, really.' She busied herself opening the box of chocolates and thrust it out to the nurse, who smiled, taking her time in choosing. When she'd gone Joy said, 'Why don't you tell me about this girl you've taken on.'

He thought about Annette, her fragility, and wondered how he might describe her to Joy in a way that made any sense. Making himself smile, he said, 'Her name is Annette, she's quite a timid little thing really. But she works hard – she's very diligent. I bought her a Hoover – bought *us* a Hoover. I don't think Mum even had a duster in the house.' After a moment he said, 'The house needs you to knock it into shape, Joy. The garden, too. The garden is like something from a Grimm fairy tale – I half expect the trees to start talking.'

She laughed. 'The daffodils you brought me were lovely. Are there flower beds?'

'Probably, beneath the weeds.'

She unwrapped a toffee penny. 'I'm looking forward to seeing it.' She handed him the opened box. As he took it she said, 'Annette – is she very young?'

'Quite...' Hastily he said, 'Although she's married, she has children.'

'And yet she works?'

'Yes, the little boys are at school.' After a while he said, 'I gave her some books – books I'd had as a child – to give to her children.' It sounded like a confession and he took his time choosing a sweet, knowing that Joy was watching him, waiting for him to give more of himself away. At last he looked up. 'I think they're very poor. I felt rather sorry for them, for her and her boys.'

'Perhaps they would like to come and play in the garden whilst their mother is working – perhaps during the school holidays.'

'Let's get you well first, eh?'

Later, as he drove home, he thought of Annette's children playing in his garden. He thought too of Annette, of how she seemed so hopeless. She reinforced the feeling he had that he was powerless to help anyone. Stopping at traffic lights he closed his eyes and breathed in deeply. 'Self pity,' he said aloud. Behind him a car horn sounded and he realised the lights had changed from red to green.

Chapter 14

I saw Mark in the hospital corridor. He was buying a drink from one of the vending machines, his head bowed, palm flat against the machine's front, his body braced as he waited for the plastic beaker to fill. He was wearing the same clothes he'd worn the night before and his hair stuck up a bit like he'd been pushing his fingers through it. He needed a shave; his five o'clock shadow made him look effete, like he was trying too hard for a certain look. I guessed he'd been up all night – he had that expression you see so often in hospitals if you work on the early shift. I thought how I would like to stand close to him and breathe in his scent, his true scent, unadulterated by soap or deodorant or after-shave. I wondered if he would smell of us, if I would recognise him by his scent alone. I stared at him as he took his drink and sipped it, wary of the scalding liquid. I stared until he looked up and noticed me. I smiled and stepped forward. Instinctively, I think, he stepped back. I smiled some more and held up my hands in that placating gesture I was beginning to perfect.

'Hello, Mark.'

He looked over his shoulder as if assessing the best escape route. He turned back to me. 'You work here. I'd forgotten.'

I could see how desperate he was to go. I could see that his eyes looked bleary like he'd been crying. His shirt was crumpled and there were sweat stains under his arms. I stepped closer and breathed through my nose. There was only the hospital stink and the smell of his black coffee. He lifted the cup to his lips and sipped again.

I said, 'The coffee from those machines is horrible, isn't it?'

'Would you excuse me?' He turned away only to turn back as though he'd just thought of something clever to say. Only it wasn't clever, it was horrible. Intently he said, 'You stay away from me, do you hear? I can't stand the sight of you and I don't want anything to do with you or your family. Is that quite clear? Have I made myself understood?'

My guts loosened, that humiliating feeling I used to get when Danny raised his voice. I found myself glancing away, a fixed, defensive smile on my face, shameful and pathetic. He stepped toward me. Lowering his voice he said, 'Why are you smirking? Do you think this is amusing in some way?'

I managed to look at him. 'I'm sorry, I'm not smirking; it's not funny. I'm sorry.' I could hear the cringe in my voice, all those creeping apologies reminding me of when I was a kid and I couldn't say sorry often enough. My lip curled involuntarily; I was disgusted with myself, my cowardly ways. I tried standing straighter as he looked me up and down.

He said, 'Did you know I was here?'

'How could I know?'

'You could have checked the admissions.'

'Why should I do that?'

'I don't know. All I know is that you're here, spying on me.'

'I wasn't spying.'

'No? You stare. Is there something wrong with you?'

'No! I'm sorry if I was staring – I didn't mean to, I didn't think I was…'

He gave this odd, harsh laugh. 'Jesus Christ. Did Ben put you up to this?'

151

'Up to what? I work here. I don't have to have an excuse –'

Sister Reeves came along. She grinned at me, then did a double take when she saw Mark, this puzzled expression on her face, hesitating for a moment as if waiting for an introduction. I said, 'This is Mark Walker, sister. The novelist.'

She looked blank, only to smile. 'Hello. Sorry – I never have a moment to read books. Steve, are you here to fetch Mr Sanderson?'

'I'll be right, there, Sister.'

When she'd gone Mark said, 'At least you didn't introduce me as your brother.'

'Well you're not, not really. Besides, I didn't think you'd want me to.'

'You're very perceptive.' His voice was thick with sarcasm; he held up the plastic cup in a little salute. 'I appreciate your thoughtfulness.'

I should have told him to piss off. I said, 'I have to go.'

As I stepped past him he caught my arm. 'How's Danny?'

'The same.' I shrugged him off.

'Don't mention me to him, do you understand?'

'Yes, although he knows all about you. He reads your books –'

'The books aren't about *me*! He doesn't know *anything* about me!'

I wouldn't have thought him capable of such anger. A thread of spittle hung from his mouth and he wiped it away with the back of his hand. He grasped my arm again, bringing his face up close to mine, his rage so animating he looked like one of the patients on the locked wards. I drew away, repelled by the sleepless stink of his breath, but he tightened his grip, jerking me towards him. 'Listen to me, you little shit, you can tell him from me I wish him dead. I wish he were burning in hell already with all the worst punishments reserved just for him. Tell him that!'

'You should tell him yourself, because I won't. I've already told him.'

He gazed at me, his beautiful eyes searching my face as though he couldn't believe what I'd just said or decide whose side I was on. He let his hand fall to his side and stepped back, and it seemed all that energy drained from him as quickly as it came. I noticed how pale he looked, how sick at heart. There was a row of plastic chairs by the vending machine and I took his arm and made him sit down. I sat beside him. I said, 'Drink your coffee. Try and be calm. Sometimes it helps if you picture yourself in a place you've been really happy.'

He made a noise somewhere between a laugh and a sob.

'I used to picture myself on Scarborough beach,' I said. 'My uncles took us there once. I imagine myself on Scarborough beach or in the maternity ward across the way, the day my daughter was born.'

'You have a child?' He seemed to force himself to look at me, his curiosity and surprise seemingly making him forget himself for a moment – like he was a little kid who had been told something astonishing in the middle of a tantrum. He must want kids, I thought, or be obsessed with them in some way. But of course he was, because so was I.

I said, 'Her name is Jade – she's nearly three. She's lovely, bright as anything.'

'You're very young to be a father.'

'Aye, that's what Mam said: *You're too bloody young to be saddled.*' I glanced at him from the corner of my eye. 'I'm twenty-two.'

He nodded. Quickly he said, 'I'm keeping you from your work.'

'It's all right. Besides, they won't be ready for Mr Sanderson yet, I'll give him a few more minutes in the comfort of his bed.'

153

After a while he said, 'You really said that to him? That you wished him dead?'

'Aye well. It was a while ago, now.'

'But you meant it?'

I glanced away, embarrassed by the way he seemed so desperate for me to tell him how much I hated Danny. Lately I'd been trying not to hate him so much; I was still hoping that I could come to some kind of peace with him, although so far I hadn't been very successful. I knew it would be harder still now that I'd met Mark.

I turned to him. 'He's really sick – dead ill. I think now I just want it to be over.'

'Yes.' He exhaled. 'Yes, so do I.' Looking down at his coffee he said, 'I didn't intend to be so rude to you.'

'It's all right, I understand.'

'No…Steven, I should have told Ben I didn't want to know about…well, about anything he discovered. Last night I didn't expect you.'

I remembered that look of shock on his face when he saw me, how it had intensified my own nervousness. I'd felt guilty for frightening him, for resembling Danny so much. But he looked like him, too. He shocked me in his turn.

I said, 'I've always known about you – ever since I can remember.'

He looked at me sharply. 'He talked about me?'

'Yeah.' I couldn't meet his eye. There was a poster on the wall opposite demanding that visitors washed their hands. A kid had drawn a smiley face on its corner, the kind of face they draw when they're asked to crayon a picture of their Mam, all yellow hair and blue, spider-lashed eyes, some bored kid, waiting in this corridor for their real Mam to finish her visit.

I felt Mark's eyes on me. Turning to him I managed to smile. 'I have to get to work.' As I made to stand up he touched my arm.

'Steven, listen, I *am* sorry.'

154

'Don't be. I understand.' I wanted to say, "*I know what you've been through – me and you – we're the same person.*" Instead I stood up and smiled, repeating, 'Honestly, don't be sorry. You don't have to be sorry with me.'

'Why not?'

I shrugged. 'I understand.'

'You keep saying that.'

'It's true.'

He looked down at his coffee. 'You *understand*, eh?' He glanced at me. 'Would you talk to me – without Ben? Ben wouldn't have to know.' He took a business card from his wallet and handed it to me. 'My mobile number's on there. Here.' He took the card from me again. Taking a pen from his jacket pocket he scribbled an address on its reverse. As I took it from him he asked, 'Do you know where that is?'

'Opposite the cemetery, on Oxhill Avenue.'

He nodded. 'I'll be there tonight. About eight.'

I shoved the card into my pocket and he stood up. Without another word he turned and walked away.

Mark sat down beside Simon's bed, cradling his hand between his own. 'Dad, I'm going home now. I'll be back this afternoon. Would you like me to bring you anything special?'

'Only the things we talked about.' Simon drew his hand away. 'Go. Get some sleep. You look exhausted.'

'Can I get you anything before I go?'

'No. Mark, don't fuss. Bad enough you got Ben out of bed –'

'He needed to know.'

Simon closed his eyes wearily.

From the other side of the bed Ben said, 'Dad, I shall go too.'

Simon turned to him. 'Will you be fit enough to operate? You've had no sleep –'

155

'I'm taking the day off.'

'Oh no – I don't want you to let patients down because of me! It's too bad Mark worried you like this!'

Ben laughed. He kissed Simon's forehead. 'I'm not indispensable, Dad. Besides, you come first.'

'Rubbish. This is too bad.'

Ben turned to Mark. 'You want a lift home?'

'Thanks.'

Ben kissed Simon again and squeezed his hand briefly. 'OK. We're going. I'll be back tonight.'

'Bring Nathan.'

'Yes.'

'I want to see him, Ben. Please.'

'I said yes, didn't I?' He smiled. 'You should try and sleep now.'

Ben drove, his mouth set in a thin, angry line, his hands tight around the wheel. Another driver cut him up and he blasted his horn long and hard. 'Stupid wanker! Jesus! Can you believe how many wankers there are in the world?' He switched off the radio that had come on automatically when he'd stared the engine. Glaring at Mark he said, 'Why don't you say something? For once in your life why don't you make a fucking effort at conversation?'

'I'm not in the mood for small talk, Ben.'

'Small talk! Fucking hell! You say what's on your mind! You say what we're both thinking!'

Mark looked out of the car window at the familiar streets. This was home, once. He felt disconnected from it, as though it represented someone else's childhood. How quickly he had got away, as quickly as he could, aged seventeen, off to training camp, never to return. Except here he was. He should have stayed in London. Ben slammed on the car's brakes, jolting him forward. In front of them at the traffic lights was a lorry on its way to Thorp Road abattoir. The legs of calves were visible through the lorry's slatted sides and he imagined how fearful the creatures would be. He bowed his head, wishing he were far away. Far away and senseless, not having to think or feel or imagine anything.

Loudly Ben said, 'I want you to say what's on your mind!'

He looked at him. 'I'm thinking that if it hadn't been for Argentina wanting the Falklands I would have been sent to Northern Ireland.' He looked at Ben. 'Do you remember the picture of the tarred and feathered Irish girl the Gazette published? I must have been about eight. It was the first time I'd heard of *The Troubles*. The IRA tarred and feathered women and tied them to lampposts. I remember feeling sick with shock.'

The lights turned from red to amber to green and Ben shoved the car into gear and moved off, too close to the slaughter house lorry's tail. Bitterly he said, 'I don't remember that. I'm not obsessed with war and pain and suffering like you are.'

'I was also thinking about a man I did my basic training with. He was killed last year – a skiing accident. I heard about his death quite by chance – ran into a mutual friend on the Heath. I was thinking how precarious life is and that perhaps I should have taken up skiing – killed myself by sliding into a tree, or falling over a ravine – however skiers die.' He glanced at him. 'Ben, do you blame me for Dad's heart attack?'

'You know I blame myself!' Another red light and Ben pulled on the handbrake. Angrily he said, 'It's me he's upset with –'

Mark laughed shortly, thinking of Simon's anger with him. 'He's not upset with you, Ben. Maybe concerned for you, that's all –'

'Concern – upset, it still adds up to stress, to a heart attack.'

157

Gently Mark said, 'The lights have changed, Ben. Look, why don't you pull over? I'll drive…'

'No! I'm fine.' He exhaled. 'If you hadn't been there, at the house, he might have died.'

'Iain was with him, too.'

'But if he'd been on his own —'

'He wasn't.'

'He should live with us, with Kitty and me. He's so stubbornly independent.'

'That's good, isn't it? Wouldn't you want to be like him at his age?'

Ben looked at him sharply. 'But we won't be like him, will we? We've got Danny's genes in us, Annette's. Do you know how old our real grandparents were when they died? They were young. And Danny — Danny's only in his sixties.'

'I didn't tell Dad what you told me last night.'

'No?' He sounded surprised.

'Did you think I would tell him?'

'Maybe.' He took his eyes off the road to look at him. 'Maybe I thought you'd tell him to win some favour. I know you think I'm his favourite.'

'You *are* his favourite, Ben. I don't mind. It's natural, I think, to like one person more than another, to have an affinity with them.'

'But parents should try to be more even-handed. If I have another child —' He sighed. 'He did his best. He did more than most men would have. Taking us on — Christ! Who in their right mind?'

Mark remembered how Simon had sat them both down in the garden of the last Children's Home, a scruffy, overgrown garden that none of the Home's staff had time to care about. He remembered that dandelions grew everywhere and that he'd picked one and crushed its fat stem between his fingers, tasting its wet-the-bed bitterness as Simon told them how they would be coming to live with him. 'Would you like that, boys?' He'd smiled, seemed desperate. 'I have a lovely, big old house with a great big garden...' He'd looked around, at the long grass, the broken crazy paving and rusting swing no one ever played on. Suddenly he put an arm around each of them and hugged them to him. 'We'll be so happy. I know we will!' Ben had squirmed away from him, but he had allowed himself to he held, afraid of offending this great big unhappy man. He had know Simon a few months by then and was nowhere nearer understanding who he was, or why he seemed so intent on being part of his life, although he had his suspicions.

Ben pulled up outside Simon's house. He turned to him. 'You go and see him this afternoon, and I'll go tonight, with Kit and Nathan.'

'Yes.'

Ben sighed heavily. 'OK. Try and get some sleep – you look awful.'

Mark watched Ben drive away. He thought of himself at six years old, of Simon, still vigorous and strong in early middle age. He wondered how a man could love a child who was so wary of him, who suspected the very worst of him, the most vile and disgusting suspicions. A man couldn't love such a child, of course, despite his protestations.

Looking up at the house he'd been brought to aged six, Mark remembered how Simon had shown him around, his voice loud and hearty, smiling. He had noticed that it was a house full of hiding places and had felt comforted by this, but Simon had crouched down in front of him and his voice became quieter and edged with concern. 'Mark? You know if you're worried about anything – *anything* at all – you can talk to me about it and I can help? You know that, don't you?'

But all he had known was that he could never talk to this man who knew him inside and out, that there was nothing to say that he didn't already know. He had wondered only

159

how this Simon-Daddy might act on his knowledge, the ideas it might give him. He'd had his own idea that he was worthless, like a shop-soiled toy; nobody would think that it would matter very much if he was damaged a bit more.

Mark let himself into the house. Climbing the stairs to bed, he thought of Steven, remembering how he had looked at him, such understanding in that look, such knowing. He lay down on his bed. He thought of Steven's knowingness and unzipped his fly, hesitating only a moment before closing his hand around his semi-erect cock.

Simon slept. He dreamt that Mark and Ben were children. He dreamt that Annette had visited him, holding her boys' hands. She asked him if they'd been any trouble. He'd been about to speak when a voice said, 'Simon. Simon? Come on now…Dear oh dear, this is no good at all! Getting all upset!'

The black nurse smiled at him. She said, 'Do you remember where you are?'

He wiped his eyes with his fingers. 'Yes. I'm not senile.'

'No, but sometimes people get confused after a heart attack.'

'No, they don't. Don't make excuses.'

'All right. I need to do some checks on you. See how you're going along.'

When she'd finished she said, 'So you're Mr Walker's father, eh? I bet you're proud of him and his brother – such handsome boys!'

'*Boys*!'

She laughed. 'Oh they're boys to me! I could be their mother.'

'You're too young.'

'Flattery will get you everywhere!'

He squinted at her, wanting to see her better. 'How old are you?'

160

'Now what kind of question is that?' She leaned close to him. In a stage whisper she said, 'Fifty-four. Now look surprised.'

'Too young. Annette would have been sixty-one this year.'

'When did she pass away?'

He pretended not to hear. 'Am I to be fed?'

'You hungry? I'll go and see what I can rustle up.'

Alone, he thought about Iain, who had been his friend for almost forty years, and had become as he imagined a brother might be, brothers who'd had the right start of course, who had been ordinarily loved.

He remembered Iain saying, 'You must be out of your mind! Simon – do you realise how damaged those children are? Especially Mark! Think about Joy – it's Joy who will have all the responsibility, all the heartbreak of it. My God, I can't believe you're even considering such madness!'

Iain, dressed in shorts and turning sausages on a barbecue while his wife Sarah wafted in and out of their glass and steel house with beers for their son's university friends. Iain, whose daughter held her baby and laughed as her husband kicked a ball about on the lawn, calling out goal! as he tackled his brother-in-law. Iain, who had all this, cursed as he bit into a too-hot sausage and frowned at him. 'Simon, have you even talked about this with Joy? Don't you think that after all she's been through –'

'Don't lecture me on what my wife has been through!'

'Perhaps you should be lectured! Perhaps you should have your head examined!'

'Those little boys need me, Iain.'

'They need specialist care – not well-intentioned middle-aged surgeons who have never had children and are too wrecked by guilt to think straight!' Impatiently he added, 'I'm sorry. But that's the truth.'

Sarah came over in her long, floaty dress printed with abstract flowers. She said, 'I'm so sorry Joy didn't feel well enough to be here.'

Iain said sharply, 'Tell Sarah what you're thinking of. She'll tell you the same as me.'

But Sarah had listened to him in her kitchen with its window looking out over the youngsters on the lawn and said, 'All children need loving homes.'

Simon touched the monitor pads on his chest. When the pains came Mark had behaved well – he had to give him that. He didn't panic, didn't fuss. He carried him to his bed, where the sheets were still warm from his body, and laid him down, reassuring him, his voice calm and steady. He remembered thinking how strong this man was, and being surprised. It wasn't so long ago that he carried Mark in his arms, a frail child, so timid it was hard not to be repelled because timidity had always discomforted him. To his shame, Simon was afraid of mice, of creatures that scuttled away.

Mark had taken his mobile phone from the bedside table and called an ambulance. Then he'd gone downstairs and fetched Iain. If he had to die in front of any one he was glad that it was Iain. Iain was used to death, he would comfort Mark. But Iain had looked afraid and he remembered that, just as Mark was older, Iain was too, and that death had regained its potency for him. And so he had tried to smile at his friend and say, 'I'm all right. Mark is fussing.'

And the chatty young ambulance man had said, 'You're both doctors! Well – I can't be telling you two anything, can I?'

And the pain was worse than he remembered any pain before. And he couldn't help telling Iain he was scared when Mark went downstairs to show the ambulance crew in. Later, as they carried him to the ambulance with its lights casting alarming shadows on the road, Mark called

162

Ben, although he'd told him not to, what would be the point? 'The point is he's your son,' Iain had said.

On Mark's eighteenth birthday, Iain had given him a first edition of some book of poetry or other. He remembered that Mark could hardly bring himself to look at it, that Joy had to remind him to thank Iain. Which he did, of course, in that terrible, stilted way he had when he was embarrassed. Mark and Iain had never got on, and he understood why. Besides, Iain always felt uncomfortable around such introverted people.

On Mark's eighth birthday, watching the other children run around as Mark sat alone and ignored, Iain had said, 'Do you think he may be autistic?'

Simon wondered where that black nurse had got to. She had smelt of Camay soap and it had reminded him of Joy: Joy tucked up in bed after her bath, a novel open on her lap, the news half-listened to on the clock-radio. And once, during the Falklands war, listening to the announcement that the Sir Galahad had been sunk, she had said, 'Oh Lord, Simon. I can't stand it! How could that dreadful woman start another war and put one of our sons in such danger?' *Our sons.* Even after so many years it had still touched him to hear her say that. Despite his worry over Mark, despite the anger he had still felt over his chosen career, he was moved. There was even a tiny spark of pride when he thought of Mark in his officer's uniform; he had been a soldier, too, and for once he felt he understood Mark a little.

In the corridor outside a nurse laughed loudly, was still laughing over her shoulder as she pushed the door open and came in. She said, 'Here we are. Breakfast!' She'd gone again before he could thank her. He struggled to sit up. He removed the steel cloche covering the plate; the little room began to fill with the smell of bacon and sausage that had stood too long under heat lamps. He placed the cloche back. He drank the cup of tea she'd brought. He wondered if Ben would bring Nathan to see him.

Ben had said, 'You don't disapprove, do you Dad?'

They had been watching Kitty and her bridesmaids have their photograph taken outside the quaint little church where Ben had chosen to be re-married. There had been a forced lightness in Ben's voice that only served to emphasize his desperation for his blessing. He had turned from the pretty picture his new daughter-in-law made to smile at him. 'She's lovely. I wish you a long and happy life together.'

Kitty was just a child. Ben shouldn't have married a child like Kitty. He blamed himself, sometimes, for making too many allowances for his sons.

Here we go in loops and circles: blame, guilt, blame, guilt. Exhausting. The nurses had taken his leg off when he arrived, without comment of course. Such an ancient wound, the skin all patched round the stump. The surgeon who had amputated had been a major. Major Harold Greenbeck. Tough as a terrier. 'Soon have you running about again,' Major Harold Greenbeck barked from the end of his bed. '*As long as the war is over by the time I'm doing the running*,' he'd said under his breath. That's all he wanted, the war over and Grace naked in his arms in their bed in their little flat near London's St Thomas's Hospital.

He should sleep; sleep was a good cure. But he thought of the nightmare the nurse had woken him from and was scared to close his eyes. He never thought of Annette any more, except occasionally when she appeared in some fleeting expression of Mark's. He hadn't had the dream for years – odd how it hadn't changed, how it had remained preserved in his brain like a corpse kept on ice. Annette had been such a pretty child, a child like Kitty. He hoped Mark would keep away from Kitty. He hoped he would keep away from Kitty and not behave as he had with Susan.

Susan and Ben married in Chelsea Registry Office. Susan wore a white trouser suit and carried orchids. She had pinned some of the purple flowers in her hair too, her long blonde hair that fell around her shoulders and was lustrous and heavy and caught the sunlight that played on the Chelsea Registry Office steps. Ben, standing on the steps beside her, looked so proud, but elated, too, as though he had won a prize. A big prize, the lottery jackpot. A trophy wife, Simon had thought, although Susan had a career; Susan loved work and London. Susan was clever and bright and marvellously funny; she made jokes; she changed his opinion of women; he thought Ben had met his match at last. He thought Mark hated her on sight.

Susan teased Mark. She teased him most about his writing. Gentle teasing, that no one else would have minded. She went out of her way to introduce him to her friends as *a novelist*, that eyebrow-raised, mock awe in her voice. But Mark was so bad at being teased. His shyness hardened into superciliousness and he couldn't see how this set him apart and made others think he was not quite normal.

And one day he had visited Mark, a surprise visit, a whim. And Mark had begged him to understand as Susan dressed hastily in his bedroom. 'What is there to understand?' He remembered asking, and it seemed a silly question now, or at least one that Mark couldn't answer, except to say he loved her. Susan had come out then, and she must have heard Mark's declaration, but she wouldn't look at him, wouldn't look at either of them, just snatched up her coat and bag and left, an ordinary adulteress who had been found out. He knew then that *love* had nothing to do with it, not as far as she was concerned.

Simon closed his eyes. He thought he would call the nurse and ask her for something to help him sleep. His father used to sing to him, lying on the bed beside him singing *Nelly Gray,* which was the saddest song in the whole world and about death. He was older than his father was when he died. Strange to think that if they met in heaven he would see a young man of sixty-two.

Mark had said, 'I always thought she imagined I was some kind of idiot-savant...but she didn't – it was just her way of hiding how she felt –'

They had been standing in the Natural History Museum. There must have been something Mark had wanted to see there, something he was researching. A dinosaur skeleton loomed above them. Simon remembered how helpless he had felt, adrift. This tall, elegant, *beautiful* man at his side made him feel as if he knew nothing but bones. All he could do was listen and feel dull with fear.

Mark said, 'Neither of us meant for it to happen. I swear, Dad.'

'It must stop. Now.'

Mark had bowed his head, that familiar shame. 'I've stopped it. As soon as you found out.'

'You stopped it because of me? Of what I might think? Mark – what if I hadn't walked in on you both? Would you have carried on? Don't you have any regard for your brother in this? My God, Mark – I despair of you!'

'So?' He'd looked at him sullenly. 'Haven't you always?'

The nurse came back. Her skin was beautiful, ebony. He and she were two opposite ends of the human spectrum. He felt like a poor pale ghost beside her.

'Simon,' she said, 'your son is on the telephone asking if there's anything you need that he can bring this afternoon.'

'Which son? Mark?'

'Yes, my love, Mark. What shall I say? What would you like?'

To be left alone, he thought. He smiled at her. 'Chocolate,' he said.

Chapter 15

Kitty heard Ben's car and went out on to the drive to greet him. On her shoulder Nathan drooled, his gums clamped on the *Peter Rabbit* teething ring that had been chilling in the fridge. She watched anxiously as Ben got out of the car and took his jacket from the back seat. Slamming the rear door he looked up and smiled at her wearily.

'It's all right. He's fine.'

'He's all right?'

Ben edged past her into the house. He walked through to the kitchen, tossing his jacket down on a chair before filling the kettle.

Kitty followed him. 'Was it a heart attack?'

'Yes. But he's doing OK now. Out of danger.'

'That's good.'

'Yes. A relief.'

'Shall I make you some breakfast?'

'No. I'm not hungry, thanks. I just want a decent cup of tea.' Glancing at her while taking the tea caddy from the cupboard he said, 'Did you manage to get any sleep after I'd gone?'

'Yes. He's been good.'

'Makes a change, eh?' He took Nathan from her and held him at arm's length. 'Well, young man, let's have a look at you. All present and correct?' He held him closer and kissed his head. Nathan grinned up at his father, giggled as he tickled him. The teething ring fell to the floor and Ben crouched to retrieve it. Looking up at her he said, 'Dad wants me to take Nath to see him tonight.'

'Oh. OK.'

'You don't sound too sure? I thought the three of us would go.'

'No – that's fine. Of course.'

'I could take him on my own, if you like.'

'That would look wrong.'

'Yes. It would.' Holding Nathan against his shoulder he turned away to make his tea. Casually he said, 'Steven was there – working, of course. I saw him talking to Mark in the corridor outside Dad's room. Quite cosy, the two of them.' He jiggled Nathan up and down as he began to squirm. 'All right, sweetheart, Daddy's nearly done here and then we can sit down. Shall we watch *Bob The Builder* or read *Teddy Where's Teddy* again? You decide. Daddy's at your command today.'

'Aren't you going to the hospital?'

He frowned at her in surprise. 'I've been up all night, Kit – I thought my father was about to die – do you really think I'd be any use to anyone?'

'I meant don't you want to be with your Dad.'

He sighed. 'Sorry. Sorry – forgive me, I'm tired.'

'Maybe you should go to bed.'

'Later. Maybe when Nath has his nap.' He held out his hand to her. 'Come here.'

She went to him and he put his free arm around her, pulling her close. He kissed the top of her head, inhaling. He'd told her once that he loved the smell of her hair, that if he could carry its scent with him he would and it would make him feel that everything was right with the world. It had been months since he'd said anything like that, long before Nathan was born. Sometimes it seemed that their short romance had ended the day she told him she was pregnant.

He smelt faintly of sweat beneath the clean, soapy smell of the detergent she washed his shirts in. She felt his arm tighten around her and she leaned against him, her head against his chest. He was a head taller than she was; he used to say they were the right height for each other. They stood, still and quiet, waiting for the tea to brew. At last he said, 'We could go to bed now, I suppose.' He looked down and kissed her upturned face. 'I love you,' he said softly. 'You and Nath. I can't tell you how much.'

She nodded. 'Let's go upstairs.'

The first time they'd made love, afterwards as she lay in his arms, she'd steeled herself to ask him, 'You don't think any less of me now, do you?'

He'd lifted his head to look down at her, almost dislodging her head from his chest in his surprise. He'd laughed. 'Any *less* of you? Sweetheart, I don't think I ever want to let you out of this bed again. How could I think less of you?' He grinned at her, kissing her as he cupped her face with his hand. 'You're wonderful.' After a moment he said, 'Do you think any less of *me*?'

'No!'

'I mean now you've seen me naked.'

She laughed. 'No! *You're* wonderful.'

'I'm old.'

'No. Don't say that.'

'Old enough to be your father. I remember the *Beatles* releasing *Hey Jude*.'

'I don't know what year that was. It doesn't mean anything to me.'

'Exactly!'

'I bet you were only a baby, though. I bet you don't really remember.'

He said, 'Yes, I do,' and his voice was sad and wistful and she'd looked up at him anxiously.

He'd smiled. 'It's all right. I was just remembering. I was about five or six. It was played all the time on the radio.' Hugging her closer, he said, 'Why did you ask me that silly question?'

169

'Sometimes men go off you when you go to bed with them too soon.'

'Do they? You must know some very old-fashioned men.'

'Lads, then.'

'Oh, I see.' He nodded sagely. 'Well, I'm no lad.'

Feeling stupid she'd said, 'I've made myself sound like a kid. I shouldn't have asked you, should I? It's not as if I've jumped into bed with lots of people –'

'*People?*' He laughed. 'Darling, I think we should drop it, don't you? Don't talk yourself into a deeper hole.'

'Don't patronise me!'

He pressed his hand to her mouth. 'Be quiet, now. Grown-ups don't talk so much after sex.' Drawing his hand away slowly he said, 'I don't care about the past, Kitty. Let's make a pact, eh? I won't talk about my ex-lovers and you won't talk about yours.'

He meant he wouldn't talk about his first wife, of course, that beautiful clever blonde, a fellow doctor, a woman who knew the insides of other women. She wondered if Susan's knowledge had excited him, if it added some extra thrill to the sex they had. Too often she imagined Ben and Susan in bed together, and their sex was always fantastic and Susan was never anything less than panting for him. Susan was never bleeding; there was never milk leaking from her breasts; she was never a bit smelly from being too exhausted to shower. Susan would never lie flat on her back as he made love to her because she couldn't be bothered to pretend even to save his ego. Susan had never listened out for her baby's cries as her husband climaxed. Susan had never wanted children, he had told her that much. 'And neither did I,' he smiled, 'until I met you.'

Nathan lay in the cot he first slept in when they brought him home, kept in the corner of their room for times like this. He was making quiet, contented noises, gnawing at the teething ring. The plastic would be warm now, soaked with his saliva. She turned on her side and smiled at him. He smiled back at her and waved his arms and legs, an up-turned turtle. She reached a finger through the cot's bars and he held it tightly.

'Lift him into bed with us,' Ben said.

She rolled over to face him. 'I thought you were asleep.'

'No.' He stroked her hair from her face and kissed her mouth. 'Bring Nathan into bed with us.'

She placed him between them and Ben propped himself up on his elbow and smiled down into his son's face. Looking up at her he said, 'I don't see enough of him, do I?'

She avoided his gaze, smiling at Nathan and handing him back the teething ring he'd dropped on the bed. He needed to be changed; his bottom was sore and Ben had told her this was because of the tooth he was cutting. He knew so much about babies, although he professed to have forgotten most of his obstetric and paediatric training.

Watching her Ben said, 'Kitty, I know I've been difficult lately –'

'No, not really –'

He touched her mouth. 'Listen. Since Nathan was born...' He laughed miserably. 'I don't know, Kit...I'm not a terrible father, am I?'

'No! Of course not. He adores you!'

'And I adore him.' Sitting up he lifted Nathan into his arms. For a while he talked baby talk to Nathan, then he said, 'I adored my father.' He glanced at her, away from looking at his son. 'Danny. He was marvellous, when he wanted to be. He was going to buy me a bike, you know, teach me how to ride it...I never thought about him much, before Nathan. Only sometimes. And then I'd make myself forget again – it was easy, I just worked harder – at exams, at work...everyone thought I was *so* ambitious!' He laughed, touching Nathan's cheek. 'Do you know your Daddy was one of the youngest consultants ever? How proud Granddad was!' He glanced at her. 'And Mum. Mum wrote me this long, lovely letter saying how proud she was of me and all I'd achieved. It was such a loving letter, and all I could do was read between the lines thinking she wouldn't have sent such a letter to her real son, she wouldn't have felt the need to write down how much she loved me if I had been her own blood.'

'That's not true.'

'No, I know. But I think mad thoughts when it comes to Joy and Simon. You know, last night, when I thought he might die...' After a moment he went on, 'I was scared. I couldn't help thinking it was my fault...that if I hadn't upset him...I know that's what Mark was thinking. He could barely stand to look at me.'

'But Simon's all right. And it's not your fault.'

He raised his knees and propped Nathan against the slope of his thighs, holding his hands. 'You are a good boy, aren't you? I think you are probably the best boy in the whole, wide world. We should make you king of somewhere. But where? Spain – Mummy likes it there.' He kissed him and began to sing, 'I had a little nut tree...Nothing would it *bear*...but a golden nutmeg and a silver *pear*...' He kissed Nathan's head again. 'The king of Spain's daughter came to visit me, and all for the sake of my little...nut...tree.' Turning to her he said, 'Danny used to sing that to me. He wasn't always mad. I want to tell Mark – he wasn't always mad – there were times...'

Gently she said, 'It's all right, don't be upset...'

He rested his forehead against Nathan's. He smiled. 'You need your nappy changed. I shall bathe you, we'll have bubbles and ducks.'

'I'll do it, you should rest.'

'No, let me.' He looked at her. 'I'd like another baby, Kitty. Before I'm too old. Simon was too old...I hated that he was so old, so much older than Danny... Oh Christ. I wish I'd never started this. Mark was right. I've broken Simon's heart.'

She hugged him awkwardly, Nathan squirming between them, and Ben drew away from her. 'I'm tired,' he said, 'it's been a long night.'

'Simon will be fine, you'll see.'

'Yes. Of course.'

'And he thinks the world of you, it's so obvious how much he loves you.'

'Have I betrayed him?' He gazed at her anxiously. 'Do you think he understands? We were never allowed to talk about Danny, you know? No – it wasn't that we weren't allowed, more that we didn't dare to...*I* didn't dare to. Mark was so secretive, and he and Simon...well, I know they kept stuff from me. I used to think that Mark...' He shook his head. 'As I said, I had mad thoughts.'

'What did you think?'

Quickly he said, 'I used to think Mark masterminded it all – you know – like Brains off *Thunderbirds*? I used to think that Simon was somehow under his control. Isn't that mad? He was just a little boy, a little frail wisp of a kid.'

'But you were only little, too...you must have been scared...'

'Yeah. I was scared all right.'

Hesitantly she said, 'Maybe you should tell Simon you've made your peace with Danny and that it's over.'

'He doesn't even know I've found him.'

'Then you should tell him.'

'I can't. Not now. I'll tell him I've stopped looking, that I'm not interested.'

He'll know that you're lying, Kitty thought. Simon was shrewd, he saw through everyone; beneath that charming, distracted air she knew he was hard as her mother was hard – both of them of them unfailingly ruthless when it came to defending their own.

She took Ben's hand and squeezed it tightly. 'It will be all right. No matter what, you have me and Nathan.' She smiled. 'We'll have another baby.'

'Are you sure?'

'We always said we would have two.'

'I know it's not long since Nath…I can't waste any more time, Kitty.'

She got up. 'I'll run the King of Spain's bath. Why don't you undress him – tell me how you think that nappy rash is doing.'

Later, as Nathan slept, they made love and he didn't use a condom and he told her how much he loved her over and over, scaring her with his intensity. He called her my Kitty, my own darling girl, my *Katherine*. No one called her Katherine except him, occasionally, when he would breathe the unfamiliar name out as though its syllables were music. The sound thrilled her; she was his Queen Katherine, worshipped and adored.

She turned her head on the pillow. Ben slept beside her, his face anxious still as though even his dreams worried him. His arm lay across her body and she lifted it away gently and placed her own hand over her stomach. She wondered if she was already pregnant. Perhaps it would be a girl this time: Sophie Joy Walker.

Ben had told her all about Joy, his mother who had died with her sons and her husband at her bedside, men who made sure she slipped away painlessly, knowing that she was loved. Ben had told her how he had held his mother's hand throughout her last night, and that it had been Christmas and outside frost glittered on the ground and carol singers could be heard from the hospice chapel. 'When we were kids at Christmas she would decorate the house at night, after we'd gone to bed, so that we'd come down in the morning and it was as if the world had been transformed. It was magical. She loved Christmas, she was

174

like a child for those few weeks and normally she was so right and proper.' He'd smiled to himself. 'Mum was always very *proper*, you know? Not cold or anything – far from it – but Mark and I were shown how to behave.'

He had told her this before he told her that Joy wasn't his real mother. When he told her about his real mother, his real father, it was in short, stilted sentences as if each word was too much trouble and made him angry.

What he told her about his real parents had kept her awake that night. Still living at home, she had got out of bed and gone down to where her mother was watching the late night film. Sitting on the edge of the settee, pretending to watch James Dean, she'd shuddered and Julie had looked at her quizzically. 'What's wrong?'

She had burst into tears. At once the TV was switched off and her mother's arms were around her. The whole story spilled out and she could hear her mother's shock in her silence. Julie had wiped her eyes with her fingers, hush-hushing her. 'He's still the same man,' she said. 'Still Ben, still lovely Ben…'

She'd strained to hear the conviction in her voice but Julie looked frightened and all her smiles and comforting, sensible words couldn't hide her fear. Ben had bad blood. Upstairs in her wardrobe her wedding dress hung covered in its protective plastic. In a week she would put on her brand new lingerie and the blue garter her girlfriends had bought her and slip the dress over her head. She couldn't imagine not wearing the dress; the dress was beautiful and it would break her heart if it remained hanging there, a terrible symbol of disappointment. She knew she was shallow to think only of the dress, but it was impossible to think about the rest of it. It would hurt too much to think of Ben and the way he bowed his head as he made his confession. He had looked like a criminal, like a man who knew how wicked he had been and craved forgiveness. He had done nothing wrong, she told him, nothing had changed. She lied and lied to reassure him, trying not to think of everything he had told her, afraid to ask all the questions she had because it was too terrifying, like thrusting a fist into a fresh wound

Leaving Ben and Nathan to sleep, Kitty got up and dressed quickly. Downstairs there was a pile of ironing to be done, a tangle of washing to be sorted, Nathan's freshly laundered babygrows to be pegged on the line, reminding her of a string of headless paper dolls as they flapped in the breeze. She would prepare a salad for Ben's lunch, tearing the leaves from the pot of basil to flavour the tomatoes. She would set the table properly and make a pot of coffee and everything would be just so, just as he liked it. He would be reassured and calmed and later they would go to the hospital together. She wouldn't think about Danny lying somewhere in another ward close by, dying his slow, painful death. Danny was a monster, a wicked, disgusting creature. She would hope that it wouldn't occur to Ben to introduce his baby son to such a man.

Chapter 16

Miss Grey said, 'Oh you stupid, *stupid* girl! Do you have any idea how much that vase was worth?'

Annette looked at the broken pieces of crystal on the hearth. The vase had shattered spectacularly, the noise it made bringing the two old sisters from the other room. She crouched down and began to sweep up the bits with the hearth brush. Her hands shook. From the corner of her eye she saw the older Miss Grey's lace-up brogues and thick tan stockings as the woman came to stand over her.

'That vase belonged to my mother.'

'I'm sorry. It just slipped...'

'Just slipped! It wouldn't have *slipped* if you were taking care! It shall come out of your wages.'

The younger Miss Grey said, 'Oh Eddie, I'm sure we don't have to go that far. Annette, dear, do be careful you don't cut yourself.'

'If she cuts herself it's her own to-do. Honestly – I don't know what's got into you, Annette. You've become as much use as, as – well – as that vase! Sweep it up properly, fetch your coat and go. We don't want you back.'

She stalked out of the room, leaving her with the younger sister, May. May said gently, 'Leave it, Annette. And do go home, you look quite exhausted. Don't worry about what my sister says, of course we don't expect you to pay for the vase – it was such an ugly old thing.'

Annette scrambled to her feet with the dustpan full of shards. 'Will you pay me for today?'

May's eyes darted towards the door as though she thought her sister was listening behind it. Timidly, she said, 'I'd have to ask Edwina – she deals with that kind of thing.'

'It's only a few shillings, Miss Grey. Only what you owe me.'

'But the vase…and Edwina is so cross with you…'

'All right. It doesn't matter.' She put the dustpan down. 'I'll go.'

On the tree-lined street outside the Greys' pretty little villa, Annette took out her cigarettes and counted them. Three left. She hesitated. She had promised herself she would save them for later, when she could sit down with a cup of tea and enjoy a smoke properly. But she needed one now. Across the road was Thorp cemetery with its benches for mourners. She would go there and sit down and smoke. She wouldn't think about anything, she would just smoke.

In the cemetery the horse chestnut trees were beginning to blossom. Its rooks were hopping between graves, using the headstones as lookout posts. They looked at her. They carried on with their business.

She sat down and tried to strike a match but her hands shook too much and it snapped against the box. She took a breath and tried again. Finally she was inhaling smoke deep into her lungs. She rested her head back and closed her eyes. She felt the sun warm on her face like a kiss. A breeze rustled the cellophane protecting the roses on a new grave and brought her the smell of wallflowers. Aloud she said, 'Please help me, God.' She listened to the quiet, suddenly broken by a rook's harsh craw.

Wallflowers grew in her grandmother's back yard, her lovely, gentle grandmother who had said, 'Don't marry him, pet.'

She'd laughed. 'Why not?'

Her Gran had sighed. She wouldn't say any more, she'd said her piece. Danny was a Carter, and everyone knew about the Carters. But she had known better than her gran:

Danny had broken away from his family, he never saw his mam, his dad was dead, and his brothers were never mentioned except to say how much he despised them. Danny had got away and was different. He liked books. He understood things she didn't even try to. And he had such a beautiful face.

Her gran had worn a navy suit to their wedding, so dark it looked black. She wore a cockeyed navy straw hat, too, battered-looking so that she'd felt a bit ashamed of her. Not that there were many guests to judge the old lady's outfit, just a few girls from the sugar factory and a man she'd never met before, a mate from Danny's days in the marines. He was Danny's best man. She couldn't remember his name because she hadn't seen him since.

A few weeks after she'd stood at the altar with Danny in his neat, blue suit, she knew that she was pregnant. She'd just turned seventeen. Danny was delighted. Everything was working to his plan. Ben grew inside her, pushing a little hand or foot against the barrier of her muscle and skin, rolling her new big belly like a wave, strong even then. Danny would press his hand to her when Ben kicked. He would grin. 'A little fighter.'

Annette drew on her cigarette. In a minute she would go and stand outside the school railings, watching for her boys. In a minute, there was no hurry. She might try to sleep – snatch forty winks like her gran used to. She'd play at her feet with her two dolls, Paula and Anne. Her grandmother would sometimes mumble from her dozing, slurring reassurances of her presence.

Annette forced herself to open her eyes. Falling asleep on a cemetery bench was the kind of thing tramps did. If Danny saw her he would go mad. Madder. Danny was mad all the time, mad in all its senses. His madness showed itself in the terrible lies he told. No one believed in his imagined fancy woman Anne-Marie, or her baby; everyone knew he'd made her up. Joan had shaken her head when she'd told her. 'Don't you think that if it were true it would have got back to you before now? You can't have a stiff shit round here without the whole world knowing! He's winding you up, pet. *Anne-Marie from Skinner Street*! Christ Almighty!'

She'd had doubts about telling Joan, but it turned out she knew already – Danny had told the same lie to the men he worked with and the grapevine made sure everyone knew. 'He wants his head testing,' Joan had said. 'He'll end up in St Stephen's the way he's going.'

St Stephen's was the lunatic asylum on the outskirts of Thorp. At school, if you were a bit slow, the other children would threaten you with its men in white coats. Even the mention of the asylum's name scared her. The idea of Danny being sent there was terrifying.

Last night Danny had said calmly, 'Fetch Mark. I want to talk to him.'

Her heart had almost stopped, only to start racing. Trying not to sound as if she might cry she asked, 'What do you want to talk to him about?'

'You'll find out won't you, when you've fetched him. Go on. Be quick.'

She went out on to the street to look for him, hoping he'd gone off with all the other kids to play on the rec. She would tell Danny she couldn't find him, he might, at a pinch, lose interest in whatever it was he was planning. The thought of one of Danny's plans made her legs feel wobbly, she had to lean against the wall of their house. She saw Mark at the other end of the street, alone. She went to him.

Mark had turned as she called his name. He'd looked at her warily, knowing that his father was home, guessing that she had come to take him inside, within a few feet of his tormentor. She had smiled at him as reassuringly as she could.

'What you doing on your own?'

He shook his head.

'Where's Ben gone, leaving you all alone?'

He looked down at the pavement and began bumping against the wall behind him. Gently Annette said, 'Don't do that, sweetheart.' She crouched down next to him. 'Why don't you go and find Ben? I bet he's playing a good game somewhere?'

He looked at her. His face was grubby and too pale, his hair cut brutally short on Danny's insistence so that it was barely more than bristles. He was still angelically beautiful, so much like Danny that sometimes she found it hard not to turn away from him.

She saw his eyes widen in fright and looked behind her. Danny stood a little way away. She drew breath, the metallic taste of fear on her tongue.

Danny said, 'Is he refusing to come in?'

'No! I've only just found him.' Brightly she said, 'Mummy's just found you, hasn't she?'

Mark stared at the ground. As Danny came closer she saw a wet patch form on the front of his trousers. Danny snorted. 'Dirty little bastard. Come on you – in. Now.'

In the kitchen *Peter Rabbit* and *The Tale of Mrs Tiggywinkle* had been placed side by side on the table. Annette stared at the books in dismay and felt her own bladder loosen so that she pressed her thighs together. Danny knelt on the floor so that his face was level with Mark's. He held on to his shoulders and at once Mark looked at her in terror, his eyes pleading.

Evenly Danny said, 'I found two books hidden under your mattress. I want you to tell me where you got them from and why you hid them away.'

'Danny I put them there! Miss Grey gave me them – you know, the old ladies on Linden Avenue –'

'Quiet! Don't you lie for him! For Christ's sake – why would you hide baby books? No, I want the truth and I want it from him.' He shook Mark. 'You stole them, didn't you?'

'No! Danny listen – I was given them, honestly!'

181

'Shut up. I will make him speak. I will if I have to beat it out of him. Now, one more time. Where did you get those books?'

Mark shuddered. He bowed his head and a tear splashed onto the floor between him and his father. Danny drew his hand back and hit him hard across the face so that he staggered and almost fell. 'You stop crying! You don't cry just because I'm speaking to you, you little snivelling bloody nancy! And don't look at your mother – she won't help you!'

Annette lifted Mark into her arms. 'Leave him! Just you leave him alone!'

Danny shook his head in mock disbelief. 'Put him down. Put him down you silly bitch. You'll make it worse for him if you don't.'

Mark clung to her more tightly, his arms around her neck, his face buried in her shoulder. She could feel his wetness soaking into her skirt, his snot and tears through her blouse. Tremulously she said, 'Danny, I hid the books, as a surprise for him when he went to bed. It was just a game.'

'Put him down.'

'Don't hurt him.'

'I won't.'

She kissed Mark's head. Setting him on the floor she crouched in front of him and said, 'Let's go upstairs and get you bathed, eh?'

As she straightened up Danny grabbed her arm. 'He's not going upstairs.'

She had almost cried. 'Please, you said you wouldn't hurt him!'

'I'm not going to. You are.'

In the cemetery Annette shuddered. The breeze became colder, wisps of cloud scuttled across the sky. She drew on the cigarette, right down to its filter; she closed her eyes.

Danny had reached behind him and picked up a bamboo cane from the worktop. To Mark he'd said, 'Because you've lied and caused your mother to lie you're going to be punished. Take off you trousers and underpants.'

'Danny –'

Danny looked at her. 'Help him. Help him get undressed.'

'No – there's no need for this. I'm going to take him out, to Joan's. Let you calm down.' She took Mark's hand and made to edge past him. Danny pushed her back, his hand flat against her shoulder. Turning around he locked the back door and put the key in his pocket. 'Get him undressed.'

He'd told her that if she caned Mark he would receive only five strokes; if she disrespected him and refused he would beat him and he would get ten, or more, perhaps. Wearily, as though tired of explaining it to her, he said, 'He has to learn, Annette. He has to learn that he can't just hide behind your skirts.'

She'd undressed him. He'd stopped crying but his whole body was shuddering. His teeth were chattering and she pressed her hand against his cheek, trying to look him in the eye and give him what little comfort she could, but his eyes seemed not to see her, too frightened even to make a silent appeal. When he was naked from the waist down he hung his head with such abject shame that she began to cry.

'Please don't do this, Danny. I'll do anything...'

Danny sat down. He said, 'Mark, come here and bend over my knee. Your mother's going to cane you.'

The cemetery rooks took off as one, startled by something only they sensed. Annette covered her face with her hands, seeing again the red weals that criss-crossed Mark's flesh.

When she'd brought the cane down the third time she'd stopped, her face wet with tears as she said, 'Danny, please don't make me go on.'

He didn't look at her, just kept his gaze on Mark's bottom. Evenly he said, 'Two more strokes. Don't worry if you draw blood.'

Danny had carried Mark upstairs when it was over and laid him tenderly on their bed. He knelt beside him and placed his hand over Mark's forehead. Softly he said, 'There. Now you know what will happen to you in the future if you're not good and don't do as I tell you. And Mammy will be even more cross, next time.' Mark had seemed comatose, he didn't even flinch when Danny leaned over him and kissed his cheek. Looking up at her standing in the doorway Danny had said, 'He can sleep in here with me tonight. You sleep in his bed with Ben.'

On the cemetery bench Annette let her hands drop from her face. This wouldn't do. Time was getting on. She had to go to the school and watch out for her boys. After their dinner they played in the yard. Ben played. Mark watched. She would watch Mark watching. She stood up and began to walk as quickly as she could.

Annette watched through the school railings as Ben and his friends chased each other around the yard. She couldn't see Mark. She tried to catch Ben's attention but he was too caught up in his game. Just beyond the railings two little girls were skipping. Annette called out to them. 'Where's Mark Carter?' They looked at her as though she was mad. An older girl approached her. 'Are you his Mam?'

'Yes. Do you know where he is?'

'Miss took him inside.'

'Why?' Panicked, she looked towards the blue doors that led inside the school. She imagined Danny had come to fetch him. Her knees felt weak and she held on to the railings to stop herself falling.

The girl turned away. 'Here's Miss now,' she said.

'Mrs Carter?' Mark's teacher stood in front of her. 'Mrs Carter, are you quite all right?'

184

'Where's Mark?'

'He's inside, with the school secretary. I'm actually very glad you're here, I was just about to take him home to you.'

'Why? He's all right. He's all right, he was this morning...'

The young woman touched her arm through the railings. 'Calm down, Mrs Carter. Look, why don't you come in. I'll take you to him.'

She followed the teacher along a corridor lined with little pegs for the infants' coats. The coats were missing, revealing drawstring cloth bags made from navy serge or checked gingham, knobbly with the outline of plimsolls; there was a faint smell of rubber and sweat. Each peg had a picture of an animal above it and a child's name written in neat, bold letters below. The name **MARK CARTER** was coupled with a picture of a panda, a long stalk of bamboo in its paw. She stopped and touched it. His teacher smiled at her. 'He chose the panda. Did he show you his drawing of it? Wasn't it good?'

He hadn't shown her any drawing. As the teacher walked on she wondered if he had shown her and she'd forgotten; perhaps she'd hidden it away, out of sight from Danny. Best to hide things from Danny.

The teacher opened a door. 'Here he is, Mum,' she said. 'Here's your poor, poorly boy!' The woman smiled at Mark and crouched in front of the plastic chair he was sitting on. 'Guess what, Mark? Mummy must have guessed you weren't feeling well and came right over to get you! What a clever Mummy you have!'

She stood up straight and turned to Annette. Lowering her voice she said, 'He's been very quiet this morning, even quieter than usual. When I asked him what the matter was he seemed not to be able to tell me. We asked Ben if he knew what might be troubling him and he told us Mark had a tummy ache this morning. Anyway, the poor little thing didn't look well at all. I think it's best that you take him home and tuck him up in bed. I don't know if you should call your doctor out, but I think perhaps I might if I were you. He's not the type of child who usually makes a fuss.' She laughed slightly. 'Not that he's making a fuss now.'

Annette barely heard the stream of words. She kept her eyes on Mark, willing him to look up at her. But he went on staring at the floor, still as a doll. She stepped towards him and he flinched.

Gently she said, 'Mark, come on now. We'll go home, just you and me. Daddy's out. Daddy's out at work all day.' She held out her hand. 'Should I carry you? I'll carry you if you like?'

He let himself down from the too big chair. He slipped his hand into hers and she squeezed it with relief. 'Come on, sweetheart. Let's go home.'

She lay with him on his bed and sang softly along to the little transistor radio, '*I left my home in Georgia, heading for the 'Frisco bay, I had nothing to live for...*' Such sad words. Her baby Mark was sleeping and she stroked his short, short hair. The music had soothed him, she hoped it had. She sang, '*Sitting on the dock of the bay, watching the tide roll in...*'

Last night, just before dawn, she'd woken from a fitful sleep beside Ben to see Danny standing over the bed, Mark naked and limp in his arms. She knew that he'd killed him and she sat bolt upright. Unable to stop herself from crying she covered her mouth with her hand.

Danny jerked his head. 'Get up.'

'Danny – what have you done –'

'I said get up. Don't wake Ben or I'll kill you.'

He'd turned and carried Mark out again. She got out of bed, stumbling in her haste to follow him. He was standing in the bathroom.

'Run the bath. He needs a bath.'

'What have you done to him?'

186

'Run the bath.'

Her hands were shaking so badly she couldn't get the plug to fit. The water poured from the tap, soaking her arm as she struggled. Danny prodded her with his foot. 'Come on you silly bitch, he's getting cold.'

'But the water's cold, Danny. There's no hot water now!' She looked up at him, crying openly. 'Oh please Danny please say you haven't hurt him.'

He lowered him into the few inches of cold water. 'Wakey-wakey, Mark.' He scooped a handful of water and poured it over Mark's head, pinching his face hard between his fingers, distorting it. 'Wake up, you little sod! Wake up and stop pretending!' He'd let go of him abruptly. Brushing past her he'd said, 'Get him dry and bring him back to my bed.'

Sitting on the Dock of the Bay ended. She kissed Mark's forehead. 'We like that song, don't we. One day you and me will sit by the sea and watch the tide roll in.' She smiled and kissed him again. 'You and me and Ben, watching the tides.'

Mark opened his eyes and looked at her. For a while all he did was hold her gaze but then he reached out and touched her cheek. 'Mummy,' he whispered.

'Yes, sweetheart, I'm here.'

'Mummy...'

'What? Would you like something to eat? Are you thirsty?'

He shook his head.

She kissed him. 'It's all right. I'm here.' She drew him closer to her and closed her eyes. Outside in the street a woman laughed. A dog began to bark. She thought of Danny hating dogs. The barking went on, dragging her back from the edge of sleep. After while the dog was silent. She thought of Danny shooting it; he would have a gun, one day. One day Danny would have a gun. She drifted into sleep and dreamt of Danny marching the streets with a rifle on his shoulder.

She woke up to find Ben standing next to the bed. 'Dad says you're to come downstairs.' He giggled and covered his mouth with his hand. Leaning forward he whispered in her ear, 'He's got a nice surprise.'

She sat up. Anxiously she said, 'What is it, Ben, what's the surprise?'

He shook his head and pressed his lips together.

'Tell me.'

'You have to come down and see!'

She glanced at Mark, still sleeping. 'Did Daddy say any thing about Mark?'

Ben shook his head. He looked at his brother. 'I don't want Mark to wake up.'

'No, perhaps it's best he has a nice sleep, eh?'

'Mark's a baby.' Still looking at Mark, his face twisted with contempt. 'I wish I didn't have to go to school with him.' Ben looked at her hopefully, as if she might grant him his wish. When she didn't say anything he added vehemently, 'He's too babyish to go to school anyway. Everyone thinks he's just a soft baby!'

'That's not true, Ben! His teacher thinks he's very clever.'

'No she doesn't!' He looked away as if he knew his mother would guess he was lying. 'Come down,' he said. 'Dad says come down now.'

In the kitchen Danny stood at the stove. An open can of baked beans stood on the sink. Toast was browning under the grill. He turned and grinned just as Ben had. 'Ben — show *Madam* to her table!'

Ben smiled at her, pleased. He pulled out one of the chairs. 'Sit down Mammy. Look what we've done.'

The table was set with knives and forks and side plates, a paper napkin folded at each of the three places. A single red rose had been placed in a vase next to the salt and pepper pots.

Danny said, 'Ben, butter this toast for me.'

Timidly, unsure where all this was leading, Annette said, 'I'll do that, Ben, you sit down.'

'No. He can do it. We're giving Mam a rest, aren't we Ben?' He turned off the grill and tumbled the toast on to a plate. 'Come on son, chop chop, you're on cook-house duty now!'

Annette sat down. The sickly smell of baked beans filled her mouth and nose and she felt her stomach cramp. She knew she wouldn't be able to eat more than a mouthful without feeling sick. She would have to force it down. Danny wouldn't stand for anything else.

'Right!' Danny poured the beans onto the toast. 'Sit down, Ben. I'll be the waiter.'

Ben scrambled onto the chair opposite her. He smiled happily and she made herself smile back at him. She cleared her throat. 'Isn't this nice! Haven't you and Daddy been working hard!'

Danny set their meals in front of them. Sitting down with his own meal he said, 'Let's say grace.'

About to pick her knife and fork up she jerked her head up to look at him. Danny said, 'Bow your heads, then.'

Ben glanced at her, anxiety creeping back into his eyes. She nodded at him and he bowed his head and closed his eyes tight. She did the same. Danny laughed suddenly, causing them both to jump.

'Look at the pair of you! *Grace*! For Christ's sake! For what we are about to receive may the lord make us truly fucking thankful!' He ruffled Ben's hair. 'You know your Mam believes all that rubbish, don't you? She'd have you down to Sunday School if she had her way. You don't want to go to school on a Sunday, do you son?'

Ben shook his head.

'No! Course you don't!' Danny looked at her. 'Eat your tea. We've got a surprise for you after, haven't we Ben?'

Her stomach rebelled at every mouthful. Fear at what was to come next made her barely able to swallow. Her hands shook and Danny looked at her pointedly.

'You had a sleep this afternoon, then? Had a nap?'

'Yes.'

'Then you should be feeling bright as a button, eh? Fresh as a daisy!'

'Yes. I am.'

'Good. That's what I like to hear! I know – we'll have some music on – make it even more of a party!' He looked to the windowsill where the transistor radio usually stood. Turning to her he said, 'Where's my radio?'

She stood up at once. 'I'll go and get it.'

He said, 'Sit down. Tell me where it is.'

She sat. Trying to control the tremor in her voice she said, 'It's by Ben's bed. Ben – you go and get it like a good boy.'

'No.' Danny sighed. Earlier he'd spread his paper napkin over his knee and now he screwed it into a ball and tossed it down. 'For fuck's sake, nothing's ever nice and easy in this house is it? Always something to spoil things.' Pushing himself away from the table he said, 'I'll go and get it. Eat your teas. Don't worry that mine's ruined will you?'

She listened to his light, quick tread on the stairs, her body stiff with fear. From the corner of her eye she saw that Ben was listening, too, his knife and fork clenched tightly in his hands. 'It's all right, Ben. You finish your tea now.' He ignored her, staring down at his plate, both of them listening to Danny's footfalls in the room above them where Mark was sleeping.

He came straight down again. He set the radio on the table and turned it on. A DJ's voice filled the kitchen. *The Supremes* began to sing *Baby Love*. Danny grinned at her.

He sang along in his lovely tuneful voice. After a few bars he sat down and finished his meal.

Later, when Ben had gone out to play and she stood washing the dishes, Danny came up behind her and wrapped his arms around her waist. 'Did you like your surprise?'

'It was lovely, Danny.'

He had bought a cake, a cream sponge. He'd hidden it in the cupboard and had brought it out with a little fanfare. Ben had looked at her, gauging her reaction and she had forced herself to pretend delight. For once Danny seemed to have been fooled. The cake had tasted of milky cardboard, clagging against the roof of her mouth as she struggled to swallow it.

Standing behind her at the sink he squeezed her tightly. 'Do you love me?'

'Yes.'

'Say you love me, baby.'

'I love you.'

'I'm going to buy Ben a bike. I told him he should have a bike, promised him.'

She closed her eyes, hating to think of Ben's disappointment when the promise was broken. Danny stepped away. He leaned against the table, watching her. Eventually he said, 'You're in a funny mood.'

'No I'm not. I'm fine.'

'I thought you'd be pleased to have your tea cooked for you.'

'I was! It was lovely! Everything was lovely!'

'I got the rose from the cemetery.' He sniggered. 'Just lifted it right off a grave. Stupid waste, putting flowers on a grave.' Reaching out, he picked the rose from its vase and handed it to her. 'There. A rose for my rose.'

The red petals were edged with brown; something had eaten away at its centre. She placed it down gently. 'It's lovely, Danny.'

191

'I don't want you being scared of me.'

'I'm not.'

'There's nothing to be scared of, anyway! Sometimes I think you're not right in the head, the way you go on. Ben thinks so too. He's a good boy. I told him – he's my good boy. I asked him how he thinks we should sort you out. Stop you being so timid.'

He picked up the rose and began plucking out its petals. When it was almost nothing he said, 'Ben should have a bed to himself. It's not right.'

As calmly as she could she said, 'We'll have to try getting another bed on tick.'

'We don't need another bed. What do we need another fucking bed for?' He came to stand close to her. He gripped her arm tightly; she felt his breath against her ear as he said, 'You're sleeping on the floor from now on.

She pressed her thighs together against her body's shameful softening; a trickle of urine ran down her leg. 'But Danny…'

'But nothing! Oh – maybe I'll let you sleep on the settee if you're a good girl, eh?' He smiled. 'Like a little dog: a little bitch, all curled up on the settee.'

He sighed and looked down at the rose petals scattered at his feet. 'Oh dear. What a mess.'

'I'll sweep them up –'

'I know you will. No hurry. First you can go and get Mark and put him in my bed. Tell him I'll be up in a minute to take care of him.'

Chapter 17

Mark drove to the hospital. He bought flowers from the florist in the foyer and a bar of Cadbury's Fruit and Nut, the largest the hospital shop sold. He also bought bottled water and *The Times* and *The Evening Gazette*. He'd brought fruit from home, an apple and a banana and a tangerine. He waited for the lift to the fourth floor and Simon's ward, and thought that perhaps he'd over-done it and that Simon would tell him again that he fussed. The flowers were beautiful, though, white roses and spray carnations, baby's breath and blue-green eucalyptus; they would cheer up Simon's drab little room. In the lift a woman smiled at the bouquet and then at him. 'Your wife will love those,' she said.

Last night Simon had said, 'I think I'm having a heart attack.' He staggered over the words, each one an effort, his face such a terrible shade of grey that Mark had been certain he would die. He had only ever seen that colour on corpses, a putty grey, no longer living flesh but something that would quickly break down into the earth. Simon's lips turned blue; he had wanted to press his fingers against them to see the pink colour return, shocked by the terror in his father's eyes and needing him to be normal again. Simon couldn't be afraid, it was unthinkable.

The lift stopped and its polite and lilting voice announced the fourth floor. Mark stepped out with his flowers and his bags of treats and followed the little group of his fellow visitors along the corridor that dog-legged past the diabetic clinic and through a set of double doors that swung both ways. He turned right, past the family room and the little kitchen. At the end of this corridor was Simon's room, close to the nurses' station; he hadn't needed Ben to tell him that this was a bad sign.

The Jamaican nurse greeted him. 'Look at you, all loaded! My goodness your father's a lucky man.'

'How is he?'

'Oh he's doing just fine. He'll be pleased to see you.' She walked in to the room ahead of him. 'Look who's here!'

Simon opened his eyes. 'Mark.'

'Here,' the nurse said, 'let me take those flowers. I'll find a vase for them.'

When she'd gone Simon made an effort to sit up, refusing Mark's arm. 'Flowers, eh? I don't remember anyone ever buying me flowers.'

Mark sat down on the armchair beside the bed. 'How are you feeling?'

'Fine. How are you – you look better than you did this morning, at least.'

'I managed to get some sleep.'

'More than I did. No one sleeps in a hospital – it's not allowed.' He looked at the carrier bags. 'Goodies?'

Mark began to unpack the chocolate and fruit onto the bedside cabinet. He handed him a bottle of water. 'Ben said you mustn't become dehydrated.'

'Did he?' He sighed. 'Yes, I suppose he's right. Do I drink it out of the bottle like all you youngsters? You're like babies sucking on dummies.'

Mark laid the newspapers on the foot of the bed. The *Gazette's* lead story was about the child that had gone missing on the Rosehill Estate, its headline *Please Bring Back My Leanne*. There was a photograph of the child's mother and Mark turned the paper over so that he wouldn't see her distraught face. Aware of Simon watching him, he said, 'I bought you *The Times*, too.'

'Thanks. I don't feel up to reading – take it back with you.' He closed his eyes. 'Mark, I don't want you to stay. Thank you for the chocolate and everything but I can't be bothered with small talk.'

'No, I understand.' He made to get up.

'You can stay a moment. I'll let you catch your breath.'

Mark sat down again. He looked across the bed to the window and its view over the Rosehill Estate to the Cleveland Hills. A huge, fat moth clung to the outside of the glass, battered by the wind. He found himself surprised that it had flown so high; he wondered if it was lost.

He said, 'Dad, we don't have to talk – I don't mind sitting here quietly if you feel you just want company.'

'I know you don't mind. I know you're a good boy.' He opened his eyes to look at him. 'I used to sit by your hospital bed for hours. I suppose you remember?'

'Yes, I do.'

'You don't have to repay me in kind.'

The nurse came back. The flowers had been placed in a too big vase so that the florist's careful arrangement was lost and the roses fell against its sides. Brightly the nurse said, 'Here we are! I'll put them where you can see them, Simon. Now – would you like a cup of tea?'

'My son's just leaving, my dear.' To him he said, 'Will you telephone Ben and remind him to bring Nathan with him this evening?'

'Yes, of course.' He bent to kiss his head but Simon waved him away.

'Off you go. Don't get caught up in the afternoon traffic.'

Mark drove to the Rosehill Estate. He stopped outside the playground and locked his car carefully before walking along the path to the swings and slides. There was a rocking horse beside the infants' slide, its red and gold metal head defaced with graffiti. He touched the horse and set it rocking gently. Its long body would carry five children, each on an individual saddle; with their combined energy the horse could rear up like a bronco. They would have to hold on tightly, their arms around the waist of the child in front. And the lead child, the child at the horse's head, would urge them to go faster, imaginary reins wrapped around his fists.

Annette sang, 'I had a little nut tree, nothing would it *bear*...' She kissed his head and held him close. 'But a silver nutmeg and a golden *pear*...' He heard the smile in her voice. She liked this rhyme and always stressed it. Shifting his weight a little she whispered, 'We're in a garden in Spain and the sun is hot and gold and purple butterflies bask in the heat and we sit beneath the shade of a tree that bears precious fruit. Just you and me and Ben. And roses grow all around and their scent is so sweet and we can hear singing, the gentle voices of the nuns who care for us...' She held his head between her hands, searching his face anxiously. 'Won't you speak?' She tried to laugh. 'Stick out your tongue so Mummy can see it's not cut off.'

He shuddered and she held him close again. 'Oh, I'm sorry. I didn't mean to scare you. Shall we sing together? *I danced over water, I danced over sea*...' Sadly she said, 'But all the birds in the air...Mark, you mustn't be so frightened...try not to be so scared and he won't hurt you any more.' She looked at him, smiling encouragingly as if willing him to understand. Her eyes were frightened and he didn't know how to comfort her.

His palm was flat on the horse's head between its goggling eyes. He pushed hard and the horse bucked on its rockers, creaking, old and rarely used – children had different pleasures nowadays. He turned away to where bunches of chrysanthemums and carnations were arranged on the spot where the missing child, Leanne, was last seen. There was a blue teddy bear with the child's name embroidered across its chest and he thought how bedraggled the toy would become in the rain that was bound to fall. The little girl was dead, of course. On the news just now in the car the police had announced that her stepfather had been arrested and charged with her murder. How obvious it was that such a relationship had proved to be so deadly, no doubt the police had known all along that this man who had such a responsibility of care had decided not to care at all. Or care too much; it was easy to imagine the man's obsessive love, his desperation.

Mark crouched down and read the cards attached to the bouquets. They told of an angel child, a precious little girl now safe in heaven. He touched the tightly closed bud of a pink rose, soft as a child's mouth.

Danny said, 'Your Mammy doesn't love you any more because of the things you make me do. Do you understand?' He had nodded and Danny pressed his hand against his cheek. 'You understand, don't you? You're mine...' He groaned softly, a noise that sounded like pain so that he'd held his breath, knowing it meant there would be pain for him, too. 'Oh Christ,' Danny groaned. 'Oh sweet Jesus Christ.'

'Mark?'

He turned, shocked at being suddenly dragged into the present, and Steven stepped towards him. He held a little girl's hand, a pretty, dark-skinned girl, her hair neatly braided.

Mark straightened from his crouch, staggering a little like a drunk because his knees had become stiff. Putting out a hand to steady him Steven said, 'I thought it was you.' He smiled shyly. 'I wasn't spying, honestly. Jade and me come here most afternoons.' Looking down at his daughter, he said, 'Jade, this is Mark. Why don't you say hello?'

She held on to her father's leg and hid her face. Steven laughed. 'She's a bit shy.'

'It's all right. Don't make her speak if she doesn't want to.'

'I wouldn't *make* her do anything.' He ruffled her hair then suddenly lifted her into his arms. 'We come here because she likes the rocking horse,' he said. 'Don't you, Jade?'

The girl nodded and turned her gaze on Mark, curious now.

Gently Mark said, 'Hello, Jade.'

She turned away again. Steven said, 'You heard about Leanne?'

'Yes.'

'Nicola's mam knows the family. It's terrible, awful.' He added, 'Nicola's my ex – Jade's mother.'

Mark turned to the flowers. 'I was reading the cards.'

'Yeah...people like to show they care...' Steven crouched down just as he had, standing Jade beside him and steadying her with a hand on her back. He looked up at him. 'Listen, Mark, Jade said she's thirsty. There's a café over the way – if you want to come and have a cup of tea.' He looked embarrassed. 'Just a thought.'

'All right.'

'Great!' He got up from his crouch gracefully and swept his daughter into his arms again as though she weighed nothing at all. 'It's this way. She loves the ice cream there, it's that soft, whippy stuff...'

'*Mr Whippy,*' Mark said. 'That's what we used to call it.'

I smiled at him. He was sitting opposite me and Jade, watching her as she played with the ice-cream because she wasn't really hungry, guessing I'd used her as an excuse to be with this strange man. She kept looking at him when she thought we weren't taking notice. From time to time Mark would catch her out and smile, embarrassing her.

Mark sipped his black tea. He put the cup down in its saucer gently and said, 'There's always been a café here. When I was a child I remember they served the ice cream through a hatch in the wall.'

'Really?' I looked at him like he'd said something really fascinating and he laughed a little, making my heart ache with longing.

He said, 'Ben and I used to play in the park here.'

'Quite a walk from Oxhill.'

'No, we came before then, when we lived on Tanner Street.'

'With Danny,' I said, and watched for his reaction.

He pretended not to hear. He said, 'Would you like another glass of milk, Jade?'

She shook her head, always mute with strangers. 'I think she's had enough,' I said.

The café was shabby, all dark oak chairs and tables with vases of tatty plastic flowers trying to break the gloom. The menus were wipe-clean and hadn't changed for years – lots of toasted stuff. The place smelt of toast and cigarette smoke – there was an ashtray on every table so it was like walking into the past, before the government decided we should all stop smoking.

Mark took out a packet of cigarettes, and then he looked at Jade and put them in his pocket again.

'Her mam smokes in front of her,' I said.

'But that doesn't make it right that I should.' To Jade he said, 'Was that ice cream delicious?'

She grinned at him and I felt relieved she didn't feel so wary any more. I'd been beginning to think that I shouldn't have introduced her to him, that it would all get confusing. But he was her uncle. It seemed weird; it was hard not to ask him what he thought of her, if he could see any resemblance.

'How's your Dad?' I asked.

'He's better, I think. Thank you.'

'He's really old, isn't he?'

'Over eighty. I'm never quite certain of his exact age – he keeps it to himself; he's quite vain, in certain ways.'

'Yeah? What ways?'

199

'He's vain about his appearance. He's a very handsome man.' Mark looked at me frankly, as if he knew all about the kind of man I thought handsome. 'Mum used to say he had a look of Charlton Heston. I don't suppose you've ever heard of him?'

'Of course I have – *Ben Hur*. Very sexy.'

Mark laughed and glanced away. 'Well, Mum thought he was, I think. Wooden leg or no.' He turned back to me. 'He lost his left leg during the war, during the Normandy Landings.'

'A hero, then.'

He ignored me again, his eyes on Jade. She'd pushed the bowl of melted ice cream away and was scribbling in the little notebook I'd given her to keep her quiet as we'd waited to be served. He said in that lovely voice of his, 'What's that you're drawing, Jade?'

It's easy to tell when people aren't easy round young kids – they ask them questions, as though that might kick-start a conversation like they were at a dinner party. Jade only stared at him and after a bit she returned to the orange and green mess she was working on. He went on watching her with that single-minded intensity he had. Desperate to regain his attention I said, 'Ben told me you were in the Marines.'

He frowned. 'Did you and Ben talk about me a lot?'

'No – not really – just the usual stuff people tell each other –'

Coldly he said, 'Usual stuff? That doesn't sound like Ben. He likes to get beyond the usual.'

'He only told me that you were in the Royal Marines, that you were wounded during the Falklands War.' I hesitated, but then rushed the words out anyway. 'Danny was in the Marines.'

He gazed at me. After a while he said, 'I was an officer, a very junior second lieutenant. I just about knew where the Falkland Islands were – *very* far away.' He smiled slightly.

'I loved that I was going to war. Terrible eh? I can hardly believe what a vicious little sod I was.'

'You were never vicious.'

He raised his eyebrows and looked like Ben for a split second.

'So, were you wounded?'

After a bit he said, 'Yes, I was wounded.'

Trying to keep my voice light, to not sound too nosy, I said, 'How long were you in the marines?'

'Am I being interviewed?'

I laughed – it seemed best to make a joke of it. 'Yes. So, Mr Walker – you were in the Royal Marines…?'

'Yes, I was. Not for very long – although I still managed to squeeze a war in. Not a very *big* war, not like Dad's, but all the same…' He sipped his tea. Setting his cup down he glanced at me. 'I wouldn't have left, I wanted to stay on but I wasn't fit enough. I had to leave.'

'And then what did you do?'

'Oh you know – drifted. Unemployed…*unemployable*.' He smiled at me. 'I was on the streets for a while – begging.'

'Really?' I was amazed.

'Terrible, eh? The way this country treats its veterans…shocking!' He laughed. 'Why are you so astonished? I was at a loss. I felt my life – my reason for a life – had been snatched away from me. I was an officer in the Royal Marines. I didn't want to be anything else. Besides – I didn't think I was capable of anything else.'

'How did you get off the streets?'

'My mother, Joy, came and found me.' He picked up a sachet of sugar and turned it over and over, his eyes fixed on it. At last he said, 'She found me – I don't know how – perseverance, I suppose. She said I'd left a trail – made me feel like a slug – although of course she didn't mean to, just a figure of speech. Anyway…she took me home. Got me on my feet.' He looked up and smiled at me too brightly. 'Got

201

me fit enough to go to university, but that was a waste of time – didn't fit in. All the other students were so anti-everything I'd been for...' He looked down at the sachet again. 'Anti-war – I used to wonder what they thought they knew about it. So I left at the end of my first term. I started to write, and that was a waste of time, too, at first. But you know – you keep trying, keep pushing at doors...'

'But you missed being a Marine.'

'Less and less, over the years.' He looked at me curiously. 'Have you ever thought of enlisting?'

'Me? You're joking, right?'

'No.'

I snorted and looked away. We were sitting by the window but you couldn't see out for condensation. I rubbed a view hole, trying to displace the anger I felt, trying to look like I didn't care that he'd got me so wrong. It had started to rain and I remembered Jade didn't have her coat. I silently cursed myself.

He touched my hand and I jerked back, shocked, like he'd pressed a burning cigarette against my flesh. I looked at him and he smiled crookedly, as if he'd realised he'd slighted me and was trying to make amends. Carl used to have the same realisations, the same sense of knowing when I was hurt or disappointed in him. Sometimes he'd try teasing me out of myself; he'd tickle me and we'd start play-fighting, end up in bed. I pressed my lips together, struck by grief as I was a hundred times a day.

Quietly Mark said, 'Steven, the time I spent in the marines was the happiest time of my life. I had purpose, direction – *respect* –'

'I don't need to wear a uniform to feel respected.'

'Well that's good. Good. Good for you.'

'I do a useful job.'

'Yes, you do.'

'A job that doesn't involve killing people.'

He laughed. 'Hopefully not.'

'You think I don't have any ambition –'

'*Do* you have ambition?'

I couldn't face him. I wanted to say yes – my ambition is to be you, to live your cool and tidy life. I imagined being his shadow – less than that – being with him without being seen so that he couldn't hide from me. I would see everything of him then and it would take my mind off this weight of grief that no one could be bothered to care about or even notice. So there – that's my ambition, to be wound up in him, to forget my useless self.

I made myself look at him and he gazed back, this soft, understanding look that makes you want to confess the worst thought you ever had because if you did you knew he would help you. I had to bite my lip to stop myself blurting something ridiculous and degrading. And all the time he watched me, making me wonder if he realised the effect he was having.

Gently he said, 'Steven, why don't you come and have supper with me tonight?'

From the corner of my eye I saw Jade put her crayon down. She tugged at my sleeve. 'Daddy, I need a wee.'

When we came back from the toilets Mark had paid for the teas and was standing by the door. He said, 'It's raining. I'll give you a lift home.'

Chapter 18

Ben slept until late afternoon and then went into his study to work on the paper he was about to publish. He'd explained briefly what the paper was about but, knowing how squeamish she was, he'd smiled. 'I won't put you off your supper, don't worry.'

She'd protested that she was interested. He'd laughed.

She ironed his shirts. She thought about their visit to the hospital later that evening, how it would disrupt Nathan's hypothetical bedtime. Lately it wasn't so hypothetical, lately she had got him down at around six thirty. The evening would stretch ahead of her. She would watch TV alone. Ben didn't watch television, except occasionally when he was too exhausted even to speak. Even more occasionally they'd eat their tea in front of *Eastenders* or *Coronation Street* and she'd feel like he'd made an extra special effort to fit in with what she was used to. It was an uncomfortable feeling, as though he was humouring her. Boredom radiated from him, making her shift restlessly, unable to concentrate on the stories. She'd think of her Mam and Alan who never used their dining table but always ate on the sofa, one at each end, the remote controls for the telly, the video and the satellite box between them, *TV Quick* open on the day's listing. Behind them the unused table reflected the lamplight, a pyramid of bright green porcelain apples placed in its exact centre.

Watching television alone was boring. She'd taken to having long baths, if Nathan allowed, or reading the newspapers Ben had delivered but never had time to look at. She liked *The Guardian* on Mondays and *The Times* on Wednesdays. She'd begun to look out for certain columnists, women who wrote about what it was like when your boss got too demanding or your friends longed for babies/husbands and you didn't, or vice versa. She found such writers laughable, they made her feel as if she had done something right with her life, although she was sure that wasn't their intention.

Ben had said once, 'I'm more old-fashioned than most men my age. Does that bother you?'

'Depends how you're old-fashioned.'

'I don't want my wife to work. Susan worked.'

Secretly she'd been pleased. She hated her job as a bank cashier. All the same she'd made a stand to test him.

'What if I want a career?'

He'd raised his eyebrows. 'As?'

That *as?* It had made her feel stupid. She had let the subject drop and he never mentioned it again. As soon as they knew she was pregnant, only a few weeks after their marriage, he suggested she gave up work. Her morning sickness had lasted all day and was horrible and she'd agreed at once.

Kitty hung the last ironed shirt in Ben's wardrobe. She went to the window and looked down on the rainy garden. When Nathan was older – soon – she would take up gardening. She pored over the catalogues that dropped out of the Sunday supplements and imagined planting fruit trees and bushes – plums and quinces, gooseberries and currants, old-fashioned fruits she could make jam from. She fancied herself making jams and chutneys. She fancied a greenhouse and a vegetable patch and a physic garden like the one Ben had taken her to see at Kew. He had laughed at her idea of having a smaller-scale version at home. 'I may have to burn you as a witch. As a surgeon I have to take a hard line.'

'Medicine isn't just about bones,' she'd told him.

Being thought of as a witch appealed to her but she kept its appeal secret from him. She fantasised about making potions that could erase memories, whole months and years of memories. She would serve him wine laced with this concoction and wipe Susan from his mind and heart and it would be like clearing a tenacious weed from a path.

One Sunday, early in their relationship, Ben had taken her to meet Simon. As Ben parked the car and she was about to get out he had said, 'Dad's old, he can be tactless – blunt, I think he terms it. Just smile. Remember he's trying to shock you.'

But Simon had been lovely. 'He'd turned on the charm,' Ben said later, 'he's probably fallen in love with you.' As they were leaving, the old man had taken her hand. 'My dear, come and see me on your own – two's company and all that. We'll have tea together and I can tell you all his secrets.'

'I don't have any secrets, Dad,' Ben had said dryly. 'You'll have to invent some.'

'Oh, I shall! Will you come, Kitty?'

She had told him she would.

She had been shy at first because it seemed so strange to be a guest of a boyfriend's father, grown up and sophisticated, *middle-class*, she supposed. He had served her tea on the lawn – he always sat outside if the weather allowed, he told her – and he had walked her round the garden, showing her the roses his wife had planted. The sky clouded and began to spit. He took her inside, into the sitting room where she hadn't been before, where the sideboard and mantelpiece were crowded with family photographs. Ben and Mark looked out at her from gaudy school photos, two little boys smart in green blazers and maroon ties; as teenagers with longish, seventies-style haircuts, but still smart and slightly nerdy. Ben in cap and gown, smiling between his proud parents; Mark in uniform, alone and deadly serious. She hadn't met Mark then, and she'd picked up the photograph and looked at it more closely.

'Handsome boy, isn't he?' Simon said.

She'd glanced at him, blushing as though she'd been caught out making eyes at another man. 'Nearly as handsome as Ben.'

Simon laughed, delighted and surprised. 'Good girl! Very well said!'

Next was the photograph of Ben and Susan on their wedding day. For this picture Simon came to stand a little closer to her. Gently he said, 'What do you make of her?'

'She's lovely.'

He took the picture from its place a little behind Mark's photo, only to put it down without care so that it was almost hidden. 'Now,' he said brightly. 'Let's have another cup of tea before you have to go.'

Later that evening Ben had asked her how her meeting had gone. She had wanted to say that she'd seen his wedding photograph and that he looked blissfully happy to be married to such a woman. She wanted to ask him if Susan was taller than he was, because it seemed from the picture that she was, a little, a centimetre, maybe. She wanted to ask how she felt that day, if he'd been nervous, if he'd been sure of her and certain she would arrive on time, or dreading her lateness, the sick fear – no matter how remote – that she might jilt him. Had Mark been his best man? Or had he chosen a fellow doctor, repeatedly asking him if he had the ring, pestering him for the time, to the exact minute. Where had they gone on honeymoon? Was it to a grand hotel, champagne on ice beside the vast, four-poster bed she pictured them in? She wanted to ask if he had loved his first wife madly and passionately but shallowly, hoping that he had and that it was the kind of blazing love that had quickly burnt out. Most of all she wanted to ask if he missed her still, half knowing the answer, half unsure.

Instead she had asked only how Susan had died, timidly, ready to suffer his pretence of not hearing her even as he made it clear she mustn't repeat the question. But he had said, 'She had an ectopic pregnancy. There were complications no one could have foreseen, an infection that took hold after surgery.'

'She was going to have a baby?' She was incredulous; the very idea of it made her feel giddy with jealousy.

'No, sweetheart.' He sighed as though he was explaining it for the tenth time to one of his thicker students. 'The pregnancy was *ectopic* – outside the womb. It was never viable.'

Viable. Her jealousy lessened and became manageable.

She went downstairs and prepared Nathan's bottle to take to the hospital then stacked the dishwasher, going into Ben's study to hunt for stray coffee cups. He wasn't at his desk as she expected; he had switched off his laptop but left the French window open and she went to close it. She peered at her reflection in the dark glass.

She was too skinny, flat-chested, with too short, elfin hair, the cut Ben liked best. She thought of Susan – of the photographs she'd seen of her – and remembered that at her own wedding she had overheard someone say that she was the exact opposite of Ben's first wife. It had been just before she and Ben were to take the floor for their first dance and she was inside a toilet cubicle, a bit drunk, struggling with the long skirt and net petticoats of her wedding dress. She had paused, standing stock-still to listen, her skirts around her thighs, but nothing else was said. Not that it mattered. She knew that she was Susan's opposite, not only in looks but in every way.

From his study doorway Ben said, 'Kitty?' He was holding Nathan in his arms, both of them dressed ready to go out, Nathan wearing the navy velour cap and matching suit that he had just about grown out of, clothes she never dressed him in any more but were still in his drawer. She told herself that Ben couldn't be expected to be up-to-date with his baby's wardrobe. He smiled at her. 'Are you ready?'

'Two minutes.'

'I know you don't like hospitals –'

'Ben, he's your Dad – don't be daft. I'll fetch Nathan's stuff.'

Ben hesitated. 'Perhaps you should stay here with the baby – we shouldn't disrupt his routine.'

'Simon wants to see him.'

'OK.' Miserably, he said, 'Let's go and get it over with.'

Mark emptied a bag of pre-washed salad leaves into a bowl. He would leave oil and vinegar on the table and the boy could dress his salad or not, as he chose. The table was set with cutlery and side plates and his mother's napkins he'd found in a kitchen drawer, unused since her death. Holding the square of yellowing white linen to his face he had breathed in deeply in case it still smelled of her. There was only a faint mustiness.

He had dropped Steven off across the road from the tower blocks that dominated the centre of the estate. The boy had slammed the car door, lifting his daughter onto his hip before stooping down to the window so that Mark had pressed the switch to open it.

'Thanks for the lift.'

'Go, quickly, before you both get soaked.'

Already the rain had plastered Steven's dark hair to his head, but all the same he seemed reluctant to go. 'Tonight, then?'

Mark nodded.

'About eight? Should I bring a bottle or something?'

'Steven, go – get your baby inside.'

Mark had watched him run across the expanse of concrete towards the first tower, thinking how young he looked, no more than seventeen or eighteen, the little girl bouncing on his hip like a rag doll. He set her down as they reached the shelter of the tower's entrance. Side by side they looked like brother and sister rather than father and daughter. Jade had held up her hand and waved to him, whether or not at Steven's bidding he couldn't guess.

He prepared macaroni cheese, making the best of what was in Simon's fridge and pantry because he couldn't face going to the supermarket, grateful as he often was that Joy had shown him the rudiments of cooking. 'One day your wife will thank me,' she'd told him. She had stood him on a chair beside the Aga; she had said, 'Now, you watch – with enough butter to melt into the flour there won't be any lumps – we just keep stirring like so...' She'd closed her hand around his on the wooden spoon. 'That's right. Nice and steady as we pour in the milk. When Simon comes home it'll be all ready and he won't complain about the lumps because you did such a good job!'

When did she stop referring to him as Simon and start calling him Daddy? Grating the hard lump of cheddar he'd found in the fridge, Mark tried to remember. He thought that it had been around Ben's eighth birthday, the first birthday to be celebrated in their new home. Perhaps this change had come about in case the hordes of children Joy had invited to the party thought them odd, teasing them for not having a Mummy and Daddy but a pair of adults called Simon and Joy. Joy hated to think she might inadvertently embarrass Ben and him.

He'd suspected Joy worried that she stood out amongst the mothers who waited at the gates of their private day school. She was older, tweedier, her salt and pepper hair set in the style she'd worn since the war. The other mothers wore mini-skirts or trouser suits and let their hair fall lose around their shoulders; some even wore jeans and looked very young, almost as young as the Mummy he was trying hard to forget and remember and forget again. He would look away from these mothers, keeping his eyes so obviously averted that Joy would glance back anxiously. She was afraid that he would be snatched away from her by one of Danny's brothers, although none of those men had shown any interest in him or Ben. She seemed afraid of so much in those days behind her brave, cheerful front. Nowadays he only wondered how she coped at all.

Mark measured out the dry macaroni and tipped it into a pan of boiling salted water, remembering Joy, the precise, careful way she went about everything she did. He remembered his mother and Susan working together in this kitchen. Just as she'd shown him how to cook, Joy had set about teaching Susan too, but in a more light-hearted way, as though conceding that modern women had a duty not to know the things she knew about sauces and cakes and pastry. Joy had liked Susan and admired her because she had been a career woman too, once, for almost as long as she had been a wife and mother. Joy wasn't disappointed, as Simon was, that Susan didn't want children, but believed it was a brave decision. 'I could never be so rational, never so free of my – what do they call it nowadays? – *biological clock ticking*!'

Bubbles rose to the surface of the boiling water. Mark stirred the pasta, remembering how Susan had admired Joy in return. 'An ideal mother-in-law – she doesn't interfere.'

They had been in bed, of course – because what else did they do together but go straight to his bed – and Susan had sat up, resting her chin on her raised knees. He'd trailed his finger along the bumps of her spine and she'd glanced at him. 'Joy's in love with you, you know.'

He remembered how shocked he'd felt. 'Don't say things like that!'

Susan had smiled, infuriating him.

'She's my *mother*, for God's sake!'

'Ah, but she isn't, Mark. *Annette* was your mother.'

'Let's not talk about it.' He'd tried to pull her into his arms but she moved away. Sighing he said, 'Can't we have an ordinary conversation for once?'

She'd laughed.

She had stayed in London when Ben had moved back to Thorp and a consultant's position in the hospital there. Thorp was a joke to Susan – it couldn't be taken seriously. She had been convinced that Ben would come to his senses and move back to London. Mark had been convinced that his brother's marriage would wither and die under such pressure, but it seemed only to flourish. 'He doesn't have to feel guilty about being at work all the time!' Susan had laughed, as though astonished at his naivety. 'And when we *do* see each other…'

'I don't want to know.'

'Of course you do! Of course you want to know how you compare.' Kissing his mouth, she drew back to frown at him. 'You're very alike. Both wishing the other dead.'

A few days later Joy had visited him and he had taken her out to lunch. He'd imagined that she could smell Susan on him, that tell-tale blonde hairs clung to his jacket to give him away. But that afternoon Joy had seemed more preoccupied with the past. After lunch they had strolled to Trafalgar Square and up the steps to the National Gallery. Looking over the square to Big Ben, she had turned to him.

'During the war I came here with my fiancé Peter. We talked about how many children we would have when the war ended. We named them. When I heard Peter had died I think I mourned those babies almost as much as I mourned him. Silly, eh?' Turning back to the view, she said, 'Sometimes in crowds like this I imagine other lives I might have lived – if Peter had lived, if I hadn't met Simon, lots of *ifs*. But then I always come back to you and Ben and know I would choose to live my life just as I have, because of you and your brother. I hope Annette would have approved of the way I brought you up.'

'Of course –'

She had taken his hand and squeezed it briefly. 'I wanted you and Ben to be close.'

He'd tried to laugh. 'Personality clash, I'm sorry –'

'Oh, it's not your fault, no one's fault.' Briskly she said, 'Anyway, you're both grown up now, living your own lives, successful...it's enough for me that you respect and care for each other.' She'd searched his face, wanting to be reassured that he did care for his brother, and he remembered being unable to meet her eyes, feeling only the intense shame of his affair. But shame was a constant in his life. Only when he was with Susan did he feel defiant enough to overcome it, to believe that nothing mattered but his love for her.

Outside the gallery he'd forced himself to smile at his mother. 'Shall we go in and see the paintings?'

She'd nodded and linked her arm through his.

In December 1983 she'd found him begging outside Victoria tube station. Begging was all he was fit for, haunted as he was by nightmares of sinking ships, of dead men rising from the sea still burning. He had begun to see the dead on the streets; they hailed him, hearty, pleased, although their skin hung off in ragged, black sheets. They stank of burning engine oil and he couldn't get their stink out of his mouth and nose. And sometimes, if he turned around quickly, he would see Danny, and the dead would recede into nothingness, and the streets would become still, although he was racing: his heart, his blood, his thoughts – all speeded up as though his body was set on fast-forward. He would crouch down and cover his head with his arms. He would close his eyes tightly and pray. Slowly the streets would return to a normal pace, feet hurrying past him, ordinary, living, contemptuous feet, and he'd dare to look up and eventually hold out his hand for pennies.

But Joy had followed the trail he'd left at hostels and Salvation Army kitchens and, by some miracle, found him.

She'd sat down at his side, and for a moment she didn't speak, as if they had only been apart for a few minutes instead of months. At last she said, 'It's so cold, isn't it? I rather wish I'd worn my warmer coat. Feel my hands – like ice!' She'd held his hand between her own, rubbing his fingers that were numb with cold. 'Shall we find a café and have a cup of tea? Shall we?' She stood up. 'Come on. We'll have toasted tea cake, too.'

Mark drained the pasta. The doorbell rang and he frowned at his watch. The boy was exactly on time, almost as if he'd stood outside the door waiting to press the bell just at the moment the hand of his own watch jerked on to the hour. It was the kind of thing he himself would do.

Going out into the hall, Mark glanced at himself in the mirror by the coat stand, a full length, unforgiving mirror that had hung in the same place since he first came to this house. It was no more than a glance. All the same, he saw that he looked terrified. He shook his head, exasperated with himself.

Steven said, 'This is delicious – you're a good cook.'

Mark pushed the half-empty dish of macaroni cheese towards him. 'Have some more.'

'Sure? You could save it for tomorrow...'

Mark laughed. 'It's all right. I'll force myself to go shopping tomorrow. Finish the salad, too.'

The boy did as he was told. He seemed to be starving but Mark remembered when he was his age that there never seemed to be enough food in the world. He'd pushed his own meal around the plate with his fork and the few mouthfuls he took tasted of nothing and were too stodgy. He concentrated on the salad, noticing that the boy ate the mixed leaves with no dressing at all. Steven liked bland dishes then, like a child. He wondered what he should give him for dessert and thought of the tinned peaches and carton of custard in the pantry. That would do. Steven would enjoy the cloying sweetness, no doubt.

Mark finished his own meal and fetched the tin of fruit. He opened it swiftly and emptied half its contents into a cereal bowl. Snipping off the top of the custard carton he said, 'I hope Jade didn't get too soaked in the rain.'

'No – she was fine. Her mam went on a bit about me forgetting her coat. I told her it was blue skies when we set out.'

Taking his cleared plate, Mark set the bowl of peaches and custard in front of him. Steven smiled. 'Aren't you having any?'

'No, I have to watch my weight.'

'You? You're dead slim.' He began to eat, but more slowly, as though aware he'd wolfed his main course. When he'd finished he set his spoon down gently in the bowl and glanced at him. 'That was lovely. Thank you.'

'Would you like a cup of tea? Coffee?'

'I'm all right for a minute.' He smiled shyly. 'You keep springing up. You should let your meal settle.'

Mark laughed. 'OK. Do you mind if I smoke?'

'It's your house.'

He lit a cigarette. 'I'm going to have to spring up again and fetch an ash tray.'

'I'll get it.' Steven was on his feet at once. 'Where is it?'

'There, beside the fruit bowl on the dresser.'

At the dresser Steven picked up a photograph of Kitty and Ben on their wedding day. He squinted at it then took a pair of glasses from a slim case in his pocket. Putting them on he studied the photo before turning to him. 'All the nurses said she was really pretty.' He put the picture down again and took off his glasses. 'They look really happy – suited. And they've got a baby boy? Nathan? That's right, isn't it? It's a nice name – unusual.' He sat down again and placed the ashtray between them. After a moment he said quickly, 'I'm nervous, that's why I talk too fast – do everything too fast...I'm not usually like this. I'm quite a calm person, really.'

'I suppose I'm nervous, too.'

'Yeah? You don't act like you are.'

'No, I'm dead cool, me.'

Steven looked down at the empty bowl in front of him, straightening the angle of the spoon. 'I know I talk rough – real Teesside.'

'Sorry, I didn't mean to take you off.'

'But you did.' He looked up at him. 'You're a good mimic.'

'I used to have the same accent, remember?'

'Danny's a good mimic.'

Mark exhaled cigarette smoke. 'Yes. I remember.'

'I *am* here to talk about him, aren't I?'

'Do you want to talk about him?'

'Do you?'

Mark drew on the cigarette deeply and wondered how he would appear to this boy if he got up and poured himself a large scotch. Affected, he thought – like he was a character in a play trying to disguise the fact that he'd forgotten his lines. But he needed a drink. 'Look,' he said, 'I'm going to have a scotch, will you join me?'

'I don't drink.'

'Could I get you a soft drink? Would you like that tea –'

'No, thanks.'

He poured himself a small scotch, noting that the bottle was almost finished, that last night Simon and Iain had been generous with their measures. He would have to buy another bottle and thought about how long he would be staying in this house to drink it. Perhaps Simon would prefer it if he went home and left the house to its own devices. But he knew he wouldn't do that, not until Simon was safely out of hospital and settled.

As Mark sat down Steven said, 'Do you drink a lot?'

Mark laughed, surprised. 'Yes. Far too much.'

216

'Really?'

'No, not really. I stay sober, most of the time. You ask a lot of questions, don't you?'

'Making up for lost time.'

'Is that what we're doing?' Mark sat back in his seat, regarding him carefully. 'You don't drink at all? Why?'

'Dunno. Hate feeling drunk? Hate not being able to think clearly? Lack of cash? Lots of reasons. My mam drank, when I was a kid. It puts you off, a bit. Well, it put *me* off.'

Mark found himself gazing at the boy. He was astonishingly pretty, such fine skin over such good bones. He had Danny's big dark eyes fringed with the same long lashes, Danny's full, soft mouth and straight, white teeth. Even his nose, which looked as if it had once been broken, was Danny's. He felt the rush of fear he got when waking from nightmares of drowning; or the nightmare of Danny, come to fetch him back – the more usual nightmare, lately. He sipped his drink, concentrating on its taste and the way it warmed him. He knew the boy was watching him, considering his own resemblance to their father. He made himself meet his eye.

'Do you live with your mother, Steven?'

'No – I have my own flat in the tower – right at the top. Dead cheap. No one wants to live there. It's quite big – big enough for a family – that's who they were built for, after all – families.'

'My mother – Annette – she used to tell me that one day we'd live in a tower. She used to make it sound like something out of a fairy tale.'

'He talks about her quite a lot.'

'He shouldn't.'

Steven glanced away. 'Can I wash up for you?' He stood up and began clearing the table. Mark got up too and began to help him. Running the hot tap, Steven said, 'I'm really tidy, I can't stand mess.' He squeezed washing-up liquid into the water. 'I tidy up Nicola's flat when I'm round there.

217

She thinks it's great, thinks I must be soft in the head. She's a slut,' he smiled at him as if to soften the word. 'But she looks after Jade really well, she's a good mother. She says she'd rather play with her than hoover under her bed. I say maybe she could do both – she just tells me to fuck off.'

Mark laughed. 'When did you split up?'

'We were never together.' He rinsed a soapy plate and passed it to Mark to dry. 'Not *living* together. I don't think I could live with Nicola. She says I'm her best friend but that she couldn't live with me, either.'

'But you had Jade together.'

'Yeah, well, you don't have to live with someone for that to happen, do you?' He frowned at him. 'You think I should live with her for Jade's sake?'

'No.'

'No – you're not that old. It's only my grandad's generation that thinks that.'

'Are your grandparents still alive?'

'Yeah. They think Jade is fantastic, although neither of them was happy when they found out she was on the way. Grandad asked me why I couldn't stick with my own race. Mam told him he was a shocking old man. Big, screaming row they had.'

'That must have been difficult for you.'

'Not really. The rows Mam's family have are more comic than anything – all sparks and noise and daft insults – *never darken my door again* stuff. They've made up the next day. It's not like, well, you know…not like Danny.'

They finished the dishes in silence. The boy worked efficiently with a look of single-minded concentration on his face that reminded him of Ben. He remembered how he and Ben had to take it in turns to wash up after a meal. Joy wrote out a rota of jobs to be done before the allotted two hours of homework and the hour of TV they were allowed each evening: *Blue Peter* or *Magpie* or *Scooby-Doo* – they could choose. Neither of them thought to complain or

218

argue. When he'd first arrived to live with his new parents he had thought that this was how all normal families behaved.

Steven washed the last fork and plate and emptied the washing up bowl. Handing him a towel to dry his hands, Mark said, 'Shall I show you around? Come on – you can have the guided tour.'

I wanted to say to him that it was all right, we didn't have to talk about Danny if he didn't want to, we could talk about anything but. I remembered what Ben had said, that Mark could be difficult and I was to tread carefully, making me think of minefields. Grandad said that during the Second World War his platoon had driven sheep and goats over land where they thought mines were buried. I felt like one of those goats, only I was driving myself forward, so how stupid did that make me?

I followed him along the hallway and into the big room at the front of the house where this Simon had his study. There were books everywhere but no novels, none of Mark's books that I could see, just great heavy medical and science books, all dusty and faded so that I imagined how brittle their pages would be. There was a skull on one of the bookshelves, a gibbon's, Mark said. He said it was very old, a Victorian gibbon. He smiled that gentle, wry smile of his. He took the skull down and moved its hinged jaw so that it looked like a ventriloquist's dummy talking. 'Poor thing,' he said. 'One day I'll give it a decent burial.'

There was another animal skull on Simon's desk and a stuffed stoat in a glass case. The stoat was baring its teeth and its jet-like eyes managed to give it an expression of fear and viciousness in one snarling look. I put my glasses on and peered at it. The bit of tree it stood on had clumps of moss stuck to it, fern, too; it all looked so real that you could imagine the stoat was about to move, that if you lifted the glass it would jump up and bite you.

219

Mark said, 'You need glasses for close work, like me.'

I took my specs off and put them back in my pocket. I'm vain about them, I think they make me look geeky, and I have enough trouble with the way I look than to go around inviting more.

Stepping toward the desk, Mark pretended to look at the stoat too. After a bit he said, 'Ben calls this stuff *the relics*. Most of it belonged to Simon's father. Simon was very close to his father.'

'Are you close to Simon?'

He looked at me. 'I love him.'

'But?'

'But Simon and I got off on the wrong foot.'

He picked up the little skull from the desk and held it out to me on his palm. 'This is a cat's skull. Ben found the cat run over on the road outside and begged Simon to help him dissect it. Mum was horrified but Simon said it would be educational. He wanted us to be doctors, you see, like him.'

'But the cat must have been someone's pet –'

'But it was dead.'

'Even so!'

He put the cat skull down and touched my arm gently. 'Out of here, now, it's depressing.'

We went upstairs and I couldn't help thinking of Carl, how he'd lead me up his stairs to bed. At the top of the house, in the attic that looked right across the cemetery, we stood side by side at the window and Mark said, 'Quite a view, eh?' He laughed. 'When we first came to this house Ben would tell me that all the dead people would cross the road in the night and come and get me.' Turning to me, he said, 'What do you think of Ben? He's impressive, isn't he?'

I shrugged, unsure of what he expected me to say. I remembered the first time I spoke to Mr Ben Walker. He had a reputation for being off-hand, of not suffering fools, but one afternoon he approached me and said, 'Are you any

220

relation to a Daniel Carter?' and he seemed nervous and unsure of himself, shifty even, as though we were about to deal.

Mark turned back to the view. Dully he said, 'He is impressive. Always was. Brave. Danny absolutely adored him. Simon did, too. They thought he was a proper boy. Someone they could play with.'

I looked at him from the corner of my eye, wanting to judge his mood so as to say the right thing, but he caught me out and smiled. 'You must have guessed that Ben and I don't get along?'

'Yeah, I suppose.'

'But he *is* impressive. A real man's man.'

'He's all right.'

He laughed.

I turned to him. I blurted, 'Are you going back to London?'

'Eventually.'

'Would you take me with you?'

I hadn't meant to say it. He looked at me, this sad, concerned look that made me want to die of shame for sounding so needy. I stared out of the window and thought of all the dead people who had lived their lives without blurting stuff out, men and women lying in the ground regretting their silences. He was standing quite close to me and my skin bristled because I thought he was going to touch me again, but he only shoved his hands into his pockets and gazed out over the graves.

He said, 'What about your little girl? What about Nicola and your mother and brothers?'

What about me, I thought. I said, 'I wouldn't abandon Jade, London isn't so far away.'

'Doesn't she need her father close by?'

'Yeah, you're right.' I smiled at him to show I was OK. In my best bright voice I said, 'I'd best be off – work in the morning.'

As we got downstairs I said, 'Thanks for the meal.'

'My pleasure.'

'*Do come again?*' I hadn't meant to sound so hurt. I glanced away. 'Sorry. I'm a cunt sometimes.'

'Don't use words like that about yourself.' He took a step closer to me and frowned as if he was seeing me for the first time. 'Look at me! Stand up straight!'

'What?'

'You cringe, you don't look at me directly. I don't know if I can trust you.'

'Trust me with what? I don't cringe!'

'When I was your age I –' He stopped himself. Incredulously he said, 'Jesus. I sound like Dad.'

'When you were my age what?'

'Nothing.' He shook his head. 'It doesn't matter.'

'Come on – say it! When you were my age you were fighting a war – you think I should join up!'

'Of course I don't! I don't think you'd last five minutes in a barracks.'

'I would!' I sounded like Jade when she knew she was losing the argument over bedtime. I felt my face burn. He reached out and placed his hand flat against my cheek and I had that weak-kneed feeling you get when someone you've fancied for ages unexpectedly takes you into his confidence. It was disgusting and disturbing and it took at lot for me not to grasp his wrist and kiss his palm. He held my gaze, giving me this tender, *loving* look so I felt myself become hard and it was appalling and fantastic and sick as can be.

Gently he said, 'Steven, does Danny know you're gay?'

It felt as though he'd slapped me. I sprang away. 'Christ you're a twat! Fucking *twat*…!' I was too angry to look at him. I would have walked out but my jacket was in his kitchen, my keys and wallet in its pocket. I tried to get past him to fetch it but he caught my arm.

'It's nothing to be ashamed of.'

'I'm not ashamed!' I shrugged him off. 'I'm not.'

'But you haven't told your father.'

'Would you tell Danny who you were fucking? You wouldn't tell him anything!'

'That's not the point – he's not my father.'

'Yes – he is! And you're just like him – a fucking twat!'

Evenly he said, 'You've got a foul mouth. You should try to control it.'

'Should I? Why's that? So I can sound like a get like you?'

'A *get*?' He laughed. 'You are an old-fashioned boy, aren't you? It must be years since anyone called me a *get* – it was probably some corporal I'd pissed off.'

I went into the kitchen and found my jacket. He watched me from the doorway so I turned to face him, defiant. Spitefully I said, 'Dad wants to see you, you know. Fucking *desperate* to see you.'

He looked like I'd hit him. 'He wants to see me?'

'Course he does! You're his little angel, aren't you? That's what he calls you – his little angel. I think he's expecting some six-year-old kid with wings and a fucking halo! Well, they say Hitler was sentimental, don't they?'

He sat down at the table like his legs wouldn't support him any more. White-faced, he put his hand to his mouth as if some really shocking thought had just occurred to him. But he was remembering, of course, like I remember – certain words or smells or sounds triggering memories so that you have to stop and try to be still and not think. My anger died like a cheap sparkler. I was back to feeling sorry for him, like at the hospital, or the first time I saw him when he looked so scared.

I sat down next to him. 'Mark? It's OK –'

He frowned at me. 'I want you to go. Get out of my sight, don't come near me again.'

'No – you should talk to me –'

'Why? Tell me why I should talk to a foul-mouthed little shit like you?'

'I'm sorry – it was the way you touched me – looked at me – you really did my head in, that's all –'

'Did I?' He sneered. 'I thought you liked me to look at you like that? Wasn't my *looking* what you came here for?'

'No –'

'So you don't want me to fuck you, then?'

I drew back from him. 'For Christ's sake!'

He looked at me, this exaggerated frown on his face. 'You make eyes at me, do you realise that? I know that it's an old-fashioned expression but that's the only way I can describe it – you make big, *take-me-to-bed* eyes. So, what would it be like, do you think? What would it be like if we went to bed together? Maybe we'd have a moment in the heat of it all when we'd meet each other's eyes. There'd be this deathly stillness, like we were both holding our breath. All at once we'd realise just what we were doing and suddenly neither of us would be any use to the other, dicks as shrivelled as if we were drowning in a frozen sea. We'd have to scuttle about putting our clothes back on, cringing apologies if we accidentally brushed skin against skin. Wouldn't that be excruciating? God – your flesh would absolutely *crawl*, wouldn't it? You'd be thinking *Jesus Christ Almighty – I almost sucked my brother's cock! What kind of bloody perverted animal am I?*'

He stood up, pacing like he couldn't keep still. 'Or maybe it wouldn't be like that. Maybe it would be sweet and tender – you're such a gorgeous boy after all – maybe I could somehow make myself forget the *wrongness* of it – maybe you could – it would have to be a joint effort, though –'

'You're not gay.'

'What? You mumble and I have to strain to hear you – it's annoying. What did you say?'

Louder, hating the sound of my voice, I said, 'You're not gay.'

He gazed at me for so long I had to turn away.

At last he said, 'I shouldn't have asked you here. I don't know why I did – I should have stuck with my first instincts.'

'So why didn't you?'

'Curiosity. Irresistible, the urge to know more.'

'What do you want to know?'

'I think we've both said enough for one night.'

'*For one night* means you want to talk to me again.'

'I need to think about that.'

'I'd like us to be able to talk.'

'Yes, I know you would.'

'I don't want anything from you. Don't think I'm on the scrounge.'

'I don't think that.' He sighed. 'Listen – I'm sorry. Sometimes...' Shaking his head he said, 'Sometimes...well – sometimes I lose control.'

Like Danny, I wanted to say, and it was as if he knew what I was thinking because on a rush of breath he said, 'I try to behave.'

I could hardly look at him. 'Yeah. I know.'

'All knowing, aren't you?' He laughed like he was in despair. 'If you know so much then maybe you'll forgive me.'

He saw me to the door. He said, 'Goodnight, Steven, thank you for coming,' as if all the things we'd said to each other hadn't been said at all.

I walked through the cemetery and stopped at Carl's grave. The flowers in the urn were wilted and I put them in the bin. He'd told me not to bring flowers, but to save my money. I told him flowers didn't cost very much, although they do. If he'd been a saint the flowers wouldn't die and his body wouldn't decompose and in a thousand years they would dig him up just to check and he'd be just as he was when I kissed him goodbye in the funeral home. I made a mental note to buy flowers the next day. There were other things I could save on.

Chapter 19

Doctor Walker said, 'Ah – Annette, there you are! Dusting my mother's horrible sideboard! My dear, leave that and come with me a moment, would you? I need you to hold on to a curtain pole while I fix it to the wall.'

She followed him into the dining room with its oil painting of dead birds and rabbits lying limply next to a jug. Looking away from the rabbits' glassy eyes, she noticed the box of books and toys on the floor. She hoped he wouldn't press more of them onto her. She would have to put them in the waste bin outside the cemetery. That's what she would do. She felt relieved to have come up with a plan.

The doctor said, 'Annette, could you hop up on that chair, do you think? It's quite sturdy and safe.'

She took her shoes off and climbed up on to one of the chairs he'd pulled away from the dining table into the bay. The chair was big and solid, made from some glossy black wood, fruit and flowers carved into its back. Annette felt the sawdust padding of its seat give a little beneath her feet, like wet sand on a beach. She stared out at the garden. She thought of Mark slumped against Danny's shoulder as he carried him to their bed.

Doctor Walker said, 'Now then. Now, is this going to work? No, I rather think not. I'm so sorry, Annette, I'm wasting your time – I really don't think you'll be able to hold it on your own, the wretched thing is too long.' He held out his hand to her. 'Hop down, my dear.'

As he helped her down she swayed a little. He frowned. 'Are you still feeling poorly?'

'No!' He went on frowning at her so she said quickly, 'I'm fine, really.'

He nodded but she knew he wasn't convinced. All the same he said brightly, 'Do you know what day it is today?'

'No…'

'My dear – don't look so worried! You haven't forgotten anything! No, *you* haven't, but everyone else has and I'm feeling particularly sorry for myself – it's my birthday, and this morning – when the postman neglected to call – I thought, blow it – I'll buy *myself* a cake! So I did. Chocolate sponge. I'd be delighted if you'd share it with me.'

'I couldn't…'

'Well I'm insisting! So, down tools. The cake calls.'

Danny had dressed Mark in his school uniform. He'd carried him downstairs and sat him beside the sink and rubbed his face hard with the dishcloth. Timidly she'd said, 'I'll wash him, Danny. Let me see to him.'

He'd glanced at her from wiping Mark's hands with the same, grey cloth. 'You have nothing to do with him from now on, you hear me? If you go near him I'll kill you.'

'But Danny…' She stepped towards him and he spun round.

'I said that if you go near him I'll kill you. Isn't that clear enough?' He grabbed a piece of bread from the sliced loaf on the table and thrust it in to Mark's hand. 'I'm taking him to school now. I'll pick him up this afternoon. Don't go in our bedroom, don't you dare.'

Doctor Walker said, 'I'm pleased to say Joy – my wife – is much better. We're hopeful that she'll be home in a few days.'

Dully she said, 'Will you still want me?'

'Of course – even more so. And I've told Joy all about you; she's pleased we've found someone so reliable.'

Annette looked down at the brown, sticky looking slice of cake he had handed her. Cake twice in two days – more than she had ever had. The idea of eating it made her feel sick. She wished she could wrap it up and take it home to Ben. It would be too dangerous to sneak some to Mark.

Mark hadn't looked at her that morning. He had stared at the floor. When Danny had lifted him up to take him to school he had only gazed over Danny's shoulder blankly.

Doctor Walker cleared his throat. 'How are your boys, Annette?'

'Fine.'

He was about to say something when the doorbell rang. He got up. 'Annette, why don't you pour us another cup of tea while I go and see who's calling?'

Simon limped along the hallway to the door as the bell sounded again more insistently. He tried to go faster and his leg throbbed. Feeling his temper rise, he called out, 'All right, I'm coming!' It was his birthday. Although he knew it was childish, he still expected this day of all days to go well. So far it hadn't. That morning he had woken and wondered where on earth he was, so disorientated that for a moment he expected his mother to come barging in to demand why he was still lazing in bed. Remembering, he had been filled with despair. Here he was – his life changed beyond all sense. As his mind cleared further he remembered Joy. He remembered his baby was lost. He rolled onto his side and pulled the bedcovers over his head, determined not to get up at all. Joy was due to come home in a few days; the house was still in a horrible state and he couldn't face its squalor and chaos. But then he had remembered Annette, and it was thinking of her that drove him to get up. He would put on a cheerful face for this girl; he would have to behave himself in front of her.

He paused before opening the front door, wanting to compose his expression so as not to give his pain away. He

228

heard a woman's voice say, 'Isn't this a nice big house, Mark? Isn't this exciting!'

Simon swung the door open hastily.

A smart, pretty young woman smiled at him. 'Doctor Walker? Hello – My name is Miss Wood and I'm this little chap's teacher. I took him home just now to his mummy but the neighbour told me she was here, working for you? I wondered if I might have a word with her…?'

'Oh, of course! Do come in.'

He stood back and held the door as wide as it would go. She stepped past him, her hand on the little boy's back, steering him gently. She smiled at the child. 'Well, here we are, Mark. I told you we'd find her, didn't I!' More quietly, she said, 'I'm afraid he's been quite poorly this morning. I really don't think he should have even been at school but his daddy said he was fine. As you're a doctor perhaps you could…but I don't want to interfere… Oh, dear, I don't know…Mrs Carter *is* here, isn't she?'

'She's in the kitchen, why don't you both come through?'

Annette said, 'Mark!' She stood up and her hand went to her mouth, her eyes widening in distress. She made no move towards her son. His teacher said, 'Mrs Carter – Mark has been terribly unhappy today. I'm sorry, but I really think you should keep him at home until he's feeling well again.' She glanced at Simon. 'I really have to go back to school – my class… I'm so sorry to trouble you like this.'

'It's no trouble. I'll see you out.'

When he went back in to the kitchen Annette was holding her son on her knee. She looked up at him at once. 'We'll get off home. I'm sorry about this, Doctor Walker, I'm sorry you've been bothered.'

'Annette, your son being unwell isn't a bother to me, I'm concerned. Would you like me to see if I can find what's troubling him?'

'Oh no, no – he says he just has a tummy ache. Best I just take him home, tuck him up in bed…it's just a tummy upset.'

Simon sat down next to her and the child hid his face in her breast. He said, 'Mark? Mark, my name is Simon and I look after children who aren't feeling well. I can make them feel better again – I bet I can help make all that nasty tummy ache go away if you let me have a look at you. How about that?'

Annette said, 'Sometimes he won't respond – I've told him it's naughty…'

'Annette, would you turn him round to face me?'

'Doctor, honestly – it's all right, he's just –'

'Please, Annette, do as I say.'

She bent her face to Mark's ear. 'You be a good boy and tell the nice man your tummy hurts. Sit up now and face the doctor.'

Mark kept his gaze fixed on the floor and Simon ducked his head to look up at him. 'Hello, there. Now then, can you tell me where your pain is?' He didn't look up and Simon put a finger beneath his chin and tilted his head back a little. There were dark rings beneath his eyes, making his complexion seem even paler. He noticed how dirty his clothes were and how his elbow stuck out of his sleeve, the waistband of his shorts held together with a safety pin. He smelt unwashed, of urine that had dried on his clothes, and looked half-starved, like one of the ragged refugee children he'd come across during the war. Simon frowned at Annette – he'd imagined Mark and Ben as lively little boys, well-cared-for and loved. She avoided his eye and for the first time he felt angry with her. It seemed to him that she had cause to be ashamed.

Smiling at her son he said, 'Mark, won't you tell me what the matter is?'

Lifting Mark off her knee, Annette stood up. 'We have to go now. I'll get him to bed and he'll be fine – no need to worry. He's fine – he'll be right as rain.'

She looked at him defiantly, the first real spark he'd ever seen her show. Suddenly he felt too weary to argue with her. Her children were her own concern and he had concerns enough of his own. Briskly he said, 'All right. Would you like a lift home?'

'No – no, we're fine.'

'Perhaps if he's not feeling so bright tomorrow you should take him to see your GP.'

'Yes, I will – but he's all right, really. He's just a bit highly strung.'

He nodded. 'Take care of him, Annette. Keep him warm, give him some good, clear broth if he can manage it.'

She lifted Mark into her arms and kissed his cheek. 'I will, doctor.' Smiling at Mark she said softly, 'He's my sweetheart, my very best boy.'

He saw them to the door and watched them cross the road and walk towards the cemetery. The child held on to her hand and after a moment she stopped and lifted him into her arms, kissing his head again. He thought of his own mother, who had never kissed him, not even on his birthday, and wondered what was more important to a child, love or care. The sense of gloom he had woken with that morning deepened. Closing the door he went back to the kitchen and threw the remaining cake on the lawn for the birds before pouring himself a very large scotch.

Danny came home with Ben. He said, 'Ben, go outside and play.' He sat beside her at the kitchen table. Lighting a cigarette he blew smoke down his nose, frowning at her as if something puzzled him. She couldn't think straight. Already she could feel her face burning in anticipation of the lies she'd have to tell him.

He reached out and pressed his hand against her cheek. 'You look scared. I've told you about looking scared, haven't I?'

'Yes, Danny.'

'So what are you looking scared about?'

'Nothing.'

'*Nothing*!' He laughed. 'Where's Mark?'

'He's upstairs, asleep. His teacher brought him home poorly.'

'Try again, Annette. Try again with the truth. His teacher brought him *where* poorly?'

She felt like she might pass out with fear. She imagined curling herself up in a ball on the floor, not even trying to stand up to his blows, just lying down and waiting, her head tucked in, protected by her arms.

He blew smoke into her face. 'Annette, I know where his teacher took him. Now – are you going to explain what you were doing at that doctor's house?'

'Cleaning.'

'Cleaning? All right. That's good. Give me the money.'

'What?'

'The money he gave you for doing his *cleaning*. Give me it now.'

'He pays me at the end of the week…'

'Oh. Pity.' He grabbed her arm, twisting the flesh in a Chinese burn. 'Was the Doctor at home when you were there? Did you let him touch Mark? Did you let him anywhere near?'

'No! I took him straight home, Danny, I promise. I just took him home, as soon as he arrived.'

'I don't want any fucking doctors looking at him, do you understand? Do you understand?'

'Yes Danny. I understand.'

He let go of her. 'Good. Good girl. I won't hurt you if you do as I say. You don't have to be scared if you just do as I say. Obedience. It's not much to ask, Annette. Now, he's upstairs in bed?'

'He's asleep, Danny, please don't wake him...'

'I'm not going to. It's good that he sleeps during the day.' He flicked ash into her teacup. Thoughtfully he said, 'I think maybe he shouldn't go to school any more. He should sleep during the day – then he's not so tired at night. Yes. That's the best way. Last night he was too tired to be any good.' He got up suddenly and she wet herself; he only glanced at her. 'I'll go and look in on him. Make Ben and me something to eat, would you? I'm bloody starving.'

As she made toast from stale bread and spread it with jam, Joan put her head round the kitchen door and said, 'Hiya, love. Everything all right?' She came in and sat down. 'I just popped in to see how that poor bairn is. His teacher brought him here then comes knocking on my door. I told her where you were. Did she find you all right? Nice kid, she was. Didn't look more than a bairn herself.'

'She found us all right.'

'How is he then? He looked white as a ghost, poor mite.'

'He's fine. He's upstairs asleep.' She looked at her over her shoulder. 'Danny's checking on him.'

Joan snorted. 'Is he? Well, at least it's all quiet. At least he'd not braying him for daring to breathe.'

Annette put the knife down. She bowed her head and her tears splashed on to the jam jar. Joan said evenly, 'Don't take on, now. You don't want the bairns to see you crying.'

They both turned towards the door as they heard Danny run down the stairs. Joan sat up straighter as if to make herself look more formidable. From the doorway Danny said, 'Joan! To what do we owe the pleasure this fine evening?'

Her mouth turned down in contempt. Pointedly she said, 'I've come to see how that lad of yours is. He looked dead poorly this afternoon.'

'Well, I've just had a look at him and you're right – he's poorly. We'll be keeping him in for a bit. Don't want the other kids catching what he's got.'

'And what has he got?'

'What did that doctor say, Annette? Mumps.' Danny smirked. Leaning against the sink he picked up a piece of toast and studied Joan as he ate it. Taking another piece he said, 'You know – you can always go up and check on him. But you know what mumps can do to lads, Joan, and you don't want to carry that home to your Ray. You don't want your Ray's balls swelling up big as melons.'

Joan stood up. 'You dirty bugger! You're a filthy, nasty, dirty bugger.'

Danny laughed. 'See you later, Joan. Close the door on your way out.'

When she'd gone Danny sat down at the table. 'That should keep the old bag away. And the beauty of it is she'll tell the whole fucking street to keep away, too – we shan't be bothered by any nosey bastards.'

'Is Mark all right?'

'Speak up! You're like a timid little mouse.' He grinned. 'Timid mouse, that's you. Squeak, squeak, squeak. I might have to buy a mousetrap, eh?'

She cleared her throat. Louder she said, 'Is Mark all right? He should have something to eat.'

'No. No food. Not yet. Later, when he's earned it. Go and call Ben in. He can have his tea then run down to the shop for some sweets. Bit of a treat for my lad.'

'But Danny –'

He got up and stepped towards her, bringing his face up close to hers. 'You want me to love Mark, don't you?'

'Yes.' She bowed her head, terrified of the bright, intense look in his eyes.

He grasped her face, his thumb and fingers digging into her cheeks and distorting her mouth. Forcing her to look at him he said quietly, 'I have to break him first, Annette. It will take time and I can't have you interfering and spoiling all the effort I'm putting in.' He let his hand fall away from her face and rested his forehead against hers. He sighed and his breath was warm and rank. 'He's like you. It drives me mad how he's so like you! Why can't you and him behave normally around me? What have I done to deserve to be treated like this?' His voice had risen and he seemed to make a great effort to calm himself. Stepping away from her he said, 'It's no good getting angry. It has to be done, that's all. He's waiting for me now. Stay down here – make sure you and Ben stay down here.'

Chapter 20

Unable to sleep, Mark made tea, staring out of the kitchen window as he waited for the kettle to boil. He thought of Steven, the way the boy moved and talked and smiled. He looked like Danny as he remembered him on one rare Sunday in July when he had taken him to the park with fishing nets and jam jars to catch minnows.

Mark frowned, thinking that this memory must be one of his very earliest, but that even now it could be triggered by the muddy smell of still, weedy water. He could remember Danny's arm around his waist as he crouched beside him, holding him steady as if afraid he might fall and drown. Danny's face was on a level with his; he was smiling and showing him how to move the net slowly though the water. Sometimes he imagined he dreamed this. Danny was never good or kind or loving; Danny was always mad. But he remembered the captured minnows swimming round and round the jar that suddenly seemed too small and cruel. He remembered how Danny held the jar up to the sun and how the light dazzled. He remembered how he had begged him to pour the little fish back into the water so that they might be free again and that Danny had solemnly agreed, holding the jar high so that the minnows flipped and tumbled through the air like tiny performing dolphins before disappearing into the dark water. Danny had taken his hand and reassured him that the fish would survive the disturbance.

The kettle whistled and Mark made tea. He sat down at the kitchen table and lit a cigarette. He remembered he had told Susan about this fishing trip and that she had listened carefully, as she always did, storing his memories as a valuable resource to draw on later. She had been lying in his arms, her head resting on his chest, her fingers restlessly tracing circles on his groin. When he'd finished the story her hand became still. She'd craned her neck to look up at him.

'This was before he began raping you,' she said, his life more real to her than it was to him. He remembered the weight of her hand, its warmth, how her fingers curled into his pubic hair and pulled gently so that the pain was mild and tantalising. He'd lifted her hand away and held it tightly and she rested her head on his chest again. 'Your heart's beating too fast,' she said.

She wore *Youth Dew* perfume, a rich, heavy scent that seemed to him to have nothing to do with youth and everything to do with age and experience and her peculiar decadence. When she left his bed her scent lingered so it seemed she was never entirely absent. Once he'd caught her scent on his telephone and he'd pressed the redial button. Ben's voice answered, quick and impatient and breathless so that Mark knew he'd interrupted his brother screwing his wife. He'd wondered if she'd showered before climbing into her husband's bed, and decided that she wouldn't have. His sweat would remain on her skin, his come still inside her; she would relish the risk of being sniffed out – a small risk, she told him. They were brothers, they smelt the same, and the babies they might make would be too similar for it to matter. 'I may even have twins,' she said. 'And one would be yours and the other Ben's. Wouldn't that be wonderful?'

Mark drew deeply on his cigarette, holding in the smoke before exhaling. From the hallway Joy's grandfather clock chimed midnight. The clock was worth a lot of money; on Simon's death such valuable possessions would have to be re-valued so that the estate might be evenly distributed between his two sons. He wondered if he should concede his share to Nathan, as recompense for past sins, and imagined telling Ben how he didn't need or want Simon's money. How grand he would sound, how much like a wanker.

The afternoon Susan bought his book, after the wine bar, they had walked across the heath to his flat and she had linked her arm through his and talked about her childhood. She told him about her father – who was a gynaecologist too, who expected – no, demanded – her to be as successful as he was. She told him her father had affairs and that her mother turned a blind eye to these women her father would be so in love with for a few charged months. She had followed her father once, to a café where he held hands with a woman across a table. She had thought how weak he looked, and vulnerable, how she could have destroyed him simply by walking into that café and saying hello, smiling, asking to be introduced. She wondered what had stopped her from shattering his conceit in such a way. Mark remembered turning to her as he opened the door to his flat and asking, 'Pity, perhaps?'

Susan laughed. She frowned at him, her eyes puzzled, curious. 'I think you must be a kind man, Mark.'

He led her through to his kitchen. He made her coffee and toast thick with blueberry jam because she hadn't eaten and this, she said, was what she craved: sweetness. Watching him as he took butter from the fridge, she said, 'Ben told me that when you were children your nightmares were so bad that he would get up and go into your room and stand over your bed, willing you to wake up. He wouldn't touch you, he said. He couldn't bring himself to, not even to shake your dreams away.'

He couldn't believe that Ben had told her this. Ben had no interest in telling tales from the past, especially tales about him. But he remembered Ben in striped pyjamas, a white-faced, angry little boy, standing by his bed, his fists clenched at his sides. Spreading the butter on the warm toast, he had looked up to find her watching him intently. She'd smiled, as though this might encourage a response from him.

'All children have bad dreams,' he said.

She'd nodded. 'Of course.'

The first time he'd kissed her he had tasted blueberry jam.

The first time he'd kissed her he had thought that perhaps that was all it would be, a kiss, something to feel a little guilty about for as long as he remembered. But she had stepped back from him and placed her hand lightly over his heart. 'It wasn't pity I felt for Daddy. I'd like you to know me better than that.'

Months later, Susan knelt beside him on his bed, the super king-sized bed, big enough for a second man, a third – if only he could bring himself to redraw the line. She leaned forward and her small, pointed breasts hung down and reminded him of the teats on the statue of the she-wolf that suckled Romulus and Remus. She had kissed him only to sit back on her heels and regard him quizzically. 'What would you say if I told you I would rather be with you than Ben?'

'I would say leave him, I'll marry you –'

'And he would never speak to you again. You would have no one but me.'

'You would be enough.'

'Simon would hate you.'

'Leave Ben.' He'd sat up, animated by the sudden possibility that she might be his alone. 'Leave him. Why should he have everything?'

She'd smiled, reaching out to brush his hair away from his eyes. 'I'm teasing. How could I leave Ben for you?'

He must have opened his mouth to speak because she'd pressed her finger to his lips. 'You know you're not your brother. You know that. How could you possibly take his place? Be realistic, my darling.'

She got up and he watched as she picked up her panties and bra from the floor and began to dress. She rolled on stockings, clipped them onto her suspender belt with deft grace, stepped into her skirt and smoothed it over her hips. Spreading her fingers across her flat belly she caught his eye and smiled. 'I hope he's your baby. That would be an interesting combination – your genes brought up by Ben.'

Dressed, she bent over the bed and kissed his mouth. 'I'll let you know the results of the pregnancy test tomorrow.'

The next day Ben rang and told him his good news and there was a note of astonishment in his voice, a rare betrayal of emotion as he said, 'We're both very pleased, of course.'

Mark remembered how he had congratulated his brother, stiffly, formally. It was all Ben expected of him, this coldness; it didn't give anything away.

Sitting at Simon's kitchen table, Mark crushed out his cigarette. He thought of Ben walking behind Susan's coffin, how his brother had held onto Simon's arm as though he might fall without his support. Walking a few steps behind them, he had wondered at his own ability to keep upright and not collapse beneath his weight of shame and guilt and grief.

He thought of Steven and his little girl who was almost the same age as his child, Susan's child, if she had lived. He had no doubt that Susan's baby had been his. And Susan would have left Ben to be with him and they would have brought up their baby together. She couldn't have gone on hurting him.

Susan said once, 'I wish you didn't exist. Because even if you were ugly and wicked I would still have slept with you because you are his brother and yet Danny chose you. I need to understand that.'

He had pulled her into his arms and held her tightly. 'I love you. That's all that matters to me –'

'How can you love me?' Pushing him away she said, 'Shouldn't you hate me for hurting your brother so badly?'

'He doesn't know about us!'

'He knows. He just can't bring himself to believe it.'

And months later, in the Natural History Museum, Simon had said, 'How could she behave so wickedly?'

The Tyrannosaurus Rex skeleton had loomed over them. He had planned to write a novel about the nineteenth century bone hunters. The bones in Simon's study had always held a fascination for him, although he pretended that they didn't. He could have gone to the museum alone, but Simon insisted on talking and he couldn't have the conversation Simon wanted to have in his flat, the air would have become too tainted. He had betrayed his brother – best to get the recriminations out of the way in this neutral place; besides, he had felt as though he was about to be flayed and so it had seemed fitting to be amongst the bones.

In the shadow of the great skeleton, Simon had become silent, words failing him. They had watched a group of children being shown around the exhibits by their teacher. Unable to help himself, Mark had said, 'I wanted children.'

'So why sleep with your brother's wife? Why not live your life decently, find a decent woman?' Simon had sighed. 'I suppose you have a raft of excuses you could use to keep yourself afloat.' Looking at him coldly, he'd said, 'But that's all they are, Mark, excuses. Take responsibility. Don't make me lose patience with you.'

In Simon's kitchen, Mark got up from the table and washed his cup under the running tap. Tomorrow he would sit by his father's sick bed and watch him fade. He thought about the bone novel he had neglected to write and knew that he wouldn't write it now. After Simon's death he would take the bones from his study and bury them and that would be the end of it, and the beginning of responsibility.

He thought of Steven and his heart ached, and he knew that he was as far from taking responsibility as ever.

Chapter 21

I saw Ben outside theatre. He was in his scrubs and he looked dead beat, although he smiled at me as though I was some long-lost pal and took me to one side. He said, 'How are you?' A nurse passed by and he looked at her fleetingly. He seemed to wait until she was out of earshot before saying quietly, 'I need to talk to you.'

I told him about the old hospice garden and we arranged to meet there. I was early. I sat on the grass and the sun shone down on me, and the birds flew in and out of the over-grown hedges and there was a scent of lilac just come into bloom. I closed my eyes and lifted my face to the sun's warmth and tried not to think of anything, just like Carl tried to teach me. 'Stay in the moment,' he'd say. I never could.

I felt Ben's shadow fall across me and opened my eyes, shielding them from the sun with my hand. 'I've brought you a sandwich,' he said. 'Roast ham.'

He sat on the grass beside me. Looking around he said, 'So, you found a secret garden?'

'I don't know if it's a secret.'

He held out the sandwich in its plastic triangle. 'I bought a cheese and pickle, too. Which would you prefer?'

'Ham,' I said. I felt shy of him, awkward like I wasn't inside my own skin. We both broke into the sandwiches and ate in silence, although I imagined he could hear my jaw working, my chewing and swallowing so that the bread seemed to turn to cardboard and the meat to gristle in my mouth. I tossed the crusts to the starlings hopping nearby;

they came closer timidly, only to fight over the scraps of bread.

Ben handed me a bottle of water from the carrier bag the sandwiches came in. He said, 'It's a lovely day. Too nice to be inside.' He laughed, and I realised he felt awkward too. Looking at the scrapping birds he said, 'Dad was always saying that – too nice to be moping around the house. He'd turf us out, set up a game of cricket in the garden or organise some long, dull walk.' Plucking at the grass he said, 'I'm afraid he's very poorly. I'm afraid he might die.'

'I'm sorry.'

He looked at me. 'He's had a long life. A good, interesting, long life. He's eighty-five. I hope I live so long, so well.' After a moment he said, 'How's Danny?'

'Same, a bit worse maybe.'

'I'll try and see him. It's finding the time – I never seem to have enough time.'

'We could go now.'

'No,' he said. 'Not now. I need to talk myself into it.'

I nodded. 'He asks after you.'

'Yeah?' He raised his eyebrows. 'Tell him next time you see him…well, tell him I'll try to pop in…'

We drank our water and all the time I could sense his agitation. I remembered what Carl used to say about waiting calmly, allowing the other person to take their time in saying whatever they had to say. So I waited and at last he said, 'You're an easy person to be with. I didn't expect you to be so easy to like.'

I tried smiling at him. 'My mam would say that's a backhanded compliment.'

'Is it? Perhaps. The trouble is that when I look at you I see Danny as he was when I was a child. I was scared of him.'

I looked away. 'Yeah, well. I can't help it if I remind you.'

'No, of course not, and of course I wasn't always scared – I loved him too. And there were times…well…he wasn't always psychotic.'

I thought of Danny. One of my earliest memories was of Mam lifting me up and handing me to him. He held me awkwardly, like he wasn't used to holding little kids. I remember he smelt of old clothes that had been stored somewhere damp, and that his skin had this grey pallor. He needed a shave – I felt the bristles when Mam insisted I kiss him – and there was this deadness in his eyes like the prison guards had cut his heart out. I was petrified of him. I thought I'd be sent to prison just because he was my father.

Ben cleared his throat. He said, 'How's Jade?'

'Fine.'

'I was thinking that she might like to come and play at our house – meet Nathan. Little girls love babies, don't they? And they're cousins, it's right they should meet, that I should meet her…'

'That would be nice. Thanks.'

'And you should meet Kitty, my wife.'

'Yes, I'd like that.'

'You don't have to come on your own – bring a friend.'

'A partner, you mean? I don't have one.'

'Fine. Just you then.'

'He died.'

'Oh? I'm sorry….'

'His name was Carl. I'm gay. I don't know – you probably guessed…'

'No. I hadn't.' He avoided my eye, embarrassed. 'Look, it's fine – you don't have to explain yourself to me.'

'I just thought you should know.'

He nodded. 'Well, thank you for telling me.'

'Am I still easy to like?'

He frowned at me. 'Your sexual preferences don't matter to me. They're none of my business.'

I concentrated on watching the starlings hop about the grass. I don't know why I'd told him. Sometimes I just have this longing to talk about Carl to anyone who'll listen, and there aren't many that will. Mam won't have his name spoken. I swallowed a mouthful of water, hating myself for being embarrassed, hating him for saying *sexual preferences*.

Gently he said, 'Steven?'

I turned to look at him. 'Carl died last year.'

'I'm terribly sorry.'

'Aye, well.' I swigged more water because suddenly my mouth was dry. 'What did you want to talk to me about?'

'I don't know, really. You, I suppose, Danny...how things were...'

'I hardly knew him. He was in and out of prison.' I looked at him and couldn't stop the bitterness creeping in to my voice. 'He was a loser, a waste of space. When I was a kid I wished he'd go away for good, but he kept coming back – Mam would always have him back. She made it obvious that the sex was too good to give up. Disgusting, eh? Are you disgusted?'

'No.'

'I am. I don't know how she could stand him to touch her.'

'She must have loved him.'

'Nah. I don't think so.'

An ambulance siren sounded. We both looked towards the road and saw its lights flashing through the hedge. As the noise died away he said, 'My mother – Annette – loved him. I was jealous of the way she looked at him because I knew he would always be more important to her than I was.' He laughed sadly as though remembering. 'She was very beautiful, you know? I had *very* handsome parents – Mark is so obviously theirs.'

I thought of Mark. I'd thought of him a lot. I'd looked for his novels in the library – there were two – the others

246

had all been borrowed, the librarian told me. 'He's very popular,' she said as she stamped the date inside the books. 'There's a waiting list for his latest. I could put your name on it, if you like.' I'd wanted to tell her that he was my brother, but I didn't think she'd believe me; she might have thought I was some kind of nutter.

I said, 'I had supper with Mark.'

He raised his eyebrows. 'And how was that?'

'All right.'

'I know he's not the easiest of men to get along with.'

'Isn't he?' I raised my eyebrows, too. 'He showed me your Dad's study; he told me about the cat you skinned.'

He laughed. 'I'd forgotten about that. What a gruesome child I was.'

'I suppose it was educational.'

'What was – me skinning a cat or you being shown my father's study?'

'Both.' Cautiously I asked, 'Has Mark ever been married?'

He looked surprised. 'Mark's not interested in women. I thought you of all people would have guessed.'

I don't know if he meant to make me feel so thick and so perverted in the same breath. I don't think he noticed how angry I was because he said evenly, 'I think he swings both ways, but I get the impression he hates women. Although they like him…more than like. They turn to look at him – they do these comic double-takes.' He frowned at me questioningly. 'So, you had supper with him, eh? I'm surprised after the way he carried on in the pub the other night.'

'That was just shock.'

'Yeah. Shock.' He snorted, as though he didn't really believe in such a thing. 'He's highly strung. Listen, Steve, I don't want you getting your hopes up. Mark's…well, I don't think he's what you want him to be.'

'What do you think I want?' I felt like punching him, the smug bastard. 'What?'

'A friend? A brother? Steven, Mark doesn't do friendship. As for being a brother, well take it from one who knows —'

'I just think you don't like him.'

He laughed painfully. 'You can't choose your family, can you? Can't pick them out of a catalogue.'

'Isn't that just what your Dad did? Simon? He chose you.'

He looked away. 'The hospital should do something with this place. It's a shame that it's left to run wild.' After a bit he said flatly, 'He didn't choose us.' He clambered to his feet. Looking down at me he said, 'Listen, we'll get together sometime, eh? You and your little girl — Jade? I'll call you.'

I watched him walk away. He has this cock-of-the-walk air about him, but he's a flimsy man, I think, underneath it. He can't bring himself to ask what he really wants to know. I felt like shouting after him, *'Yes, Danny raped me — any other questions?'* I stared after him. Quietly I said, 'He chose me, and Mark. I don't know why he didn't choose you.' Although I did, of course. Stand Danny's five sons in a row: it's obvious.

I went back to work. I tried not to think about Mark or Ben. There's only one person to think about, anyway. Carl. I miss him. Missing him feels like getting over flu, only you know you're going to feel like that for the rest of your life.

I met Carl in a gay bar. I'd been working myself up to going there for weeks, even getting as far as the door one evening. There were bouncers on the street outside; they looked me up and down and then held the door wide open for me without a word. I couldn't bring myself to go in after that, not that night at least. I couldn't stand how they just took it for granted I was queer when I wasn't totally sure

248

myself. Besides, I didn't know what to expect. Somehow I imagined I'd get jumped on. Carl laughed when I told him that. '*You* should be so lucky!'

It was only a gay bar on Tuesdays. Tuesdays the DJ played seventies disco music: *I Will Survive* and *I Feel Love* and stuff like that. Stuff Mam danced to in the kitchen. When I finally, finally plucked up my courage and got past the smirking bouncers I stood at the bar drinking Bacardi Breezers from the bottle and watching the men dance together on the jam-packed floor. There was this one man; he wore tight jeans and a tee shirt that showed off his six-pack. I just stared at him, stared and stared until this sweet voice behind me said, 'He's taken. Don't look any more, it will only make you heart-sick.'

I turned round, ready to say I wasn't looking, ready, if I'm honest, to tell whoever it was to fuck off. But this lovely man held up his hands as if he thought I was about to punch him. He laughed. 'All right – I'm just teasing. Look, if you want to, everybody else does.'

He bought me a drink. I bought him a drink. He told me he was an architect. I lied and told him I was a student because I didn't think he'd look twice at a hospital porter. He didn't ask me what I was studying – I think he guessed I was lying. Later he told me that he recognised me from the hospital, that he'd seen me once or twice when he was there having his usual check-ups and that he'd thought how sexy I was. 'Actually,' he said, 'I thought you had a beautiful face. Angelic. Not my type…' He grinned at me. 'Which is really my way of saying that I thought you were out of my league.'

I said, 'I'm nothing much,' and he laughed like I'd said the most endearing thing ever.

'You're something,' he said. 'Quite something.'

He lived in a big old house a few streets from the bar, all wooden floorboards and plain walls. Not a swirly carpet or a stripey wallpaper in sight, just a load of good taste so it felt cold, as though he didn't really live there. He had the biggest bed I've ever seen. He'd had it made, he said, especially. I said, 'Especially for what? Orgies?'

'I gave them up years ago.'

Carl turned nineteen in 1983 and ran away to London. He told me it was a wild time and that nothing was taboo except celibacy. I tried to imagine those wild times, the clamour and crush of bodies, all that heat and smell, the frantic pace of it, like sex was an assault course that had to be got over with as much show and bravado as possible. Carl said, 'There was a lot of sex, a lot of drugs, a lot of me thinking that this was liberation. I could fuck two or three or ten men in one night and often it was fantastic but sometimes...' He looked down at the wedding ring he wore, twisting it round and round, the ring was lose, easily slipped off. After a while he said, 'There's a certain kind of grey light in London, in the early morning. It shows you up and casts you down and you think *Christ*...' He laughed as though he was embarrassed. 'Just that: *Christ.* I don't have any words for it – I wasn't ashamed or guilty. I love sex. I love that feeling you get when a stranger's hands start tearing at your clothes like nothing else matters in the world to him but your body. It was just, well...that certain light.'

He thought I understood.

He told me he had HIV. He told me as we were watching TV in his bare front room, some awful panel game where the guests think they're dead clever, dead funny, but they're not. He squeezed my hand and said, 'Do you know how much I love you?'

'Yep.' I remember smiling at him. 'But you can tell me again, if you like.'

'Steve –' And for a while he was lost for words and we sat there holding hands until I began to worry that he was going to end it. He cried and it was the first time, he said, the first time he'd cried since the day the doctor told him the test was positive. I said everything would be all right and that it didn't matter to me. I said all the stupid things people say when it's best to keep your mouth shut. Secretly I worried that he'd given the disease to me, of course I did.

He hadn't. He was always so careful, like he said he would be that first time. After he'd confessed I moved in with him and I saw how many pills he had to take. It became normal that he should have a cupboard kept especially for his medicine, normal to talk about viral loads and cell counts and how best to kill the time spent waiting in hospital corridors. Worry was kept on a short leash like a badly trained pit-bull, or at least I thought it was. Sometimes in the middle of the night I'd come down and find him staring into space. I'd make him a cup of tea. I'd think about the light, that greyness in the sky that could take him away from me so easily.

I wonder what Carl would have thought of Mark. They were about the same age, same build, same height – same class. I doubt they would have got on. Mark's strangeness would have got to Carl. He liked people to be straightforward, easy. I think he would have thought Mark was a creep.

The grey light Carl talked about – I understand it now.

Chapter 22

Annette knelt by the bed and watched Mark sleeping. Danny had tied pyjama cord around Mark's wrist and fastened it to the headboard and she had imagined untying it and lifting him into her arms. But she didn't want to wake him. He would cry. He would be hungry. Her hand hovered over his head; she was afraid to touch him. Best if he slept on. Sleeping meant that he was all right. She would leave him sleeping, peaceful in the land of dreams. Her hand hovered over his head, afraid to touch him, as she would be afraid of touching a wounded animal, in case she hurt him even more. Danny had tied pyjama cord around his wrist and fastened it to the headboard. She had imagined untying it, imagined the feel of him in her arms, and couldn't bring herself to do it.

Annette got up. She went to the window and looked out on to the street. No one was about, everyone at work, at school. Danny was at work, emptying bins. Danny would lift the bins onto his shoulder, although he looked too frail for such a weight, and tip the stinking rubbish into the dustcart. He would think about Mark. He would think about what he could do next to Mark. He would whistle, as he did when he was happy.

Danny had said, 'It's only what my father did to me.'

The room smelt of Danny – that dirty man stink that came after sex and clung to the sheets and made the air thick. She pushed the window open and breathed in the clean outside. Looking down, she saw that there was dog muck on the pavement and saw herself sweeping it away into the gutter. She looked up at the cloud-streaked sky and saw herself flying towards the shrouded sun. Danny would clutch at her ankles but she would kick free. She would carry Mark in her arms and he would be her solid little boy again and not the broken animal on the bed.

Mark stirred and cried out. Kneeling by the bed she hush-hushed him, her hand hovering over his head. She couldn't bring herself to touch him but she put a smile in her voice and willed him into sleep again.

Simon brought Joy home. Showing her around the house, he found himself smiling too much, making his voice too bright, laughing rather too loudly over nothing very much, all the time making excuses for their new home as he tried to fathom Joy's expression, the way she held herself. She looked pale and thin and tired. As he led her from room to room she kept her coat on as though she was very cold. At least she looked around with interest. She lingered at windows to gaze out over the garden. In the room that had been his father's surgery she rubbed at the condensation blurring her view. He stood beside her and shyly took her hand.

'Joy, is it all right?'

She turned to him, only to look out over the garden again. 'It's all right, Simon. It's fine.'

'It's a big house. Too big, perhaps. We could sell it, buy something cosier...'

'No. We'll stay. The house is fitting, I think.'

'Fitting?'

'For your position.'

He thought of all the empty rooms they couldn't fill and knew that she was thinking of them, too. He squeezed her hand tightly.

Through the spy hole in the condensation, he saw Annette open the gate and walk up the path that led to the back door. He let go of Joy's hand and heard the idiotic brightness in his voice again. 'Here's Annette, the girl I told you about. Right on time, as usual!'

Joy seemed to stand up taller and straighter. 'Good,' she said. 'Time to get busy, I think.'

The first time she set eyes on Doctor Simon Walker, Joy had thought that here was a frivolous man: a silly, light-weight man with a roving, restless eye and an opinion of women that was at once too high and too careless. She had watched as he chatted to Clare, her fellow secretary, at a Christmas party. Although he seemed to listen intently to what Clare was saying, although he laughed in all the right places and was attentive and charming, Joy knew he was thinking only of the best way to get the girl into bed. He had that *air* about him: predatory, ruthless; he was the fox in *The Tale of Jemima Puddleduck*, a story she read to her brother's children on weekend visits. She found herself smiling as the doctor touched Clare's arm: so empathic, so caring! He seemed genuinely interested in whatever it was the girl was telling him. Joy had noticed earlier how he had moved away from the group of fellow surgeons gathered at the bar as soon as he politely could. Doctor Simon Walker was a ladies' man, a womaniser if the rumours were to be believed. Joy chose not to believe quite yet, but to bide her time until she could trust the evidence of her own observations.

She observed how handsome he was, of course: tall, blond, muscular as a butcher – which he was, in his way – just as used as a butcher to sawing off limbs, which took strength and, she imagined, unflinching determination and boldness. These traits were to be admired in a man, and she did admire them. And she thought about Simon Walker as she lay alone in bed, when the street outside her window had settled for the night and her empty flat beyond her bedroom door was dark and silent as a tomb. She lay on her back and allowed her hand to stray between her legs and sometimes her fingers were idle and sometimes not. Always her thoughts strayed to Peter, whose photograph she kept by her bed. Peter would not have taken to Simon Walker. Peter was a different breed.

Peter had been shy and it had been her idea that they should go to bed and cement their relationship in a way that seemed most real and satisfactory to her. Remembering, she wished he hadn't been so awe-struck and that they hadn't lost their virginity to each other but to the kind of people who took the business of sex less seriously – the kind of people who could laugh when they were naked. Her instinct was that sex didn't have to be so deadly earnest and it would be better if it wasn't. She knew that a more sophisticated man than Peter would smile more in bed. It was his smiling, his casual *sexiness*, that drew her to Simon. She was sure that Simon treated sex with a light heart.

Simon smiled when he first asked her out on a date, his eyes twinkling as though he was including her in an ironic joke. In an Italian restaurant over minestrone soup and lasagne, he gossiped with breath-taking indiscretion about his fellow surgeons, the nurses and hospital managers. She felt her eyes widen; she had to remember to close her mouth on her astonishment. Leaning across the table he drew her into his confidences and secrets and it was an expert lesson in seduction, if she'd been aware enough to think of it as such. But she only found herself gazing at him. Between them the candle in its Chianti bottle flickered and gave off too much heat and too little light, and she imagined him in her bed as she had for so many nights before: smiling, easy, experienced. She needed his experience. She had become a virgin again, healed over with scars.

And in her bed he'd stroked her hair from her face and asked her if she was sure, because, he said, he wasn't the type of man she needed. How infuriating he was, just as she'd suspected he would be. But infuriating was something she could cope with, she could be firm and straight with him and he would accept that she wouldn't be patronised and be straight with her in turn. After all, he was a good, sensible man beneath his bluster and charm and silliness. And he'd been a soldier, like Peter; an army captain, like him. Perhaps not such a different breed, then. Perhaps Peter might even have understood.

Her GP had said, 'My dear, I can only confirm what you already know, that you're pregnant and that everything appears normal and healthy.' The old man had looked at her over the rim of his spectacles just like her father used to. Not unkindly, he said, 'You're a little older than most girls in your position...most *are* girls...young, foolish...' He'd sighed and taken off his glasses and pinched the bridge of his nose as though terribly weary of all the life that paraded through his door. 'Joy,' he'd said, 'you're the very last person I would have expected this of. Will the father stand by you?'

'I don't know,' she'd said, and truly didn't. Not that she expected Simon to stand by. Sitting in the doctor's surgery, on the hard, wooden chair that seemed designed for the penitent, she had thought of Simon in her bed, asleep because lovemaking seemed to exhaust him. She'd thought that his exhaustion was justified now that he was to become a father: hard work, being a stud.

And on the train, as she lost her baby, her most beloved thing in the whole world, he had been calm and efficient and she could have taken this as coldness, and for a while, in hospital when the pain was unbearable, she had. She had hated him, a loathing that made her cringe away from his touch, the comfort he seemed so desperate to offer her as if to make up for his early detachment. In hospital he had sat by her bed for hours and hours and sometimes she didn't have the strength to pull her hand away from his, but allowed him this small intimacy. Occasionally he would lift her hand to his mouth and she'd feel the dry brush of his lips. It took hours of his silent handholding for her to recognise the depth of his sadness, a leap of imagination not to treat his pain as nothing, although she still felt that it was nothing compared to her own.

Joy followed Simon into the hallway of their new house, a few steps behind him as he went into the kitchen and answered the timid knock on the back door. He said in his hearty voice, 'Ah, Annette! My dear, come in. Joy – this is Annette, who has very kindly been helping me out this past fortnight or so.'

The girl smiled shyly, hardly able to meet her eye. She looked no more than eighteen or nineteen, her long dark hair loose around her shoulders, her complexion pale as ivory. Too thin, she could be one of the new type of waif-like models, all sharp angles and huge, startled eyes rimmed with kohl. The tartan skirt she wore was too short, her sweater cheap and garishly cheerful so that it seemed wrong on her because she looked so sad. Still too full of her own sadness, Joy stepped back from the girl. She heard Simon laugh to cover his embarrassment.

'Well,' he said, 'why don't we have a cup of tea?'

Unable to bear his fussing, Joy had sent Simon to buy a newspaper. Opposite her at the kitchen table, Annette Carter sipped her tea self-consciously; the girl's hand shook so that each time she set her cup down it rattled against the saucer. Joy noticed the love-bite on her neck, an ugly purple bruise she had tried to cover with face powder. In Joy's head she could hear her mother saying *common! So common!* The word and its disgusted intonation made her feel old.

Forcing herself to smile, Joy said, 'My husband tells me you've been a great help, Annette. Now I'm home I wonder if we could formalise the arrangement? Would three mornings a week suit you?'

'Yes, thank you, Mrs Walker.'

Her voice was little more than a whisper and she touched the bite on her neck as if to hide it. Joy saw that her nails were bitten to the quick and that her hands were cracked and angry-looking. Her wedding ring slid towards her knuckle and she pushed it back, twisting it round and round. Timidly she said, 'I should get on. Where would you like me to make a start?'

Joy looked around helplessly. The house was worse than she had imagined; its dereliction made her want to weep in despair. She remembered Simon's mother from their brief meeting early in her relationship with her son; the old woman had been imperious and haughty and she had imagined that her home would be tightly run, that she would have a cohort of bullied servants to keep the place in order. Simon had told her how grand the house was, how lovely its garden. In hospital it had helped to think of this garden. Seeing it so overgrown and choked with weeds had made her feel overcome with weariness. She would need a man to help her with the heavy work; she knew how difficult it was to find reliable men.

Aware that Annette was waiting for some direction, Joy said, 'I don't suppose your husband needs a little extra work, does he? The garden...'

Annette looked horrified. 'Oh, no. No – he couldn't –'

'All right, just a thought.' She smiled, wanting to reassure her even as she wondered at the vehemence of the girl's response. Perhaps her husband was the kind of man who felt casual work was beneath his dignity, no matter how much his family needed the money. Such men were a waste of the air they breathed. She felt her anger rise, like bubbles in a shaken pop bottle, she could do nothing to stop its useless expansion. Too sharply she said, 'But why not? I'd pay him good money –'

'No, no, I don't think so...really, it's very kind of you.'

Joy's anger had more to do with herself than this anxious girl, she knew that, she understood the shock her body had been through, its hormones raging as though desperate for a purpose now that her baby was lost. She tried to breathe steadily, as the understanding nurse had taught her. Her anger only seemed to increase and she got up, wanting to find something to fling at the wall. She paced to the window and back again. The girl watched her as though terrified.

Joy turned on her. 'What does your husband do?'

Annette bowed her head. 'He's a bin man.'

'And that takes up all his time, does it? He doesn't care to earn a little extra money?'

'I'm sorry…'

'Why? Why are you sorry? Honestly – what good is it?' Anger swelled inside her, so animating she could imagine jumping and spitting with rage; but she pictured how mad she would look, how scary, and the girl already seemed terrified, like a child unjustly reprimanded, the kind of child who couldn't say boo to a goose. All at once Joy felt deflated and foolish. She sat down again. Grudgingly, the anger still retaining a little of its grip, she said, 'I'm sorry. Of course it's up to him what your husband does and does not do.' She attempted a smile, to make a joke of herself. 'I tend to become rather over-wrought, at the moment. You must bear with me.'

The girl nodded. 'It's all right.'

'Is it?' Joy sighed.

'I should get on, Mrs Walker, if you tell me where…'

'Oh I don't know! Where do you usually start? You know this house better than I do. Don't you have any initiative?'

Annette stood up. 'I'm sorry, Mrs Walker. I'm sorry if you're angry with me.'

She was so pale, her hair hanging in greasy rat-tails around her face, her cheap clothes looking as though she had slept in them. Earlier, Joy had caught the unwashed smell of her. It was difficult to believe that she could do anything as efficiently as Simon insisted she could. Joy thought of this girl's children and imagined them ragged and snotty. It was unfair that God had given children to her to neglect when her own child would have been so loved. Unable to help herself, she said, 'You have two little boys, I hear?'

'Yes.'

'Then you're very blessed. I hope you realise how blessed you are.'

'I do.' She bowed her head and tears fell down her face. She swiped them away with her fingertips. 'I'm sorry,' she said. 'I'm sorry.'

Joy stepped towards her, only to hesitate, at a loss to know what to say or do. She knew that other women would take the girl in their arms to comfort her, their voices soft with there-theres. She thought of the nurse that had held her so tenderly when she had wept, and the soft stream of sounds she made, sweet and sad as a lullaby. She had held on to that nurse and had not felt ashamed of crying as she usually did. She remembered how she had stained her blue uniform with snot and tears, a dark, wet patch above her breast. 'You're all right,' the nurse said. 'You're going to be all right.' She had almost believed her. At least she had held on to her words as if she had thrown her a lifeline.

Now she stood before this girl and could say nothing, offer nothing. Her heart was too hard. How often her mother had told her that − her heart was hard with practicalities, she was cold and unfeeling. Joy clenched her fists at her sides, trying to dispel her mother's voice from her head. She stepped forward.

'Annette...' Joy held out her hand and touched the girl's arm. 'Don't cry.'

Annette pulled a handkerchief from her sleeve and quickly wiped her eyes. 'I'm sorry.'

'And don't keep saying you're sorry!' Joy laughed awkwardly. '*I'm* sorry! I was abrupt...'

The girl gazed at her. Suddenly she said, 'He's going to kill my baby.' Her hand went to her mouth as if to recapture her words and force them back where they came from. She closed her eyes and Joy was catching her in her arms as she fell.

Chapter 23

Mark sat at Simon's hospital bedside. A few moments ago the hospital chaplain had left, smiles and handshakes all round. As soon as the door swung closed behind the man's back, Simon had closed his eyes and his mouth became a thin, angry line. 'I'm a stinking hypocrite,' he said. 'I should have told him what I really think.'

'What do you really think?'

He had opened his eyes and looked at him as though he was appraising his ability to understand. At last he said, 'I think that it's all make-believe and stories. But then, why should I offend the man? And if he finds comfort in his make-believe, who am I to question it? I know it gave your mother comfort – when I meet men like him that's what I keep reminding myself of – their stories helped your mother at the end.'

Simon closed his eyes again and at once Mark said, 'Would you like me go?'

'No. Stay. Stay a while, bide with me.' He opened one eye to smile at him.

Simon slept and Mark picked up the newspaper he'd brought only to put it down again after a quick scan of the headlines. He got up and went to the window, but the rain that had been falling all morning made the view grey and even bleaker than usual. In the distance the church spire was shiny-black with rain, the cross at its pinnacle stark against the leaden sky. This was the chaplain's church, St John's. Mark had found himself asking him about the size of his congregation. It seemed an impertinent question now, and he wondered what had come over him to ask. But the man had seemed pleased at his interest, and had proudly told him that the church had a lively, active membership. *Membership*. From the corner of his eye he had seen Simon's lip curl in contempt as the chaplain described how he saw the church's role in such a challenging community as Rosehill. Only able to bear this kind of talk for so long, Simon had said briskly, 'Reverend, you know my son's a novelist, don't you? I'd be careful of his interest.'

The man had looked alarmed.

Mark remembered the day his first novel was published. At the launch party he had watched his parents move around the room, practised, gracious guests. 'Our other son Ben is an orthopaedic surgeon,' he'd heard his father say to his agent, and Joy had cut in, 'We're very proud of both of them,' as if to dispel any doubt.

Resting his forehead against the cold window, Mark looked down on the car park several stories below. He should be at home, writing; already one deadline had passed, although his publisher had understood. He should be at home, writing, but it seemed impossible to imagine himself at his desk, summoning the concentration needed to work. He had begun to imagine how he might not write. He had made calculations in a notebook, a list of expenditures balanced against a list of savings and pension funds and the equity in his London flat. Added to these calculations was the money he knew he would receive following Simon's death. Writing down an estimated figure, he had felt only a little mercenary. Lately, his heart seemed absent.

A young family walked across the car park: mother, father, a toddler dragged by the hand, a baby in a fashionable three-wheel buggy. The father wore a baseball cap in Burberry tartan and white jog-pants. He was smoking. Mark watched him stride across the tarmac, the child trailing behind him until he jerked its arm to hurry it. Thinking of Steven, Mark turned to the mother. Her head was bowed, her dark hair streaked with blonde and tied in a high ponytail. The father looked up and seemed to stare right at him. Instinctively, Mark stepped back from the window.

Last night Ben had phoned and told him that he was thinking of inviting Steven to Sunday tea. Sunday tea had made him think of tinned salmon sandwiches and cocktail sausage rolls, fairy cakes and jelly and ice-cream, the kind of tea Joy would prepare so diligently when they were children. They would be allowed to invite a friend or two and often Ben did and Michael or David or Geoff would join them and eat more than their fair share. Mark never invited anyone, although in the early days Joy had encouraged him to, even inviting little boys on his behalf. These boys became Ben's friends for the afternoon, just as he knew Steven would because it was easy to like Ben, to imagine that he liked you.

Mark sat down again. Simon's hand was closed in a loose fist on the hospital blankets, its blue veins raised so that he imagined they would yield to his touch like water in a plastic bag. But he knew he would only feel bones beneath the papery flesh, hard and uncompromising.

Simon had said, 'I am so disgusted with you, Mark. So disgusted I can hardly bear to look at you.'

This was days after Simon had discovered his adultery, days for his father to become so angry he couldn't speak Susan's name. From that day she was always *Ben's wife* or *your brother's wife*. This last was said with hard-edged stress. 'Have you no scruples,' Simon asked, 'no moral sense?' and he had sounded like the tyrant father in a Victorian morality play. He always was an old-fashioned man.

And Susan had asked, 'So why did you agree to discuss it with him?'

Although she knew why, and had even laughed at him. It had never occurred to her that Simon might tell Ben.

264

He had finished their relationship and he had felt that his life was over so that when he went back to her he knew he would rather sacrifice Simon's respect than lose even a moment with Susan. He treated those desolate weeks as a lesson he had learnt. Susan treated them as nothing at all.

Mark hunched forward on the hard, hospital chair and buried his face in his hands. 'Oh Christ,' he said softly. 'Sweet Jesus Christ.'

'Mark?' Simon's voice was tender. He reached out and touched Mark's shoulder. 'My boy.'

'I woke you...'

'No.' Gently he said, 'You looked so like your mother for a moment.'

'Annette?'

'Of course Annette. The first time I saw her...' He sighed.

'The first time you saw her...?'

'She was lovely.'

Annette knelt by the bed. She reached out to touch his wrist where the cord bound him, but drew away as though scolded. He tried to find his voice but fear smothered it and besides, she seemed too far away, like someone in a dream. Perhaps he was dreaming. He heard her breathing, sharp, quick breaths.

'Mark?' Anxiously Simon said, 'Mark, are you all right?'

Annette clambered to her feet. She hesitated, only to turn away. She closed the door softly behind her as though afraid to wake him.

Mark stood up. He crouched in front of the bedside locker and began packing Simon's laundry into a carrier bag to take home.

Simon said, 'Leave that, Mark. Sit down. You're upset...'

'No, no I'm not. Ridiculous, anyway, after all these years.' He thrust a pair of pyjamas into the bag. 'I'm fine.'

'For God's sake boy!'

Mark straightened up. He knotted the handles of the carrier bag together. He said, 'I should go.'

'Sit down, Mark.' More carefully he said, 'Sit down.'

Mark sunk down onto the chair. He wrapped the bag's handles round and round his fingers tightly, welcoming the pain. At last he said, 'Ben's found Danny.'

Simon nodded. 'I'd guessed that he had.'

'I keep thinking I shouldn't care so much.'

'It's bound to be unsettling for you.'

'I feel five years old again.'

'Oh, Mark –'

'I know – pathetic, isn't it? It feels like I've failed, that no matter what I do I'll always be...I don't know – *Danny's*...'

He could feel Simon's gaze on him. Expecting him to speak, instead his silence went on, so that Mark forced himself to look up.

'You're my son, Mark,' Simon said. 'Danny was just...' He shook his head. '*Nothing*. He was nothing, just a deranged boy. You're not his, no more than Ben is his. You're my sons. I brought you up. What is Danny compared to that? How can you believe he has any influence on the kind of man you've become?'

'He's in my blood.'

'Blood! So what? What kind of Fascist rubbish is that?'

'Did you know that Danny had another family? Three sons? The youngest...his name is Steven...'

'And?'

Quickly he said, 'He's such a good-looking boy. I couldn't help thinking, wondering...I wanted to ask him... Well, I suppose you can guess what I wanted to ask.'

'Can I? Mark, keep away from them, for your own sake...'

'Danny wants to see me.'

266

Simon snorted. 'I bet he does!' He shook his head in disgust. 'I bet he wants to see you.'

Mark thought of going to see Danny, of walking into his ward and scanning the beds. He wondered if he would recognise him at once, knowing that he would, of course. Danny would look up as though sensing he was being watched and for a moment he would be afraid, not expecting him to have grown so tall, into such a powerful-looking man. Anyone could see how capable he was. And Danny would be weak and tremulous and the tables would be turned.

Gently Simon said, 'Mark, you realise, don't you, that Danny would have hurt any child in his care? It wasn't anything to do with you personally –'

'He didn't hurt Ben.'

'Don't you think he would have, in time? You must stop thinking about him – tell Ben you don't want anything to do with Danny or his family. Try and forget.'

Mark laughed painfully. 'How do I forget, Dad?'

'You stop yourself from remembering.' Closing his eyes he said, 'I'm tired, Mark. I would like you to go.'

Walking down the hospital corridor, Mark saw the signs for the ward where Danny waited to die. In the lift his finger hesitated over the buttons. Finally, he made his decision and the lift's mechanical voice announced his destination with cheerful goodwill.

So, Simon thought, Carter had sired other sons. He thought how criminal it was that such men were allowed to breed once their wickedness was known. He thought of castration, of brutal, just, biblical punishments, but felt only disgusted with himself, as though he had sunk to Carter's level.

That afternoon, just before Mark arrived, a vicar had visited him. The man remembered Joy, and told him what a good, Christian woman she was. Joy believed in redemption, he knew that much. She believed, too, that

Danny Carter should be forgiven. 'By whom?' he'd asked. 'By Annette? By that damaged child?' He had turned against God. Now, in his final days, he told himself he should be brave and stand by his non-believing. It was more difficult than he had thought it might be because there was the terrible, shaming temptation to hedge his bets and allow himself to pray with the man who spoke so kindly and was so convinced of the comfort of an after-life. In the end, it was this obvious conviction that hardened his heart. Besides, he didn't want his consciousness to live on, if that was what heaven meant.

Simon looked at his watch. Soon it would be time for the supper trolley to come round. He had ordered fish pie and caramel custard to follow. Nurse Fletcher — Sally — was amazed by his appetite, and, idiotically, her amazement and praise of his cleared plate pleased him. Next he would be telling her that he had all his own teeth. He was old. At least his father, someone he thought of often lately, had been spared the shames of age.

Fish pie. He wondered what had possessed him to order such a dish. It would be foul, he knew. He thought of Joy, who had been a good, plain cook. Aloud, he said, 'I wish you were here, my darling girl.' They wouldn't meet in heaven; for a moment he was sorry he didn't believe in the stories.

Joy had made toad-in-the-hole the first evening the boys came to visit them. The social worker had smiled and said, 'Something smells delicious!' Grinning at the boys, the woman, who looked too young for such responsibilities, had added, 'Gosh, I wish I was staying to tuck in, too!' At once Mark had looked frightened, turning to hide his face in the girl's coat. She had ruffled his hair. 'Oh don't be shy, Mark! Remember we talked about how lovely it would be to stay here with your new Mummy and Daddy?' Looking up at Joy, the social worker had smiled as though she needed to apologise for Mark's behaviour. And Joy, who he discovered later, was more frightened than she had ever been in her life, smiled back.

They had talked and talked and talked about taking on Ben and Mark. '*Taking on*!' Joy had laughed in despair. 'As if they are our enemies, as if we are entering into a war! They're just two little boys…'

Sitting up in bed, the alarm clock ticking away the long minutes between three and four in the morning, he had lifted her hand from the eiderdown and kissed it. 'Darling, if you have any doubts…'

'No. It's the right thing to do.' After a moment she added, 'I *want* them. I daren't admit to the children's home how much I want them.'

Joy had fallen in love with Mark, of course, that beautiful, angel face. 'Such a gentle little boy,' she kept repeating after their first meeting. 'How could anyone hurt such a child? How could his mother…' She'd trailed off. Annette could not be blamed. Annette was beyond blame, now.

Simon remembered Annette in her tartan mini-skirt. He remembered her sitting on his backdoor step, smoking a cigarette, watching the sparrows flit about the garden. He remembered imagining her in his bed, and he remembered the guilt of such imaginings. Guilt was always close by whenever he thought of Annette, becoming less over the years, only to make its presence felt more forcefully after Joy's death, when his defences were down. In those days he had, eventually, been able to put the guilt to one side. Now he knew it would not be shaken, he would take it to his grave.

He pressed the buzzer for a nurse, hoping it would be Sally who answered the call. Sally was cheerful and made him laugh. Desperately, he pushed the buzzer again, struggling to sit up as an almighty wave of pain swept over him.

Chapter 24

Joy said, 'She fainted, Simon.' Her heart was hammering, as if she had run a mile, and her hand went to her chest as she watched Simon stoop over the girl and take her pulse.

'Annette,' he said calmly, 'Annette? It's all right, my dear.' He looked up. 'Joy, would you fetch a glass of water?'

Fumbling around looking for a glass, Joy told herself to be sensible, to breathe normally and not panic. The girl was fine. She had fainted, that was all. Simon was here now to take care of her, walking in just in time, tossing the paper he'd bought on the table as he hurried across the room. Such was her relief at seeing him she had almost cried. At least he was too concerned with Annette to worry about her; she was tired of worrying him with her unruly emotions.

The tap coughed and spluttered out brownish water. Waiting until it ran clear, Joy filled a glass, taking a swift sip herself before carrying it to the girl. Annette was even paler than before and she watched as Simon pressed his hand to her forehead. 'Annette,' he said, 'What are we going to do with you, eh?'

'I'm sorry, Doctor Walker.'

'Nonsense! You have nothing to be sorry about! But you haven't eaten, have you? Now that's not good, is it? Haven't we talked about this before?'

'Yes, Doctor.' The girl's voice was barely a whisper. She crossed her arms over her chest as though freezing cold. At once Joy said, 'I'll go and fetch a blanket.'

Upstairs on the landing, Joy looked around her, trying to remember in which room she'd seen the blanket box. It was the room at the front of the house, she was sure. Hurrying along the faded carpet runner, she felt the benign ghosts of the house crowd around her.

Downstairs again, Joy handed the blanket to Simon and he draped it around the girl's shoulders. He said, 'Annette, I'm going to drive you home. Joy will come with us and see you safely to bed.' He glanced at her. More quietly he said, 'Is that all right, Joy? I think it would be best.'

'Yes, of course.'

Annette struggled to stand up. 'It's all right, Doctor, I'm fine. You don't have to go to any trouble. I can manage...'

'No.' Simon's voice was firm. 'You'll do as I say, Annette. My wife and I will take you home and make sure that you're cared for. Is there someone who can come in and sit with you? Someone who can collect your boys from school?'

'Really – I'm all right.'

He ignored her. 'Is there any way I can contact your husband?'

Annette looked at him as though he had slapped her.

'Annette...' He sighed. 'He should know that you're poorly.'

'I'm not! Please don't say anything to him.'

She began to cry and Simon turned to her. 'Joy, would you stay with her? I'll go and get the car out of the garage.'

As soon as he'd gone Annette said, 'Please let me go home on my own. I'm all right, really and truly...' She wiped her eyes and made an effort to sit up straight, even attempted a smile, her mouth trembling. 'I don't want you to go to any trouble.'

'But it's no trouble.' Joy crouched down beside her and took her hand. 'Why don't you tell me what the matter is? Perhaps I can help.' Gently she said, 'Who's hurting your baby, Annette? Is it your husband?'

271

Annette's eyes filled with tears again. She shook her head. 'Please don't say anything to Doctor Walker.'

'But Annette – he can help you…'

'No – Danny will be angry!' As if a solution had suddenly presented itself she said, 'I'll leave him, I promise. Like Joan said – I'll go to Joan's.' She smiled, wiping her eyes quickly. Her voice lightened as though everything was solved. 'There. You don't have to worry. I'll go home now, Joan will take care of us.'

The girl got to her feet shakily. Lacking the strength of body or will to stop her, Joy allowed her to go.

When Simon came back, he frowned around the kitchen as though she was hiding her. 'Where is she?'

'She's gone. I couldn't make her stay – she didn't want us interfering.' Joy sat down. Wearily she said, 'We can't make people do what we think is best.'

'That girl's ill! Honestly, Joy – couldn't you at least have kept her here until I came back?'

'No – I couldn't! If you take on some unstable girl in my absence it's not up to me to sort her out! I don't have the strength or the inclination to care about your lost causes.'

Coldly he said, 'She's not a lost cause.'

'I don't care, Simon. I'm sick and tired and I just want to go to bed.'

'I'm worried about her.'

She forgot about not wanting him to be concerned for her, realising that in fact it was all that she wanted. Her voice rising she said, 'Worry about me! *I'm* your wife – me! *I* need to be taken care of and worried over! For once in my life I want someone to worry about me!'

'I am taking care of you, Joy, but that girl –' He looked towards the door as if he had half a mind to chase after Annette. Turning back to her he said, 'You saw how frightened she was. I think she's scared of her husband…'

Joy laughed scornfully. 'You think?' She remembered the fear in the girl's eyes; the husband was obviously a bully who took his temper out on his wife and children. But there were millions of such men, millions of wives who stayed with them, stupid and feckless to the last. If Annette did leave this Danny then it would be for the best, best that she took her life into her own hands.

Simon sighed. 'So, she went home?'

'Yes. And it's none of our business.'

'No, I suppose you're right.' He smiled sadly. 'Shall I help you to bed?'

Simon undressed. Naked, he climbed into bed beside her and when she shied away from him he said, 'Please let me hold you, that's all I want.' Very carefully, he touched the scar where they had cut out her womb, an expert's touch. He held her and he was gentle, he told her that he had missed her and that he loved her and how sorry he was for everything, although he didn't mention their baby, just kept his voice soft and kissed her breasts that ached still.

But he gave off too much heat and she moved away from him. He smiled at her as if seeking reassurance that she loved him, that he had made amends. Misery crept over her, like the cold that comes over the dying, as though her body was a towel drawing up water. She said, 'We'll never have children.'

'No, we won't.'

'What shall we *do*? What?' Her voice rose and he took her hand and squeezed it. Pulling away she said, 'It's all I think of: how empty my life will be.'

'It won't be – there are other things –'

'But what? You can't even say! Or you'll say *work*, or *charity*! I don't want to help other people!' She knew she sounded like a child but she couldn't help herself. Tears streamed down her face and she thought of Annette, weeping in that miserable kitchen when she had no right to, no right at all with two healthy little boys of her own at

273

home. Fiercely she said, 'It's not fair! That girl can have children easily and she doesn't even care about them –'

'I'm sure she does care –'

'How can she? How can she stand by and let her husband hurt them if she cares so much? It's wicked!'

Simon propped himself on his elbow to frown at her. 'He hurts her children? How do you know?'

'She told me!'

His frown intensified. 'What did she tell you? What exactly did she say?'

Joy felt ashamed suddenly: she should have been kinder to the girl, she should have made her stay. Thinking of the children, the shame turned to guilty panic. Anxiously she said, 'Do you know anything about him? Is he violent?'

'Joy, what did Annette say? It's important.'

She got up, too agitated to keep still. 'She said something about him hurting her baby...Oh, Lord, Simon...'

'Did she say anything else?'

'No – oh, I don't know! She looked half-mad, I didn't know what to think...'

Simon went to her and drew her into his arms. 'I don't want you to worry about this. Listen, you hop back into bed, try and get some rest. I'll drive round to her house and make sure she's OK.' He held her at arms' length, smiling to reassure her as he searched her face. 'Is that all right? Or would you prefer me to stay here?'

'No, no, I'm fine. You go.'

In bed, she watched as he dressed quickly, becoming the brisk, conscientious doctor. All at once she felt shy of him, she hardly knew him, after all, had spent only a few nights in his bed since they met. And yet he had seen the worst of her, the monster that anger and pain had made of the self-contained, calm-seeming woman he had married. He knew her, inside out; the pornography of grief had left her wide open. She wondered how he could bear to look at her.

He tugged on a pullover. It made his hair stick up and as he stooped over the bed to kiss her she smoothed a heavy strand back from his face. He smiled.

'I love you,' she said.

'Do you?'

'Tell her I'm sorry if I seemed brusque.'

He kissed her again. 'I love you, too.'

'Go on – I'm worried about her.'

Lying on her side in the bed that smelt of him, that still retained the heat from his body, she thought of him going to that girl. No doubt Annette Carter carried children easily, bore them easily; she would push them out in to the cold air and think so little of it, little enough for it hardly to matter if they were kept safe. Jealousy felt like a weight on her chest, felt like raw, impotent rage, a useless, destructive energy that would keep her from the oblivious sleep she craved. Tossing the bedcovers aside, she got up. Rage and jealousy had made her defiant, full of agitating fearlessness. Alone in the house she would confront its ghosts and claim it as her own.

Danny was home. Annette could hear him moving about upstairs and with every thud and creak of floorboards she would jump, fear jolting through her like an electric shock. She drew her coat around her more tightly, too cold to take it off. Besides, keeping her coat on made her feel ready to escape, if she should need to; it lent her a little confidence, knowing she was ready to run.

Creeping out into the passage, she listened, ears straining for any sound of Mark. But he was such a quiet little boy, so good. He never gave her any trouble – even his teacher said how good he was. Feeling shaky, she leaned against the wall. There were no sounds from upstairs now. Very quietly, she sat down on the first stair and huddled inside her coat.

Her dolls sat in a semi-circle around her: Paula and Suzie and Anne. Anne was her favourite and she had made her a purple dress from crepe paper and she was pretty, with blonde, curly hair and blue eyes that closed when she was laid on her back. Reaching out, she picked Anne up and cradled her in her arms. She sang softly, 'I had a little nut tree, nothing would it bear...' Anne's big blue eyes flickered and closed. From her chair by the fire her grandmother snored and mumbled from her sleep. The room had become dark and the fire burnt out; shadows crept up the walls. She would stay very still and she would listen and listen and it wouldn't matter how stiff and cold she became if the darkness kept away from her little circle. She held Anne more tightly and sang a little louder, 'The king of Spain's daughter came to marry me...'

Upstairs the bed creaked and banged against the wall. A man's voice groaned, like he was in pain and about to die. Anne's hard little hand stabbed against her chest as she held her even closer; her voice quavered over the words of her song. There was something big and frightening she had to worry about, she knew, and she knew that she should try to remember what it was. The words of the song faltered so she went back to the beginning again, and the words helped to dampen the clamouring feeling that there was something terrible she had forgotten.

Chapter 25

The lift doors opened. Mark hesitated for a moment, only to step forward quickly when the doors began to close. In the corridor he hesitated again, unsure whether to turn left or right. A nurse approached, casual in a short white overall and trousers; she smiled at him. 'Are you lost?'

The Tesco carrier bag bulging full of Simon's dirty laundry felt heavier suddenly and more noticeable; it marked him as someone who would dither in corridors, who would appear all too obviously lost; a person diminished by domestic responsibilities, cowed by them. This is the person he would have been, he knew, if it hadn't been for Simon and Joy: poor, voiceless, pathetic – his true nature revealed, rather than hidden by a middle-class education and encouragements. Feeling his fingers tighten around the bag's handles, he said, 'I'm looking for Mr Carter.'

'Danny?' The nurse smiled as though Danny was a joy to her.

Mark nodded and his mouth felt dry with the metallic taste of fear.

'This way.'

He followed her along the corridor, turning right and through double doors that swung noiselessly behind them, and right again, past the nurses' station where a porter dressed like Steven lounged and chatted to a nurse whose eyes scanned a computer screen even as she smiled at the porter's joke. They both looked up as he followed his nurse; he could feel their eyes on him, but knew that this was just his imagination. They could have no interest in him; they couldn't know the momentousness of this visit. His legs felt weak. The metallic taste became more pronounced.

The nurse pushed open a door. 'Here we are!'

The room was exactly like Simon's room: a high bed, a visitor's chair beside the locker, a sink in the corner with the same warning notice about hand washing above it. The window looked out on the same view of distant hills. Get-well-soon cards were pinned on the same cork notice board. Standing in the doorway as the nurse went in ahead of him, he noticed all this even as he kept his eyes away from the figure in the bed. He thought he might be sick. He thought his knees might give out on him. The nurse said breezily, 'Danny, you've got a visitor! Isn't that nice?'

Danny's mouth and nose were covered by an oxygen mask. Lying on the bed, only his eyes moved, flickering to the side to look at Mark. But even this small effort seemed too much for him. His eyes closed. Beneath the obscuring mask his face had taken on the look of a man who has already given himself up to death. He was too late.

The man in the bed didn't look like Danny: this man was too small, his hair was grey and too thin. Mark found himself going to the corkboard and reading the messages inside the cards to confirm his identity, thinking that the nurse had made a mistake. One of the cards was signed from Steven and Jade. He turned back to the diminished figure on the bed; it might just as well be a stranger lying there: less than a stranger, something not human, a teaching aid, perhaps. Turning away, he stepped out into the corridor. No one was about. He walked back to the lifts quickly, the carrier bag bumping against his leg.

I was reading one of his novels when he came. If I'd known it was him knocking at the door I would have hidden it away, but there it was, open and face down on the floor by the chair. I don't think he noticed it. I hope he didn't.

278

He knocked at the door and I took my glasses off and sat stock still, listening, because sometimes it's just kids who knock and run or shove something disgusting through the letterbox. I waited to hear the thud of feet running away, but instead the knocking went on, insistent. I began to worry that something had happened to Jade, so I tossed the book down and half ran to the door. Through the spy-hole I saw that it was him and I could hardly get the chain unhooked quickly enough because my fingers were suddenly clumsy. I heard myself call out, 'Just a sec,' and I sounded too excited, too pleased, so that I wished I was cooler and didn't wear my heart on my sleeve so obviously.

He came in. Without a word he went to the window and looked out. You can see for miles from my lounge window, right over to the Cleveland hills, but it was pouring with rain and he just stood there, staring into the greyness. Rain splattered against the glass and the wind roared like it does around the tower blocks, as though it wants to tear them down for getting in its way. Unsure of myself, I laughed my daft, embarrassed laugh. 'All right?'

He turned to look at me. 'I'm intruding.'

'No you're not! Do you want a cup of tea, or anything? Look, sit down.' I cleared the settee of a pile of books and newspapers. 'Here.'

I made him a cup of tea. I forgot and put milk in it, and had to pour it down the sink and start again. Through the hatch from the kitchen into the lounge I saw him sit down on the settee. He looked around like he wasn't sure how he'd come to be there. There was a sadness about him that filled the whole room.

As I handed him his black tea he looked up at me and smiled. 'Thank you. I'm cold, I need something to warm me.'

'You got caught in the rain.' His hair was wet and I had an urge to reach out and touch it. 'Do you want a towel, dry yourself off a bit?'

'No. I'm fine.' After a moment he said, 'I saw Danny today.'

I wasn't sure what to say so I said nothing, and waited for him to go on. He laughed awkwardly. 'I don't think he recognised me...he didn't speak. I felt foolish, not what I expected to feel.'

'And how do you feel now?'

He sipped his tea. 'You remembered I don't take milk.'

'I put milk in the first cup – I had to throw it down the sink.'

He gazed at me, a long, searching look. I squirmed, thinking how self-conscious he made me feel, as though I was everything and nowt at the same time. Putting his cup down at his feet he got up and crossed the room to my bookcase. He took down my copy of *Ulysses* and flicked through it, only to put it back again. He did the same with some of the other books, like he was looking for something I'd hidden between their pages. After a bit he turned to me.

'Which is your favourite?'

'I dunno. Changes all the time.'

Looking at the books again he said, 'No poetry.'

'Nah.'

'No Shakespeare.'

'Big gaps in my education.' I went to stand beside him, not too close. 'Tell me what poets I should read.'

He laughed like I'd said something stupid. 'What would he say when he saw you reading?'

'Danny? He didn't say anything, I kept out of his way.'

He nodded and slid back the copy of *Animal Farm* he'd been leafing through. 'Reading used to be an escape,' he said. 'Even when I was a very young child I could read a story and cut myself off from everything that was happening around me. In the children's home...Well, even in the most chaotic of places there are always quiet hide-aways.'

'You hid away?'

280

'Did you?'

I found myself staring at my small collection of books gathered from car-boot sales and charity shops, and even one or two I'd actually gone into a bona-fide bookshop and paid full whack for. I didn't know whether to be proud of the books or not, or what he thought of them. People are judged by their books, or their lack of them. You're either too clever or not clever enough. But I knew he wasn't thinking about books, wasn't even seeing them. He seemed not to be able to focus properly.

Suddenly he said, 'In the home where they first sent us I found this huge cupboard they used to store bedding. I'd hide in there. There was a smell of washing powder from all the piles of clean sheets.' He smiled. 'Something about that harsh, clean smell made me decide I was safe in there, that it was the last place he would look.'

'You thought he was coming after you?'

'Of course!'

'But they must have told you –'

'I can't remember that they did.' Frowning at a row of books he said, 'Have you read Hemingway? Steinbeck? Roth? You seem to have neglected most American writers.' He glanced at me. 'Where did you hide?'

'It wasn't hiding, not really. I'd go to my Nana's. He was scared of her.' Cautiously I said, 'Did you really think he was coming to get you, even when they took you away?'

'He told me that he'd always find me, no matter what. I believed him more than I believed strangers.'

'You must have been scared stiff.'

He laughed, his eyes scanning the book spines. 'Scared stiff. Yes. My mother – Joy –' He stopped himself and I was afraid to prompt him.

He went to the window again. The rain had stopped, the sun starting to break through the clouds. 'May I ask you something?' He glanced at me. I nodded and he said, 'Do I remind you of him?'

281

'No!' I couldn't say what I wanted to say, that I was afraid of the truth of him, scared he might be Danny after all. Eventually I said, 'You look like him, but then, so do I. I suppose I could ask you the same thing, do I remind you –'

'Yes. Yes, you do. It's why I'm here. I'm drawn to you. It's like you're a puzzle I have to keep returning to again and again until it's solved.' He stepped toward me. Quickly he said, 'I wouldn't hurt you, you know that, don't you? I only want to be close to you –'

'How close?'

He ignored me. 'You and me – what he did to me he did to you. I'm right, aren't I?'

I couldn't speak, I knew that my voice would break and I'd be ashamed. He moved closer to me and I felt his hand brush against mine so that I squirmed.

Insistently he said, 'It was only you and me, wasn't it? Don't you wonder why? Don't you ask yourself all the time? He didn't hurt Ben, I know that – and your brothers – he didn't hurt them, did he?' His voice rose as he repeated, 'It was just you and not them, wasn't it?'

I stepped away from him. My skin was crawling. Like an idiot I said, 'Your tea's going cold.'

'Steven…' Desperately he said, 'We can help each other, I'm sure – the first time I saw you –'

'You couldn't stand to look at me!'

'I was shocked by you, by how much you're like him, like me. Since then I can't stop thinking about you.' Reaching out he touched my hand. 'Steven, I am right, aren't I? You haven't denied it…' His hand closed around mine, such a cool, strong grasp he had. Gently he said, 'Why don't we lie down together? It's safe here, so high up, away from everything.'

I nodded, speechless, feeling only the strength of his fingers around mine and the sudden, quickening excitement in my guts.

*　　*　　*

The boy's bedroom was empty expect for a double bed and a chest of drawers, and so tidy it gave nothing away. Mark had expected more books, had dreaded the sight of them and the hopes they represented. He had expected photographs, too, pictures of the little girl, Jade, and he had dreaded these even more. To be reminded that this boy had fathered a child would have made what he was about to do impossible.

Steven took off his shoes and lay down on the bed. The duvet cover was white, the pillows too, and when Mark lay down beside him he caught the smell of fabric softener, the same brand that he used. He breathed in deeply and remembered the oxygen mask over Danny's face, the flickering eyes above it, so that he tried to concentrate on the ordinary, comforting smell of the pillow.

Softly Steven said, 'You all right?'

The bed dipped as the boy moved closer. They were both lying on their sides, face to face, and Steven rested his hand on Mark's hip, smiling at him. Awkwardly Steven said, 'We're just going to talk? That's all. It would be wrong, wouldn't it? Anything else would be wrong.'

Outside the wind howled. Mark imagined he could feel the building swaying, giving in just enough to stop itself being destroyed. The howling was terrible; he wondered how the boy could stand it. Quickly he said, 'You must make more of your life.'

'Must I?' Steven rolled away from him to lie on his back. Staring at the ceiling he said, 'You're not my dad. Don't talk as if you are.' He turned to look at him. 'If you *were* my dad my life would be brilliant.'

'In what way?'

'You should hear yourself talk – so *proper*.' He laughed. 'If you were my dad my life would be brilliant *because*...I don't know – it's obvious, isn't it?'

Steven was silent for a while. Eventually he said, 'I know I should make more of my life. But then, Jade came along...I always wanted kids. Maybe I got Nicola pregnant accidentally on purpose. I wanted to prove to everyone that I could be a good father. I didn't need to prove it to myself – I knew what was inside me.' Propping himself up on his elbow, he looked down into Mark's face. 'Danny didn't get into my heart. You understand, don't you? He didn't touch my heart or my imagination, or my soul. Just my body. Bodies don't matter – you can leave them on the bed and go away somewhere he can't reach you.'

Mark closed his eyes, unable to look at the boy. Tears spilled down his cheeks and he felt Steven brush them away.

'Mark?' Drawing him into his arms, Steven whispered, 'You can tell me what he did to you and I will say yes, he did that to me, too, and so what? He was just a dirty bastard and sick in the head, and we were unlucky –'

Mark pushed him away. He laughed brokenly. '*Unlucky*?'

'Yes. Unlucky to look like we do, to be his sons...we were little kids...' He fell onto his back and threw his arm across his face. At last he said, 'Five. I was five when he first...I thought I was being punished for something. I thought it was my fault.' Lowering his arm he turned to him. 'I'm not...*normal*. You know that. It's why we're both here, on this bed. I've got a hard-on like a sick fucking bastard because you're so fucking gorgeous and I'm thinking *but he's your brother!* And then I'm thinking, no – he's not, not like Graham is, or Colin is. He's just some gorgeous fucking stranger. But you're not. You *are* my brother. And this is fucking mad and sick – and I think...'

He exhaled sharply. He got up and sat on the edge of the bed, holding his head in his hands.

'What do you think?'

Steven turned to look at him. 'That you're sicker than I am. Maybe because what he did to you was worse, I don't know.'

'You don't know what he did to me.'

He snorted. Looking away again he said, 'No, I know nowt, me. You can just come here and play your sick games and keep me guessing. Well, I'm pretty good at guessing. I know Danny – better than you do.'

Mark moved across the bed. He touched the boy's shoulder and felt him tense. Expecting to be shrugged off, instead Steven kept very still. Carefully, Mark said, 'Shall I tell you everything? Then you won't have to guess.'

Steven turned to look at him. 'I don't think you have the words.'

'Lie down,' Mark said. 'Let me hold you. I'll tell you everything.'

Chapter 26

Driving to Tanner Street, Simon almost turned around and drove home, worried about leaving Joy alone. She had seemed less frail in hospital, more ready to face the world. But patients in hospital took the trouble to convince their doctors they should be allowed home and he should have recognised the signs, he had seen them often enough. Women like Joy put on a little lipstick and brushed their hair, they made sure they were sitting up in the chair rather than in bed when he made his rounds. They smiled and made their voices bright, just as Joy had. And their husbands, if they were about, smiled too and told him how ready they were to look after their wives and how much the little woman was longing to be home. He had become just such a husband, aching for his wife and for some semblance of normality to return to his life. Selfish, he had always thought these husbands selfish, and childishly dependent.

He sighed, driving the car on through the traffic lights in the High Street, knowing that he wouldn't turn round, that he would go on until he reached Tanner Street. He imagined parking the car and getting out, knocking on number seven's door and waiting for Annette to answer. She would be shocked to see him, and afraid, no doubt. He tightened his grip on the steering wheel, angry suddenly and unsure where his anger was directed. At himself, he thought. Somehow he had become useless, sunk in the concerns of women.

Tanner Street was a short terrace of two-up, two-down houses, the road cobbled so that the car rattled and bumped along. He parked and locked the car, ashamed that he was so ready to believe that Annette's neighbours were thieves. Number seven was half way down the terrace. He looked up at it, noticed that its curtains were drawn, not quite meeting in the middle even though the cloth was tightly stretched. Even from the street there was an air of neglect about the little house. Simon found himself sighing again, uselessly. He glanced back at the car; he could go home, he could tell Joy that it was best they didn't interfere.

Remembering how worried Joy was about the girl and her child, he walked quickly to Annette's door and knocked sharply. Flakes of paint fell at his feet. He glanced at the bay window and saw that there was a hole in its glass, taped over with a torn cornflake packet. The windowsill was rotting, its wood spongy-looking so that he could imagine breaking off huge clumps with his bare hands. No doubt the house was damp. He knocked on the door again, then crouched down to peer through the letterbox.

Annette was sitting on the stairs, so rigid and still he was reminded of an animal about to run for its life. Through the letterbox he could see the petrified look on her face. As her hand went to her throat, she seemed to mouth something – but no sound came.

'Annette? It's Doctor Walker. Why don't you let me in...?' He laughed self-consciously, feeling his alarm undermined by a sense of foolishness as he crouched there, knowing that all she could see were his eyes or his mouth as he spoke. He could smell the breath of the house, damp and dirty; it mixed with the metal smell of the letterbox and sickened him. Taking a deep breath of fresh air, he called to her again. 'Annette, please. Let me in. I only want to see that you're all right.' She began to back up the stairs, her eyes fixed on the door. 'Annette,' he said more gently, 'please let me in – there's nothing to be afraid of –'

He heard a man's voice. Straightening up, Simon knocked again. 'Mr Carter? Would you open the door please? It's Doctor Walker, Annette's employer.'

There was a silence. Simon waited, sure that in a moment the door would be opened and Carter would appear. He could guess what this boy would be like: a swaggering bully, smiling excuses and assuming that he shared his posturing, man-to-man attitude towards women and their ways. Or he would be aggressive, demanding to know what right he had to come looking for his wife, sticking his nose in. Simon felt his anger rise, knowing that whatever type Carter was he would want to smash his teeth down his throat. The man hurt his children and his wife, he scared them to death. Thinking of the silent little boy the teacher had brought to his house, Simon began to pound on the door with his fist, causing it to swing open. He found himself face to face with a naked man.

'For God's sake!' Simon frowned at him, surprise disarming his anger a little. 'Go and make yourself decent!'

The boy pushed him, the flat of his hand against Simon's chest. 'Fuck off out of it.'

'I will, when I'm certain Annette is all right.' He looked past Carter to the terrified girl. 'My dear, we were worried about you –'

Turning to his wife Carter said, 'Is this the bastard you've been fucking? Is it?'

Simon gazed at him in disgust. 'Go and get dressed.'

Ignoring him, Carter said, 'Tell me who he is. Don't lie to me now. Don't you dare.'

She looked at Simon. 'Please go. Please, I'm all right.'

'I won't go until I know you're safe.' To Carter he said, 'I'm Simon Walker. Your wife works for me. Today she gave me cause to be concerned for her, which is why I'm here. Now, you go and get dressed and calm yourself down and I'll make us all a cup of tea.'

He made to step past Carter, turning his face away to avoid looking at him, already he had seen enough. The boy was slight, his skin deathly pale against the dark hair covering his chest. He didn't seem to care about his nakedness, his exposed cock shrivelled in its nest of pubic hair. Simon caught his musk-like scent, darkly sexual, and suddenly he couldn't control his disgust. Turning on the boy he said, 'Don't you have any decency? You have two young sons – what if they were to see you like this?'

'Two sons? Is that what she told you?' He laughed. 'I've one, only one.'

There was a muffled cry from upstairs. Annette's hand went to her mouth and she turned to Carter; he shot her a quick, silencing look.

'Is there someone upstairs, Annette?' Simon stepped towards her. Cautiously he said, 'Annette, there's no need to be frightened –'

She began to cry. 'I wanted to give him something to eat, but he was asleep –'

'Shut up, you silly bitch!' Carter turned to him. 'She's talking rubbish – there's no one here.'

'Are your boys upstairs, Annette? Are they poorly?' As he stepped towards the stairs, Carter barred his way.

'Where d'you think you're going?'

'Get out of my way, unless you want me to call the police.'

Carter laughed as though astonished. '*You* call the police? Who broke into my house – who came in here shouting the odds?'

Simon shoved him to one side but the boy caught his arm. 'You're not going up there. This is my house – you've no right!'

For a moment they stood face to face. Carter's nakedness had come to seem almost normal, making him think of the time he'd spent working on the mental wards when he was training and how lunacy could all too easily become unremarkable. And Carter was so slight, boyish – he could knock him down with one swipe of his arm. Only his eyes gave him pause; they betrayed the boy's madness and he knew that mad men often had the strength of devils.

Softly Simon said, 'Listen, my boy, why don't you show me upstairs yourself? I just want to satisfy myself –'

Carter stepped aside. 'Go on then. Go and *satisfy* yourself. He's asleep, but if you want to disturb him, go ahead.'

Looking at Annette, Simon said, 'Will you show me where he sleeps, Annette? Best if his mummy is there if he wakes – I don't want to scare him.'

She shook her head, her voice barely a whisper. 'I can't.'

'Oh, come now!' He attempted to smile at her, to be patient, even as his growing anxiety made him want to rush to the child. 'Annette, I'm sure he'll want his mummy.' Holding out his hand to her he said, 'Come on. We'll go and see him together.'

Leading her up the narrow staircase, Simon thought of his father and how his work as a GP took him so often into his patients' homes: uncontrolled, unpredictable places, the front line. Drunkenness, madness, squalor – his father took it all in his stride. Simon knew he wouldn't have had his father's forbearance. He needed the conformity of hospital wards, the mediating nurses. Here, in Annette's little house, he felt a weight of foreboding he had never experienced before. Whatever he was about to be confronted with, he would have to deal with it alone.

At the top of the stairs the itch-inducing stink of unwashed bodies became stronger. Simon turned to Annette, still hardly able to believe she could keep such a house. Her husband was close behind her, his eyes darting from side to side as if he was a thief in his own home, ready to run at the slightest hint of discovery. They're children, Simon thought, and the pretence of being adults has driven them both mad. Gently he said, 'Which room, Annette?'

She pointed at a closed door straight ahead. Turning the handle Simon found that it was locked. 'Do you have the key?'

'You're not going in there.' Carter pushed his wife to one side. 'If you don't get out –'

'Be quiet, now.' Simon spoke as calmly as he could. 'Listen, it's Danny, isn't it? Danny, I want to help you. I want to help you and your wife and your boys. No one's going to hurt you –'

'I don't want you taking him away! You'll take him away and I won't have it!' Carter stood in front of the locked door, his arms out-stretched to bar the way, and Simon thought how easy it would be to lift him away bodily and simply put his shoulder to the door. Instead he touched his arm. 'Danny, let me see your little boy. I only want to see him and make sure he's all right.'

'He is! He's fine!'

Annette was weeping and Carter's eyes darted to her. 'You stop crying! Stop crying, you hear? There's nothing to cry about!'

'Please let the doctor in, please.' Reaching out to Danny, she sobbed, 'Doctor Walker will know what to do! He'll die, Danny. Don't let my baby die...'

'He's not going to die!' Carter's voice rose hysterically and he looked at Simon as though he would confirm this. 'Tell her – Mark wanted me to do it – you should see how much he wants it! He loves it!' Grasping Simon's arm he said conspiratorially, 'I think he's possessed. He *makes* me do things to him! He's not just an ordinary little kid, I'm warning you!'

Shrugging off his grasp, Simon said, 'Move out of the way.' Carter shook his head and Simon pushed him to one side before standing back and putting his shoulder to the door. It gave easily and he staggered into the room.

At once Simon covered his mouth with his hand, overcome by the stink. It was the smell of the filthiest brothel, of sweat and semen and soiled bedding. Across the window thin red curtains filtered the sunlight so that the room was bathed in a pinkish glow. Simon gagged; stumbling, he went to the window, tearing the curtains to one side and shoving it open. He turned to the bed.

The child lay on his stomach, his arms raised above his head, each wrist tied to the bedstead, his mouth gagged with a rag. He was naked. As Simon went to him, he saw that his back and thighs were covered in red weals as though he'd been beaten with a cane. Kneeling by the bed, Simon untied the gag and the cord that bound his wrists, all the time keeping up a soft stream of words as he felt for his pulse. The child was barely conscious, his breathing shallow. Almost overcome by pity, Simon clenched his jaw; he could not be weak, he must not give in to the pain and grief he felt at the sight of this child and the remembrance of his own.

Standing behind him, Carter said, 'It's like a devil's inside him – I had to keep him quiet, what else could I do –'

Simon lifted Mark into his arms. Half-starved, he seemed to weigh nothing at all. His eyes flickered and Simon made himself smile to reassure him, stroking his shorn head.

Stepping in front of him Carter said, 'Don't take him. He's mine.' His voice was pleading, and he touched his son's body so that Simon stepped back, disgusted by this naked creature. He turned to Annette who stood in the doorway, her hand covering her mouth, her eyes wide. Again she reminded him of a little girl that had been discovered in some forbidden place. She seemed to be waiting for him to be angry. Gently he said, 'Annette, you must come with me and your little boy to the hospital in my car – it will be quicker than calling an ambulance –'

'He doesn't need an ambulance!' Carter shouted, 'You give him back!'

As Danny made to snatch Mark from his arms, Annette pulled him back. 'Don't you touch him! You've hurt him enough.'

Danny turned on her. Grasping both her arms, he shook her violently. 'Why did you bring him here? Why? This is your fault, you stupid bitch!' He pushed her, both hands flat against her chest so that she staggered. He pushed her again, screaming obscenities as she stumbled through the open door and fell backwards down the stairs.

Simon waited in the hospital corridor. He had wanted to stay with the child, but Iain had gently insisted that he should wait outside while he examined him. He was pleased it was Iain – the first doctor he'd seen as he followed the ambulance men into the hospital. Iain was a good man, a fine man, he had taken charge of the situation whereas he had been useless, on the brink of tears, of making a real show of himself. 'You're in shock,' Iain had said, and he'd taken his arm and made him sit down, here, on this chair in the corridor, a visitor's chair, a chair for those who waited and prayed, uselessly.

A nurse brought him a cup of tea. It grew cold at his feet, too milky, too sweet. Sweetness was good for shock. He should drink it. The smell of that hellish room was still in his nose and mouth, it might take the taste away. He closed his eyes, seeing Annette again, broken at the bottom of those stairs. Slumping forward, he held his head in his hands and groaned softly.

He couldn't remember going downstairs. He remembered holding the child and the feel and smell of him as he crouched over Annette's body. He'd kept his hand firmly on the back of Mark's head so his face was pressed to his shoulder and he wouldn't see. And then a woman appeared at the front door. She said, 'What's going on –' and she stopped, her hand going to her chest as though her heart had stopped along with her words. This was Annette's neighbour, he discovered, Joan. He remembered that he had told her to call an ambulance, and he remembered his voice was quick with impatience as though it was her fault that Annette lay there at his feet. He'd looked up at the woman because she didn't seem able to move and more sharply he'd said, 'Hurry up – go!' At once she was running, and it seemed only a moment before she was back again, taking the child from him, rocking him in her arms and singing softly as though he was hers. She sang *I Had A Little Nut Tree*, because, she said, Mark knew the words and it always comforted him. They sat on the stairs together, he and Joan, Mark cradled in her lap, and she told him all this as they waited for the ambulance. He had covered Annette's face with a clean handkerchief, taken from his drawer that morning. Joan had grasped his hand tightly. He felt as though he had known Joan all his life, for ever, and that they didn't have to speak to comfort each other. At the top of the stairs Danny crouched, groaning, his arms covering his head as if shielding himself from expected blows. They ignored him, almost forgot him. The ambulance came, the police. The door to the street was open and the little hallway filled with noise and blue light. Joan staggered to her feet, clutching Mark to her as though she would fight rather than give him up.

Simon sat back in the hard, hospital chair. He breathed out, trying to be calm and think clearly. A statement had to be made to the police. The young constable, who had crouched beside Annette's body and checked for a pulse, as if he hadn't already searched for it, had told him he would have to go to the station and make a written statement. By then Danny had been handcuffed. From somewhere a blanket had been found and thrown over Danny's shoulders to hide his nakedness so that he looked like a savage dressed by missionaries so as not to offend God. How small he seemed, and slight. Simon had told the police to go easy on him as they bundled him away; his pity was raw and indiscriminate and he felt consumed by it. Besides, the boy was mad, and he thought of his bare feet, blackened by the filthy street and wanted to weep because they had seemed so pathetic.

Iain came out of the examining room. Simon stood up at once and Iain smiled the kind of smile he himself used on those who waited in corridors: ready to give reassurance but grave, doling out hope in small measure. Taking his arm Iain made him sit down again and sat beside him. After a moment's hesitation he said, 'Simon...' He sighed, and suddenly all his professional front was lost. He rubbed his hand over his face and groaned softly. 'Oh, Christ, Simon. That child – what he must have suffered!'

'Tell me.'

Iain looked at him. 'You already know what he did to him. You know that it's unspeakable.' He exhaled sharply. 'Christ! I'd like to kill him! He should be hanged! His *own* son! How could a man do that to his own child – to any child? He must be sick!'

'That has to be your answer, that he's sick.'

Iain snorted. 'And so he'll be sent to a nice, quiet asylum?'

Simon bowed his head. He thought of Danny hunched inside the police car, imagined what would happen to him in a cell before it was decided that he should be in a hospital. He turned to Iain. 'Can I see Mark?'

'He's sedated.' He hesitated again. At last he said quickly, 'I don't think you should get any more involved.'

Simon stood up. 'Let me see him, please.'

'Why? Simon, I think you've done enough, best to leave it to the social workers now.'

'*It?*'

Iain sighed. 'All right. Just for a moment. I don't want him upset.'

*   *   *

Later as he lay sleepless in bed, he wished he hadn't seen him and that he had gone straight home and tried not to think about Annette's son. But he had followed Iain into the room and stood by the trolley where Mark lay on his side, a drip in his arm, his eyes closed as if he slept an ordinary sleep. He touched his cheek gently, relieved to see that some colour had returned, a little at least.

He'd turned to Iain. 'It's my fault – I should have guessed what was going on –'

Iain had been dismissive, said that the child wasn't his responsibility, that anyway he had acted in time to save his life, and what more could he have done, in the end?

'His mother's dead.' He had wiped his tears away impatiently, fumbling for his handkerchief only to remember what he had done with it.

In bed he turned on his side. Joy was sleeping, exhausted. They had sat up late and he had talked and she had listened and he had been reminded of why he'd first been drawn to her: she calmed him. He had an urge to wake her and ask if she believed he could have done more. But in the end he knew it wouldn't matter what she said, if she lied to him or told him the truth, he would always believe Annette's death was partly down to him, that he should have guessed sooner how frightened she was and saved her and her children.

Chapter 27

Kitty found Ben in his study. Standing in the doorway she waited for him to look up from his book. 'That was the hospital,' she said. 'It's Simon, they think you should be there.'

He put his book down, closed it on a bookmark. Standing up he said, 'Will you come with me?'

'Yes, of course!'

'The baby –'

'Mam's on her way.'

He stepped towards her. 'Kitty...' Glancing away, he laughed painfully. 'What if we don't go?'

'We have to.'

'But if we didn't make it in time?'

'We will.'

He sank down into his chair. Holding out his hand to her he said, 'Come here.'

He pulled her down onto his knee and she rested her head against his shoulder. She thought that it had been a while since he held her like this and that being held on his knee made her feel like a little girl, made her feel that he was so much older and stronger, like a father, although not like her father. Her father was shy of such closeness, had never touched her, not once.

Stroking her hair he said quietly, 'I wish I was younger, Kitty. I wish I were your age. All this, this house, my career – I would give it all up if it meant I could start again with you. When Dad dies perhaps we should go away, somewhere completely fresh, where no one knows anything about me –' He laughed bleakly. 'I thought that by living here I could square up to the past, confront Danny, confront Simon, as though the past could be sorted out and tidied away, forgotten, if only I asked the right questions. But I went at it half-cock – I couldn't decide how much any of it *mattered* any more. I'd look at you and Nathan...'

The doorbell rang. Her mother called out, 'Hello? Only me.'

'That's Mam.' Kitty stood up. 'We have to go.'

'Kit –' He caught her hand. 'I don't know if I can face him...'

'You can. I'll be there, I'll help you. Everything will be all right,' she said. 'Everything will be fine.'

Steven said, 'Mark, are you OK?'

Mark turned his head on the pillow to look at him, realising that he had been silent for a while, had felt that if he closed his eyes he might even go to sleep. He was so tired always and the boy was such an easy person to be alone with. He stared at the ceiling. A crack ran from the door to the window as though linking escape routes. In his mind's eye he saw Annette fall down the stairs just as he'd described it to Steven, a graceful fall, because it was her gracefulness that he remembered most about her.

Carefully Steven said, 'Mark, you don't have to tell me any more –'

'There isn't any more. After Annette died, well...that's where I would end the story, if I were writing it.' He thought how he would write Simon in those final few pages, how he would burden him with a ton of guilt. To him, Simon had never suffered enough for what he did.

Taking his hand Steven squeezed his fingers gently. 'It's late. You could stay the night, if you like, if you feel you need some company.'

Mark turned on his side so that they lay facing each other, almost touching. 'We would ruin each other, have you thought of that?'

'We're already ruined. Damage done.'

Drawing away from him a little he said, 'Do you want me to stay?'

'I don't think of you as my brother.'

'Steven...' He pressed his palm against the boy's cheek. 'I wish I could have saved you from him. If I'd known you existed I would have taken you away.'

'Been my Dad?'

'Looked after you, at least.'

'And if you had we'd be proper family and you wouldn't be here, on this bed. I think I'd rather have you here now.' Moving closer to him Steven took his hand and kissed it. 'What if we'd met on the street – in London say, near where you live, or in some club? I wouldn't have been able to keep my eyes off you.'

'Steven –'

Steven put his fingers to Mark's lips. 'Imagine it. Imagine I'm a stranger. Imagine buying me a drink and using some line on me. Imagine asking me back to your flat.' Moving still closer he whispered in his ear, 'Imagine me naked on your bed at home and you're just about to fuck me, and you're so hard because I've been sucking your cock...' He took Mark's hand and held it against his erection. 'I'm good, you know? Really, *really* good.'

Mark gazed at him, saw how his dark eyes were hard and bright with lust, saw how young he was, and raw, his eagerness to please making him innocent despite himself. He unzipped Steven's flies and held his cock. The boy groaned, closing his eyes, an expression of intense pleasure on his face so that it seemed to Mark that he was play-acting. Drawing his hand away he began to unbutton Steven's shirt, bowing his head to his nipple and biting gently. Blindly, he reached for his hand and guided it to his

299

own erection. The boy fumbled with Mark's belt buckle, impatience making him clumsy, but finally Mark felt Steven's fingers close around him, heard him make a noise like a sob. Suddenly Steven was pushing away from him and rolling onto his back. Hiding his face with his hands he said, 'I can't.'

Mark lifted his hands away. 'Look at me,' Mark said. He kissed his mouth softly. 'Look at me.'

'I can't!' He sprang away and sat on the edge of the bed. 'Fucking hell! Fucking, *fucking* hell!'

Mark lay on his back. His cock was still semi-erect, still hopeful, at odds with his heart, as ever. He shoved it back inside his pants and zipped his fly. He thought of Danny forcing himself inside him, groaning and grunting with the effort of it. And if he cried out Daddy would press his face into the pillow so that it felt like he was drowning, so that he learnt to keep silent and not plead and beg as he had the first time, although even then his voice had been too small and he wasn't sure what he was asking him not to do. The first time Danny had asked him if he loved him. How scared he had been, but also hopeful because he had never asked him that before. Of course he had said yes, whispering it but emboldened, brave enough to take his hand, the bravest thing he had ever done, and Danny had said, 'Good boy. Good boy,' and lifted him on to the bed.

Steven turned to look at him. His face was smeary with tears, bleary and smudged so that he looked even younger. Painfully he said, 'The first time, with Carl...I think he thought I was a right head case...'

'Carl? Your first lover?'

'The first man...well, you know. The first man...' He turned away again. 'You know what I mean.'

'Yes, I know what you mean.'

'He was lovely. Patient – he didn't run a mile. I would have. I would have run from a nutter like me.' Looking at

300

him over his shoulder he said, 'I didn't tell him – you're the only one who knows.'

He thought of Susan, who had said, 'Tell me about Danny. Ben's told me a little – you know Ben, how much words cost him.' She'd gazed at him, smiling, curious. It had been only the second time they'd made love, the first time being too frantic, too astonishing for words, at least for him. This second time he had begun to sense her restlessness and had waited for her to make an excuse to leave. But instead of leaving she had asked about Danny. It was difficult to resist such an opportunity to keep her in his bed.

Steven lay down beside him. After a while the boy said, 'Would you have gone on? Buggered me?'

Mark winced at the word, still fastidious. 'I don't know.'

Steven began to cry again but more openly, and Mark pulled him into his arms and held him as tenderly as he could, afraid of his body's reaction. 'I'm sorry,' Mark said, 'I'm sorry.' He kissed his head. 'Don't now, don't cry.'

Steven moved away from him and wiped his eyes quickly. 'What shall we do?'

'Do? I don't know.' Mark reached for his hand. Holding it against his chest he said, 'You asked me if I would have gone on, made love to you. I think that yes, I would have, if you'd wanted me to. It's what I came here for – I had this idea that it would help us both to banish ghosts…that if we made love and it was sweet and tender and *loving*…' He exhaled sharply, not knowing if what he was trying to say was a lie or the most profound truth. Desperately he said, 'I thought we would comfort each other. There – I suppose that's what it comes down to. We would comfort each other, knowing what we both know.'

Steven seemed to be going over his words in his head. About to speak, he closed his mouth and bit down on his lip. Then, when Mark was about to try to explain again, Steven said, 'We're both fucked up, aren't we?'

Mark laughed bleakly. 'I am, at least.' Squeezing his hand he said, 'Steven, tell me what you want most in the world – if I could do anything for you, anything at all –'

The boy drew his hand away. 'There's nowt. What I want – well, it's impossible to have.'

'Tell me what's impossible.'

'No. Why should you help me, anyway?' He looked at him, his lip curling in distaste. 'All that just now, it was lies, wasn't it? That crap about comforting each other, about *banishing ghosts. That's* impossible! You'd have fucked me just because you wanted to fuck me and gone back to London and nothing would have changed – except I'd feel worse about myself because what we'd done was so wrong – not just wrong – *illegal!*' He laughed harshly as though coming to a realisation. 'We'd be *criminals*, like Danny! No better than him!'

Mark closed his eyes. He felt Danny's breath on his shoulder, his tongue flashing against his ear like a dog's. He was being smothered, snuffed out. Unable to lie still, he got up, aware of the boy watching him as he buckled his belt. He turned to look at him. 'I'm not Danny.'

Steven gazed at him. At last he said, 'You know what I thought when I first saw you outside that pub? What I thought for a split second? I thought that you were. I thought you were Danny. My heart turned over and I didn't know if it was fear or what. Fear or lust.' He snorted. 'There. Freud would have a good time with us, wouldn't he? A fucking field day!'

A mobile phone began to ring and Steven grabbed for it on the bedside table. About to switch it off he frowned. 'It's the hospital,' he said.

Chapter 28

I used to think that when Danny died I'd go to St John's and offer up a prayer of thanks. Then I'd pray for his soul and light a candle and that would be the end of it. Then, after Carl died, I stopped thinking of God, of hell and heaven, of souls. I just felt sick with despair and I knew that I wouldn't give a fuck when Danny died, and I wouldn't go through any daft, superstitious rituals in the hope of finding peace. There was no peace any more, not after Carl died.

The hospital telephoned – Sister Allison, who's kind and efficient and good – more than Danny deserves. She said, 'I think you should be here, Steve. The morning will be too late.' Too late for goodbye, good riddance. I put the phone down and looked at Mark. 'I have to go,' I said, and straight away he said he'd take me. I thought how handsome he looked. I thought how I couldn't have made a bigger mess if I'd put all my heart into it.

Driving to the hospital, he kept up this silence. Once he took his eyes off the road for a second to look at me. I said, 'I'm glad you're here,' and he nodded. It began to rain and he flicked on the windscreen wipers and a fan to clear the condensation, calm, concentrating. Realising I was staring at him, I looked away. I wished he would put the radio on. The wipers swished back and forth. Lights turned from red to green as we approached because it was late and there was so little traffic, but it seemed they changed just for him and I wondered how it could be that I was still in love with him, despite the fact that he'd used me, or failed to use me, failed to do whatever I wanted him to do. Whatever that was.

He'd asked me what I wanted most in the world. I suppose I wanted him not to ask but just to take charge, like a Dad, a proper Dad.

We took the lift to Danny's ward. I kept saying that it was bound to be a long night – this had happened before, a false alarm a couple of weeks earlier when they were sure he wouldn't last until morning. Then I'd stayed until four, holding his hand, willing him to die, not just for my sake. As Mark and I got out of the lift I repeated, 'It might be hours. Don't feel you have to stay.'

'I'll stay,' he said. 'I'll stay as long as you want me to.'

I smiled. As lightly as I could I said, 'A long night, then.'

'Maybe.'

As soon as I walked into his room, I knew that this wasn't a false alarm. I even thought we were too late, that he was already dead, and suddenly I felt sick that I'd missed it, that he'd been alone. Sitting beside the bed I took his hand, it was still warm. His eyes moved towards me, he seemed to make this massive effort to smile but just couldn't manage it. Beneath the oxygen mask his face looked as though it was collapsing in on itself, like the face on one of those poor sods mummified in a bog for a thousand years.

Mark went to the window and stared out at the rain. It was falling in sheets now – we'd got soaked walking from the car. He hadn't even looked at Danny, and he stood there, his hand clasped behind his back. After a bit he turned to me. 'Would you like a drink? I noticed a vending machine along the corridor.'

'Coke,' I said. Truth was, I just wanted him out of the room. I wanted to be alone with Danny for a while.

When Mark had gone I moved the chair closer to the bed. 'We're both here,' I said, 'Mark and me.'

I thought I saw some recognition of my voice flit across his face, but maybe not. When Carl was dying he just seemed absent, and even though he was still breathing he was far away, somewhere I couldn't reach him. Danny had gone there, too, that place between life and death, a nowhere. I bowed my head, and thought that to someone passing the door it must look like I was praying. So I prayed, and I asked God to forgive him.

I was five when he started on me. Five when he started calling me Mark, saying I was his angel and thanking Christ that I'd come back to him, how he'd never let me go again. He would come into my bed in the night and his hands would be all over me, his hands and his mouth and his breath, his prison stink, a stink he never washed off. I'd lie dead still, because I'd learnt that was best, still and quiet so that he said how good I was. I remember his weight, like it would crush the life out of me, his weight and his stink of despair. I remember being Mark, and putting Steven away.

Prison must have softened Danny. I think it must have, after what Mark told me. I was never beaten, never bound or gagged, never burnt with cigarettes, starved or left naked to freeze on a bare mattress. When Mark was telling me all this I wanted him to stop. I wanted to call him a liar, to say that wasn't how it happened. But that wasn't how it happened to *me*, I had to keep telling myself he wasn't talking about me. All the same, I couldn't help thinking that he was lying – making up a story – it's what he does, after all. That would make Mark mad, I suppose.

Mark came back with a can of Coke for me and a bottle of water for himself. He sat down on the plastic chair in the corner of the room as though he wanted to make himself as unobtrusive as possible. I smiled at him to make him feel more comfortable and he said, 'Are your brothers coming? Your mother?'

'They won't be bothered.'

He looked relieved. He took a swig of water and wiped his mouth with the back of his hand. He smiled awkwardly. 'I can taste the hospital. Horrible.' After a minute he said,

'My mother was on this floor. Joy, my mother. Just along the corridor here, before they moved her to the hospice. I've only just realised.' He looked as though he wanted to run.

Sister Allison put her head round the door. Quietly she said, 'Hiya, Steve,' and gave me this sad, *I-know-what-you're-going-through* smile. She came in and did the things nurses do to those they know are dying – nowt, very much. I was grateful for the diversion, though. Mark watched her intently, and she looked up and caught his eye; he obviously impressed her, given the way she smiled at him. They exchanged these soft *hellos*, as though Danny could be wakened. When she'd gone I said, 'You're on there.'

He laughed, this quiet, sexy laugh that made me jealous of her, of him – of everyone in the world.

We sat in silence, listening to the wind lashing the rain against the window, straining to hear Danny breathe – or at least I was straining. I realised I was sitting on the edge of the seat, still holding his hand. Self-consciously, I drew my hand away.

Mark said, 'Would you prefer it if I left you alone with him, Steven?'

'No. But if you want to go –'

'I'll do whatever you want me to.'

'Will you come and sit closer, next to me?'

He stood up and carried the chair over, setting it down within an inch or two of mine so that I had an urge to lean close to him, breathe in his clean, subtle scent. He showered twice a day, he told me, an aside as he talked about what Dad had done to him. He remembered Danny's stink too, the way it seemed to cling to your hair and skin.

After a while he said, 'I'll pay for the funeral.'

'Hush!' I frowned at him. 'Don't talk like that, not yet.'

'He can't hear us, Steven.' Sitting forward a little he smoothed a crease from the bedcover. Without looking at me he said, 'I'll pay – I want to help you, Steven. I've been wondering about the best way of helping you and besides, I have more money than I could ever spend, it should be put to good use.' He smoothed another crease, his fingers almost brushing against Danny's. 'I have money – I've worked hard for it, I suppose – for the proof of success. I did everything I could to make Simon and Joy proud of me, to be *their* son, not Mark Carter any more.' Very quietly he said, 'Not yours any more.'

His hands became still; at last he looked at me. 'I think I should leave you to say goodbye alone now.'

'Say goodbye to him.'

Getting to his feet he stood over the bed and I watched him, hoping that he would do or say something that would make me feel that everything would be all right now. He just stood. After a bit he turned and walked out.

Simon carried Mark to the ambulance. Such a small child, and so silent. He murmured that he was safe now and hoped that he could hear him in that place that he'd escaped to. The ambulance man had given him a blanket to wrap him in and he had been careful to make sure he was wrapped snugly, decently, all of his nakedness covered. Only his beautiful face showed, framed by the rough blue wool. He kissed his forehead, and realised he had never kissed a child before, had never known anything about children until this moment. He felt his heart change, his soul. He held him closer. 'You're mine,' he whispered. There was awe in his voice. He knew that it was true.

And Joy held the boys, her arms around their shoulders, the three of them bunching up for the camera he held. He was proud of her, loved her more than he had believed possible; their marriage a wonderful, surprising gift he didn't deserve. 'Stand closer,' he said, 'smile!' He took the Polaroid picture, held it in his hands. His family, his wife and his sons, developed from blackness into bright, glorious colour.

Ben said, 'Where the *hell* have you been? Where?'

Kitty said quickly, 'Ben, it's all right, he's here now –'

Ben turned on her. 'Now is too late! What's the point in him being here now?' He began to cry. There was a line of chairs in the corridor outside Simon's room and Kitty led her husband to it and made him sit down. She crouched at his side. Looking up at Mark she said, 'Come and sit down.' More gently she repeated, 'Come and sit down, Mark.'

Mark stood beside the bed. Someone had combed Simon's hair and closed his eyes; they had arranged his hands so that they lay folded together on his chest. Death seemed somehow to have diminished him, as if only the force of Simon's personality had sustained the illusion that he was a powerful man. But Mark remembered how strong he had been, how he would carry him on his shoulders, his hands grasping his ankles. He had steadied him when he set him down on the ground with a firm hand on his back. When he rode on Simon's shoulders he must have been no more than six, still small, still frail, still believing that Simon, this man he had to remember to call Daddy, was not quite human but something fantastical. He was still afraid of him, ashamed of this fear that bobbed in his belly whenever Simon took his hand.

Mark sat down on the chair next to the bed. 'I'm sorry I wasn't here, Dad.'

'Where were you?'

Mark turned to see Ben in the doorway. Stepping towards him Ben said, 'I phoned. I phoned you at Dad's, I phoned your mobile – I left messages…'

'I'm sorry.'

'So – you just weren't answering your phone? Why?'

'Ben, let's not argue now, please.'

'I'm not arguing with you –'

'Your voice is raised.'

Ben turned away as though he could hardly bear to look at him. 'I'm taking Kitty home.'

'Wait.' Mark stood up, catching Ben's arm. 'Ben...' Unsure if he should tell him about Danny he hesitated and Ben shook him off.

'If you've got something to say, Mark, keep it for another time – I'm tired – it's tiring sitting at your father's bedside, watching him die. You know, he asked for you – the last thing he managed to say – *Mark*! Christ knows why! Christ alone knows!'

'Ben, I think you should keep your voice down.'

'And I think you should go to hell.'

'I was with Danny.' He gazed at his brother. 'That's where I was.'

Ben laughed, a short, incredulous burst of noise. 'Jesus!' He shook his head. 'With him, eh? That creature. Well, I think you probably deserve each other, so it makes sense.'

He turned away and Mark followed him out into the corridor. Again he caught his arm, forcing him to stop. 'Ben, have you forgotten who started all this? Who found Danny in the first place? It wasn't me who decided to dig up the past! It wasn't me who had to remind Dad where we came from!'

'Oh, he didn't need reminding by me – he only had to look at you – you're a living, breathing reminder, Mark! Look in the mirror – no, look inside yourself. You're the same twisted bastard Danny was.' He stepped closer to him, backing him against the wall. Searching his face as if seeing him for the first time he said intently, 'I know what you did to me, Mark. Susan told me – she used to laugh about you.'

Mark placed his palms flat against the wall to steady himself. 'She lied to you.'

'Don't you dare say that. Don't you dare.'

Fearfully Mark said, 'Was it revenge? Was finding Danny revenge?'

Ben looked away, smiling bitterly. 'Revenge!' He turned back to him, a sneer transforming his face into Danny's. 'Why should I go to so much trouble for you? All I wanted to do was uncover the lies everyone told me.'

'No one lied to you –'

'No – maybe not, but no one told me the whole truth either.'

'You didn't need to know the whole truth! You were just a child! '

'So were you!' Ben breathed out heavily, some of his anger seeming to subside into weariness. 'I don't want to talk to you about your so-called truth, Mark. To be honest you turn my stomach. I should feel sorry for you, I know, and at the best of times I did. But even when I felt pity for you I still found it hard to look at you because I just see him.'

After a moment Ben went on, 'I used to think that you killed Mam – our Mam, *Annette*. You killed her and made Dad take the blame so they'd take him away.' He laughed, as though he hardly believed that he'd ever thought such things, but his eyes were bright with pain. 'I thought that Simon was your dupe.'

'Ben...'

'I know you were just a child – not much more than a baby, really. I *know* none of it was your fault. In my head, as an adult, I know. But I missed Mam, I *miss* her.' He glanced away, as though such a confession was somehow shaming. 'Kitty's waiting in the family room. She'll wonder where I am.' About to go, he hesitated. Turning to him, he said, 'Susan lied to me, lied like it was a party game. I'm still not sure about so much of what she told me – even ordinary things. Would you tell me the truth if I asked you one question?'

310

Mark nodded. Hollow with grief, his fear of his brother seemed like a pitiful thing, not worthy of the fuss his heart was making.

'Christ.' Ben shook his head, as if his question hardly mattered. Exhaling he said, 'Why? Why did you do that to me?'

'I loved her.'

Ben gazed at him. At last he said, 'She used to come home to me and there'd be this *air* about her, this excitement in her eyes and voice, this prurient, *childish* interest in Danny. She didn't love you, Mark. All you were to her was living, breathing pornography.'

'I know.'

'You know? Then I can't hurt you, can I?' He laughed painfully. 'I can't have my revenge.' After a moment he said, 'Did she break your heart?'

Mark nodded.

'Good. Then you know how it feels.'

'Ben –'

About to walk away he turned to look at him. 'Goodbye, Mark. 'Tell Steven I'd rather not see him again. It's over. I have no interest any more.'

Chapter 29

Mark packed Simon's clothes into charity bags. He found a wardrobe full of Joy's clothes and packed them away, too. Sitting on his parents' bed, he looked around the room. The familiar, dark, old-fashioned furniture was as ugly as ever but had taken on a poignancy he found difficult to bear. He wondered if he could get rid of it, if he could really make this his home. His own furniture would be lost in its rooms. It would look fey and insubstantial. Perhaps he should sell the house. Too many memories crowded round him, like ghosts.

The eiderdown on Simon and Joy's bed was soft and silky, the purple of damsons; his fingers worried a line of stitching that had begun to unravel. At his feet the charity bags with their bright, childish logos sagged and bulged. There were still the drawers to sort — underwear, handkerchiefs, all scented with bars of soap so that the smell would take him back, add to the memories. He remembered Joy taking soap from its wrapping and tucking the pink bars beneath his father's socks. No one else did this, no one else had underwear that could make you sneeze. He smiled, and caught sight of himself in his mother's dressing table mirror. He looked away quickly.

Standing up, he went to the drawers on his mother's side of the bed. He opened the first one. It was empty, except for the faint smell of Camay. The next drawer held a large envelope, its stamps torn off to be given to charity, its seal sliced clean open by Joy's paper knife. The envelope was stuffed full and he lifted it out and spilled its contents on the bed.

Birthday and Christmas cards fanned out, bright greens and reds and golds against the dark quilt. Between the cards were letters, some still in their original envelopes, but some not; these were dog-eared as though they had been read and re-read. He recognised his own handwriting on these letters, and that of Ben. Fanning the letters and cards out, his fingers hovered over an envelope with his name printed boldly across it, the date in smaller print below. He breathed in, wanting to steady the sudden quickening of his heart preparing him for flight. Inside this envelope were the letters Joy had sent to him.

In hospital after his rescue from Danny, he had received a letter from her everyday. Each letter ended with the word *Joy*. When he had grown strong enough he would trace his fingers over this word, thinking it could only be a code for something. The man who brought the letters and read them to him in his bright, jolly voice never explained. He wondered who the man was but was too shy to ask, and too ashamed because this stranger seemed to know everything that made him dirty but nothing else. Slowly he began to realise that the man knew nothing else about him because there *was* nothing else, just this great big, black shame.

Except the person who wrote the letters seemed to know more. The letters were about ordinary, everyday things, about his teacher and the children in his class and his brother Ben. He'd thought that Ben had been taken away. Everyone had been taken away, everyone he knew, replaced by strangers, who all the same knew all about him. The world had shrunk to the size of his hospital bed. He tried not to cry for his mother because he felt he didn't deserve to. The man had told him she had gone to heaven, that she was safe now. The letters came with each visit and were better than the chocolate and the books the man brought:

they connected him to Ben, and to their mysterious writer, the only people who knew him properly.

Mark turned the envelope over in his hands. He had opened it once before, when he was sixteen and had found it when he was looking for a pen in Joy's desk. Not wanting to, he'd read one of the letters. He'd felt then as he did now, sick with self-pity. But then he'd felt angry too, hating Simon for being so careless of his five-year-old self. It had been easy to hate Simon when he was sixteen, normal, even. Now he only felt the pity, but pity for Simon too, who had tried so hard; he supposed this feeling was a small step forward, that he must have grown up a little.

He bundled the cards and letters together again and shoved them back in their envelope before shutting it back in the drawer.

Someone was ringing the doorbell. Not expecting anyone, he got up and went to the window that looked out on the front garden, deciding not to answer if it was another of his father's friends or ex-colleagues offering condolences. There had been a steady stream of them over the last few days. He was tired of small talk, of their reminiscences that made him feel he didn't know Simon as well as he'd thought. His father had had a life other than just being his father. How strange that seemed, lately.

Outside he saw a child in a pink anorak and pink jeans, a pink bow in her black hair. He gazed at her, watching as she picked the tiny horse-chestnut blossoms from the path with studied concentration. When Jade looked up he stepped back, unsure that he wanted to be seen. The doorbell rang again, polite but somehow urgent, too. It was like the boy, Mark supposed, to have an edge to his patience. He went into the hall, deliberately taking his time, trying to think only of the things he had to do for the funeral to keep his mind off his visitor.

Steven smiled at him shyly then glanced over his shoulder towards the cemetery; he shifted from one foot to the other. Managing to look at Mark again he said, 'Hiya.'

'Hello.' Mark turned to the little girl. 'Hello, Jade. How are you?'

'She's shy,' Steven said quickly when his daughter ignored him. 'Say hello, Jade. Be a good girl.' Lifting her up he said, 'Say hello to Mark, Jade.'

Mark held the door open wider. 'Come in.'

'Is that all right? I'm not disturbing you?'

'No. Of course not. Come through to the kitchen – I was about to make myself some coffee.'

In the kitchen, Steven set his daughter on her feet, immediately taking her hand as if he was afraid she'd run away. 'We were going to the park at the end of the road here…we were just passing…you don't mind?'

'No.' He smiled at him. 'You don't have to make an excuse to see me, Steven.'

The boy avoided his gaze. 'I just thought you might think…'

'It's nice to see you both. Listen, why don't I make us this coffee and we can drink it in the garden? There's plenty of space for Jade to run about out there.'

I led Jade out to his garden, following him as he carried a tray set with a pot of proper coffee, cups and saucers, a plate of biscuits and a glass of milk for Jade. I was pleased he'd made the effort for us. I'd had this feeling that I wouldn't be so welcome. But he's a nice man. I keep forgetting, at the same time reminding myself, that good manners mask real feelings in people like Mark. It was confusing, all these conflicting thoughts. I didn't know what to think, to tell the truth, only that every time I saw him I wanted things to be ordinary between us, ordinary as they could be, even though I kept making them more complicated. But I felt myself getting more and more

315

awkward, like I do in dreams where I've gone to work naked, thinking it was a good idea at the time only to feel humiliated. I didn't know where to look, except at Jade. I made her sit on my knee, although she squirmed and fretted because she wanted to be off, exploring this exciting new place she'd suddenly found herself in.

He said, 'I saw Danny's death notice in the paper.'

I nodded. 'Short and sweet, wasn't it? I didn't want one of those poems they print. None of them was right.'

'And the funeral's tomorrow?'

'Yeah.' I glanced at him as though it didn't matter. 'Will you come?'

'Yes.'

'And Ben?'

'No, I don't think so.' He held out the plate of biscuits to Jade. 'Jade, you know there's a little bird that lives in this garden, up there – see?' He pointed at the big tree by the wall and she turned to look, forgetting to fidget for a second. Smiling, Mark said, 'He's very shy, but sometimes, when little children come here and eat biscuits on the lawn he'll fly down and eat up all the crumbs, friendly as you like! Why don't you take a biscuit and see if he'll come down?'

She scrambled off my knee straight away. Taking a digestive she ran to where Mark was pointing. He watched her, smiling still, but then he turned to me and his smiled melted away. 'I'm sorry,' he said. 'I meant to come and see you – but when my father died...'

That formal *my father*, it hurt a bit, like he was trying to distance himself from me and Danny. Sullenly I said, 'It's all right.'

'Ben's taken it very badly.'

'And you?'

He looked to where Jade was running around the tree. After a while he said, 'I miss him.' He smiled as Jade tossed her biscuit into the air, calling out for the bird to come down. Turning back to me he said, 'She's lovely. I'm glad you brought her with you.'

We drank our coffee. Jade ran back and took a handful of biscuits to throw on the ground beneath the tree. I told her not to be naughty, that she should sit down and drink her milk, but Mark said it was OK, she could throw all the biscuits to the birds and save him from eating them all. He couldn't keep his eyes off her. I watched him watching her and suddenly I couldn't hold back any more.

'Mark?' He tore his gaze away from Jade to look at me. On a rush of breath I said, 'Mark, I'm sorry – sorry I cried, and everything...'

I looked down at my coffee, too embarrassed to look at him. I thought of the way we'd held each other on my bed and the shame I'd felt then was as strong as ever. From the corner of my eye I saw him put his cup down. He took out a packet of cigarettes and held it out to me, forgetting I don't smoke.

He lit his cigarette. He said, 'You have nothing to be sorry about. It was my fault – my responsibility.'

'And mine –'

He frowned at me. 'Steven, listen to me, now. All my life I have behaved badly and made excuses for myself. I don't want to behave badly with you. And yet...' He laughed despairingly. 'The way you look at me...I have to hold myself back.'

'I can look at you differently –'

He watched Jade, his eyes narrowed against the sun. At last he turned to me. 'What do you want from me, Steven? I would like you to be honest with me.'

'I don't know...'

'Sex?'

I squirmed. 'No...I don't know...no. I don't want to be that person.'

'No.' He sighed. 'Neither do I.' He smiled crookedly. 'I want to be above board. Above board, everything ship-shape and Bristol fashion.' Looking down at the cigarette wasting its smoke between his fingers, he said, 'This house,' he glanced back. 'When I was first brought here I knew they'd made a mistake, that this couldn't be my home. Well, it wasn't, not really. No matter how hard Simon and Joy tried I felt like an impostor, that I was Danny's and had no right to anything decent. I was not a decent human being.' Quickly he said, 'I still think that. It's best that we don't see each other.'

'Please don't say that —'

'Steven…Don't cry —'

I wiped my eyes impatiently. 'We could be different, now Danny's dead. We could start again like the other night hadn't happened.' I forced myself to look at him. 'Prove that Danny can be defeated.'

Jade ran towards me. She pulled at my hand. 'Find the birdie, Daddy.'

'In a minute. Mark and me are talking.'

Mark stood up. 'How about if I help you find him, Jade?' She stared at him, but he held out his hand to her. 'Let Daddy finish his coffee, eh? You and I will find the bird.'

He stood beneath the tree, holding my daughter's hand, the two of them so still, and all at once he swept her into his arms. There, a few steps from them, a robin had flown down to peck at the crumbs Jade had thrown. She turned to him in amazement like she believed he had made the bird himself, just for her.

The robin flew away. Setting Jade down, he took her hand and led her back to me.

He said, 'I think you should take Jade home now, Steven. I'll see you at the funeral tomorrow.'

I stood up. 'You'll definitely be there?'

'Yes, of course.'

'And it will be the last time we see each other?'

It was as though he couldn't bear to look at me. Turning away he walked quickly back to the house.

Danny said, 'Say you love me.'
'I love you.'
He untied him and pulled him into his arms, pressing his face against his chest so that he could hear his heart hammering, its noise filling his head, his scent filling his nose and mouth; he was part of Danny, a slick of his sweat, his blood, his semen. He was melting into him, becoming nothing but a stain on his skin. Soon he would be washed down the drain. But first Danny was kissing him and his hands were all over him and nothing was private or secret, no matter how dirty or shaming. 'Say you love me,' Danny said. And he tied his wrists and gagged his mouth so his last words were *I love you, Daddy*.

Outside the crematorium, Mark walked away from the other mourners to where Danny's wreaths were laid out. There were two, a cross of white chrysanthemums and a circle of yellow roses, soft, plump cushions of flowers. He read the cards. He glanced back at the men and women who stood around in small groups, obviously wanting to be away to the social club where the wake was to be held, not wanting to seem in too much of a hurry. His half-brothers, Colin and Graham, stood either side of their mother. Strangers, he thought. He wouldn't recognise them if he bumped into them on the street.

Steven stood a little way away from his family. He wore a dark suit and a white shirt, the knot of his black tie neat at his throat, whereas his brothers had loosened theirs, unused to restriction, no doubt. Steven looked up and caught his eye. His face was pale, fragile-looking. Mark thought how beautiful he was and, as if the boy read his thoughts, he looked away, an expression of contempt transforming him.

Mark turned back to the wreaths. The roses were from Steven. The card read, *At peace at last.*

Behind him Steven said, 'I didn't think you'd come.'

Mark turned around, noticed how the boy stepped back from him. 'I said I would.'

'Are you going now?'

'Do you want me to?'

Steven laughed shortly. 'Do what you want.'

'It's not far to the club is it? Perhaps you and I could walk there?'

Steven glanced towards his mother. One of his brothers had put his arm around her shoulders and she was weeping, dabbing her eyes with a tissue. Steven shook his head, his contempt meant for her now. Looking at Mark he said, 'All right. Let's get away from here.'

They walked along Thorp Road, past the abattoir where their grandfather had slaughtered and butchered. Mark stopped, touching Steven's arm so that he would stop too. He said, 'I spent the night thinking about you.'

The boy snorted. Looking away he said, 'Careful – you'll go blind.'

'It wasn't like that –'

'No? Then tell me what it was like – tell me how you *think* about me.'

'Obsessively?' He laughed bleakly. After a moment he said, 'I just want to do the right thing. The right, *decent* thing.'

'And what would be the decent thing?'

'I don't know. Behaving as a father would? A proper father...' Mark looked away. He thought of Susan and the child she had allowed him to believe was his, his seed, sown so fatally. He fumbled in his pocket for his cigarettes and his hands shook and Steven touched his arm.

'Mark?'

320

He met his gaze. He thought again how beautiful he was and the pride he would feel if he were mistaken for his son. He thought of Simon, who told him how little blood mattered, that the only true ties were those of love.

A group of mourners caught up with them. A woman caught Steven's arm and pulled him along. She would buy him a drink, she said, they would raise a glass to his Dad. Mark was left alone on the pavement. Over his shoulder the boy looked back at him, and he looked so much like Danny that he had to turn away. He heard the woman laugh, felt himself jostled by a group of black-suited men. No one knew him, he was a stranger, an intruder. Mumbling apologies he walked back against the on-coming crowd.

Chapter 30

Kitty said, 'It will be strange to see your Dad's house so changed.'

Ben didn't speak. He glanced at her. He thought how astonishing she looked: blooming. Her pregnancy showed now, a neat bump. This morning he had felt the baby kick and he had such an overwhelming feeling that he must keep her from harm that he was speechless. Words were often useless, too trite, too sentimental – or at least they were in his mouth. He hoped she understood how much he loved her. She smoothed her skirt then clutched her hands together in her lap, glancing nervously out of the window. Wanting to reassure her, he said, 'You look lovely.'

She laughed. 'I look fat.'

'Beautiful.' Gently he said, 'Steven's nice. Easy to get along with.'

Kitty looked at him. 'I'm not worried about meeting Steven.'

Turning the car into Simon's drive he switched off the engine. 'Well,' he said. 'Here we are.' He thought about the last time he had seen his brother, at Simon's funeral. Mark had behaved as if it wasn't their father they were burying but some distant relative so that he could easily afford the energy to charm Simon's friends and ex-colleagues, to make sure that each mourner was properly attended to. All except him. Out of some sense of propriety Mark had kept a respectful distance from him, just as he had at Susan's funeral. Once, Ben had caught his eye and Mark had held his gaze blankly, as he used to as a tiny child in Skinner

Street Infants. Beside him, his father's friend Iain had said gently, 'He's not really here, is he? Never quite with us.'

Ben had torn his gaze from Mark's to look at him. 'It's just an act,' he'd said. Later he thought how childish he must have seemed to this urbane man. Iain had placed his hand on his shoulder as if to steady him. 'Try and make your peace,' he'd said. 'For your father's sake.'

Ben lifted Nathan from his car seat. He kissed him. Holding him close, Ben turned to look at the house, half expecting to see Simon at the sitting room bay. He felt nervous suddenly, and a sense that if he stopped behaving with such determined reasonableness grief would overwhelm him, that brutal mugger that robbed him of his voice, his courage. He held his son more tightly. He felt Kitty's hand on his arm. Softly she said, 'It's all right. Everything is going to be all right.'

'Kitty...' He laughed tearfully. 'Oh, God...'

She took Nathan from him. 'Why don't you sit down out here?' She nodded towards the bench that years ago Simon had placed in the sunniest spot in the front garden. 'I'll go in and let them know we're here.'

Ben sat. He stared out at the cemetery across the road, remembered that as a child he had been scared to live in a house so close to the dead. He remembered that Simon must have guessed at his fear because one day he helped him on with his coat, crouching in front of him to fasten its buttons. He'd smiled at him. 'I thought we'd go for a walk, Ben. Just the two of us.'

He hadn't ever allowed Simon to hold his hand, and so they walked with a careful distance between them across the road to the cemetery gates where Simon stopped to smile at him. 'Ben, would you mind very much if we took this short-cut into town?'

He had shaken his head, determined not to be a baby in front of this man, and so they had set out along the wide path that cut through the cemetery's heart, past the stone crosses and marble obelisks, past the occasional weeping angel or mourner carrying flowers. Horse-chestnut trees shaded the path, their heavy, candle-like blossom subtly scenting the air. From time to time Simon smiled at him encouragingly. Then, at a vacant bench, he stopped and sat down.

'It's very peaceful here,' Simon said. He glanced around, smiling at a little bird that hopped out from behind a grave. 'Last week I saw a squirrel – running straight up that tree there.' He turned to him. 'Maybe we'll see one today, eh? If we're lucky.' After a while he said, 'The little creatures, the squirrels and the birds, they know that it's quiet and peaceful here and that there's nothing to be afraid of because there's nothing here but the trees and the stones and the certainty that we're all safe, in the end.' He laughed a little. 'I think of my daddy when I come here. He used to watch the birds that live in these trees.'

'Where is he?'

Simon had gazed at him. Perhaps he realised that this was the first time he had spoken to him directly. Reaching out, Simon had brushed a strand of his hair from his eyes, the first time he had touched him so intimately. 'He died,' he said. 'A few years ago, now. I think about him every day – just ordinary thoughts, ordinary memories, wondering what he'd think of this or that. I don't feel so sad any more, only sometimes. Most of the time I have only happy memories of him, like now, when I see the birds he loved so much.'

Ben remembered getting down from the bench. 'Birds are stupid.' He'd glared at him defiantly. Simon had only nodded. Getting up too, he'd said, 'Well, there are birds and birds. I know where there's a nest of a particularly clever bird.'

And he had shown him a nest with a clutch of speckled blue eggs, holding him firmly as he lifted him up to look. He had tried not to be impressed but the eggs were too astonishing. For a while his anger with this man couldn't be sustained. Only when they returned to the house, when he saw Mark watching anxiously for him at the window, had his anger returned.

Ben closed his eyes. He thought of the speech Mark had made at Simon's funeral, how he had talked about their father's extraordinarily generous love for them. He had listened, his head bowed because he couldn't bear to look at him, thinking only what a good actor his brother was, what an exceptional liar. Simon had never loved Mark generously; there was something that stopped their father's heart when it came to Mark. But Simon had loved him, and as a child this had felt right: he was the victor in a just war.

As an adult he had tried to like Mark and put aside all the confused feelings of pity and shame and raw, protective love, and just *like* him, as it seemed other brothers simply liked each other, tolerating their peculiar ways. There were times when he had even admired him, but he realised you could admire a man and still know that whatever it was you admired them for it was not something you had any wish to emulate. Mark's bravery, for instance, seemed particularly useless to him.

Simon phoned him. He said, 'Mark's been wounded.' Ben wondered now if he had imagined the exasperation in his father's voice. Such a little war that Mark had got himself involved in, that had him fighting for his life on a hospital ship. Simon had said, 'Ben – I'm afraid it's quite serious.' And he remembered thinking that he had talked like this before, when he was six years old and Mark had mysteriously disappeared from his life. It was as if Simon believed that Mark was too frail to survive. He had known better: Mark was strong, invincible, even; he knew his brother much better than this man who found it so impossible to hide his pitying distaste, as though Mark was a particularly horribly injured animal spilling its guts in the road.

Susan said, 'Your brother's very...*odd*.'

She'd only just met Mark at some party or other. He remembered laughing at her barely concealed curiosity. Most women were curious about Mark, he seemed so unreachable, a challenge. He should have been more on guard, he supposed, but he'd believed that Susan was different from most women. And she was, of course, only different in a way that he hadn't allowed for.

And he had asked her, 'What is it with you and him?' That was in the early days, when he could bring himself to ask, when her difference – her *oddness* – made her the sexiest woman he'd ever met. He was like a thirteen-year-old discovering pornography. He couldn't be sure what was normal any more.

Ben became aware of someone watching him and he looked up. Mark took a step forward, smiling awkwardly. He said, 'Sorry – I didn't mean to disturb you.'

'Mark. How are you?'

'Fine.' He laughed a little. 'Well – OK, I suppose. May I?' He sat down beside him, at once looking up at the sun breaking through the clouds. 'Dad used to say this was the sunniest spot in the whole garden. He would sit here for hours, remember?'

'Yes.'

Mark glanced at him only to look away again. 'Kitty and Steven are introducing Nathan to Jade. They're all getting on so well I felt something of a spare part so I thought I'd come and find you. Say if you'd prefer to be alone for a while longer.'

'No, I'm all right.' He made to get up but Mark touched his arm. 'Ben, let's give them a few minutes.'

As he sat down again Mark took an envelope from his pocket and held it out to him. 'This is for you. Photographs. I found them in a drawer when I was sorting Dad's study.'

'Photographs of...?'

'Annette. Danny. Wedding pictures. Snaps of you as a baby – you and Annette and Danny. Before I was born.'

Ben shook his head. 'I don't want them.'

Gently Mark placed the envelope between them. 'No, OK. I'll keep them, anyway.'

Ben picked the envelope up. All at once he was tearing at its seal, spilling the pictures out. Annette smiled up at him, her back to a brick wall, a bundled baby in her arms, its shawl spilling down past her short skirt, white and frothy and clean looking – pure, incongruously so. He shuffled through the rest of the pictures, saw Danny smart in a suit, a carnation in his lapel. He put this picture to the back, shoved the whole lot in the envelope again.

Mark said, 'The children will be here soon. All Jade's friends from her play group, and their mothers.' He smiled at him and for a moment Ben thought how much he looked like the child he once was, shy, unsure of himself. 'Steven seems to have everything under control – he even made cakes.' After a moment he said, 'He's pleased you're here.'

'Nathan likes parties.'

'So does Steven – he's more excited than Jade.'

Ben looked out towards the cemetery. He thought of Simon, who ran their birthday and Christmas parties with the kind of good-humoured firmness that made him believe that everything in his life could be so well ordered and nothing could ever again be out of control. He smiled, remembering how Simon had taught himself to twist balloons into animal shapes, how the balloons would sometimes leap from his hands to jet around the room, control lost only for theatrical effect. And afterwards, when all the guests had gone, Simon would collapse into a chair and say, 'Well now – I think that went well – don't you think so, boys?' He must have been eight, nine, ten, and at some point he had accepted Simon as his father, which seemed to him unremarkable, only a gradual getting used to his new life, the periods of not remembering becoming

327

longer and longer. There were times when he even imagined he had dreamed his old life: a bad dream his father – Simon – had woken him from. Then he would look at Mark and know the truth of it.

Simon said to him, 'You mustn't blame Mark, Ben. Try to understand –'

But he couldn't understand, only that there were lies and secrets considered too big and dirty for him, and so he had raged and shouted and kicked at Simon's shins as he tried to reason him out of one of the many tantrums he threw in those early days. How much he had hated Simon then, and Joy, these adults who allowed him his hate and his rage, who held him so tightly as he screamed and shouted. Even during the worst of his rages, the strength of Simon's embrace made him feel that he was understood. Only his hatred of Mark wasn't understood and had the power to hurt Simon and Joy. Only this hatred made him feel ashamed when all of his other excesses were forgiven.

Ben turned to his brother. He said, 'So, Steven's living with you now.'

'Yes, while he's at university.'

'You've taken him on.'

Mark laughed. 'I think he's taken me on. But I'll support him though his degree.'

A little girl ran from the house. She scrambled onto Mark's knee, resting her head against his chest and contentedly sucking her thumb. Mark kissed her head, drawing her closer, settling more comfortably. Looking at him, Mark said quietly, 'She doesn't know what to make of me – uncle, grandfather – who?' He smiled, kissing her head again. 'We are friends, at least. That's important.'

A couple of cars pulled up. Young women lifted toddlers from back seats, calling out to each other. Mark set Jade down and stood up, taking the child's hand. 'Well, sweetheart, we must welcome your guests.'

Ben stood up too. He touched Mark's arm so that he turned to him. 'I'll take the photos, Mark,' he said, 'I'll take them from you.'

Mark nodded. After a moment he smiled. 'Come on. Let's see if we can live up to Simon's birthday parties.'

You want to know what happened to Kitty. She became a gardener. She modelled her first design on the physic garden at Kew, and it was admired, and people asked her to come and transform their gardens, and a newspaper asked her to write a column on gardening and her life began to seem like a seedling rushing towards the sun. After a while she was writing books about medieval gardens, about gardens and plants that were lost and rediscovered. She became famous – you've most likely bought a trowel or a garden fork or seeds and herbs branded with her name. She travelled the world, a garden odyssey. Sometimes, on a plane, or waiting in a foreign station or port, she had a feeling of being outside herself, watching, because she could hardly believe that this was her life, that she had grown all this from barely anything, just a thought about gardens, a nurtured seed.

In her own garden, hers and Ben's, she grew such plants that centuries ago would have been used in evidence against her, had she been on trial as a witch. She served Ben teas brewed from her physic garden plants, their leaves and seeds, experimenting. She watched his reactions. He didn't change, not very much, although he became calmer, she thought, and more in tune with her. He remained the man she had married, and she realised this was enough.

I sit with her in her garden sometimes and we have tea. I ask her for love potions; she just laughs.

THE END

About the author...

Winner of the first Andrea Badenoch Prize for Fiction in 2005 for *Paper Moon,* Marion graduated with distinction and won the Blackwell Prize for Best Performance for the MA in Creative Writing at Northumbria University in 2003. She currently teaches creative writing through the Open College of the Arts and has had poems and short stories published, most recently a pamphlet of poetry about her father and childhood entitled *Service.* Her first novel, *The Boy I Love*, was published in July 2005 to much critical acclaim.

Marion is 43, married with two children and lives in the Tees Valley

The Boy I Love

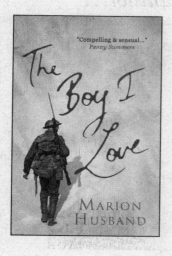

"Compelling & sensual..."
Penny Summers

MARION HUSBAND

ISBN 1905170009 £6.99

Superbly written with engaging characters that are simultaneously strong and weak, compassionate and flawed. The book is a controversial but compulsive read and readers will find their sympathies tugged in unusual directions as they engage with the lives of the characters.

The Boy I Love is the first of a two book series – the second book, Paper Moon is set in World War 2 and follows the life of Mick, now a war poet, his son and Robbie, son of Paul and Margot.

Paper Moon

Winner of the Andrea Badenoch Fiction Award

ISBN 1905170149 £6.99

Following on from *The Boy I Love*, Marion Husband's highly acclaimed debut novel, *Paper Moon* explores the complexities of love and loyalty against a backdrop of a world transformed by war.

The passionate love affair between Spitfire pilot Bobby Harris and photographer's model Nina Tate lasts through the turmoil of World War Two, but is tested when his plane is shot down. Disfigured and wanting to hide from the world, Bobby retreats from Bohemian Soho to the empty house his grandfather has left him, a house haunted by the secrets of Bobby's childhood, where the mysteries of his past are gradually unravelled and he discovers that love is more than skin deep.